SECRETS IN THE BONES
THE CURSE OF BLOOD BAY

RYAN HOLDEN

RYAN HOLDEN BOOKS

Copyright © 2023] by Ryan Holden

All rights reserved.

No part of this publication may be reproduced, distributed, or transmitted in any form or by any means, including photocopying, recording, or other electronic or mechanical methods, without the prior written permission of the publisher, except as permitted by U.S. or UK copyright law. For permission requests, contact www.RyanHoldenBooks.co.uk

The story, all names, characters, and incidents portrayed in this production are fictitious. No identification with actual persons (living or deceased), places, buildings, and products is intended or should be inferred.

Edition Number: One/2023

About the Author

I fell in love with the idea of writing many years ago. Then I grew up, fell in love with many other things, and had to learn how to be an adult with responsibilities. Two teenage sons later, things didn't turn out too bad, and now I have a little more free time to reunite with my first love... I want to create a world that readers sink deep in and never want to get out. A supernatural detectiverse with intriguing cases and loveable characters. Join me on this rollercoaster.

Also By

The Detective Reynolds Series (4 book series)Kindle edition by Ryan Holden (Author)

This supernatural detective crime thriller series will draw you in with its gripping suspense. Detective Reynolds is thrown into a world of the supernatural, one he never knew existed and must keep his identity as a werewolf a secret. As a member of the Murder Task Force, each new case is filled with murder, suspense, and a unique thread - the murderer is anything but 'normal'. With others around him aware of his true identity, Detective Reynolds must face many challenges ahead. Follow along as he fights to keep the streets safe in a battle between good and evil. If you enjoyed the thrilling suspense of books like "The Girl With The Dragon Tattoo" or the realm of "Jim Butcher," then you'll love this series. Buy now and join this exciting journey into a supernatural world that is so grounded it could exist.

Secrets In The Bones: The Curse Of Blood Bay.

A dark, supernatural crime thriller steeped in the chills caused by things that go bump in the night. (The Detective Reynolds Series Book. The sleepy fishing village of Cruden

Bay hides a centuries-old dark secret deep beneath its bewitched surface. After solving the case of the Black Widow, Detective George Reynolds and forensic pathologist, Ellena Walker are off to Cruden Bay, Scotland. But what they think will be a romantic getaway soon turns into a mission to save the village from an ancient and deadly enemy—forced to investigate a string of unexplainable occurrences and discover the truth. One steeped in the supernatural that leaves George struggling to know the best path to take. With the help of Ellena Walker, George must discover the connection between the ancient village, Ellena's family history and why ADI Locke would steer them to danger. While also trying to stop centuries-old vampires from roaming the streets. George's awakening to the world in the shadows has been a baptism of fire, but this battle will set him on the path to hell, tormented by sin. As George and Ellena uncover more secrets, facing the danger of a hidden past, their burgeoning relationship is threatened by something so sinister and dark that it scares George to his core. But he won't go down without a fight, especially after being given a second chance at love. If you enjoyed the thrilling mystery of "Black Widow" and the idea of vampires battling vampires in an age of corruption and organised crime, you'll love this emotionally dangerous roller coaster with fangs bared and bloodshed. Buy now to continue your detectiverse journey!

The Devil's Pages

"Demons are real, and it's time to sell your soul".
Are you ready to journey into the darkness and explore the terrifying power of 'The Devil's Pages'? In this thrilling horror novel, Gerald Ackerman is a good man from Newport Pagnell, England, struggling to cope after a tragic car crash took the life of his beloved wife.
When he stumbles upon a mysterious leather book at a seedy flea market in Northampton, England, he finds himself able to exact revenge - but at what cost? Read on to find out if Gerald will be brave enough to pay the price for justice or if someone can stop him and the mysterious book. If you enjoyed "The Detective Reynold's Series" by Ryan Holden or Stephen King's "The Stand", you'll love "The Devil's Pages"! Buy now if you have what it takes to beat the devil.

Dedication to Nana

To our Nana, our shining light. A shoulder to cry on, an ear to share secrets with. A home from home. Most of all, a heart made of gold that was never too full for a lost or struggling soul. Forever loved, and you will live on in every person's life you touched and are grateful to have known and loved and been loved by you. Lots of love from us mere mortals that greatness left behind too soon. You will always be the air that we breathe, the stories we share and the jokes we tell. I. like everyone else, have been privileged to call you Nan, to others, mum or great nana. The list would be endless because that's how many souls you reached. We love you, now rest because you've earnt it xxxxx

Contents

Prologue	XI
Chapter 1	1
Chapter 2	7
Chapter 3	11
Chapter 4	16
Chapter 5	22
Chapter 6	28
Chapter 7	33
Chapter 8	38
Chapter 9	43
Chapter 10	48
Chapter 11	54
Chapter 12	59
Chapter 13	64
Chapter 14	69
Chapter 15	73
Chapter 16	79

Chapter 17	85
Chapter 18	91
Chapter19	95
Chapter 20	100
Chapter 21	106
Chapter 22	111
Chapter 23	117
Chapter 24	122
Chapter 25	128
Chapter 26	134
Chapter 27	139
Chapter 28	145
Chapter 29	154
Chapter 30	160
Chapter 31	167
Chapter 32	174
Chapter 33	181
Chapter 34	190
Chapter 35	199
Chapter 36	212
Chapter 37	218
Chapter 38	226
Chapter 39	232
Chapter 40	240
Chapter 41	248
Chapter 42	257
Chapter 43	265
Chapter 44	273

Chapter 45	282
Chapter 46	287
Chapter 47	294
Chapter 48	301
Chapter 49	310
Chapter 50	318
Chapter 51	325
Chapter 52	332
Chapter 53	341
Chapter 54	351
Chapter 55	358
Synopsis	368
Epilogue	370
Acknowledgements	373

Prologue

'Dear Georgie'

'First of all, thank you for the hard work you and the team have pulled off lately. It's been two gruelling cases quickly, and I understand the ballache I caused by dumping the 'Black Widow' case on your lap. It was an immense favour in a realm that I knew nobody else would understand or be able to see through the smoke and mirrors.

I know you need a well-deserved break yet, what I will say next. Well, sort of a request. Maybe more a merciless beg that you could find it within you to help again. I will owe you. Part of that I'm working on now. It will be a surprise, and that's all I will say about it for now. Until then...

Fuck...I should probably apologise first—the little manipulation of where to go. I'm sure Cruden Bay wouldn't have been your first choice. Or should I say 'Blood Bay' as it used to be called? I needed you there. Your mind and the way you see things are unique. I need you to solve a murder.

A very old and bizarre murder of my ancestor Jean Martin Cortez. In seventeen twenty-five. He'd travelled the world mapping countries with his assistant, Frederick Lasille. They were intrigued by the different cultures and looked into the mythology. They came through Romania and the countries between Scotland to explore Great Britain and Norway. -

-Until he met Countess Anna Farrington, the only daughter of six children from Earl Andrew Farrington and Countess Sophia Farrington. Anna and Jean hit it off after Anna became intrigued by his recordings. Only Jean was also a druid, collecting special herbs *from those countries and had been somewhat of a healer. Especially in Cruden after sailors brought an outbreak of scurvy through the port. Jean won favour with the Earl until he became aware of his fondness for Anna.-*

- What they all failed to see was Frederick getting sick. Until it was too late. No herbs worked, not to cure him. He developed a liking for blood. An unusual parasite in Romania brought on that he'd kept from Jean. First, it was alleviated by animals. Jean began to notice physical changes in Frederick. Large fangs, paler skin. Hot then cold sweats, until only cold. Jean attempted to hide the condition from everyone, including the Earl and his family.-

-Meanwhile, Anna and Jean's relationship intensified. They were in love. Even the moments it became hard to see each other. They found a way to message each other—symbolising their unrelenting love. Then people began disappearing, at first, sporadic. Then some would be found torn to pieces. Each day, the amount of blood painting the Village became greater.-

-Eyes turned on Jean, thinking his methods to cure sickness had turned the villagers rabid. Little did they know Frederick had started it. He'd been sneaking out at night. In every sense, Anna and Jean were forbidden by the pain of death. The villagers sought to eradicate the problem they saw as a curse. Realising stabbing the heart with spikes made from mountain ash would all but desiccate them to what they believed was dead. Most had been friends, so they couldn't bring themselves to destroy the bodies. Instead gave them coffins. Yet also didn't believe their abominations warranted burial.-

-On orders of the Earl, a group of villagers entombed the coffins in the caves and tunnels deep under the Village through the cliff front. All went quiet for a month or so. Jean occupied Montague House, keeping Frederick, his friend and assistant, a secret. Sadly, Jean had been blinded. Believing what Frederick had said about the parasite, and that's how the town got sick. Jean worked tirelessly for a cure. He built a tunnel from the house to the castle and the tombs. He was taking samples and experimenting. It also allowed Anna and Jean to reconnect.-

-Jean was struggling for a cure, so in the meantime, he cursed the Village and those afflicted by what he called a savage virus—binding them to the Village. So if somehow one or Frederick escaped, they could never leave. Two years later, on a lunar eclipse, Jean ritualised a talisman; if he ever got the virus, he wouldn't be affected like the others. What he hadn't realised was he'd not only bound himself to the Village. He'd missed how the villagers were turned through a bite. The parasitic toxin is released through tiny holes at the tip of their fangs.

This is where the information gets sketchy. It's said Anna and Jean were seen together. The

Earl turned on Jean even more. He was inciting the villagers to go after him. They didn't get him. Yet he disappeared all the same. Anna was distraught, especially after she discovered she was pregnant. If to be believed as true. The Earl had the baby aborted. Then no less than two hours later, Anna was banished to the dungeons.-

-A big mistake. Nobody found Frederick. He'd become rabid. He was starved of blood because Jean wasn't around. Frederick grew strong, too strong. One night he escaped through the tunnels fueled by rage and set on revenge. Found himself in the dungeons... The first hint of blood in over two weeks and even stronger in light of the abortion. He found Anna first. Yet in her blood, he felt Jean, his friend. So he didn't try to kill. Saw her as a victim who may want revenge. Frederick bit Anna and turned her. They tore through the castle. Bled the family and servants all but dry.-

-Until they all became obedient savages. The Village didn't expect the second wave. They were caught off guard, but that didn't mean they weren't prepared. The villagers fought back and drove them into the tunnels and Montague House. The Earl, the rest of his family, and others were desiccated and interred with the rest. Anna and Frederick were the last. Each with a mountain ash spike laced with mistletoe buried in their hearts.-

-No other infected can bare to touch it; no one normal in their right mind would dare. The Village sealed everything off; the buildings became shrines to what the Village endured. Even embellished with stories to make into tourist attractions to help bring in money and revamp everything to start over. Jean never reappeared, nor did his secrets. Georgie, his bloodline, mine. It's also cursed. He may have been bitten but had resistance because of the talisman.-

-My bloodline feared anything coming out in us down the years. It fucking came out in me... It's managed with some herbs and things. I need you to find Jean. I read if his body rests on hallowed ground. It severs his ailments from our bloodline. Solve what may have happened. Lay him to rest. Help set us free, please. I will owe you so much.-

-I understand if you've read all of this in disbelief and thought, holy shit, it can't be real. Remember, you're a werewolf. Aside from that, everything I've told you is a mix of history books, some gossip, worked whispers, fragments of the very few texts to escape the 'Bay of Blood', no pictures, just scared scribbles if you need anything at all. Maybe even your grumpy sidekick. Just call. I promise you will get a rest soon. Be safe.'

'Sincerest regards, Frank Locke,'

Well, that was a kick in the balls. If the shoe had still been on the way down. The letter most definitely made it drop. This Village was quite literally hell on earth. Or at least, waiting to happen with what's below. With each echo made, the little 'dots' suddenly make sense. The cave, the house and the coffins. Yet the biggest and by far the scariest. Who I assumed to be a vampire version of Ellena was, in fact, Anna. The normal ghost was her before the 'turn' leaving a rose.

I felt for Locke; I did. The Village too. With Amos and whoever else roaming by night to hunt. Yet by day tries to blend in as if the world was none the wiser. Ellena looked like Anna, and now I had to find out why vampires would want a lookalike. While I got my head around everything Locke had said in the letter. Not to mention Mary. I could've disregarded and run at that point. Now I couldn't.

I had an itch I couldn't scratch; Locke had made me worry—more than I was already. I lay in bed wrestling with the urge to ensure Ellena was okay. At the same time, I wasn't sure how she'd react if I told her what Locke had said. Until, for the second time tonight, I bit the bullet. I flipped off my covers and headed for the adjoining door.

'Knock knock'

I wrapped on the door as non-threatening as possible, even if my angst made me want to open it. She'd been unusually tired this evening. I had to carry her to bed and barely stirred as I staggered the steps. I didn't think at the time. Now it seemed strange. There was no stirring now, either. Not even a roll across the mattress. If it was anything like mine. It would make a slight squeak. I listened deeper, so I could spare the embarrassment of barging in. I drifted through the door into her room…No heartbeat…I couldn't hear her, so I barged in after all.

The be's was empty, covers pulled open, and the pillows scrunched. Her boots and coat were still there. My heart raced as I was consumed with panic. Ellena was missing…

Chapter I

'5th of November 1987. Detective Reynolds Scotland bound.'

Somewhere quiet and out of the way. With everything I've been through, it didn't feel like much to hope for. We have bounced, leapt and damn well dragged ourselves from one traumatic murder to another with little time for much else in between, which hasn't been kind to my weary body—or fragile grip on reality. Nor was getting shot at and nearly blown up trapped in that blood-covered limousine amongst the chaos of Trafalgar Square.

What we craved, more than anything, was a semblance of normality. A place untouched by serial killers, sadistic demons unleashed from stolen Egyptian relics, stranded ghosts, or other bizarre and scary supernatural entities that had plagued our lives thus far. Perhaps a ghost or two wouldn't be so bad if they weren't tethered to a fresh corpse. The nostalgia of witnessing something old could add to the mystique of where we're headed, but that's all I wanted on this trip—a chance to recharge and explore without looking over my shoulder for trouble, especially from a wolfsbane-laced bullet, like what happened to Michael.

Yet, my feeble attempt to shift my restless, paranoid gaze towards the bustling motorway or muster excitement for the Scottish adventure ahead was failing miserably. Second chances in life were a rarity, at least for me. The opportunity to love again, to be swept up in intoxicating romance, was a thrilling prospect I wanted to seize with both hands. I still remember the first kiss between Miss Ellena Walker and me by the Grand Union Canal; the electricity felt between us. I yearned for more of that, and I'd like to think I had earned it. What better place to try than over seven hundred miles from London, in the endless chill of the countryside? If only I could clear my mind.

As the traffic flowed around us, my thoughts inevitably drifted back to our last case. I was haunted by the gruesome details that had yet to sink in fully and the fate that had befallen those poor girls. Guilt gnawed at me, an insidious force fueled by things beyond my control. If only the detectives had done their jobs properly the year before, if only they hadn't covered up the first death and had the backbone to take on Westminster politicians, Selene and the others might not have been transformed into rampaging monsters, exacting brutal vengeance on those who had cruelly exploited them. They had been daughters, transformed into something monstrous by greed, need, and neglect.

Whether a seasoned detective like Michael Dalton or a newcomer like me, a disconcerting constant haunted us all—the chilling details of our cases. Those tiny, overlooked threads of evidence, woven into the seedy fabric of society, often went unnoticed by untrained eyes or were dismissed as unimportant. For me, they become another brutal murder on the dark streets of London, which grew darker with each case we put to rest.

We had toiled tirelessly to maintain the illusion of normality, knowing all too well that more blood would inevitably be spilt. It was enough to drive the latent werewolf within me wild. Yet, as we uncovered the growing evil lurking in the shadows, I couldn't help but listen to the echoes of pain that had already come to pass and those that still loomed on the horizon. I wondered whether my supernatural abilities were a blessing or a curse. I watched as the light slowly faded from the eyes of another victim, hoping that, someday, we could make a difference. Too many cases had ended this way, all because those tiny details were now shrouded in the supernatural.

Twenty-four hours had passed, and we found ourselves on the road to the Aberdeenshire coast, heading east of Fyvie towards a little fishing village called Cruden Bay. It was a place I hadn't considered or heard of before, but a small advertisement in a magazine had piqued my interest. The village's history had drawn me in, with tales of battles and ancient ruins. I had a soft spot for history and exploration, and this seemed like the perfect opportunity to satisfy that curiosity.

The village had a rich history, including a battle where King Malcolm II led the Scots and defeated the Danes. It might not have been my main draw, but added a unique touch to our destination. More importantly, Cruden Bay offered an escape from the chaos of London, a chance to distance ourselves from the gruesome cases that had become all too familiar.

But what truly captured my attention was that in the 19th century, Cruden Bay had been a holiday haunt for Bram Stoker, the Irish author of Dracula. Stoker had found inspiration in the spooky ruins of Slain Castle, perched ominously on the headland, and had used it to shape his vision of Count Dracula's Castle. This detail, I thought, would particularly appeal to Ellena, with her penchant for the macabre. I couldn't deny her anything, especially when she filled the air with the comforting scent of coconut, instantly putting me at ease.

However, despite the allure of the Scottish adventure ahead, I found it difficult to shake off the remnants of our last case. The memories and the guilt weighed heavily on me. Suppose only the detectives had acted differently, and we had unravelled the mystery sooner. Those innocent girls might not have been turned into vengeful monsters in that case. Their tragic fate haunted me, and I couldn't help but feel responsible for not preventing it.

As we drove on the M1, with traffic flowing smoothly and the promise of an open road and sunshine ahead, I struggled to find peace. The world appeared calm, and there was a rare sense of tranquillity, yet something nagged at the back of my mind.

And then it happened. A black Mercedes Sprinter van changed lanes, passing us on the motorway, and a shiver ran down my spine with my claws sliding forward. My senses heightened, and I felt an inexplicable unease. Oblivious to my worry, Ellena smiled as the wind tousled her hair and brought the scent of diesel and sunlight into the car. Every glance in her direction usually filled me with joy.

But the unease persisted, gnawing at me from within. I should have been relishing this moment, finally getting a chance to escape the darkness that had consumed us for so long. I had devoted five years to the memory of Helen, my late wife, and our baby boy. They were now nothing more than memories, cruelly taken from me. Their brutal murder had been orchestrated by my foster brother, Ethan, who had hidden his true identity as Charlie Masters throughout the years I had known him. He had known my secrets before I did and used them to snuff out the light in Helen's eyes. Closure had come, but the scars remained, a constant reminder of my pain.

Ellena had entered my life, embracing both sides of me without hesitation. She had accepted my flaws and the supernatural aspect of my existence, never wavering or turning away, even when my fangs had emerged. Yet, there were secrets she kept hidden that I was slowly uncovering. Her past was a puzzle, and I was still unlocking the pieces. Ellena was intelligent, skilled, and undeniably beautiful. Still, the journey to Scotland made me wonder if I was letting my guard down too soon.

Once bitten, twice shy, or so the saying went. At times, she had offered glimpses of her true self, fragments of her past, but she only bared her soul when she was ready. As the miles rolled on and the Scottish countryside beckoned, I couldn't shake the feeling that something was amiss. The unease persisted, a prickling sensation at the back of my neck. My instincts screamed at me to be cautious.

But then, with a sharp glimmer of grey, a shadow loomed overhead. A suffocating blackness swallowed the cream interior of the car, and the smell of salty seawater cut through the diesel-scented breeze. It was an echo, a haunting replay of a moment in time. The windows vanished, the seats faded away, and Ellena's appearance gradually shifted. Her golden hair turned dirty black, her skin mottled grey. I felt tiny hairs on my body become needles as the echo of torment grew louder.

Chunks of pointed rocks hung menacingly from the ceiling, casting eerie shadows. We were in a cave, and Ellena lay in a crumpled heap among uneven stones and puddles. Fortunately, there was no blood, but the sight was far from reassuring. Every rasping breath I took was laced with the saltiness of the air and the sickening stench of death as I tried to comprehend the situation.

Ellena's eyes had turned jet black, and she remained unnaturally still. And then death descended upon us. The source of the putrid odour became apparent as I gazed upon a grotesque sight—coffins stacked haphazardly, reaching from floor to ceiling. They appeared ancient, perhaps a century old or more. Each coffin had ornate carvings adorned with floral motifs and a large cross. It sent shivers down my spine.

My attempts to use my other senses were useless; my supernatural abilities were impaired, much like when I had encountered the bestiary. Ellena was alive, but her condition was far from normal. Her heartbeat was shallow, weaker than it should have been. Supernatural senses were not required to tell that something was wrong. I couldn't move, couldn't escape. I was an unwilling passenger on this harrowing journey, uncertain of what awaited us. I spotted a glimmer of light across the cave wall, a faint but ominous echo.

A haunting message revealed itself carved into the stone: "Only the dead rest." The words sent a chill down my spine, and I couldn't help but wonder what they meant. Ellena began to move. Her right arm twitched, followed by her left. She flipped upside down, and then the unthinkable happened—her neck snapped, a sickening sound reverberating in the darkness. Her head rotated clockwise, her mouth stretched impossibly wide, and I saw sharp, thin fangs emerge unlike anything I had ever witnessed.

Ellena moved ominously towards snapping steps, and I remained frozen, unable to escape. There was no wolf to call upon, no one to help me. Panic coursed through me as I watched her fangs poised to strike. Her body convulsed, and my blood turned to ice. I had never been more terrified in my life. As she drew nearer, my eyes fixated on the unsettling details, hoping it was a manifestation of my mind. And then came the bone-chilling voice, the words seeping into my soul: "Secrets and the dead are imprisoned amongst the rocks. A key will set them free, and the dead will rule again."

We were trapped in a nightmarish scenario until Ellena suddenly returned to her seat, and everything returned to normal. Her face was etched with shock, just in time for me to swerve sharply to the right, narrowly avoiding a collision with a forty-foot trailer lorry.

"What the hell, Georgie? Are you okay? Your eyes... they looked ghostly again," Ellena stammered, her voice trembling with fear. Relief coursed through me, but the unease lingered. My instincts warned me that we were not out of danger yet.

"It... it happened again. We were in a cave filled with coffins, and you... you looked like death, with fangs and everything," I recounted, the memory still fresh in my mind.

"A cave? Fangs? Mine? Not that bad," Ellena replied, attempting to reassure me with her comforting smile.

"You said, 'Secrets and the dead are imprisoned amongst the rocks. A key will set them free, and the dead will rule again.' After a message on the cave wall, 'Only the dead rest.' It was utterly bizarre," I explained, watching Ellena's expression shift from disbelief to contemplation. Her fingers fiddled with brochures for Scottish attractions that she had been perusing.

I couldn't tell if Ellena was wrestling with regret or fear. Her heart remained calm, but we had just been reminded that the supernatural world had a way of intruding into our lives, no matter how far we ventured to escape it. The question lingered: would these ominous details be our downfall? Unfortunately, the signs were bathed in an eerie darkness, and only time would reveal whether the road ahead would be dangerous. Ellena and I had learned enough to understand that the devil resided in the details.

Chapter 2

The landscape before us was nothing short of breathtaking, a blend of rolling green hills, orange-yellow sands, and tranquil waters that seemed to hold a hint of mystique. We were nearing Peterhead-Cruden Bay, a historic fishing village with a population of just over fifteen hundred. It was where everyone knew each other's business, and the arrival of strangers like us didn't go unnoticed.

While the village did get its fair share of tourists, it was a far cry from the bustling streets of London. The weather here mirrored the English capital, with an average temperature of two degrees Celsius most days and rainfall on thirteen days of the month. However, the day seemed promising, with clear skies and a pleasant atmosphere.

As we approached, a road bridge spanned the low tide trenches, with seagulls diving into the clay brown sludge below. The acrid smell of diesel had given way to the clean, salty air, and the winter sunbathed the surroundings in a warm, golden glow. In the distance, the bulky beige stone ruins of Slain Castle stood proudly atop a cliff, and the crashing waves against its chalky walls were audible even from here.

The village was like a page out of history, with its colourful terraced houses lining the quiet streets. It felt like we had driven into a ghost town, and I couldn't help but sense the potential for secrets lurking in the shadows. Cruden Bay was the perfect place to let my inner wolf roam freely, away from prying eyes. However, it also reminded me how much I still had to learn about myself.

As the iron bridge rumbled beneath our wheels, I couldn't help but jump in my seat as we crossed a cattle grid. My coat pocket bounced on the edge of the seat, and my right sleeve snagged on something—a white envelope.

Amidst the rumbles and the worn cobbles on the adjoining road, we passed detached houses amidst uneven fields on the right and terraced homes, shops, and a quaint village pub on the left. Our destination, 'The McDowd Family Bed and Breakfast,' awaited us, marked by a brilliant white pebble dash facade and a rustic black sign that swayed gently in the breeze. Three hundred yards ahead, an arrow on the side wall pointed toward parking. Ellena's heart leapt with excitement, and her smile was infectious.

I couldn't help but glance at the mysterious envelope in my pocket, which bore the simple but enigmatic inscription, 'Sorry.' The handwriting I recognised was 'Locke'. Why would he choose to convey a message through a letter rather than in person? The unanswered questions from the cave and the eerie sight of the coffins still lingered in my mind. It was six o'clock, and after a seven-hour journey, we had finally arrived at a haven for the week. Unless, of course, there was more to what I'd experienced. The setting sun served as a reminder of the mysteries that lay ahead.

Although I longed to open the envelope, I resisted the temptation. I didn't want to cast a shadow over the excitement of our arrival with potentially unsettling news. But the feeling that something significant was concealed within nagged at me. One's an accident, two's a coincidence, and I couldn't shake the unease that this might be the third incident, forming a troubling pattern.

Ellena noticed my fidgeting with the envelope, and I quickly stashed it away. Instead, we decided to embark on a leisurely walk, a chance to breathe in the fresh air and change the images in our minds after the past few days' events.

Ellena shut the rear car door with a flip, and we began our stroll—the beauty of the surroundings and the sense of tranquillity washed over us. I thought about the fireworks display at 'Slain Castle' later in the evening that Ellena had mentioned. While fireworks weren't my thing, I was willing to embrace the idea of a drama-free night and the chance to see her smile.

Yet, despite the idyllic setting and the promise of an enjoyable evening, a lingering feeling of unease gnawed at me. I couldn't help but wonder if the third incident, whatever it might be, was on the horizon, ready to disrupt our newfound peace.

As we wandered, I couldn't help but contemplate Ellena's past love life. We had never delved into the skeletons in her closet, and I regretted my hesitance. We were now in a remote place, far from our usual lives, and it seemed the right moment to open up.

"So, little Lamb," I teased, "How did your husband feel about you going away for a week with another man?"

A mischievous smile crossed Ellena's face, and she replied, "Well, my sadistic wolf, you could say I'm married to many men."

I laughed, understanding the reference, "Ah, to the job."

"Yep, my wonderfully furry man, I'm otherwise married to the job. It's been that way for the last seven years. I came close once, but he didn't understand our work. He wouldn't listen to my day when I vented. So it stayed pent up. All the bad stuff I'd seen began to eat away at me. Things needed to change."

Ellena's voice had a hint of regret, a reminder that we all carried our battle wounds. I could relate, especially considering my own experiences and the support I had received from people like Sgt. Morris and Andy.

"I didn't mean to pry," I said sincerely. "I just thought now was a good time to open up."

"It's okay," Ellena replied. "We all have battle wounds. I took up a more administrative role in a crime-tasking unit in Camden for better hours, but it didn't help. Then, about when you came onto Locke's radar for that..."

I finished her sentence, "It's okay. Call it what it is. A shit show. A murderous shitstorm that nearly ended my career before it started. That and my vengeful foster brother."

Ellena had scars; I didn't want to pry too much into her past. We all had our burdens to bear; for now, it was enough to know that we were in this together.

As we walked, our surroundings began to change. The ground grew steeper, with lumps and bumps covered in lush grass extending as far as the eye could see. The ruins of Slain Castle loomed ahead, casting eerie shadows. I couldn't quite explain it, but something about the castle drew me in as if it held secrets waiting to be uncovered.

Ellena continued to share stories about the castle's history, how it had inspired Bram Stoker's "Dracula," and the eccentric author himself. I listened intently, appreciating the rich history and the sense of macabre that clung to the place.

However, my thoughts kept returning to the mysterious envelope in my pocket. It was a persistent itch, a question mark that demanded answers. I couldn't resist fiddling with it, and Ellena noticed.

"Georgie, you're here one moment, and then you're not. Your hand keeps going to your pocket," she remarked.

I chuckled, realising that I had been lost in thought, "Yeah, sorry about that. I don't understand why Locke would hide a letter in my pocket."

Ellena's response brought me back to the present, "We both know Locke has peculiar habits, and we're already assuming he's some kind of druid. It's probably something he didn't want others to hear."

Her words made sense, and I nodded in agreement. Locke was indeed a mysterious figure with his quirks. The envelope would have to wait for now.

As we continued our walk, the landscape became even more rugged, and the ruins of Slain Castle loomed ever closer. The sight of the dilapidated castle sent a shiver down my spine, but it also held a certain allure. We might not have been in Cruden Bay for long, but I felt an inexplicable connection to the place as if it held secrets waiting to be uncovered.

Yet, as my fingers continued playing with the envelope in my pocket, I couldn't shake the nagging feeling that trouble might lurk in the shadows, waiting to disrupt our new-found peace.

Then, I saw her—a young woman with long, dirty hair wearing an ankle-length black dress. She seemed to move silently, without the sway of the breeze that ruffled Ellena's hair. I blinked, hoping to clear my vision, but she was dangerously close to the cliff's edge. It was as if she was about to jump, and I couldn't believe my eyes.

I turned to Ellena in alarm, "Don't you see the woman?"

She looked at me with confusion, "No, why?"

I couldn't believe it, but there was no doubt. I had just witnessed a ghost, and Cruden Bay was beginning to reveal its secrets in ways I couldn't have imagined.

Chapter 3

She vanished from our sight in a fleeting moment, leaving a lingering sense of mystery and wonder. Ellena, my steadfast companion, refrained from judgment and embraced me with a strength that threatened to crush my ribs and compress my lungs. She empathised with the weight of the supernatural burdens I bore, and I was profoundly grateful for that. Admitting the peculiarities of my existence as a demon wolf aloud felt strangely disconcerting.

The abrupt disappearance of the mysterious lady left me pondering the intricacies of her manifestation. Her attire whispered of a bygone era, perhaps from the late eighteenth to the early nineteenth century. I couldn't help but wonder if others had witnessed her ghostly presence. A curious part of me yearned to approach the edge where she had vanished to unravel the mysteries behind her eerie visit. But I hesitated, fearful of following in her shadowy footsteps.

"Well, that was indeed unusual," I remarked, my chin resting gently on Ellena's head.

"A tad unusual, yes. But given your unique abilities and the previous vision, I half-expected something. Don't you think it adds a touch of excitement to our week?" Ellena's voice held a note of anticipation.

She had a point. Our presence here was not tied to a pressing case; it was merely an exploration of a historical death with the veneer of a suicide. We had the luxury of delving into the history of this place, unravelling its secrets at our own pace. Perhaps the lady might choose to communicate with me as others had. The wind picked up, the sky darkened, and my curiosity led me to desire a tour of the castle's exterior before we checked in at the local B&B.

As we stepped outside the castle's weathered walls, a blend of chalky white and charcoal-black stone surrounded us. Some sections retained their roofs and provided access to the castle's interior, while others stood as formidable, shadowy walls. The castle's vast perimeter seemed impossible to encircle as one side melded into the sheer cliff's edge. Our proximity to the grand entrance revealed a peculiar symbol—a goat's head—carved into the top step. Ellena noticed it, too and ventured closer for a more detailed inspection.

A robust Scottish voice broke the silence, "Ah, you can't enter. There's an event underway, and preparations are in progress." It emanated from somewhere unseen, carried by the swirling winds. No other sounds reached our ears from within the castle. Then, as though by magic, a tuft of grey hair materialised over the cliff's edge, followed by a man in his sixties. He wore a green hunter's coat, light brown cargo trousers, and black fibrous boots.

"Apologies, we couldn't discern that. We've just arrived today and were exploring," I shouted through the gusty winds.

"No bother at all. The last thing we need is tourists having their faces blown off. Quite the sight, though, isn't it?" The man's enthusiasm was palpable as he gestured toward the castle.

Suddenly, the wind changed direction, and a pungent odour assaulted my senses—blood. It wafted from the man's direction, though no obvious source was visible. It was an older scent, not distinctly human or animal, and a strange sense of discomfort settled in my bones. His hunter-style coat hinted at the animal association, yet something felt amiss. Like hackles raised in vigilance, my instincts echoed my unease as they greeted the peculiar scent.

Undeterred, the man continued toward us, his right leg slightly limp. His face sported a grey beard reminiscent of Santa Claus, but his eyes captured my attention. His left eye appeared ordinary, a shade of warm brown. Yet, his pale blue and slightly glazed right eye drew me in. It was impossible not to be captivated by its unusual appearance.

As he approached within a few feet, it became evident that his gaze was fixated on Ellena. It was not the typical admiration or lustful gaze; it seemed to swallow her whole. I heard the audible gulp of saliva as his heart quickened, and his complexion transformed from wind-flushed red to an eerie, pallid hue. His expression oscillated between shock, surprise, and the look of someone caught in an unforeseen revelation. He stared unblinkingly for what felt like an eternity, leaving Ellena visibly perplexed.

"I apologise; I merely wished to get a closer look. It seemed quite impressive as we drove by," he stammered, his words tinged with nervousness.

"Aye, she's got her fair share of tales to tell," he finally responded, his gaze still locked on Ellena.

"Intriguing. What kind of tales? Ghosts and such?" Ellena inquired, her grip on my arm tightening, a shared understanding between us.

"She could send shivers down your spine with tales that would make your hair stand on end. Ghosts are but the tip of the iceberg. So, who am I addressing?" He finally tore his gaze away from Ellena and directed his attention to me.

Ellena's heart fluttered with fascination, drawn to the prospect of supernatural encounters. The man's intriguing pitch had ignited my curiosity. We had entered this quaint village without any clear purpose. The prospect of delving into history and the unexplained tugged at our senses. Still, how the man had fixated on Ellena raised an undercurrent of unease within me.

"I'm George Reynolds," I began, hesitating to reveal my profession as a detective, sensing no immediate need or advantage in doing so. Unlike London, where such an introduction would invariably invite verbal abuse, here it seemed irrelevant. I also refrained from speaking on behalf of Ellena, partly because I was unsure how to introduce her and partly because I wanted her to feel comfortable and validated after her earlier revelation.

"I'm Ellena Walker, George's... well, sort of partner. It's still early days, and our work keeps us rather occupied. So, we decided to take some time for ourselves," Ellena added, her voice reflecting our shared sentiment.

"Yes, it's all quite new for us, and labels haven't been a priority," I concurred. "But we're grateful to be here together."

Throughout our conversation, the man's eyes remained fixed on Ellena, her presence seemingly ensnaring his attention. Her subtle discomfort in response to his gaze did not escape my notice, prompting me to consider a discreet intervention.

"Indeed, you won't be the first to find romance in this idyllic setting, and I doubt you'll be the last," the man, whom he introduced as Amos McKinnon, spoke warmly. "I'm Amos McKinnon, born and raised here in Crude Bay. It's a small place, but you won't want to leave once you get accustomed to its charms. I'm certain of that."

If Amos had spent a lifetime in this village, he undoubtedly possessed a treasure trove of stories to share—tales as captivating as the one he had just hinted at. Refraining from any complaints, I welcomed the opportunity to learn more about the history and secrets concealed within the ancient castle. As he referred to it as "she," it was evident that he attributed a living essence to the old stone structure.

However, a lingering question gnawed at me. How could Amos recognise Ellena's face? Such recognition implied that he had seen someone who bore an uncanny resemblance to her, but where and when? This puzzle beckoned for exploration, likely igniting Ellena's genuine interest in history.

"Mr. McKinnon, I couldn't help but notice your expression when you first saw Ellena. Does she remind you of someone?" I inquired politely, mindful of the need not to upset the residents during our initial hours in this charming village.

"Aye, no offence intended," Amos responded. "But the lovely lady does indeed bear a striking resemblance to someone from a bygone era."

Ellena's curiosity was piqued, and her voice rose with eager anticipation. I could sense the flames of her excitement flickering within her.

"Really?" she exclaimed with curiosity.

"Aye... a long, long time ago, she resembled a noblewoman from a powerful family. Unfortunately, her life met a tragic end under mysterious circumstances, or so the stories go. When I saw you, it was as though I were gazing upon the lady from an old tale," Amos revealed, opening the door to a realm of historical intrigue.

The echoes of that cave scenario, the enigmatic "Echo," and the haunting beauty of Ellena herself had already placed me on guard. Now, the revelation that Ellena bore a striking likeness to someone from the annals of history promised to unlock a tapestry of secrets. With discreet inquiries and the prospect of intermittent rest, we embarked on a quest to unearth the truths concealed within this charming village.

"That's remarkable. It seems such occurrences transcend borders and time. Speaking of which, with the evening descending and the eerie landscapes around us, do these cliffs and fields often attract lingering spirits if one could perceive them?" I asked, casting a furtive glance around, feigning a slight unease at the thought.

As if in response to my words, a sudden gust of sea wind carried the unmistakable scent of blood. Though fainter than before, it was enough to ignite my transformation. My hands began to shift, one concealed from view, the other tightly held by Ellena. A claw edged forward, and I knew we needed to change our location before my inner "wolf" was unwittingly unleashed.

"Aye, it's not for the faint-hearted, especially if you possess the gift to perceive the supernatural. Not everyone is blessed with such a sight," Amos commented, his words tinged with wisdom.

"Well, it sounds like we're in for an intriguing experience later," Ellena noted, her excitement palpable. "George, we should check in at the B&B before it gets crowded. Mr. McKinnon, thank you for your insights."

With a nod of acknowledgement, I struggled to keep my burgeoning fangs at bay, refraining from revealing my true nature. Amos's parting words were a solemn reminder that not all supernatural aspects were kind, particularly when wielded by those with vengeful intentions or lust for power. As we turned away, I could sense Amos's eyes burning into our backs, leaving me with an unsettling thought that lingered in the air.

"Could it be?"

Chapter 4

'5th November 6.45 pm.'

We stood by the car, and I flexed my fingers, trying to shake off the lingering sensation of retracting my claws. It always felt peculiar that transition from the primal instincts of a demon wolf to the mundane reality of human existence. Ellena had already retrieved her bag, grinning like a Cheshire cat. Everything appeared to be unfolding according to her plan, for the most part. This was an opportunity for us to spend quality time together. Now, Ellena believed she might resemble someone from history.

The most I could muster in the realm of resemblance was a faded black-and-white photograph of a skinny child rescued from a burning building—hardly a noteworthy comparison. Then again, in my eyes, few could hold a candle to Ellena's unparalleled beauty and charm. Yet, Amos intrigued me, much like the castle intrigued Ellena. He possessed knowledge, and I yearned to delve into his thoughts and uncover a way to explore what lay beneath the cliffside.

Was I inviting trouble? Most likely. And as much as we tried to avoid meddling in someone else's affairs, the lingering scent of blood wasn't the fragrance of an expensive cologne.

"What do you think lies down there?" I inquired, observing Ellena as she pulled her hair into a bun. It seemed she was entering a curious state of mind.

"I'm uncertain. Whatever triggered your transformation had to be malevolent, and I trust your instincts. On the other hand, Amos exudes an air of deception," Ellena replied.

I couldn't help but chuckle at Ellena's newfound determination and assertiveness;

it was a marvel. We were in sync, a harmony that could spell trouble for anyone else. I couldn't help but notice how she had acted meek and mild around Amos, only to transform once we were out of his sight.

"I concur. If that blood has any tale to tell, there's more to Cruden Bay than 'Dracula Books' and a woman taking a plunge," I added.

That thought lingered. Had I been selective in my perception? I had assumed the lady had leapt from the edge, but what if she had descended the way Amos had ascended? All I had witnessed was the ghost's trajectory. The wind was strong where we stood, but hardly gale force. Picture a slight woman at the precipice; she might have toppled at an angle, and the gusts could have influenced even a leap. I saw a straight path in the ghost's image, then sudden disappearance.

"Well, my dear wolfie, let's explore and see what we discover. Neither of us should venture alone, just in case," Ellena smiled, and I had no intention of letting her out of my sight.

"Well, my sweet lamb, how about you lead, and I follow? After all, you possess both the brains and the beauty in this partnership. I'm just teeth and claws. As for not separating, that seems wise. Amos seemed too interested in your resemblance to someone," I replied.

A woman in her early fifties with curly black, shoulder-length hair suddenly appeared, smiling at us through the rear window of the B&B. Then it happened again. Ellena turned to follow my gaze, and the lady's smile transformed into profound confusion. That made two for two. "Coincidence and accident" were becoming a pattern.

I waved casually, pretending not to read too much into her odd behaviour, as if something unpleasant had transpired on her doorstep. Then, another puzzle piece slapped me in the face, and a swift breeze grazed the front door frame. A large piece of wood attached to the frame was a piece of Mountain Ash. The block itself and the latch were adorned with the Ash wood.

"Mountain Ash," I muttered.

"What? Really?" Ellena asked.

"Yes, the wood on the door," I replied.

"Oh, dear. Judging by the configuration, the ash barrier is likely in effect when the wood is lowered. But don't worry; Ellena is well-prepared," she said, revealing another bag. I couldn't hide my surprise.

"And what might that be, my dear lamb?" I inquired.

"This is my werewolf first-aid kit, with a few extras," she replied.

"Why the extras?" I asked.

"Call it women's intuition, or perhaps I didn't want anything to happen to you. That last case shook me to the core. The moment with the limousine, thinking it might be the end. It opened my eyes, and I realised I'd been fooling myself," Ellena explained.

I had almost forgotten about the explosion. So much had transpired recently, and I had grown accustomed to the idea that nobody cared whether I was alive. It hadn't occurred to me how Ellena felt; I knew she was the first person I wanted to speak to once I was safe.

"And what's that?" I inquired.

"Do I need to spell it out? Well, this is all new to me, coming quickly. I'm hooked. I can't pinpoint one particular thing; it's everything about you. You always put others first, even those who don't deserve it. It's high time someone did the same for you. After all, if you face these risks against things that terrify others, you need someone in your corner. I want to be that someone," she confessed.

For the first time in perhaps forever, I was at a loss for words. But I had learned that actions spoke louder than words. So, I approached Ellena and pulled her close. Static electricity crackled over my skin, sending a shiver down my spine. Our eyes locked, and we kissed like no one else. I could feel the warmth radiating from her body, and her heartbeat raced like a runaway train. I could have stayed locked in that moment forever if not for the curious eyes still upon us. I saw that lady's expression again; perhaps she was a prude or a nun.

"Well, Mr. Wolf, that was unexpected. Shall we head inside before she has a heart attack or summons the convent squad?" Ellena quipped, and we laughed like teenagers, grabbed our bags, and strolled hand in hand to the front door. My stomach fluttered with butterflies, and an unusual feeling washed over me—happiness. Everything felt right. Yet, true to form, the peace didn't last. Something always came along to shatter it.

For us, it had been a murder. But this time, we were in a tranquil village with no expectations. Surely, life could grant us some normalcy before delivering another blow.

As we reached the front pavement again, people were beginning to head toward the castle—more than I had anticipated for an outsider looking in. We were about to enter the door when my hand instinctively pushed it open. Then, a cascade of lights enveloped the castle—laser-like blue, white, and red beams. They highlighted the grand structure, making it appear alive, like a colossal head.

Darkness had descended swiftly, and the village looked eerie at night. Only a few street lamps were scattered around, one on either side of the bridge and a few down the street.

The rest of the light emanated from homes coming to life. Then I turned to Ellena and wondered who else would look at her as if she were the second coming of 'Jesus.' Amos had likely spread the word by now, and our soon-to-be hostess was probably wracking her brain.

"Are you ready, George?" Ellena asked.

"Yes, of course," I replied.

The door swung open, revealing a space larger than it appeared outside. Dark wood flooring stretched throughout, with an open area to the right featuring a roaring fireplace against the back wall, comfortable seating, and a coffee table in front. It exuded cosiness. The rest of the room was filled with dining tables and chairs, at least eight of them, each set for four.

To the left was a counter, a fusion of a bar and hotel reception. Just beyond that, a swinging door likely led to the kitchen. The "Beef Stew" aroma wafted through the air, making my mouth water. For once, my craving wasn't for blood.

Ahead, there were restrooms and a back door, while a broad staircase graced the left side. But what caught my attention were the photographs. They adorned every available space, mostly black-and-white images documenting the village's history. They were committed to preserving their heritage. Ellena clung to my arm, sensing the captivating ambience.

But that ambience might be about to change. The swinging door swung open again, and a pair of women's feet shuffled toward us. The woman couldn't have been older than her mid-fifties, with bobbed hazel hair. She wore an apron over a sky-blue dress. She wasn't the one who had been eyeing Ellena earlier; her smile remained unchanged, and her green eyes gleamed warmly behind small brown-framed spectacles. She exuded hospitality and appeared genuinely welcoming. She was joined by another woman, presumably her sister, Dianne, who had a slightly longer mane of hair with hints of grey. Dianne wore black trousers and a white blouse.

"Hello, my dears. You must be Mr. Reynolds and Miss Walker," she said.

"That's correct. How did you know?" I replied.

"This time of year, we have very few guests, and you were the only ones we expected today. Others arrived yesterday. I'm Mrs. Mary McDowd, and I run this place with my sister, Dianne. She's the curious one who had been watching. Please excuse her; she can be a bit intense," Mary explained.

"That's not a problem. We would have come in sooner, but we wanted to take a quick look at the castle," I said.

"No worries. We understand. It's a beautiful sight, isn't it? Why don't you both warm up by the fire? We have coffee, hot chocolate, or tea waiting for you," Mary suggested.

Mary's words were like a melody to our ears. She led the way, and we followed, eager for a much-needed coffee. We reached the sofas, and my eyes were drawn to a collection of pictures hanging above the mantelpiece. Slain Castle was featured prominently, with candid shots of village residents going about their daily lives. Some dated back to the seventeen and eighteen hundreds. Some were downright peculiar, like a festival where people wore bizarre masks. But what intrigued me most were several masks that bore a striking resemblance to the goat's head symbols we had encountered.

"Mrs. McDowd, can you tell us about these pictures?" I inquired.

"Oh, those. We've had them for a while. They were in the cellar when we acquired this place. We thought they'd help us connect with the village's history and show our commitment to preserving it," Mary replied.

"So, you weren't born and raised here, then?" I asked, curious if Amos had been right about Ellena's resemblance.

"No, dear. We're from a small village near Dundee. We're both widowed. Our husbands worked together on an oil rig that exploded ten years ago," Mary said, her voice quivering as she recalled the tragedy. The loss was a sentiment I could relate to.

"I'm so sorry to hear that. How do you find it here?" Ellena inquired.

"Oh, not a problem at all. You couldn't have known, dear. As for this place, it has its quirks and is steeped in history, with a few ghosts here and there," Mary chuckled, her voice carrying a smoky undertone reminiscent of Michael.

"Have you seen any of these ghosts?" I asked, recalling Amos's mention that not everyone could.

"Oh, indeed. It can send shivers down your spine. You'd be surprised how many spirits linger in this small village," Mary said.

"The lady at the cliff?" I asked, my curiosity piqued.

"Yes, you've seen her too? I sensed something about the two of you. As for that lady, there's much more to her story, but perhaps it's best saved for another day," Mary replied.

Ellena paused while pouring me a coffee, her interest fully engaged. I was equally intrigued.

"Yes, I saw the lady in the black dress jump off the cliff. But what do you mean by 'sensed something about the two of us'?" Ellena asked.

Ellena moved to the edge of her seat, and Dianna watched from a distance. I couldn't help but be drawn to the floor, where I noticed light patches scattered amid the dark wood. Some were curved, and there seemed to be quite a few. Like pieces of a jigsaw puzzle seen from a different angle. A jigsaw puzzle to what, though?

Chapter 5

'9 pm Cruden Bay - Guy Fawkes Night,'

Separate rooms were unusual, considering how close Ellena and I had become. Mary's expression mirrored our uncertainty. We hadn't put a label on whatever "this" was between us, and we were fine with that. We both agreed to take it slow and let our connection develop naturally, without any pressure. We didn't want to rush things just because we happened to be spending a lot of time together. Our time together has been incredible so far.

What added to the intrigue was that our rooms were connected by an unlocked door, a temptation that was hard to ignore. I wanted to show Ellena the respect she deserved as an amazing person. There was also a nagging feeling in my mind that this seemingly peaceful fishing village held some hidden secrets, potentially ominous ones that could involve Ellena and me in ways we couldn't predict.

My room, a comfortable double, was positioned at the front of the house, offering a view of the small row of houses, the quaint bridge, and the lush greenery leading up to the castle and cliffside. It was a serene night, illuminated by a quarter moon. The next full moon was a couple of days away, and Ellena, always meticulous, had taken it upon herself to track the lunar phases so we could be better prepared. It was a task I knew I'd have to familiarize myself with eventually, but it felt like a world away from our usual routine of solving cases.

Everything was as expected inside the room, reminiscent of the chain hotels near the motorway. It had a shower, bath, toilet, wardrobe, dressing table, and a side unit with a kettle and television. I couldn't help but get intrigued when Mary mentioned the age of the building and the village itself. Although the structure had undergone remodelling, it had an air of age, possibly dating back a century or more. I had caught a fleeting glimpse of an oval stone tablet on the front of the house, presumably indicating its construction date. Unfortunately, I hadn't had the chance to read it, as my thoughts were already preoccupied with the mysteries of this place.

The enigmatic patches on the flooring downstairs continued to linger in my thoughts. When Mary and Diane had stood up to escort us to our rooms, Diane's proximity had been unusually close, almost uncomfortably so. She seemed to hover over us, not playfully or eerily, but intrusively. It was odd, considering her heart rate and chemo signals appeared typical. However, her behaviour made me wonder if she was trying to detect a particular scent. That was typically my area of expertise, and I couldn't determine whether she was acting strangely out of eccentricity or for some other reason.

All these details added up to an atmosphere of intrigue and uncertainty. The "mountain ash" door barrier and the enigmatic demeanour of Mary and Diane hinted at hidden secrets. I couldn't help but wonder what or whom these ladies were guarding themselves against. As we left the bed and breakfast, the night sky came alive with a mesmerizing display of colours and shapes. Laser lights danced gracefully over the front of the castle, creating intricate patterns that captured our attention. It was remarkable how quickly the atmosphere had transformed.

Navigating the footbridge in the darkness proved tricky, as the street lamps offered minimal guidance. Ellena had wisely chosen sturdier walking boots, considering the drop in temperature. The frosty crunch of grass beneath our feet reminded us of the chilly Cruden Bay breeze.

I pulled Ellena closer to share our body heat, our breath forming a visible mist in the night air. We had managed to distance ourselves from the nearest crowd, so I seized the opportunity to activate my wolf-like eyes briefly. I wanted to see if anything peculiar stood out among those who had braved the cold to witness the fireworks. The heat signatures were abundant, with each person's veins pulsing with lifelike miniature streams of molten lava.

My gaze wandered across the castle's front as we approached, and I noticed something that caught my attention. A trail of footsteps led to the far left corner of the castle, but there was no accompanying body heat signature. It was a baffling sight—how could footprints be without a physical presence? I should have ignored it, shrugged it off as a curiosity, and enjoyed the dazzling display of colours with Ellena.

However, my insatiable curiosity got the best of me. Ellena had been blissfully unaware until she noticed my change in direction and the quickening of my pace.

"Are you okay, Georgie?" Ellena's voice was filled with the excitement of a child in a candy store. I tried to maintain an air of nonchalance, but she could see right through me.

"Yeah, of course. I'm here with you," I replied, intentionally omitting that the closer we got to the fireworks, the louder the echoes reverberated in my eardrums. I watched her eyebrows furrow slightly, creating a dimple under her right cheek.

"Then why does it seem like you're on a mission? I noticed your strides quickened as our path changed. What have you seen?" Ellena's perceptive gaze bore into me, and I knew I couldn't deceive her. It was a moment for honesty.

"Footprints, but no heat signature from a body," I confessed, fully aware of how absurd it sounded. After all, how could there be footprints without a physical presence? Her frown shifted, and it was in moments like these that I appreciated Ellena even more. She didn't pout or sulk; instead, a smile spread across her lovely face, and her excitement for the fireworks returned.

"That can't be right; they'd have to be invisible. Oooh, this could be fun," she exclaimed, her curiosity matching mine. I was about to agree with her when the wind suddenly changed. The brisk breeze from Cruden Bay did an abrupt about-face, kissing my face and chilling us both.

I brought us to a halt, and Ellena gripped my left hand with hers. The popping of fireworks faded into the background, drowned out by the amplified heartbeats of the hundred-plus people around us. Each heartbeat pulsed at its rhythm, their veins resembling tiny rivers of molten lava beckoning my attention. My claws itched fiery, their tips glowing a vibrant red.

Ellena's voice reached me, a soothing whisper amidst the chaos within me. "It's okay, breathe. Come back to me, Georgie. Focus on my voice and only mine." Her words grounded me, and my frantic heartbeat gradually slowed. The fiery sensations receded, and I could again focus on the world around me. The footprints and the strange bloodstain had unsettled us, but we allowed ourselves to feel that unease.

Moments like these reminded me that life wasn't just about solving the mysteries of dead bodies. Ellena's smile, filled with the reflections of shooting stars in various colours, brightened my world. She was a beacon of happiness amid uncertainty. As much as I longed to kiss her, an inner restraint held me back. My fangs and claws remained ready, almost defensively.

One by one, they appeared in the darkness—shadows trembling with an unsettling presence. Each shudder put us on guard, and searing heat rippled through our bodies. Static coursed through our nerves, and I could feel danger approaching. My mouth closed instinctively, shielding me from view, while my eyes darted around, searching for the source.

"Blood and death," I whispered, and Ellena pulled me closer, forming a protective barrier between us and whatever was lurking in the darkness.

A sudden gust of wind and an unwelcome presence rushed toward us, disturbing the stillness of the night. They came without warning or a sound, like phantoms at night. Either they were exceptionally swift or had an uncanny ability to drift on the wind. Darkness shrouded them, making it impossible to discern their identities. However, one thing was certain: their aura was tainted with death and blood.

"Ah, Miss Walker and Mr. Reynolds. So pleased you decided to join the festivities," a voice greeted us, sending a shiver down my spine. Amos had materialized seemingly out of thin air, his smile oozing with an unsettling charm.

"It's quite the stealth you have there, Amos," I replied, unable to hide the unease in my tone. Ellena felt the fear, too, and we had to find a way to distance ourselves from him.

"Well, it comes with practice," Amos replied cryptically, his words dripping with an eerie undertone. Ellena and I exchanged wary glances, and our holiday in Cruden Bay had taken a dark and unexpected turn.

Reluctantly, we agreed to join the festivities, but our instincts told us this was far from the relaxing vacation we had envisioned.

Amos led us toward the upcoming festivities with his unsettling demeanour and enigmatic comments. The fire would be on the opposite side of the castle, and he mentioned something peculiar about this year's "Guy Fawkes" being exceptionally lifelike. Ellena shuddered at the thought, and I couldn't blame her. The entire situation had taken a disturbing turn. I couldn't shake the feeling that Amos was hiding something that might be connected to the inexplicable footprints and the fresh blood we had discovered.

As we walked with Amos, surrounded by the jubilant crowd and the colourful display of fireworks overhead, I couldn't help but notice a pattern among the onlookers. Those who wore expressions of excitement similar to Ellena's were likely tourists like us, while the locals had a more sombre and resigned look. It was as if they were going through the motions, perhaps feeling obligated to participate in the festivities for the sake of the visitors.

The fireworks lit up the night sky, revealing more of the village and the nearby port. I couldn't help but wonder about the cargo ship docked there; it seemed out of place in this quaint fishing village. The scent of gunpowder and burning wood filled the air, momentarily distracting me from the mysteries.

I focused my attention back on the small bloodstain we had discovered earlier. Ellena, ever perceptive, shielded my view while I inspected the immediate area. The aroma of Ellena's hair and her comforting presence helped calm my senses, bringing me back from the brink of a predatory instinct that had briefly taken hold.

The situation remained peculiar and unsettling. The trail of footprints leading to a point and abruptly stopping at a small blood splatter defied explanation. It was fresh blood, not more than half an hour old, and an irresistible scent stirred my primal instincts. But I couldn't allow myself to succumb to those urges; I was here to protect, not to harm.

Ellena and I exchanged glances again, silently acknowledging the unease between us. We had stumbled upon something inexplicable that didn't fit into the peaceful image of Cruden Bay. The question was whether Mary and Dianne knew more than they were letting on.

"Do you think Mary and Dianne know things?" Ellena asked, her voice low and filled with uncertainty.

"There's something about Mary. She seems to sense things. As for Dianne, she's a bit odd, and I can't get a read on her," I replied, voicing my suspicions. The enigmatic behaviour of the bed and breakfast's owners had been nagging at me since our arrival.

"So, it's human blood, Georgie?" Ellena's concern was evident, and I tried to offer a glimmer of doubt to ease her worries.

"I believe so," I answered cautiously, not wanting to jump to conclusions. But the unease in the pit of my stomach told me that there was more to this than met the eye.

The situation grew more unnerving by the second as Amos continued to exude an unsettling aura. We were led closer to the massive bonfire, where the lifelike "Guy Fawkes" effigy was about to be set ablaze. The crowd's excitement was palpable, and the flickering flames cast eerie, dancing shadows across Amos's face, making him appear even more sinister.

As we drew nearer, the acrid scent of gunpowder and burning wood filled the air, momentarily distracting me from my attempts to make sense of the strange occurrences of the night. Ellena pressed in close to me, her presence providing some comfort amidst the growing sense of unease.

The mysterious footprints and fresh bloodstain remained at the forefront of my mind, and I couldn't help but wonder if they were somehow connected to this bizarre celebration. The abrupt stop of the footprints, with no sign of a staggered trail, defied explanation, and I couldn't detect any scent to lead me to the source. Ellena, too, drew a blank in scanning the crowd for any unusual chemosignals.

I tightened my grip around Ellena, and we exchanged glances conveying unease. Cruden Bay was hiding secrets, and we had stumbled upon them unwittingly. The villagers' strange behaviour and the unsettling events of the night were all pieces of a puzzle that refused to fit together neatly.

Despite the overwhelming feeling that we should leave this place immediately, we knew we couldn't simply walk away without arousing suspicion. Amos's invitation to join the festivities felt more like an imperative, and we had no choice but to play along for the time being.

"Well, it would be rude of us, as guests to your village, not to witness such finery," I replied, doing my best to maintain a facade of politeness while my senses remained on high alert.

Amos's response did nothing to ease our concerns. "The fire will be underway shortly on the opposite side of the castle. I heard the 'Guy' this year is quite lifelike, and much preparation has gone in."

The mention of the lifelike "Guy Fawkes" figure sent shivers down my spine. It was clear that there was more to this event than met the eye, and I couldn't help but feel that something evil lurked beneath the surface.

Amos's presence continued to exude a sense of dread, and I knew that we needed to find a way to distance ourselves from him and the crowd. As the effigy of "Guy Fawkes" was set ablaze, casting its eerie glow over the village, I couldn't shake the feeling that we were stepping into a darkness we might never escape. Our only choice was to stay vigilant and uncover the truth behind Cruden Bay's secrets, no matter how terrifying they might be.

Chapter 6

'9.30 PM BONFIRE TIME.'

Arm in arm in the middle of a crowd with a chilly sea wind blowing through crackles, bangs, and lit-up faces. We were amongst the masses, and I couldn't have felt any further from being safe. The scent of human blood hung in the air, mingling with the acrid stench of gunpowder and Amos's pungent aura. If we had left after the invitation, it would have seemed suspicious.

The towering stack of wood was set ablaze with ease. It had been meticulously arranged in the shape of a mountain, with a figure strapped to the top, wearing a white mask and a black hat, a macabre tribute to the infamous Gunpowder Plot conspirator. A black sack enveloped the figure's feet and lower legs, drenched in gasoline, and the arms were eerily positioned behind its back. My instincts, though irrational, prompted me to listen for a heartbeat. Would there be one? I couldn't be sure. My mind was weaving together a web of crazy dots, but I kept my thoughts to myself; Ellena might think I was going mad. Then again, perhaps I was.

The details I had gathered led me from the enigmatic bloodstain to the realization that this "Guy" was shockingly lifelike. Had Amos thought we wouldn't pick up on his cryptic words? The trouble was that my senses were being thrown off balance. Amos was nearby, engrossed in conversation with a group of older villagers, and his scent, a cocktail of chemicals and the unmistakable aroma of gasoline, clouded any specific identification. Except for the gasoline, there seemed to be no logical reason for other chemicals. What perverse pleasure could one derive from burning a lifeless body? My thoughts were a tangled mess of mysteries, and my dots refused to connect, leaving me increasingly frustrated.

Ellena appeared deep in thought as well. A smaller fire, off to our right amid a stone pit, was being kindled. A substantial spit suggested the roasting of a hog, and the initial sizzles of its flesh added to the cacophony of confusion. Occasionally, I noticed Amos directing the gazes of a few older individuals in our direction, particularly at Ellena, who turned to me with a questioning look.

"Georgie, if you want to leave, we can. I mean, really leave," Ellena spoke, her eyes scanning the scene. Initially, I thought she meant leaving the display behind, but I soon realised she meant leaving the village.

"Do you think we should?" I inquired.

"Honestly, something feels profoundly amiss here. It's been that way for some time, I suspect. The place appeared quaint when we arrived, but I followed your example and started tracking the 'little things' that felt off. I fear that if we leave now without investigating further, nothing will ever change. I think people are dying here—being killed, perhaps. What kind of person would I be if I deprived this quaint village of the one person uniquely reckless enough, the one with an uncanny detective ability to see solutions where others don't?"

"You'd be the kind of person I'd follow, and the last thing I'd want is to put you in harm's way," I replied.

"Well, remember that this 'lamb' is just as reckless," Ellena quipped with a smile. "So, I'm with you, no matter what. The only question is, where do we start?"

Ellena's words struck a chord. She was right. We needed to uncover why Ellena had attracted unwanted attention and whether my visions were mere nonsense or eerie echoes of past events or worse—forewarnings of what was yet to come.

"Let's find someone in this village willing to talk to us, someone who might shed light on why 'Mr. Old and Creepy keeps trying to bore holes into you with his eyes," I suggested, casting a wary eye toward Amos to ensure he remained within our sight.

The aroma of roasting hog filled the air, making my stomach rumble with hunger. Trays of drinks were passed around, and I assumed it was the special mulled wine Amos had mentioned. Ellena and I watched the crowd as they revelled in the festivities, all while keeping a watchful eye over our surroundings. A moment of peace washed over us. I held Ellena close for a few minutes, forgetting the mysteries that had brought us here and savouring the moment.

Then, amidst the revelry, someone caught my eye—a woman standing at the back of the crowd, seemingly unperturbed by the loud bangs and colourful flashes. It was the same woman who had gone over the cliff earlier. This time, she didn't head toward the castle but instead ventured down a winding pathway that seemed to lead to some outbuildings about half a mile away. Ellena appeared intrigued, and we were about to follow her when a tray of drinks was thrust into our faces.

I detected the scent of spices and alcohol, along with another unfamiliar ingredient that, while almost familiar, was masked by the other aromas. Ellena reached for an old-fashioned brass goblet when a whisper, so low that only I could hear it, drifted on the wind. A woman's voice, older and ethereal, sounded near and far.

"Somebody told us not to touch those drinks. They whispered at a level only I could hear," I whispered to Ellena, gently guiding her hand away from the goblet. She looked at me, her expression a mixture of curiosity and confusion.

The decision loomed before us: follow the enigmatic ghost or uncover the identity of the mysterious whisperer who knew I could hear them. The ghost continued down the path, and Ellena joined me in scanning the area, growing unease about the engineered nature of our presence in this village settling over us. I couldn't help but think about the unopened letter from Locke.

"I knew you were different," the whisper came again, and this time, it felt as though I had heard the voice before, just moments ago.

"Don't worry. You're safe with us, despite how things may appear," I replied, recognizing the voice as Mary's from the Bed and Breakfast.

"It's Mary. She knows I can hear her. I suspect she knows more about what I am," I explained to Ellena, who kept a vigilant watch for her, although Mary remained elusive.

"Alright, let's go follow her," I said, deciding as we cut a path through the crowd.

"Be careful. You have eyes on you, and Amos is nothing good. Dianne confirmed my suspicions about you. This is fate. We believe you're here to help rid this village of the evil that's plagued it for centuries," Mary's voice carried through the air, leaving me to wonder about the nature of the evil she spoke of. Dianne's earlier actions, like her peculiar sniffing, began to take on a deeper significance. The notion of fate gnawed at the edges of my mind, and I couldn't help but question whether I had been manipulated into coming to this remote corner of Scotland for a specific purpose. The answers might lie within that unopened letter from Locke.

As we headed toward the ghost and Mary's whispered guidance, I turned to Ellena. "It's a bit of a walk. Can you keep an eye out for Amos while I guide us to the ghost?

Also, did Locke ever mention..."

I began to articulate my suspicions, although they seemed outlandish, and I didn't want to sound accusatory. One thing was certain: Locke had orchestrated our journey here.

We quickened our pace, my senses attuned to Mary's presence and the ever-present stench of blood and death emanating from Amos. No amount of washing could conceal it, suggesting that he had recently been near a mortuary. Mary had labelled him evil, but his actions' full extent remained a mystery. Our focus shifted to Mary and the gravel path that led to an unknown destination.

Near the outbuildings, an old cemetery emerged, adorned with mausoleums, headstones, crosses, and other grave markers. The ghost continued its ethereal journey, leading us to a solitary stone cross beneath a tree in the corner of the cemetery. As we drew closer, I noticed Amos in motion.

"He's following us from a distance, Georgie," Ellena whispered, her voice tinged with worry. My thoughts circled back to the dots I had been trying to connect. Could Amos have abducted someone, leaving no trace but his footprints? A shiver ran down my spine at the thought of those deadly claws.

Old black iron railings enclosed the cemetery, providing an eerie ambience. The ghost stood beside the cross, then vanished into thin air. We had left the chaotic crowd behind, and everything became eerily quiet, providing an unsettling backdrop for what was to come.

Footsteps approached three sets of them. The first set signalled the leader, slightly ahead of the others and moving swiftly. Their face was obscured in the darkness, but their stature revealed their identity—Amos.

We opened a heavy, creaking gate, its age evident in the tortured sound it produced. Inside the cemetery, fear clung to us like a shroud. Having encountered a ghost, I dreaded what other supernatural entities we might encounter. Cautious and vigilant, we knelt by the stone cross for a name, an inscription, anything that could explain why the same ghost that had gone over the cliff had led us here.

Suddenly, a hoot echoed through the night, causing Ellena and me to jump. As the adrenaline coursed through my veins, I looked up to find a large owl perched in the tree above us.

"Can you see anything, Georgie?" Ellena asked, her voice still slightly trembling from the scare.

"I'll check in a moment," I replied, glancing outside the railings to ensure we remained undisturbed before returning my attention to the stone cross.

The scene before me held an eerie sense of mystery. There was no name, no sign that anyone had ever been buried here. No flowers or offerings adorned the spot. It was a silent, enigmatic grave, and my red-hued sight failed to uncover anything unusual—except for a series of numbers etched into the stone. These numbers were unlike any date; they seemed excessively long and featured a decimal point after the initial two digits.

"Ellena, write this down," I urged, and Ellena retrieved a pen and a small pad from her pocket.

"Go on," she encouraged.

"51.81904, with an arrow pointing upwards. Hurry," I instructed.

Ellena scribbled the numbers down just as the approaching footsteps grew nearer. The significance of these numbers remained a baffling puzzle, and I couldn't help but wonder what secrets they held.

Chapter 7

Ellena swiftly concealed the paper. I moved closer to her, and we strolled out of the gate together, attempting to appear casual. Seeing, let alone following a ghost, was anything but normal. Ellena held my hand, her steady heartbeat grounding me.

My claws receded as I scanned our surroundings, alert for any surprises. The last thing we needed was another shock, like the unexpected appearance of Amos McKinnon just seconds after passing through the gate. His face was unreadable. I couldn't discern much about him. Ellena and I didn't need a creepy guy tailing us, especially with the mystery of those numbers on the cross to unravel.

How many times had that ghost materialised here over the years? How many villagers could see her? And if they could, what had they done about it? Amos was an enigma, and all I could smell was death and putrid blood. Could he be blocking my abilities? Was that what Amos was doing? I couldn't detect his heartbeat or chemical signals. Amos looked pale and sad. Or perhaps I was mistaken, and there was no heart to detect.

"You okay?" I whispered to Ellena, trying to escape my racing thoughts. The notion of confronting a heartless creature was hard to believe. It would make him the 'walking dead,' but I had no idea where the boundaries of the supernatural ended.

"Yeah. What do we do? He has us cornered."

"I can't read him. I can't hear a heartbeat."

"What? That's not possible. Right? Strange shit in the middle of nowhere," Ellena shared my disbelief. Then, a thought clicked in my mind, echoing Ellena's words about being in the middle of nowhere. Location. The way the numbers looked.

"Longitude and latitude."

"What?"

"That number."

"Oh, I see. And what might that number be, boyo?" Amos inched closer. We had been whispering, so he shouldn't have heard us.

"The square root of 'PI'. I've never been good with math. Although I know that three is a crowd," I attempted to flip the situation around. After all, Amos had followed us. How could he possibly know where we were headed? We didn't intend to take a solitary stroll.

"I thought you might be lost. As you said, you're new here."

"Well, we're not. So, if you don't mind, we'll be off," I held Ellena tightly and moved forward, attempting to create some distance.

We'd barely taken five steps when my instincts went haywire. A stronger breeze carried that foul stench to us. I turned, and Amos was suddenly right there, only a few feet away. I could move faster than an ordinary person if I chose to, but Amos, with his limp, had closed the gap instantly. The uncertainty was the most frightening part—an ironic twist, a werewolf filled with fear. Yet, I had deliberately suppressed that side of me for the sake of others.

Yet, here we were, in the middle of nowhere, under a cold, biting wind, beside a graveyard, an eerie owl hooting in the background, and Amos closing in on us with a speed I had never witnessed before. Speed...check. No heartbeat...check. The stench of death...check. I didn't mention this to Ellena; I didn't want to frighten her more than she already was. Amos was just two feet away—his face paler than when we first met, with dead, jet-black eyes.

"Why leave so soon? I could show you around. There's so much more to see. You haven't even discovered the secrets yet. Your wee lass here might be surprised by the history... Your destiny is calling," Amos's words sent shivers down my spine. What disturbed me more, his words or the chilling tone he delivered? A part of me longed to shift, but I hesitated. What if I was wrong? What if Amos was merely a twisted human, not some undead creature? I didn't want to reveal my true nature without certainty. So, instead, I allowed the wolf's presence to surge within me while keeping the rest at bay. I turned and stepped up to Amos, who exuded an unnatural cold.

"If it's all the same to you, we don't need a tour guide. Kindly piss off," I asserted. For a split second, I noticed a change in Amos's eyes. They had already been black, but now the whites had vanished, too. Then he smiled and stepped back, leaving Ellena trembling slightly. All I wanted was to distance her from whatever Amos represented.

"There you two are. We've been looking all over," Mary's voice echoed through the darkness. We turned to see her approaching, and when we glanced back, Amos was gone. I couldn't even catch his scent anymore. Whatever Amos was, to move that quickly, with his lifeless eyes and the chilling cold he radiated, he was far from normal. I hugged Ellena, and she nestled her head under my chin. Deep down, I knew it wouldn't be long before I had no choice but to unleash the wolf.

Coffee with a shot of whiskey. Flames flickered and danced within the wood logs, gradually turning from light brown to black. The aroma of burning wood was my refuge, allowing my mind to escape. I felt drawn into the never-ending abyss of red and yellow flames, my thoughts consumed by those jet-black eyes. That fleeting moment when the whites had disappeared. The wall of morbid cold emanated from his very being. Who was Amos McKinnon, and why had we ended up in Cruden Bay, of all places?

Ellena rested her head on my lap, her legs and feet curled up like a prawn. The sound of her breathing was a comfort amid the chaos. Across the wooden floor, solid heels clacked, and metal clinked against porcelain. The comforting aroma of beef stew filled the air as Mary approached, carrying a tray with two bowls of stew and a plate of bread. It felt like we were being placated before the impending storm. Perhaps I had missed it. Maybe it had already begun when we arrived, and I had failed to notice. Or perhaps it had started when Locke discreetly slipped that letter into my possession—the same letter I now held as I sipped my coffee.

Mary placed the tray on the table with a warm, grandmotherly smile, though I couldn't shake the feeling that she was about to deliver some unsettling news. Despite everything, the moments spent gazing at the crackling fire felt serene, a strange irony considering the turmoil engulfed us.

"What's that you've got there?" Mary inquired, taking the seat opposite me.

"To be honest, I'm not sure. I've been putting off opening it, fearing I won't like what's inside," I admitted. I had already had my fill of challenges from one direction, and I wasn't eager to invite more.

"Surely, it can't be worse than what's happening outside? What's happening out there? Not every written word spells trouble. Sometimes it brings good luck, fun, or a request for help," Mary offered a perspective I hadn't considered. Of course, my mind immediately jumped to the worst-case scenario—that Locke was asking for a favour.

Mary reached into a box by her feet and retrieved an ornate, dusty, black-and-white photograph. She handed it to me, and I couldn't immediately discern its significance.

"Look to the right, at the back of the group, behind the Lord and Lady in the chairs," Mary instructed.

The photograph bore the date 1867, and upon closer examination, I noticed a man in a two-tone suit with hair parted to the right. His smile and the intense, penetrating stare were unmistakable. I couldn't believe my eyes. It defied logic and reason. It upended everything I thought I knew. The boundaries of the supernatural had shifted once again. Amos McKinnon stood among a group surrounding what appeared to be nobility or royalty—over a century ago. Was he an ancestor, or was I simply being naive?

"Is this him?" I asked, still in disbelief.

"Oh, it's him, alright."

"How is that possible?"

"The same way you're possible."

"Me?"

"Dianne, turn up the heat," Mary instructed. Dianne, standing nearby, flipped a switch and watched with a smile. It wasn't an evil smile but a confident, slightly cocky one reminiscent of Michael.

"What are you doing?" I asked.

"If you get too hot, you can always turn the switch off," Mary replied. The smiles on their faces didn't seem threatening. My hackles were raised slightly, and a familiar scent began to waft through the room. Mountain Ash, but with a subtle difference.

"It's okay, George. You're safe. We're merely demonstrating that we understand and anything is possible. Including someone alive after one hundred and twenty years, especially if they're vampires."

My jaw dropped, and a loud thud echoed on the wooden floor. Movies, books, and folklore had romanticized what lurked in the shadows. A vampire. Seriously.

"What the hell? Of all the places to end up, we find vampires and an impassable circle on the floor. What are the odds?"

"Well, not too different from a werewolf coming to a cursed village. And Amos is just the beginning," I realized that my one-week escape from death and the bizarre was rapidly unravelling. There would be no respite, except perhaps for Ellena, who remained blissfully asleep. And now, someone else knew my secret—I was a werewolf. Did Mary expect me to have a magical solution to our predicament by showing me that photograph? Truth be told, I was far from understanding my abilities, let alone this new level of strangeness.

What else did Cruden Bay have in store for us? It was smaller than London by a long shot, but this obscure village suddenly felt more dangerous than any metropolis. All because, on that first day, it had appeared to be the picturesque image from a travel magazine: an idyllic castle against the backdrop of the sea, endless green fields, sunshine, and blue skies. But as night descended, Cruden Bay transformed into an entirely different beast.

Chapter 8

Mary dragged out half a dozen pictures. To anyone else, it would seem like a stroll down memory lane. This was anything but. Instead, Mary emphasised her news, and my shock deepened. I, a stranger who had just wanted a peaceful week away, was now confronting the existence of vampires. Suppose there was any saving grace, it was that Ellena slept peacefully on the chair.

I found myself back by the fire, feeling that whiskey-induced edge, and I didn't have the cockney prince to keep me focused. Each picture Mary flashed as part of her morbid slideshow featured Amos. Only they went as far back as 1769. Over two hundred years old. Christ, he had to be fossilised by now. I mean, did vampires even digest their meals? Surely, the red liquid lunch had to go somewhere.

One too many coffees, and I'm pissing like a racehorse. So what's the difference? Aside from being undead. That's what they are, right, undead? It would account for the absence of a heartbeat. The gimpy bastard looked the same in each shot. That made me think about our hosts; who were Dianne and Mary? Ten years they'd been in Cruden, or so they claimed. Their house was fortified like supernatural Fort Knox.

At least they hadn't laced the cups with LSD or wolfsbane. That number on the cross wasn't normal and seemed to be a map grid reference, which was no good without the other sequence. 'Longitude and Latitude,' Mary seemed deep in thought, contemplating what else she would share or if I intended to wake Ellena and flee their cursed village before it was too late. That would have been the smart move. Then again, I'd never been accused of being smart.

Besides, it wasn't much of a leap from a parasitic politician to a vampire. Their victims got bled dry if any of those stupid myths were true. I had to know where else that ghost had been seen and how Amos had been allowed to roam unchecked. More to the point, were there others? I stood leaning against the mantelpiece, soaking up its warmth, when I caught a scent. It was here. 'Death' was outside the house.

For whatever reason, I didn't hide myself this time. My claws emerged with the anticipation of danger. Because I hadn't resisted, the stench was strong, thankfully, the one thing I could pick up on. All this felt a little out of my depth, and I had more than myself to think about. If Amos had given anything away by following us, for whatever reason, Ellena was important. Or at least he believed her to be.

Something I wasn't okay with. The idea that some spooky, dark forces had aligned, and Ellena had become a target for something I never imagined possible. Then again, who'd have thought a werewolf could be a detective?

"It's okay, George. They can't get in."

"They?"

"It isn't only Amos. And this is far darker and more complicated than you'd think. This isn't your usual wheelhouse, and you may struggle with things you will learn. We feel fate has made this possible, and whatever way the chips fall, the village will either be saved or destroyed. And if it's the latter, this place could only be the beginning. Anyway, they have to be invited in. This house is protected throughout."

"So that part is true? How many?"

"At the moment, three. Elder familiars. What they wanted had been elusive…until now."

"What might that be? And what the hell is a familiar?"

"Enslaved people. Butlers. Servants. And spies."

"For whom?"

"I didn't want to know. With every phrase, I was becoming more creeped out. I now had more than Amos to worry about. My money was on the others we saw him with at the fireworks. One thing is for sure: there wasn't an ounce of shock from Mary or Dianne as she walked in.

"This village is steeped in many things. In the early days, it was blood. Until something changed, and things got covered up. The how and when I don't know. Only, that what's below is scarier, deadlier, and will stop at nothing until they achieve their goal."

"What the hell. I can't believe I'm asking this, but what's their goal?"

The ground we walked on was nothing more than the roof for evil, and it scared me shitless. Especially the fact they could stalk the house like we were prey. The only thing stopping them was a few little words. Little details that could get us killed.

"To be in the world properly and probably spread like wildfire."

"So what the hell is stopping them?"

"Many things, apparently, but not least a curse. We should leave tomorrow. We're safe, and you need to rest."

"Won't he or they just try again?"

"Not in daylight. That's what took so long to figure out. A detail is different from the stories. For the familiars, at least. In the day, they seem normal, act normal, and interact as we do without wanting to hunt. Come nightfall, it's like a switch gets flipped. He toyed with you two earlier. Wanted to get your measure. Don't let the limp fool you. He's powerful."

"Do they know you know?"

"I'm not sure. For the most part, they've operated anonymously. Only when a pattern of visitor disappearances was noticed years ago did we start to dig and piece it together. As I said, too much for now."

Too much, indeed. Nightmares were coming, whether I wanted them or not. I could only picture the creepy, damp cave and how Ellena looked. The creaking and cracking, her beautiful face, deathly pale with fangs. The dirty old coffins in the shadows. Those bony grey fingers. Everything Mary had said so far matched what I saw. I didn't want to believe it to be true.

It was cold. Icily bitter. The streets were empty, nothing but strips of grey bobbled roads and sheets of bristling green. The castle, in all its splendour, was engulfed in purpling black. Nighttime made it seem even more daunting. A blanket of smothering white was rolling in from the sea.

The lighthouse to the windy west disappeared amongst the white curtain, with only its bright yellow light able to pierce its veil strongly enough to guide the ships heading into port. I lingered in the street, looking towards the graveyard and the outbuildings. Every house light was out, and there was no hint of death, stench, or creeping limp scuffing across the stones.

The burgeoning tree became a fixed point for my gaze, almost charming. Until I saw a faint glow further behind those rickety old buildings along another pathway. It was the lady I still didn't know the name of or when she died. Like a moth to the flame, I followed out of morbid curiosity.

My feet endured the cold with each step. Naively, I'd stepped out barefoot and in pyjamas. Perhaps the lure of the unknown felt too great. Everything I didn't know about this village scared me. The idea of vampires below the streets filled me with dread. Yet, I had to see.

Each house I passed I hadn't noticed before. They seemed older, almost trapped in a forgotten time. Timbers and thatched roofs stretched as far as the eye could see, with the smell of horse manure in the fields behind. It made me wonder how else a place like this could survive. Tourists like Ellena and me are one thing, but still not a conveyor belt of masses. If what Mary said was true, any newcomers were getting snatched. Like the footsteps and the splash of blood, I saw.

The glow meandered through the path, gradually flowing down a stretch toward some farmland, seemingly on the back road that led to the port. The farm seemed grand, a huge all-black house with angled roofs. I was a quarter of a mile behind and following mindlessly, not for the first time. Yet the house held the same lure for me as the castle. I couldn't explain how or why, but there was a strange magnetizing pull towards its imposing silhouette.

The glowing, ghostly lady breezed through the night and the yard. A large tree spread like a creepy arm towards a flight of rickety steps. I drew closer as the ghost stopped at the steps. She had something in her hands: a single white rose. Then she faded into darkness. I was at the timber slats, and there was a carved message instead of a flower.

'Love is eternal.'

A strong wind swirled, and a rush of pain pulled and grew into an angry gust. Screams echoed all around until I was pulled to stare at the tree. The ghost stood to the side, looking up at the thick branch. A crowd appeared with pitchforks and lanterns. A rope swung over the branch before a noose was whipped around a man's neck, who stood atop a ladder. I couldn't describe what they looked like. Everyone was a blur. In the blink of an eye, the ladder was knocked away.

I heard the snap. His body writhed in the air. The crowd cheered before they all faded away. Echoes of pain roared through the wind once more. Confused, I stood in front of the house until the ghost appeared ten feet in front. She was dressed in an elegant yet dirty white dress. Her head stooped as she walked. I could smell death again. Closer and closer until that's all, I could breathe in. A sudden burst forward, and she jolted up. It was the same as in the cave...Ellena with fangs bared. She screamed, piercingly high-pitched. Before her pale, gaunt grey face stared deep into my soul.

'We...will walk amongst the gardens of man and woman again. Blood is all you'll see.'

Then she squealed, her mouth wide, fangs gleaming and dirty black liquid oozed from her mouth. It was deafening, to the point I could take no more and dropped to my knees.

Chapter 9

'4 am 6th November 1987,'

"Huh...w...w...what happened?"

I jumped up in a panic. It seemed to be a familiar theme these days. My pyjamas clung to my body. All I saw was the moon beaming through the window. Everything was vividly at the forefront of my mind. Too real not to be.

'We will walk amongst the gardens of man and woman again. Blood is all you'll see,'

That's what she said. That's what Ellena said. I didn't want it to be true. The idea of her becoming one of those scared me senseless. That big house and the way the ghost laid the rose. I never saw the face; I couldn't figure out how the two connected. Or who the bloke was that got hanged. The next biggest question mark was, why did I see them?

It was hard to decide what to do next. As Mary put it, we seemed to be guided here one way or another—fate. Or otherwise. Two echoes have come my way now. Both have shown me, Ellena, in a way that makes me sick.

I slumped back onto my pillow; the ceiling didn't hold much in the way of hypnosis that could help me drift again. All I had was an old brown lampshade with frilly tassels hanging down. There was no point in going over every detail again. That would only drive me crazy. I knew less than nothing anyway. My wheelhouse was the streets and trying to stop the bodies from dropping. For that, we had teams of people.

Then I saw the letter on the side table. I decided to bite the bullet in light of what could be ahead. A quick flick of the side light and I grabbed Locke's parting gift. I can't lie. My body was riddled with apprehension. We'd put it off long enough.

"*Dear Georgie,*

First of all, thank you for the hard work you and the team have pulled off lately. It's been two gruelling cases quickly, and I understand the ballache I caused by dumping the 'Black Widow' case on your lap. It was an immense favour in a realm that I knew nobody else would understand or be able to see through the smoke and mirrors.

I know you need a well-deserved break, yet what I will say next. Well, sort of a request. Maybe more a merciless beg that you could find it within you to help again. I will owe you. Part of that I'm working on now. It will be a surprise, and that's all I will say about it for now. Until then...

Fuck...I should probably apologise first—the little manipulation of where to go. I'm sure Cruden Bay wouldn't have been your first choice. Or should I say 'Blood Bay' as it used to be called? I needed you there. Your mind and the way you see things are unique. I need you to solve a murder.

A very old and bizarre murder of my ancestor, Jean Martin Cortez. In seventeen twenty-five. He'd travelled the world mapping countries with his assistant, Frederick Lasille. They were intrigued by the different cultures and looked into the mythology. They came through Romania and the countries between Scotland to explore Great Britain and Norway.

-Until he met Countess Anna Farrington, the only daughter of six children from Earl Andrew Farrington and Countess Sophia Farrington. Anna and Jean hit it off after Anna became intrigued by his recordings. Only Jean was also a druid, collecting special herbs from those countries and had been somewhat of a healer. Especially in Cruden after sailors brought an outbreak of scurvy through the port. Jean won favour with the Earl until he became aware of his fondness for Anna.-

- *What they all failed to see was Frederick getting sick. Until it was too late. No herbs worked, not to cure him. He developed a liking for blood. An unusual parasite in Romania brought on that he'd kept from Jean. First, it was alleviated by animals. Jean began to notice physical changes in Frederick. Large fangs, paler skin. Hot then cold sweats, until only cold. Jean attempted to hide the condition from everyone, including the Earl and his family.*

-Meanwhile, Anna and Jean's relationship intensified. They were in love. Even the moments it became hard to see each other. They found a way to message each other—symbolising their unrelenting love. Then, people began disappearing, at first, sporadic. Then, some would be found torn to pieces. Each day, the amount of blood in the Village became greater.

-Eyes turned on Jean, thinking his methods to cure sickness had turned the villagers rabid. Little did they know Frederick had started it. He'd been sneaking out at night. In every sense, Anna and Jean were forbidden by the pain of death. The villagers sought to eradicate the problem they saw as a curse. Realising stabbing the heart with spikes made from mountain ash would all but desiccate them to what they believed was dead. Most had been friends, so they couldn't bring themselves to destroy the bodies. Instead gave them coffins. Yet, they also didn't believe their abominations warranted burial.

-On orders of the Earl, a group of villagers entombed the coffins in the caves and tunnels deep under the Village through the cliff front. All went quiet for a month or so. Jean occupied Montague House, keeping Frederick, his friend and assistant, a secret. Sadly, Jean had been blinded. Believing what Frederick had said about the parasite, and that's how the town got sick. Jean worked tirelessly for a cure. He built a tunnel from the house to the castle and the tombs. He was taking samples and experimenting. It also allowed Anna and Jean to reconnect.

-Jean was struggling for a cure, so in the meantime, he cursed the Village and those afflicted by what he called a savage virus—binding them to the Village. So if somehow one or Frederick escaped, they could never leave. Two years later, on a lunar eclipse, Jean ritualised a talisman; if he ever got the virus, he wouldn't be affected like the others. What he hadn't realised was he'd not only bound himself to the Village. He'd missed how the villagers were turned through a bite. The parasitic toxin is released through tiny holes at the tip of their fangs.

This is where the information gets sketchy. It's said Anna and Jean were seen together. The Earl turned on Jean even more. He was inciting the villagers to go after him. They didn't get him. Yet he disappeared all the same. Anna was distraught, especially after she discovered she was pregnant. Supposed to be believed as true. The Earl had the baby aborted. Then, no less than two hours later, Anna was banished to the dungeons.

-A big mistake. Nobody found Frederick. He'd become rabid. He was starved of blood because Jean wasn't around. Frederick grew strong, too strong. One night, he escaped through the tunnels fueled by rage and set on revenge. He found himself in the dungeons... The first hint of blood in over two weeks was even stronger in light of the abortion. He found Anna first. Yet in her blood, he felt Jean, his friend. So he didn't try to kill. Saw her as a victim who may want revenge. Frederick bit Anna and turned her. They tore through the castle. Bled the family and servants all but dry.

-Until they all became obedient savages. The Village didn't expect the second wave. They were caught off guard, but that didn't mean they weren't prepared. The villagers fought back and drove them into the tunnels and Montague House. The Earl, the rest of his family, and others were desiccated and interred with the rest. Anna and Frederick were the last. Each with a mountain ash spike laced with mistletoe buried in their hearts.

-No other infected can bear to touch it; no one normal in their right mind would dare. The Village sealed everything off; the buildings became shrines to what the Village endured. Even embellished with stories to make into tourist attractions to help bring in money and revamp everything to start over. Jean never reappeared, nor did his secrets. Georgie, his bloodline, mine. It's also cursed. He may have been bitten but had resistance because of the talisman.

-My bloodline feared anything coming out in us down the years. It fucking came out in me... It's managed with some herbs and things. I need you to find Jean. I read if his body rests on hallowed ground. It severs his ailments from our bloodline. Solve what may have happened. Lay him to rest. Help set us free, please. I will owe you so much.

-I understand if you've read all of this in disbelief and thought, holy shit, it can't be real. Remember, you're a werewolf. Aside from that, everything I've told you is a mix of history books, some gossip, worked whispers, fragments of the very few texts to escape the 'Bay of Blood', no pictures, just scared scribbles if you need anything at all. Maybe even your grumpy sidekick. Just call. I promise you will get a rest soon. Be safe.

Sincerest regards,
Frank Locke"

Well, that was a kick in the balls. If the shoe had still been on the way down. The letter most definitely made it drop. This Village was quite literally hell on earth. Or at least, waiting to happen with what's below. With each echo made, the little 'dots' suddenly make sense. The cave, the house, and the coffins. Yet the biggest and by far the scariest. Who I assumed to be a vampire version of Ellena was, in fact, Anna. The normal ghost was her before the 'turn' leaving a rose.

I felt for Locke; I did. The Village, too. With Amos and whoever else roaming by night to hunt. Yet, he tries to blend in daily as if the world was none the wiser. Ellena looked like Anna, and now I had to find out why vampires would want a lookalike. While I got my head around everything Locke had said in the letter. Not to mention Mary. I could've disregarded and run at that point. Now, I couldn't.

I had an itch I couldn't scratch; Locke had made me worry—more than I was already. I lay in bed wrestling with the urge to ensure Ellena was okay. At the same time, I wasn't sure how she'd react if I told her what Locke had said. Until, for the second time tonight, I bit the bullet. I flipped off my covers and headed for the adjoining door.

"Knock knock."

I wrapped on the door as non-threatening as possible, even if my angst made me want to open it. She'd been unusually tired this evening. I had to carry her to bed and barely stirred as I staggered the steps. I didn't think at the time. Now, it seemed strange. There was no stirring now, either. Not even a roll across the mattress. If it was anything like mine. It would make a slight squeak. I listened deeper so I could spare the embarrassment of barging in. I drifted through the door into her room... No heartbeat... I couldn't hear her, so I barged in after all.

The bed was empty, the covers pulled open, and the pillows scrunched. Her boots and coat were still there. My heart raced as I was consumed with panic. Ellena was missing...

Chapter 10

I spun on the spot. Damn, near slipped on the thin carpet. My eyes glowed, and claws shredded lines in the floor as I just about kept on my bare feet. First came the two heartbeats of Mary and Dianne as I raced through my room and the door to the hallway. There was another. In an end bedroom. Calm, a little less than sixty beats per minute. They're asleep.

By the time I'd reached the top few steps, I was already feeling the cold air rush through. My panic was at its peak. Then I saw the front door open. Without thinking, I'd allowed myself to part-shift, clearing most of the stairs to land with a thud. Irrational thoughts were running riot. With what Mary had told me about vampires not being able to enter without permission.

Leaves blew through across the wooden floors; could Ellena have invited one in by mistake? If she'd something and was half asleep. A simple 'please come in' would probably work. That would allow Ellena to be snatched. It was freezing outside, and still in my pyjamas was bad enough. Ellena would be much the same without boiling demon wolf blood to keep her warm.

Everything was moving fast. In my panic, I couldn't focus. Too many details from my dream kept playing over and over. Partly because I couldn't be sure I wasn't still dreaming. After all, it was foggy, just like in my dream. If not a little thicker. My hackles were on fire like I was out in the open. Exposed and vulnerable with nobody normal around to intervene. I was at the mercy of anything lurking in the shadows. My hearing was a whirlwind of a million sounds at once.

Only I struggled to filter through them. My heightened emotions to do with Ellena stopped me from doing what I wanted. There were so many heartbeats to work through, and I knew I couldn't detect Amos or the other two that way. The smell would be the only way, and Ellena's was locked into my senses. Even this cold, I could tell that Coconut shampoo anywhere.

The same house from my dream was in the distance, distracting me for a minute. 'Montague House' was called. With Anna's ghost laying the rose. Until a blast of wind rushed past. 'Coconut' and it was coming from the edge of the cliff. I walked mindlessly, feeling first the rough cobbles and then the frosty grass beneath my bare feet—another moment to reminisce. I cut through the sheet of red and grey. Listening. Ellena was ahead; I heard her heart. It beat the same rate as the sleeper in the B and B.

I could do more than hear her, though; I could feel and sense everything about Ellena, and it got stronger the closer I came. We were connected, or at least I was to her. Maybe because I wasn't second-guessing my werewolf instincts. My fear for Ellena meant I acted instead of doubting; now, I felt her chemosignals strong. Ellena was in trouble. The sound of gravel scraping under her feet filled me with dread, yet even with my wolf eyes, the fog was too thick to rush through. I had to rely on the other senses.

There was no end to the bristling of my hackles either. With each step and each second, the situation began to wreak a trap. The blanket of fog across the bay was a perfect guise for the village's fanged fiends. A few steps further, I sensed the looming presence of the castle. That wasn't all. 'Death.' and it came from three different places. Behind and on either side. My claws grew longer and thicker as Ellena's scent whipped towards me. A sudden realisation hit: I didn't know what supernatural abilities Amos and his friends had. All I knew were the stories and movies. Hardly the stuff to have me well-armed for a fight.

If the movies were true, they had speed, strength, hearing and much more. I'd reached the right flank of the castle that opened to the edge of the cliff, and the fog-covered fields had become a 'kill box', and I was the unwilling victim lured into trouble. Their stench was strong, and so was their untamed lust for blood. I could already smell some. It flipped my heart in my mouth at the thought that they'd already gotten to Ellena.

'Click click...click. Click.'

'Click click...click click,'

'Click, click...click click,'

Skin-crawling clicks echoed. They bounced left, right, and left again before darting behind me. Then came the screeches. Fluctuating, stomach-churning screeches, with each one, a shiver rocked down my spine. Sheets of pimples popped up throughout my arms; I gazed at my claws, trying to focus and bring back the fire that had suddenly ebbed away. At the thought of blood-sucking vampires circling us like prey. If only I didn't have Ellena to get a hold of and make safe. I'd feel more secure to go all out, werewolf.

Gravel shuffled under Ellena's bare feet again. I could hear the rattle of her gold bracelets. With each sway. The flicker of the diamond ball on her small hooped earrings. That showcased her cute ears as her head rolled back and forth. My throat felt tight. I struggled to breathe, consumed by a giddy lightness, trying to get to her. The thought that we could get torn apart by vampires any moment... It scared me shitless. For Christ's sake, I was a werewolf, yet my six-foot world suddenly became a never-ending black hole of fear of the unknown.

A deep breath inhaled their putrid 'death' stench and became a wake-up call to focus. Finally, much like the castle's silhouette, I caught the outline of Ellena and the cliff's edge. Swirls of wind felt stronger the closer to the edge I came.

'Click click...click click,'

That haunting, preying clicking came again. A quick blast of wind whipped past, tearing a chill through my pyjamas, and the silhouette of Ellena slowly rocked forward, scraping gravel, then backwards, then forward again. There wasn't much time. Ellena swayed one last time, and I lunged unthinkingly through the thick fog. My arm flung wildly forward in desperation. Her body toppled at the edge...

Thin cotton pinched between my fingers. I landed on my side with a shower of stones and gravel dust dug into my skin. At first, it stung with dribbles of blood. I felt the scratches quickly heal. Only my blood had screeches in a frenzy. Ellena was bundled in my arms, lifeless. Then I got the shock of my life. Ellena's eyes had turned completely ghostly white. Her heart still beats at sixty bpm.

We were in a heap, and the vampires had us at their mercy. They'd breezed closer. They were circling, screeching, clicking. We were their main course in waiting. A look at Ellena's expressionless face had me empty inside. Her eyes...

The sight of them...the sight of her brought a tear to my eye. All I could think was, I did this. Ellena was in harm's way because of me. My worst fear came true. And I fucking hated myself for it. Not as much as I hated those pasty-faced, dust-farting, hole punchers on legs.

"It's so nice when dinner wanders onto the plate so willingly," Amos crowed in the wind. His menacing voice grated through my bones. I stayed quiet and slowed my heart. I could see three outlines, smoked shadows in the fog edging forward. They had each side covered.

"Nothing like a wee fear in the blood; it tastes all the sweeter. And boy oh boy, mmmm," A woman's voice. Older, similar to Amos, one of the two with Amos at the fireworks. Only I hadn't got a good enough look then.

"Isn't it past your bedtime? I mean, you pensioners surely need your rest, right? Besides, I heard seventy-five per cent of injuries to the elderly, like a broken hip, are caused by slips and trips. If you fuck around in the fog, who knows what you might break," Me and my big mouth. I tried not to show I was scared. A front, even though deep down, I was petrified.

"Oh aye, this one has some fight for sure. Now that really will intensify the blood as your shitty wee life slowly ebbs away, and the light gradually diminishes from your eyes," My eyes bounced side to side, looking for a weak spot. We were trapped, but I couldn't give up; I had to get Ellena to safety.

"Well, you wouldn't like mine. It's toxic. You see, I'm a reformed junky. You name it. I probably stuck it in my veins. Fuck me; one day, I was so high; I tried to inject sugar. I'd be so bad for you,"

"Oh, aye. Is that right? Do Ya take us for fools? Mr Reynolds. Your blood made the hairs on my balls tingle with excitement. It oozes power. There is nothing like a boost to blow the cobwebs away. Besides, it's the wee lass we want,"

"No chance. Why would you want her? I get it. She's beautiful and all. You're far too old for her,"

"Och, you funny wee bastard. You have no idea the history here. Your lass is key in more ways than you know. I'll make ya a deal. Surrender, and we won't kill you; we'll drain and turn you. So you can join our army,"

Amos cackled, but his words stuck, 'Army.' Were they snatching victims for food and hiding them for some big event? Amos seemed far too confident. We had to break for it, live to catch a limp Amos in daylight. They hadn't picked up on me being different for some bizarre reason. There was one thing I could try…

A look toward Ellena again. Her ghostly eyes and blank expression fed my pain of her being in harm's way. Even if she didn't mind. I hated the thought Ellena was being lined up in a sadistic game, like how I did in the Kanaima case. I dug down deep. My claws were long, and the shape of my face felt different. I'd shifted a little more than normal. The bowls of hell flew through the pit of my stomach, and I let rip with a 'soul-shaking' roar, rattling the fragile chalk foundations we stood on.

It echoed loudly. My roar rocked around the bay with menace. Timbers in the castle shook. Cattle in the furthest fields woke with a fright. The red-blazed bright. This time, it felt a little different. My claws felt strange. Then, I noticed a slight trickle from the tips. It was new and had to be part of my ongoing evolution. Whatever it was, it smelt different to what the Kanaima had. The droplet landed on a patch of grass, and it seemed to die off.

Well, it's more like decayed, not like the black widow. Dare I say it, desiccated. Only it lasted a few seconds before the grass returned to normal. A surprising change that could turn out to be useful in this fight. I imagined a deep claw wound, and the venom seeped into their bodies. Enough to slow them down. It smelt strong, too. Now, I don't know if it was that or my roar.

Perhaps both. The vampires began to back off. I hooked Ellena to her feet as I got up. My body was alive with adrenaline. I scooped Ellena into my arms and slowly moved forward.

The vampires gathered momentum, making more and more space as I pushed on. For the first time, I sensed their fear.

Ellena breathed as though she had slept, yet her eyes told a different story. How and why she went, there was another story. There were a couple of clicks between them, and then whoosh. Nothing. They disappeared, and I couldn't smell them anywhere nearby. At first, I thought the clicks were the vampires trying to scare me. Just then, with a short burst of clicks, they suddenly fled. That had to be how they were communicating.

We picked up the pace and soon returned to the B and B. I laid Ellena on the sofa in front of the fire to warm her up while I gave the front a once-over before closing the front door. I could only hear the same heartbeats as before, plus Ellena's—no stench of death. We'd survived, yet nothing about how Ellena looked seemed like she had survived.

The yellow ripples painted across Ellena's body made her face look all the scarier. I stared in a traumatised daydream, not knowing what to do. When I notice Ellena's lips move.

Ellena began to whisper words. The same over and over.

'Secrets in the bones. Secrets in the bones. You'll only find the secrets in the bones,'

Louder and louder until an abrupt stop. Ellen jumped upright with a loud inhaling of air. Her eyes flickered back to normal. Yet the startled expression told me Ellena had no idea what the hell we'd escaped by the skin of my fangs.

Chapter II

'4 AM.'

Ellena was in my bed, half snoring. She fell back to sleep rather easily. She remembered very little, and I told her even less. For now, anyway. That was a conversation over strong coffee and perhaps the company of our hosts. I thought we were up the creek without a paddle. That's not to say we still might be. Yet, having the vampires taunt, hide in the fog and be on the brink of picking us off. That had me scared, the most I'd ever been.

On my own. It wouldn't have mattered. If I came unstuck, there was no other risk. Ellena was the one I had to protect. While she looked blissfully passed out and cosy. I sat in the chair near the window on guard. My skin glistened in the moonlight, and I forgot our troubles for a second. Until I looked at my fingers. The smell of that venom was different, and if it could be replicated, I needed Ellena to run some tests.

Whether it was my imagination, I could still hear the fluctuating clicks and piercing screeches. My brain attempted to piece together those terrifying moments. Their movements as the vampires surrounded us. Did any wave coincide with a click? It seemed that way in the end. Unique. How they could form a dialect that way.

Assuming I didn't see 'dots' that weren't there. Lock's letter was a heavy favour to ask. How could he expect me, on my own, to be able to take these creatures on. Unless he also knew about Mary and Dianne. A detail I wouldn't put past him. The fact he admitted to suggesting where to come. It made me think he knew more about what goes on than he crammed into his message.

I slumped into the cushions of my chair and pulled a blanket up to my neck. Locke wanted me to find the body of Jean Martin Cortez and lay him to rest in the cemetery. Mentioned solving his murder, assuming that's what had happened. Had he even been bound to the village, or was that to make the story sound more elaborate. Although suddenly disappearing amidst the chaos sounded ominous and could've gone some way to enrage Frederick Lasille.

Montague house was the next stop I wanted to visit. I had to search the grounds, looking for clues. We had the numbers on the cross, and I saw Anna at the edge of the cliff and dreamt of her on the steps of the house. Now I've found Ellena at the cliff. She was making me wonder if she would repeat Anna's pattern. How many other places were there?

And where might they take her? The vamps might have had their fangs in if I hadn't been as restless. The thought of a vampire army amassed over the centuries. All are waiting to swarm the free world. It chilled me to the core.

How many the caverns and caves underneath us were holding had my arse puckering just a little. Not to mention what might dwell within that house. It looked huge. Perhaps that's where Amos and the other two were hidden. Seventeen twenty-five. That's two hundred and sixty-two years this village had endured. My head was going around in circles. For some reason, Locke's story felt a little fanciful.

A man met a woman and fell in love only to be pulled apart by tragedy, a little too much for the tourists. I feared the real story was far scarier and deep-rooted than we could imagine.

I looked at Ellena and pictured being a second too slow or a fraction off in my aim at her silhouette. Ellena swayed in the cold breeze and almost went. The image of her broken and bloody among the sharp rocks at the foot of the chalky cliff had my stomach turning. It was Ellena's eyes. They were freaky. Mary indicated Ellena had something about her. Could she be supernatural and not know it? After all, I didn't remember I was a werewolf until recently. For the moment, Ellena was safe.

I could feel myself drifting. My eyes were heavy; I had to stay awake. I had to make sure no vampires got in. There was a chill in the air; I only had a thin crocheted blanket, while Ellena had a quilt. My arms bristled; I hadn't realised the temperature had dropped in the night, and it had to be the sea air cutting through the fog. My senses were doing my head in trying to settle. I could smell the age in these buildings.

A dampness I hadn't noticed before was far more prominent. That shift to protect Ellena opened me up. It wasn't just the acidic overtones of the venom from my claws.

Mouldy water, soaked in the foundations, had a grim, salty sludge-like essence. My eyes barely held open, fixed on the shadows. Drips echoed in the darkness as my lids kept dropping—one after the other, louder and louder. Every little bump was a boom in my eardrums. The black appeared endless. The smell became slightly intoxicating.

That salty sludge slowly turned a little sweeter. I pulled my shoulders in to trap any remaining body heat. Grey rippled walls reached from beyond strips of nothingness. Stoney and cold, with a bitter wind rushing all around. Even with my eyes so heavy, I couldn't settle. Waves crashed against the cliff wall with the ferocity of an untenable beast. I stood to grab my coat for warmth. My feet were stung by a startling chill.

Rough shards of stone pressed into my flesh. Damp was now blood. Old, dirty blood that had me on the hook and being pulled toward the dark. Screams grated through the empty to my ears. A look at the bed, Ellena remained asleep. A bluster of salty seawater whipped the covers. White froth painted the sheets. Screams got louder. Someone was in trouble, and their blood was intoxicating. Cave arches led my path with a litter of stalactites lining the ceiling.

An endless cavern that reeked of death. Scared, yet I couldn't stop. Moth to the flame, I continued through the empty. Until finally, it opened up into another world. A huge, scary mausoleum, grey-stoned and damp. More or less a village-sized cavern. Littered, floor up to a two-hundred-foot high ceiling, cutouts from the walls. Hundreds of them are full of coffins.

Death was all around, and I suddenly feared this was the future—overwhelming pain and suffering. In the middle of the cavern, all on its own was another. The lid was open, and I continued to walk toward it. Another scent drifted toward me. Strong yet nothing like the rest. I reached for the lid. A musky, powerful chemo signal fired off. This was the moment I should've stopped, turned around and headed back, but my body wouldn't. Then I peeked in the coffin…

My legs became jelly, causing my feet to slip from under me. I landed in a heavy, sharp stone heap, gasping for air, but none would come. Frantic, panicked inhaling that was getting me nowhere with bile surging into my mouth… The person in the coffin…was me.

My body flopped limply in shock, and my head whipped backwards, catching another view of the death around me. Suddenly, I was back in the chair. My eyes bounced open. The blanket was tucked up still, and Ellena was fast asleep. Another fucking dream. Another bloody glimpse of death. And it was coming whether we wanted it or not.

'8 am,'

Daylight beamed through, and warmth from the sun's rays painted across my skin steadily woke me. A teaspoon rattling in a cup pounded my eardrums from downstairs. I was half asleep and groggy until I remembered Ellena. My eyes shot open. She was gone again. Panicked, my instinct was to run to the cliff's edge again. Until I heard her heartbeat, it stood out from the others. Her scent, too. Whether it was my panic causing the wolf to keep track or we were now connected on some level. Either way, I had a fix on Ellena, who was talking to another woman. A voice I didn't recognise compared to those we'd met so far. That wasn't all... Power, not strength, different in a way we hadn't encountered so far. It wasn't threatening either, yet it felt supernatural.

They were laughing, bloody surreal compared to what I went through last night. Not taking any chances, I finally pulled myself from the chair and crept out of the room. There were voices in the streets, too, nowhere near the house, and it seemed like the world was moving as normal. By the time I'd reached the mahogany-stained handrail, I had got a read on their heartbeat and chemo signals. Their heart was steady, and signals relaxed.

The smell of coffee and toast was too great, and I was starving. I breezed down the stairs as if nothing was wrong. Ellena smiled. She would've realised something happened last night for her to be in a different room. Her demeanour didn't show it. Ellena, Dianne, Mary and an unknown lady sat around the coffee table in front of the fire. That strange scent grew stronger. Enough to make me slow down.

'Don't be afraid,'

A whisper came out of nowhere. Real low-pitched. My hackles ruffled. Not enough to have me worried, though. I looked straight at the lady. Slim, possibly taller than the others. Hard to tell sitting down. She wore a navy three-quarter dress and black boots. Quite smart, actually, with a two-tone blonde bobbed hairstyle. She seemed quite professional and assured of herself. It was the neck jewellery that got my attention. An assortment of chains at different lengths. All were old, but two had rather unique-looking pendants or accessories.

'Locke' sprung to mind. The symbol on one had me confused because I knew it from somewhere. Then I remembered the tattoo described by Andy about Locke and what was on that bestiary we recovered from Etherington. And she knew enough of me or sensed enough to whisper.

"How did you know?" I whispered back. Ellena continued to smile between sips of her coffee as she tucked her knees up to get cosy.

'There's so much we need to discuss. You'd be surprised just how much I know and can be an ally- The names Ruth, by the way,'

"Morning, everyone," I nodded to Ruth and announced myself.

"Hey, Georgie. I'd been saying I must have been sleepwalking. You, being the gentleman, slept in the chair and kept guard,"

"Ah, Yeah, about that. There's a little more to it," I said, trying to come across as calm even if I was anything but.

"Like what?" Mary said, looking startled.

"I think George here is trying to be delicate. But Amos and the other familiars were skulking around, attempting to test the boundaries," Ruth spoke up, well-spoken and educated. What's more, Ruth seemed to hold seniority over Mary and Dianne.

"Much more than that. Ellena. You had walked to the edge of the cliff. And the three of them seemed ready to pick you off," Ellena paused open-mouthed. She couldn't remember.

"What the hell is a familiar, and why can't I remember?" Ellena seemed and sounded far more stressed now.

"A vampire," Ruth exclaimed; Ellena's expression changed again. A little excited mixed with fear.

"Ellena, there were three of them, and they wanted you. Only you seemed to be asleep, but your eyes were open with a ghostly white glaze," it was Ruth's turn for surprises. Her hand reached for the chain with the 'druid' symbol.

First impression: Ruth knew much of what went on in Cruden Bay and had an idea of what the ghost eyes meant for Ellena. Her heart sped up as I mentioned it. The clutch of her chain emphasised it. Only, I didn't think it was going to be good news.

Chapter 12

'8.30 am 6th November 1987.'

Ellena couldn't stop fidgeting. Nor did Ruth. She circled each curve of the emblem with a deliberate scrutiny that betrayed her belief in Ellena's unique abilities. As for me, Ruth's reaction left me with the impression that she knew more about the situation than she was letting on.

Who would've thought a quiet fishing village in Scotland could harbour so much supernatural intrigue? I couldn't help but wonder how widely known the vampire epidemic was. Whatever had kept these creatures at bay all these years had spared the world from untold pain and bloodshed. But how much longer could this seemingly peaceful village remain untouched?

"So vampires are real, too?" Ellena finally spoke, her voice tinged with a hint of fear. She may have seemed a little scared, perhaps due to her walk to the cliff's edge, but I couldn't be sure. Was it because of ancient bloodsuckers lurking nearby?

Ruth's response was cryptic but unsettling. "And a hell of a lot more. Forget any stories you've heard. The reality is far worse." She nodded to Dianne, who hurried to the drinks cabinet and retrieved a decanter of what appeared to be whiskey and glasses.

Ruth then turned her attention to Mary. A single glance from Ruth prompted Mary to press a concealed stone on the fireplace, causing it to spring open. From within, Mary produced a rolled bundle of blood-red silk adorned with ceremonial decorations. As it unfurled, it revealed a small, ornate knife with black and gold accents. Arrayed beside the knife were small pots containing various coloured herbs and a separate black dish.

Dianne began pouring whiskey into the glasses, and it wasn't lost on me that such early morning drinking usually signalled trouble or the imminent delivery of unsettling news. I'd often found that whiskey had a way of momentarily concealing one's sins, but it never truly washed them away.

My curiosity got the better of me, and I couldn't help but ask, "What's all this for? I can understand the drink, but what's with the knife and these... herbs?" My confusion was mirrored in Ellena's expression.

Ruth's response was startling, adding to my growing sense of bewilderment. "Consider it a test, and the drink as preparation for the story. However, you haven't seen Cruden Bay yet and what lies beneath its surface. The contents of your letter only scratch the surface." I tried to respond, but my mind was in turmoil. How did she know about the letter? And while I had heard rumours of vampires lurking beneath the village, what other supernatural surprises awaited us? Zombies from the graveyard, perhaps?

"We came here for a break, not a test," I protested. "And as for the letter, how did you come by that information?"

Ruth's response was nothing short of astonishing. "My dear boy, I already knew you were coming. I have glimpses like your visions, which you're still learning to control. Especially when there's so much untapped potential within you. A demon-werewolf detective—now that's quite a unique combination." Her revelation left me speechless, and I exchanged glances with Mary and Dianne, who had yet to acknowledge my true nature, let alone my profession, openly.

But Ruth brushed aside my concerns. "Don't worry about them," she said reassuringly. "You see, not all secrets are malevolent. My abilities are more of an aid, or perhaps a diversion, even an early warning system. I'm afraid Mary and Dianne are what's known as golems. Infused with magic to walk, talk, and perform all the functions of running a bed and breakfast. They cannot die or be injured, and they've been instrumental in protecting this place for quite some time." This revelation only added to the surreal nature of our circumstances.

I had struggled to come to terms with my identity as a werewolf, and now, with each passing moment, it seemed I was being thrust into a world filled with even more supernatural complexities. There was Michael, a shapeshifter with fox-like traits and an intriguing aura—Locke, a druid whose presence we had encountered during our battle with the Black Widow. We had sought Cruden Bay for a peaceful break, only to stumble upon vampires. Now, I was confronted by these creatures, golems, and the charming Ruth.

As my heart raced with uncertainty, Ellena's intrigue was palpable. Her right eye twitched nervously, but her gaze remained fixed on the knife and the assortment of powders and herbs. Dianne slid a glass before us, and I instinctively reached for mine. My heightened senses detected something unusual—an additional layer of complexity within the swirling, woody tones of the whiskey. It was a subtle nuance that would have gone unnoticed by normal senses. The more I scrutinized it, the more suspicious I became. Though Ellena's smile only added to my internal dilemma, my gaze remained fixed on Ruth. Did she prefer the wolf or the man within me?

Seeing my apprehension, Ruth reassured me, "It's alright, George. This concoction won't harm you. It's merely a blend designed to conceal your supernatural blood. You'd be surprised at how keen a vampire's sense of smell can be. It's akin to your ability to pick up on chemo signals and heart rates. They can detect a living supernatural being, even without the scent of fresh blood. Your presence is rich and potent to them."

Ellena, too, displayed similar characteristics, which put me somewhat at ease, though I remained uncertain about Ruth's perception of Ellena's unique qualities. How Ruth handled her chain and the herbs hinted at her possibly being part druid.

As I tried to process the flood of information, I asked Ellena with genuine concern, "Ellena, are you alright with all of this?" Her hands trembled, and I sensed the fight-or-flight response kicking in. I reached out, slowly cupping her hands in mine. What happened next was a revelation—I felt an inexplicable surge of energy and calmness. My hands tingled with an almost euphoric sensation before they began to glow, veins turning red. Ellena's trembling ceased, and her smile returned as her body relaxed. It was yet another enigma in a string of unexplained events.

"I am now," Ellena replied, resting her head on my shoulder.

Ruth then introduced another intriguing concept—an emissary. She explained, "George, you will need an emissary, someone to guide and assist you in this new, strange world when you return home. Events are unfolding that will redefine the rules we live by. There are 'Ley Lines' crisscrossing the world, mystical pathways that connect the supernatural with the human realm. Locations like Stonehenge and many others in the UK are beacons for these energies. Someone has opened a doorway that threatens to disrupt the delicate balance and, in doing so, has painted a target on your back."

I was filled with a barrage of questions. "How? Why? How do you possess this knowledge?"

"Some I have seen, others I have sensed," Ruth replied. "A year ago, I received a letter, an invitation to join a team investigating how to harness the mystical for real-world problems. However, I soon discovered their unethical experiments, particularly on young girls, like the ones you recently encountered—the Black Widow. It could have ended disastrously. I sympathize with their plight, but too much death has already occurred. As you often say, "Secrets will get you hurt, and the details will get you killed."

As Ruth spoke, the pieces of the puzzle started to fit together. She had insights and knowledge that were beyond my comprehension. But there was a deeper revelation—Ruth believed I was destined to accomplish something significant. She spoke of a never-ending adventure, alluding to the challenges ahead.

Ellena and I exchanged glances, realizing our journey was far from over. Ruth's guidance was invaluable, and her words carried weight. But there was more—Ruth hinted that others could assist.

I pondered aloud, "Well, I'm not a fan of flying. And a druid, I know one. Or rather, we do."

Ruth smiled knowingly, and as she unravelled the mysteries surrounding us, I couldn't help but feel a growing sense of assurance. Perhaps we were exactly where we needed to be.

Ruth raised her glass, signalling a toast. "Let's set aside these weighty matters and savour the moment." As we sipped our drinks, I couldn't ignore the faint taste of blood in the concoction. It was unmistakable, and it left me with lingering questions.

I inquired, "So, is there a genuine story about this place, or is it all hearsay?"

"Plenty of time for that, my dear. For now, I need a little of Ellena's blood,"

Ellena nudged my hand forward to comply—still, no shakes or nerves. And like the saying, Ruth stole. It's the details. The little things. And this was another to an already steep list. Which side of me was doing these things, the wolf or the demon? Surely, humans had to factor in somewhere along the way if this was all wolf, heaven forbid, what would come from the demon.

Ruth had the knife and carefully pricked Ellena's finger. A little bubble formed, and that's all it took. My claws then fangs. It was Ellena's turn to reassure. She stroked my face, and I felt calm. Suppose one thing had become clear. Ellena was my calm in the storm.

"You two are good for each other in so many ways. The fact you can centre a werewolf like George means you have a connection very few in life can get. Some never achieve it. For what's to come, you're going to need that bond. Because they will come and keep coming. Ellena holds the key to set them free, or so they think,"

Ruth was right. I'd felt it when I woke—the way I could find Ellena without trying. I could feel her so vividly I could almost reach and touch her. Her scent was a radar. If that's what it's like for me, the vampires had to fall over themselves to taste her.

Ruth squeezed Ellena's finger into the pot; each dribble made my mouth water. Joanne topped up our drinks while we sat on tenterhooks. My ears kept listening outside and anyone coming. I was trying to focus my senses away from the blood and to look for Amos. So far, no stench of death.

Ruth's eyes sparkled with anticipation as she prepared to reveal another facet of our extraordinary world. She poured a viscous, green-brown liquid onto a stone, and it sizzled like a hotplate—the room filled with a strange energy that heightened the suspense.

Ellena leaned forward, her curiosity piqued, and asked, "What does it mean?"

Ruth's response sent shockwaves through us all. "It means you're a witch, Ellena, but not just that. The ghost's eyes hinted at your unique abilities. You possess the power to dream, walk, to enter someone's subconscious, and to influence their thoughts. There's so much more to learn about your abilities. You've been intrigued by the supernatural all your life, haven't you?"

Ellena's delight at this revelation was evident. She couldn't contain her excitement at the newfound knowledge. The secret was out, and it was a secret I had no intention of letting slip.

Chapter 13

'9.30 am 6th November.'

It felt like I was the day watchman, soon to turn into the night shift. My face was inches from the windows, my gaze fixed on the world outside. I was on lookout duty, scanning the landscape for signs of death or, perhaps, the undead. What a morbid task it was to stand guard against the walking dead, or were they truly undead? In a way, we were all a form of the undead. As I watched the oblivious faces beyond the glass, these sad reflections weighed on my mind.

Amidst the ordinary scenery, a peculiar structure in the distance captured my attention—the black house. It stood there, hauntingly ornate, surrounded by vast, open space. Its incongruity in this otherwise antiquated landscape struck me as strange. It was as if this part of the world had been preserved in the 1700s, and the house defied time's relentless march. My thoughts involuntarily drifted to Anna and Ellena, and I couldn't help but wonder if my eerie dream was a glimpse of what lay beneath the surface.

A part of me wished we had turned back when I first had visions of the cave. Since then, we had slowly descended into a nightmarish abyss. With a cup of coffee in hand, acquired through a trade for the whiskey that had fueled the previous night, I had sunk so deeply into my thoughts that I nearly missed it. The hairs on my neck stood on end, a tingling excitement signalling her approach—Ellena's scent, which could brighten even the darkest moments. It was almost taken from me too soon.

Ellena breezed up to me, and I felt the rush of wind as she drew closer. Her arm encircled my waist, and her chin rested gently on my shoulder. She seemed content, perhaps having found answers to questions that had long haunted her. Meanwhile, I couldn't shake the curiosity about what had drawn her to the cliff's edge. Her identity as a witch and a dream walker explained her ghostly eyes and occasional non-responsiveness. But what had beckoned her there? Whose dream had she walked into? These questions gnawed at me, filling me with a sense of unease.

Moreover, the revelation that Locke and Ellena shared matching tattoos troubled me. It seemed that Locke had not been entirely forthcoming with his story. My thoughts and fears spilled out as I spoke to Ellena.

"You saved me last night, Georgie," she assured me. "We're in this together. We don't need labels. I feel the connection we share. I sensed it the night we met. It just took us a little while. And before you overthink things, know that I've fallen for all of you—human, wolf, and demon. But most of all, I fell for your heart. You're a good man, trying to make the world better. Georgie, you balance me."

Was it a manifestation of her witch-like abilities that allowed her to read my thoughts? Or was it the profound connection we shared that made my innermost feelings transparent to her? I confessed my worries.

"I don't know how to cope with this revelation," I admitted. "I could sense my body changing. The only choice I had was to roar. It felt different, and then the claws dripped with venom. A single drop could desiccate a patch of grass temporarily."

Ellena examined my hand, scrutinising my fingers and nails as if trying to comprehend the incomprehensible. The changes I was undergoing were beyond explanation, as were her own.

"How are you dealing with your newfound abilities?" I inquired.

"I'm not sure," Ellena confessed. "It might explain how I've been able to create the things I've used so far to combat the effects of wolfsbane."

Ellena raised a valid point. Her unique abilities had always set her apart. Locke had hinted that she possessed other skills we would discover in due time, and perhaps this was what he had foreseen.

"Whatever the reason," I concluded, "we'll face it together."

Just then, Ruth reappeared, holding an ornate box that exuded a palpable aura. The scent of blood, infused with something else, filled the air.

"Are you ready to uncover the secrets of Cruden Bay and understand what's truly at stake here?" Ruth asked, her hand resting on the box, locked with an elaborate clasp resembling a skull, with chains forming the shape of a druid symbol.

What followed was another surreal moment akin to the blood test on Ellena. The surface beneath Ruth's hand glowed with a deep purple, and suddenly, the clasp released. It was as if magic itself had granted us access. The chains retracted into the skull, and the clasp glowed a blood-red before unfastening. Ruth opened the box smiling, revealing a collection of pages from a very old journal. Each page had a weathered, leathery texture, a testament to its age—traces of dried blood stained some pages.

"Fear not, my dears," Ruth reassured us, "it's all perfectly safe. You haven't seen anything yet. The real spectacle is yet to come."

"What's this?" I asked, noting the bloodstains.

"Just a small taste of what lies beneath the surface," Ruth replied. "I believe your ADI may have been misinformed."

Ellena and I exchanged puzzled glances, ready to delve into another layer of this strange puzzle.

'Wednesday 12th August 1725,'

'Travel Log of Frederick Lasille,'

'*We arrived in Scotland today. Jean has been his usual buoyant self. However, things have progressively changed since Romania. He's spending more and more time with the specimen. All the herbs and artefacts we'd gathered on our journey paled in comparison.*

I still don't know how to describe it. Only in the pit of my stomach, I fear our fortunes may take a drastic turn for the worse. I'm left with a moral dilemma: should science prevail at any cost? Our grand pursuit. Or should I say—the grand pursuit of immortality and the cure for all sicknesses.

What's it worth? Notiarity within the scholars of the world? Should we have disturbed something buried so deep within the caverns of Bucharest? Because the small stream we discovered flowing through the cavern wall displayed healing properties for superficial wounds. A chance find after Jean sliced his hand on a rock. The hole in the wall could be seen through, and Jean believed what he saw entombed on the other side to be the answer to the world's prayers.

It took two days to excavate—Centuries-old and, for all intents and purposes, a unique discovery. At the moment, not enough is known. Only the days we travelled since have been plagued with nightmares. All I see is blood. Flashing images of streets turned into bright red rivers. Jean appears most affected. Obsessing over its security. The carved scriptures within the wood are made from 'ghost' mountain ash.

Are equally testing Jean's fragile patience. He feels we're on the cusp of greatness. Yet, I feel we could be on the cusp of oblivion. Then Jean laid eyes on young Countess Anna Farrington. However, Earl Andrew Farrington and Countess Sophia Farrington were gracious enough to welcome our stay in their village indefinitely. Jeans' attention to their daughter will not be welcomed. We were offered Montague House as it was on the outskirts of the village, away from prying eyes that could disturb our work. It's also twofold in that it needs renovations and is believed to be haunted. Ordinarily, I would argue against such things. The chance of privacy somewhere so grand felt too good for Jean and me to turn down.

Jean didn't disclose what we were carrying. He saw no point because 'they wouldn't understand'. In truth, I barely have a grasp. For now, we have seclusion. Yet, I feel anything but. I hear the calls. They're in my head. Jean thinks I'm talking nonsense. Yet I see him. He twitches and nervously glances as if he's being watched. We can only pray that this turns out to be every bit the miracle Jean believes it is,'

We now had two versions of a story. This page Ruth gave felt and looked too old to be fake. And it came from the assistant that Locke mentioned in his letter. What's more, Frederick Lasille didn't mention once about being sick or bitten by a bug in Romania.

Although it sounded like they found something they thought would be the holy grail, the question is, what? Frederick's tone in his writing sounded rattled, a little unsure of what they were doing and transporting. Being called to was different in Fredericks's head. Their troubles had started before they arrived in Scotland.

"Do you think this is real?"

"Oh yes," Ruth said, nodding her head enthusiastically.

I played over my dream again, and Anna placed the Rose on the steps. Somebody was hanging from that big tree nearby. I began thinking that elements of Locke's story could be true—the romance between Jean and Anna. Only what went wrong was caused by what Jean and Frederick had discovered; one was hung by the neck until dead. Ruth handed me another page, dated a few days later.

'Frederick's Log Sunday 16th August 1725,'

'It's been a few days since we arrived, much like the days that occurred before. Jean is obsessed with two things: Countess Anna Farrington and our discovery. Jean has begun to look paler. Long hours have begun taking their toll. Montague House is nice enough. It's quite bigger than anticipated what we hadn't been told, aside from the hauntings. Was that it had been built on the original graveyard site.

The original was moved because the graves were too shallow due to the hollow space beneath. It seems a necropolis-sized space had been tunnelled into the cliffs centuries ago and then covered unused. Jean wants to use it as a hiding place if we could make a passage. A few outcries of cattle are going missing, and so far, the village believes it's outsiders stealing livestock.

I've seen it differently. Enough to know there's something else going on. Pools of blood near where they were going missing from. And splashes near the house. Jean denies knowledge, but he's not been himself. He's playing with fire, and the Earl isn't stupid,'

Chapter 14

Ruth had many more entries in that mysterious box, and my curiosity had reached its limit. The narrative had been a slow dance, a tantalising lead-up to the main event, and Ruth had me hanging on every word. I was eager to unravel the intricate connections within this dark tapestry.

As I absorbed the contents of those entries, it became clear that Jean and Frederick, two individuals from the past, were at the heart of this enigma. Frederick's words, "I hear the calls; they're in my head," hinted at a disturbing discovery. They had stumbled upon something, or perhaps someone, with the potential to heal. But what they believed to be a miraculous panacea had a sinister origin – the first vampire of Cruden Bay, imprisoned for a reason.

I couldn't contain my curiosity any longer and had to ask Ruth, "What is going on in this place?" Her response was ominous, and she clutched her chain, a subtle signal that there was more to this story than met the eye.

Ruth beckoned me to take a seat, and as she did, I refilled my coffee with a splash of whiskey, needing something to steady my nerves. Ruth began to narrate the history of Jean-Martin Cortez and Frederick Lasille's journey, which had started in Romania. They had discovered something unique, a wellspring of water with seemingly miraculous properties. They could have exploited this discovery as a miracle cure, but their curiosity led them further.

In a matter of days, they unearthed an ancient, centuries-old sealed crate covered in inscrutable scriptures, soaked by a leaky water stem. Ignoring the warnings that something evil lay within, they embarked on a perilous journey to Scotland, where they met Earl and

Countess Farrington.

Jean and Frederick, skilled in herbs and natural remedies, were invited to serve as healers in the village of Cruden Bay. They were entrusted with Montague House, a building with a dark history, as it was built on an old, shallow graveyard. Beneath the house lay a hidden secret—a tunnel leading to a necropolis-like structure with a powerful telluric current running through it.

However, their insatiable quest for knowledge led them to uncover an even darker secret: a cursed cargo within the crate. Jean's relentless research strained their partnership, and Anna, the Earl's daughter, became a point of contention between them. Love, experimentation, and sickness entangled their fates.

Cholera ravaged the village, and the populace's thirst for the miraculous water turned into a bloodlust. The infected transformed into creatures with fangs and insatiable hunger. Chaos ensued, and Frederick, bearing rope burns from a lynching, walked among the bloodthirsty mob.

The villagers took refuge indoors, and those infected were beheaded, including Frederick. Jean vanished, and Anna was presumed dead, but rumours of her ghost persisted. The village seemed cursed, destined to repeat a cycle of death and transformation.

I couldn't help but wonder about the discrepancies in Ruth's account compared to Locke's version. In Ruth's tale, Frederick hadn't fallen ill, which raised questions about the authenticity of these accounts. I leaned back in my chair, contemplating the narrative and trying to discern which version held the truth.

Ruth's eyes welled up with tears as she paused in her storytelling, clearly emotionally invested in the tale. It was a story of heartache and tragedy, and I couldn't help but empathise with her.

"Are you okay?" I asked, concerned about her well-being.

Ruth composed herself, coughing to clear her throat before replying, "Yeah, sorry. Some stories aren't easy to tell, especially when history only knows the half of it, and centuries later, the nightmare lives on."

Her emotional connection to the story was evident, but there was more to come, and Ruth hinted that she would reveal additional details when the time was right.

The tale continued with an onslaught of horrors. Bloodthirsty villagers laid siege to Slain Castle, with some turning into monsters and others tearing apart. Frederick, bearing the marks of his gruesome execution, descended from the castle steps. His return was nothing like revenge—it was a descent into madness.

The village had descended into chaos, but it was only the beginning. Disappearances occurred once more, this time at night. Anna, once presumed dead, was seen looking like death incarnate. Some believed it was Frederick's return, while others thought the village was cursed.

My questions about Jean, Anna, and the mysterious crate remained unanswered. Ruth had been there during those tumultuous times, serving as Anna's handmaiden. Frederick had recognised her latent power and had taken it upon himself to nurture her abilities, much like he had sensed potential in Ellena.

Ruth's admission of her inability to save Frederick tugged at my heartstrings, adding another layer of tragedy to this complex tale.

"But... what happened to Jean, Anna, and was the crate ever found?" I inquired, my thirst for knowledge growing stronger.

"At first, the crate was rumoured to be deep within a cavern," Ruth began, her voice tinged with mystery. "Then came the ghostly apparition of Anna, leading to the presumption of her demise. But Jean's fate remains a mystery. I cast protective spells over most of the village, shielding them from supernatural threats. That's why you've only seen a fraction of the supernatural world that lurks beneath the surface. Years later, vampire sightings and disappearances continued until only Amos and his two familiars, survivors from the Farrington family, remained. In 1825, an accord was struck to prevent further bloodshed, allowing vampires to coexist with the villagers."

I was intrigued by this accord but baffled by one aspect. "An accord with whom?"

"Evil itself," Ruth responded cryptically, leaving me with more questions than answers.

My mind raced as I tried to process this new information. The story had taken a chilling turn. Ruth revealed that the crate contained an original vampire elder, Count Elias Diminescu, who had been imprisoned from the moment they discovered the water.

I couldn't help but feel a sense of impending danger. "Why haven't they taken over the town if they're so powerful?"

Ruth again clutched her chain before responding, "The curse binds him and most vampires to the necropolis. Amos and his companions feed them. By day, they may appear fairly normal, but by night, they become savage—their transformation results from being bitten, unlike the origin of the water. Believing the Farrington family line had ended, I ensured that a descendant could only break the curse. However, I've learned otherwise. The gods have sent you someone strong enough to sever the Elder's head before they find a way to break free before the 'calling' begins. I fear they will assimilate everything in their path."

As Ruth's gaze shifted slyly toward Ellena, who fiddled with her chain, I couldn't shake the feeling that there was more to her story than met the eye. It seemed we were all players in a larger, more sinister game.

"That would make you centuries old, wouldn't it? How is that even possible?" I asked, my mind racing with the implications of her ageless existence. "And how can we see the rest of the village?"

Ruth explained, "Witches draw power from the earth and currents. The closer to a telluric current I am, the more powerful and ageless I become. Similarly, as a werewolf or demo wolf, you will age at a fraction of the rate of humans. As for the rest of the village, it's taken care of. Brace yourself because what you've experienced is only a fraction of the truth. The bigger picture reveals a town with a mayor, police, a hospital, and all the trappings of a modern society. To the vampires, however, we remain stuck in the stone age."

I couldn't help but chuckle at the absurdity of the situation. The idea of a fully functioning town hidden beneath the surface, unbeknownst to most, was mind-boggling. I wondered whether the rest of the village knew the truth or if we were the sole witnesses to this supernatural world.

The puzzle pieces were falling into place, but the mysteries surrounding Cruden Bay were far from solved. The shadows of the past loomed large, and the impending threat of Count Elias Diminescu and the cursed vampires cast a long, ominous shadow over our future.

Chapter 15

We yearned for respite; the mysterious box we carried harboured untold secrets, leaving us with an overwhelming sense of intrigue. Ellena's curiosity burned, driving us to explore this enigmatic place further. As the front door of our refuge closed behind us, we were greeted by a sight that left us agape.

We had ventured into an alternate reality where the familiar sights remained, yet a profound transformation had occurred. The bridge, the fields, the ancient castle, and the precipice overlooking the sea remained constant. My gaze lingered momentarily on the bridge; a curious symbol etched into my memory, its significance now eluding me.

Our earlier conversations had been rife with revelations, and the veracity of these claims remained uncertain. Time alone would reveal the truths hidden amidst the tales we had been told.

The path we had traversed earlier expanded, stretching further and wider than we remembered. The graveyard and the fields surrounding Montague House had retained their essence, but the backdrop had grown. What was once a quiet village had blossomed into a bustling town, its heart pulsating with life. In the distance, a grand white edifice with majestic pillars and a splendid clock tower stood, exuding an air of officialdom—perhaps a courthouse, municipal building, or even a library- its purpose unknown to us.

Our quest continued to unveil intriguing facets, seemingly tailored for a more populous denizen than we had initially encountered. Even the firehouse, typically unassuming, now exuded an endearing charm. Yet, amidst this lively scene, my thoughts were haunted by the memory of the cross in the graveyard—a haunting presence that demanded our scrutiny.

Ellena, however, remained silent, her demeanour an oasis of tranquillity amidst the turbulent sea of revelations. Her arm was intertwined with mine, her hand resting comfortably in my pocket, a fleeting moment of serenity in our turbulent existence. Life, for that brief interlude, felt remarkably good.

We reached the gate where we had stood the previous night. My nerves compelled me to scan the surroundings, searching for any sign of Amos and the others. They were there, as expected, but provided little clarity. The arrow on the parchment still beckoned us "north," though deciphering its true meaning eluded us.

"Georgie," Ellena's gentle voice broke the silence, "why don't we set this aside for now and savour this moment of peace?"

"Of course," I replied, my senses keenly attuned to our immediate surroundings.

"Where would you like to go?" I inquired, casting aside the worries that lingered in the recesses of my mind.

Ellena's eyes sparkled with excitement as she spoke, her tone adopting a playful lilt. "Well... I did notice a sign on a community board for the local art gallery. Could we visit, pretty please?" Her request carried a charming innocence befitting a princess—or perhaps a witch.

"Why not?" I responded, a sense of adventure kindling within me. "It would be a refreshing change from our ongoing discussions of vampires. Let us seize the opportunity while the sun still shines."

Ellena, momentarily puzzled by my choice of words, chuckled in response. "I have no idea where that phrase came from. It must be something Michael used to say about making the most of favourable weather."

We both shared a moment of laughter, the memory of our absent friend lingering in our hearts. Strangely, I found myself missing the old rascal.

"Very well, let's embark on this new adventure. And remember, you can always call him if you're concerned," I reassured Ellena, despite my internal quandaries.

"Call who?" she responded, though her awareness of the truth lingered beneath the surface.

"Michael. We both share concerns for him. We left him to fend for himself, and the full moon looms just two nights away."

With a nod of understanding, we continued our journey on foot. Ellena's words had stirred a poignant reminder of our responsibilities, and the looming full moon added an unsettling layer to our unease. The thought of Detective Sargent unleashed on the world was a grim spectre we wished to avoid.

Our stroll through the vibrant streets offered a therapeutic reprieve, untethered from the grim spectre of crime scenes. Greetings and waves from the cheerful locals greeted us—a slice of idyllic countryside life I yearned for. In just fifteen minutes, we arrived at our destination, each encounter leaving us with a sense of warmth and welcome, starkly contrasting to the predatory vampires we had encountered.

The art gallery stood before us, its pristine white façade reminiscent of the grander structure we had glimpsed earlier, complete with a flight of immaculate steps adorned with decorative bunting. A sign advertising the "Soulless Eyes" exhibition was decorated with black and red balloons, and a steady stream of people flowed inside.

As we ascended the steps, a disquieting sensation pricked at my senses, and my instincts went on high alert. A brief, unexplained unease coursed through me, prompting a glance over my shoulder, scanning the crowd for any conspicuous figures.

Ellena, perceptive as ever, noticed my momentary disquiet. "Are you alright?" she inquired, her concern evident.

"Yes," I replied, my voice tinged with surrealism. "It's just... surreal. To think we're experiencing holiday-like activities amid our extraordinary circumstances."

"I know," she concurred, her voice filled with enthusiasm. "Let's make the most of it."

With that shared sentiment, we entered the gallery, paying the five-pound entrance fee, and an unexpected transformation occurred within me. At least ten points had suddenly augmented my intellect as the elegant and sophisticated surroundings enveloped us, far removed from our previous realities. An hour ago, we had been oblivious to the existence of this gallery and the wonders it held.

Ellena was drawn to the bustling activity on the far left, where the main event seemed to unfold amidst a sea of black and red balloons. A crowd of visitors had gathered, their hearts pulsating with excitement and anticipation. Unable to resist, I extended my supernatural senses to scan the crowd, detecting no traces of death—only heartbeats and adrenaline rush.

The exhibition itself, however, did not align with my tastes. Art, it seemed, was subjective. The "Soulless Eyes" theme was aptly named. Six striking artworks adorned a wall, a fusion of portraiture and landscape, their oil-based strokes blending diverse tones. I, admittedly, possessed limited knowledge of art, but these pieces exuded a profound darkness. In stark contrast, the backgrounds were vibrant and colourful, showcasing the village's scenic beauty.

Among the portraits, one stood out in stark black and white. A pale, emotionless visage with jet-black hair and attire to match, its defining feature was the eyes—darker than black, with subtle hints of crimson. They seemed to possess an eerie semblance of life, an illusion that captivated the beholder.

I became entranced, my surroundings fading into a distant murmur. Only the sound of a popping cork could pierce my reverie, though I remained unfazed, still entranced by the hypnotic allure of these enigmatic eyes.

"Shall I fetch us a drink?" I offered, eager to clear my thoughts and regain my composure.

Ellena's response was an enthusiastic "Yes, please," her gaze fixed on the mesmerizing artwork.

Joining the queue for champagne, I marvelled at the unexpected turn of events. The sparkling, fruity bubbles tantalized my senses, and I found myself smiling—an unusual sensation amidst relentless challenges, gruesome cases, and our inexplicable relocation to a Scottish town. This newfound contentment felt ethereal, akin to a daydream where one's presence barely registers.

And then, it happened—a sensation of unease, a subtle ruffling of my instincts. My head spun, the crowd engulfing me in a sea of bodies, making it nearly impossible to discern the source of my disquiet. The scent of death remained conspicuously absent.

Panic coursed through me as I frantically searched for the cause. The new exhibit had garnered even more attention, with eager spectators jostling for a better view. Amidst the chaos, I could not locate Ellena. Fear and confusion swirled within me, amplified by my inability to sense anything beyond the disquieting ruffling.

However, a memory surfaced—a moment from earlier when I had found Ellena without physical proximity. Closing my eyes, I inhaled deeply, blocking the cacophony of voices and sights that besieged me. Then, the familiar scent of "Coconut" reached my senses, carrying a palpable excitement. Her heart beat steadily, without the telltale signs of fear or anxiety. I knew where she was once again.

My eyes reopened to reveal a tall, impeccably dressed figure. His jet-black hair was neatly parted, and he sported a black suit with a blood-red pocket square. His complexion, though slightly pallid, exhibited a well-groomed goatee. But his eyes transfixed me—a mirror image of the captivating exhibit. I blinked repeatedly, searching for any sign of deception, yet they remained unchanged, their haunting darkness unyielding.

Without delay, I navigated through the bustling crowd, my heart racing. The venue was overcrowded, making it impossible to discern the telltale rhythm of a heartbeat. A group of towering individuals obstructed my path, and I fought my way through the gap they provided.

Finally, I stood within sight of Ellena, nearly at her side. But the enigmatic figure had vanished as if he had never been there. My hackles continued to prickle, a persistent reminder of the unsettling encounter.

"Hey, Georgie," Ellena greeted me, her enthusiasm undiminished. "Oh, thanks. These paintings are peculiar, not to my taste, but undeniably clever and morbid."

I nodded in agreement, suppressing the urge to reveal what I had witnessed. Ellena's happiness was fragile, and I hesitated to shatter it with my disconcerting observations.

We continued our exploration of the gallery, sipping champagne as we moved along. My vigilance remained unwavering, my hand gently clasping Ellena's, a silent assurance of her safety. As we approached an abstract sculpture of a skeletal figure with distorted limbs—a piece provocatively titled "Reflection in a Twisted World"—I once again sensed the unsettling ruffling.

And then, he appeared again, standing near the champagne station, his gaze fixated on Ellena. He stood out conspicuously from the crowd, yet my heightened senses failed to discern the source of his peculiarity. In the mere moments it took to shift my attention from him to Ellena and back again, he had vanished again.

"Are you certain you're alright, Georgie?" Ellena inquired, her concern palpable as she pulled me back from my inner turmoil.

"Yeah," I replied, offering a reassuring smile. "It was that exhibit. It gave me the creeps. Those eyes haunt me now."

I attempted to downplay my unease, pondering how long I could maintain this facade in light of Ruth's revelations. My understanding of what a witch was capable of remained shrouded in uncertainty.

In my mind's eye, I could only conjure images of children dressed in Halloween costumes or the iconic witch from "The Wizard of Oz," complete with broomsticks, green faces, pointed hats, and an unfortunate rendezvous with a house. After all, "Toto, I feel we're not in Kansas anymore" seemed an apt description of our current predicament. Yet, I refrained from uttering the infamous words, "There's no place like home," as our return awaited us with the grim spectre of more lifeless bodies and the ever-elusive ADI, whose presence had grown increasingly infuriating.

A few minutes passed, and my disquiet began to ebb, replaced by the sight of Ellena's blissful happiness. The gallery's contents began to blur together, making it increasingly challenging to discern between the extraordinary and the mundane. As we approached another exhibit, those haunting paintings again attracted my attention.

"Shall we find a café and enjoy a cup of coffee?" Ellena suggested, her words infused with an infectious enthusiasm. "Perhaps we can sit outside and let the world pass us by, if only for a little while—before the storm inevitably descends."

I was captivated by her spirit, her desire to savour a moment of calm amidst the stormy currents of our existence. The prospect of coffee and tranquillity beckoned, offering a brief respite from the enigmatic forces surrounding us.

Chapter 16

'11.30 am 6th November 1987,'

Plush-looking, white metal tables and body-cupping seats. We had the perfect view of the world drifting by. Ruth had hidden so much of the town, and it looked nice. Considering what we knew. It seemed safe.

Then I got to thinking perhaps this was the real illusion. A front for what lurked beneath. They'd even erected a bronze statue on a pedestal outside 'Crusen Bay Town Hall,' a group of imposing men with swords stood on a platform. Yet, beneath the platform was a step too far. A load of dead bodies and smashed skeletons. As if they were being victoriously trampled over.

A reminder of what the town had overcome. They were walking on the battered remains of vampires. If Amos knew, if he and the others could see that. It would make them push back and maybe test the accords. It also represented their current arrangement. The town above ground and the vamps in the caves. Ellena didn't hide her grimace looking at it. The town hall was only across from us and busy enough with a few people coming and going.

People-watching was a bad habit of mine. Even when trying to relax, I couldn't help but watch. Only now, I kept looking for the guy from the gallery. At least the coffee was good—enough to wash away the image of those paintings. I looked around the other tables. Some were chatting. Others read either a newspaper or a book. The news was a few days old and had nothing remotely interesting. Ellena had her nose in a tour guide leaflet and was fully immersed.

"Seen anything good?" I said, trying to be curious even if I wasn't really.

"Not really. Much the same as any other. The port occasionally has boat rides to explore the bay. Mentions the usual monuments and how the current mayor, Duncan Campbell, is up for re-election in a battle with his counterpart, David McNally, to keep 'Montague House from being demolished. He wants to register it as a historical landmark.
Along with the ground it sits on. If successful, Campbell plans to use it as his mayoral office to be easily available among the town folk. 'Family values at his core' apparently. As opposed to McNally, who wants it torn down and the land redeveloped for an 'ever-expanding' town. Maybe even relocate the nearby homes as part of a modernizing initiative," Ellena said, smirking.

"It seems we can't even escape politics here," I said, with the cogs turning. I looked around the town and where the road was headed. There seemed ample space for development on the outskirts and more than enough buildings and homes. Why would either of them be concerned about an old home not far from the edge of the cliffs? Christ, hadn't they heard of coastal erosion and landslides? Maybe not now, but long in the future, it could happen.

That was my thinking, anyway. Ellena looked at a picture of the statue before us with that same grimace again. While I was stuck on the article, Ellena had read to me. And something Ruth had mentioned to do with telluric currents. Call me a cynic, but a house nestled above an untapped, natural, mystical power source. Make it a registered landmark and the mayor's office. Nobody could enter, and Mr Duncan Campbell would have unrivalled access, aside from whoever he allowed.

Yes, there was the small matter of vampires. I got to thinking about how conniving the politicians in London are. There's always a deal to be made. With each sip of my coffee, I focused across the road at the town hall. My head slipped further down the conspiracy habit hole.

'E…ll…e…na. Oh, Ellena,'

"What Georgie?"

"Eh, I never said anything. I was too busy wondering if the mayor was corrupt,"

"Yeah, okay. Behave, mister," Ellena smiled, but I genuinely had no idea what she was going on about.

'Ellena. Oh, Ellena.'

"Georgie…Knock it off, or I will get Ruth to give you fleas or something," Ellena looked a little more serious this time. Although I still didn't know what she was talking about.

Fleas though? She had to go there.

'Oh, Ellena. Such beauty deserves to grace the most esteemed of walls,'

"Right. No jokes now,"

"Ellena, I'm not doing anything," Ellena began teaching her head, acting paranoid. All the while, I paddled in confusion.

'Poor, beautiful Elena. Why so confused?'

Ellena furrowed her brow. She wasn't kidding. I hadn't heard a thing, and Ellena was adamant I'd tried to get her attention.

'What are you looking for, Ellena? I'm already in your head. I'm right where you want me to be,'

"Hey, are you okay?"

"Georgie, somebody keeps calling my name,"

"Seriously? Could it be anything Ruth did?" I sounded it out even though it seemed unlikely. The bigger problem was how on earth it could be happening. First, I saw the guy in the black suit. Now Ellena hears somebody call her name.

"No. I mean, I don't think so,"

Ellena dragged her chair close, leaned her head on my shoulder, and closed her eyes. Her heart was flying. I'm looking but not seeing anything.

'Ellena. You invitingly opened the door to me; you're intrigued. Imagine the feel of my fingers tracing your skin. Your neck throbs with anticipation. All you have to do is find me...'

Ellena squirmed in her seat, biting her bottom lip. Her arms were alive with goose flesh rippling through her skin. Ellena's breathing labored hoarsely. Whatever was happening had her squeamish. Was it even possible? I kept asking myself. Until I remembered Jean as Frederick's story. The Vampire was in their heads.

"Shall we walk some more? Might clear your head,"

"Yeah, sure," Just as we went to stand up. Suited great trousers stopped at our table.

"Ah, just the people I'm looking for. Detective Reynolds and Miss Walker," I was stunned to hear our names being said. Especially calling me a detective. Only Ruth, Mary, and Dianne knew that of me.

The suit in front was five foot nine at a push. All but bald. He chose to cling to the few strands on top and the faded rug around the sides. A blue tie propped up his double chin, and his portly belly swung over his belt line. If I were a betting man, he would be the mayor. Duncan Campbell.

"Erm, yes, but how did you know? More importantly, who might you be?" I said, gauging his demeanour. Rose-red blush across his cheeks and nose told me he was a drinker. His Scottish accent was the weakest I'd heard so far. Who the hell told him, though?

"Och! My apologies. Little Ruthie mentioned we had a detective visiting to ensure you are well looked after. I'm Mayor Duncan Campbell," Ruth had told him, which was a strange thing to do. But why? We didn't need any special treatment—just the chance to relax.

"Sorry, but why? And why tell you I'm a detective," just as the words slipped out of my mouth. The penny dropped. The mayor wanted a favour. "Well, we're meant to be here resting, and so far, the place has been full of surprises, shall we say,"

"Ai. Nae bother. I understand the need for rest. But I have some valid fears, strange ones, too. All I want is an opinion. See a couple of things and give a little insight. Because I'm finding there's not many around here happy to stick their necks out,"

"Does Ruth know about whatever this is?"

"No way. You'd be surprised how quickly the whispers spread once she knew anything. No, if I'm right. Then this is delicate,"

I had to admit. I was curious and would take our minds off the vampires and hopefully get Ellena thinking about something else. After all, it wasn't like we could do much other than look and be honest. Suppose the local police weren't helping their mayor. It was either bullshit, or somebody was in the background making sure nothing came to light.

"Why not Georgie? At least we could see more of this place," Ellena spoke up, finally sounding more like herself.

"I guess the lady has spoken. Where to first?" I said, taking a quick look around for two things.

That guy in the black suit. And anyone who could be watching the mayor. I had the feeling Duncan was about to introduce a can of worms. And if I knew anything about small towns. When somebody is up to no good and gets wind of someone like the mayor taking an interest, the person up to no good would want to know just how much the 'mayor' or anyone like it knew.

"Fantastic. It's just a wee drive on the outskirts by the cliff's edge. Then the port. It must seem strange, but I know most of the normal folk in this town. What I'll show you, laddie, is nae way straightforward,"

Duncan nodded to his right, and I heard an engine fire up—two point six litres with a slight fuel injection. The front left tire was slightly underinflated—a slight sluggishness of the wheel. The rears were further back... I knew what car was coming, and my mind carried a haunting from the last one I was in.

"So a limousine then," My mouth blurted. More out of surprise that I'd heard that much. My hearing felt dialled up a level. We were close to a huge telluric current, which made me think it didn't just amplify Ruth's powers. Duncan raised his eyebrows.

"How did you know?" he said with a stared smile.

"Erhum....the engine. Georgie likes his cars and thinkers with engines when he can. Probably knows what litre too," Ellena interrupted to save my blushes.

"Oh, is that right, laddie? Pray to tell? I'll bet you a wee bottle of my finest scotch you can't," Duncan chuckled; his heart was calm, and he oozed confidence. Ellena smiled, cuddling my arm. She winked. That was all the encouragement I needed to showboat a little. Besides, I fancied winning a bottle. Anything that wasn't bloodthirsty bloodsuckers.

"I hope it's as fine as you say. Two point six litres Mitsubishi. With a modified addition of fuel injection. 85 model. Three-speed automatic gearbox. I'd get your spark plugs checked. One's misfiring. And a slightly flat front left tire," Everyone was silent and for a moment, I thought I had overdone it, and Duncan would ask other questions.

"Well, check out the clever wee fucker. Ai, she's a bit of a pig. I preferred a normal Mercedes, but the town hall insisted on a limo. Especially as I also cover Boddam, Peterhead and Hatton. Luckily, I have an assistant in each. This place is the centre of them. Oh, lucky me, eh? But bets a bet, laddie,"

Duncan chuckled loudly. Funny thing, though. Nobody was flustered or obsessed that the mayor had stopped at a cafe. In London, photographers and journalists were trying to sneak a peak at what they may order. Thank God this wasn't the case. Ellena had a huge grin and seemed somewhat impressed. I only hoped it took her mind off other things.

On cue. A black limousine rolled to a stop in front of us. The driver ran around to open the rear door. My throat dried up as I stopped dead with Ellena hooked on my arm just ahead.

"It's OKokay, Georgie. I'm with you,"

"You okay, Laddie?" Duncan looked concerned, I felt queasy, and the chauffeur was a little confused.

"Georgie was in one a few days ago on a case, and it blew up. He just about made it clear in time," Ellena spoke confidently to battle by my side.

"Och laddie, why nae say?" Duncan approached with a reassuring hand on my shoulder. Reminds me of Andy. Then, that made me think about what he could be up to. Andy had come up good when we needed it for the last couple of cases—and seemed to be on a mission of his own for now. He is still looking for his missing daughter.

"It's okay. Come on, let's go. Besides, I'm looking forward to that bottle," I smiled before looking around to ensure nothing lurked nearby. Not that I could sense anything. Then to Ellena and mouthed 'thank you', getting a hug in return.

"In that case, laddie, let's get going. More to see of 'Blood Bay' and the tide is coming in," Duncan waved us in, but I'd him clear as day saying 'Blood Bay' is not typical to say to tourists.

This limousine smelled normal and far more luxurious. Three glasses of the brown stuff had already been decanted. By the time we got comfortable. The car was moving. I clutched Ellena's hand tightly; all I could think of was the bomb and LSD. We could only hope our trust hadn't been misplaced.

Chapter 17

The ten-minute drive whizzed by, the town unfolding before us as if we were navigating a labyrinth of secrets. The road meandered, twisting left and right, ascending and descending, until it finally veered left, leading us to the precipice of a cliff.

Before us lay a breathtaking vista of sun-kissed waters, where azure ripples caressed the rugged cliffs, the relentless wind, fierce and untamed, churned the sea into a frothy frenzy as if awakening some primal, ferocious beast. The limousine came to a skidding halt thirty feet from the edge, and an unsettling sense of foreboding washed over me.

Our situation bore the ominous hallmarks of a scene from the underworld—mob-style body disposal, with the eerie possibility of us being the unwilling participants in our demise. These thoughts raced through my mind, but Duncan's timely offer of fresh glasses diverted my attention. I begrudgingly admitted that the drink was exquisite, a rare pleasure compared to the garbage Dianne had been serving.

Catching me gazing out the window, Duncan remarked, "Quite the view, isn't it?"

"I'd say so. But it begs the question: why are we here?" I replied, my brow furrowing as I scanned the surroundings, searching for clues.

Duncan pointed toward the base of the cliff and said, "It's what's down there that's important."

Intrigued, I stepped out of the car, greeted by a bitter blast of sea air. As the gales subsided, I heard another sound—raised voices and the relentless metal clanging against stone. Pickaxes, it seemed. I cast myself into the grass and mud, crawling closer to the edge, wary of the treacherous precipice. The others, wiser than I, remained safely inside the limousine.

Ellena's tension resonated in her trembling breath against my ear. Nearing the edge, the object of our intrigue came into view. A scaffold-like frame rose from the ground, extending six feet from the cliff's top. At its pinnacle, a black metal platform and a ladder beckoned, a testament to the ingenuity needed to withstand the relentless coastal winds while preserving secrecy.

Within this frame, a cargo-style lift powered by a generator stood guard, overseen by a burly sentinel armed with a rifle. The stakes suddenly rose, and I couldn't fathom what warranted such elaborate precautions.

"Guns? Really? You could've mentioned that," I muttered.

"Aye, but that's not the crucial part," Duncan replied.

My attention shifted back to the commotion below, where the source of intrigue lay. A hole in the cliffside opened like a gaping maw, with workers perched atop a mound of rubble. A chain bolted to the wall descended the slope, guiding the procession of wheelbarrows loaded with debris. Four men worked tirelessly, their pickaxes relentlessly pounding away. They were tunnelling into the cliff.

"What the hell is happening here?" I exclaimed, bewildered by the unfolding spectacle.

"A tunnel is being carved toward the cliffs beneath that grand house," Duncan explained. "It's one of the reasons I've been fighting to have it designated as a historical landmark. That way, the house and the land cannot be tampered with."

"But why tunnel from this distant spot? I fail to grasp the logic," I mused.

Duncan's voice was uncertain as he replied, "I'm afraid I don't have all the answers yet. My counterpart is involved, and it's not for mere development. He seeks access to something beneath that house for reasons unknown. But this operation is only the tip of the iceberg."

Returning to safety, my thoughts whirled, and a dreadful notion surfaced. The cavern, the telluric current, the vampires—the pieces began to align. David McNally might unwittingly unleash an ancient evil, clearing the path for chaos. We were far from Ruth's watchful eye, and McNally seemed to be playing a dangerous game, assuming Duncan's suspicions were valid.

The presence of an armed guard, perhaps to prevent workers from escaping, further fueled my concerns. I circled back to Duncan's cryptic expectations of what I could do alone and Ruth's mysterious agenda. Nothing added up, and a lurking sense of impending danger hung in the air as if the dots were misaligned, and an impending reckoning loomed.

"Where to next?" I inquired.

"Visitor's choice. The port or the garage warehouse?" Duncan replied.

"Which is closer?"

"The garage."

We all re-entered the limousine, consumed by the enigmatic puzzle unravelling before us. The tales from Ruth, Locke's letter, Frederick's diary entries, and now this, each thread seemed to point in a different direction. What could be believed, and what was mere fabrication? If the cavern beneath held such significance, why were vampires coerced into it and held there, assuming that part of the narrative held?

Ellena leaned in, whispering, "Someone is lying, Georgie, and they're doing it skillfully. I suspect Ruth has her agenda involving that cavern, and now there's tunnelling activity."

"So, what's our plan?" I replied, my thoughts racing.

"We observe, we listen, and we stay vigilant. We may need to contact Michael," Ellena suggested.

"And calling Michael would not only bolster our ranks but also make you stronger," she added.

"What do you mean?" I asked.

"I read that pack Betas make the Alpha stronger," she explained.

The idea hadn't occurred to me before. The prospect of gaining supernatural strength was enticing, and it added a layer of complexity to our already convoluted situation. However, the decision to involve Michael came with its own concerns, as he also needed respite from the ongoing turmoil.

Duncan, ever the gracious host, poured us another round of drinks, drawing our attention to a walnut-finished door next to the minibar. His collection of bottled scotch stood proudly on the shelf, a testament to his refined taste.

"Twenty years old, that one," Duncan remarked, handing me a bottle. "A fine choice, indeed. Your willingness to entertain the musings of an old man with a penchant for paranoia means a great deal."

Grateful for the distraction, I accepted the drink, my mind swirling with questions and uncertainties. Duncan's sincerity was apparent, and I couldn't help but wonder how much of the supernatural darkness he was aware of, concealing my knowledge of the mystical druidic spot beneath the house, inhabited by ancient vampires.

"Thank you," I replied, choosing my words carefully. "And I must admit, Duncan, I don't think you're paranoid."

"Is that so, laddie? And what makes you say that?" Duncan inquired.

I hesitated, wary of revealing too much about the supernatural undercurrents. "From my own experiences, anyone guarding a rickety lift at the base of a cliff with a rifle usually has something significant to hide. But the larger question remains—why haven't the local authorities investigated this?"

"Because, my dear lad, I've lost faith in them," Duncan replied with a sigh. "The police here function differently, led by an elected sheriff who assembles his crew. Sheriff Bernie Doyle, a close friend of McNally, hails from the previous administration. Need I say more?"

Duncan's words resonated, painting a picture of corruption akin to the darkness that clung to this seaside town. Now, more than ever, I leaned toward contacting Michael for assistance despite the complexities and conflicts that would arise. The situation was spiralling, and the puzzle pieces were far from fitting.

"Where do we go from here?" I asked Duncan, my thoughts racing.

"Well, it's your choice as visitors. The port or the warehouse garage?" he replied.

"What's the nearest option?" I inquired.

"The garage," Duncan said.

We settled back into the limousine, and my mind continued to churn, questioning the integrity of the information we had gathered. It was a tangled web of half-truths and hidden agendas, and I couldn't shake the feeling that another shoe was about to drop in this sinister drama.

We embarked on the next phase of our journey, leaving behind the enigmatic cliffside operation for now. Our destination was "McNally and Son's Auto," and we wisely parked a street away from the establishment, avoiding the conspicuous presence of the limousine in the immediate vicinity. The garage, now transformed into a warehouse of secrets, stood hidden off the main road. Its sprawling yard harboured towering stacks of scrapped automobiles, partially visible behind wire fencing and the tops of the boundary wall.

The forecourt, reminiscent of a derelict outpost, showcased a few petrol pumps and a selection of second-hand vehicles up for sale. We were on the outskirts, where Cruden

Bay and Peterhead met, with an old-fashioned motel, a café, and a pub nearby. The sense of community was palpable, with locals who seemed to know each other and their dogs. The motel, draped in flaking paint and adorned with dirty windows, barely clung to its tattered three-star rating, with the third star appearing on the verge of desertion. It was a stark contrast to the pristine appearance of Cruden Bay—or "Blood Bay," as Duncan had earlier dubbed it.

Maintaining our ruse as sightseeing tourists, Ellena and I strolled hand in hand, playing the role of a couple interested in exploring the area. The weather, at least, was cooperating, even if Ellena's blonde hair danced wildly in the wind. She seemed to have shaken off her unease, her apprehensive glances over her shoulder fading. The local pub exuded an atmosphere of camaraderie, while the nearby motel wore its three-star rating with a mix of pride and neglect.

Our attention temporarily shifted to a battered "A Reg" Sierra Cosworth on sale for £595, its driver's seat window revealing a discrepancy in the displayed mileage—54,000 miles instead of the advertised 48,000. As we scrutinized the vehicle, we overheard a heated conversation in the nearby office—a confrontation between two men in their late twenties or early thirties who bore a striking resemblance to each other, likely brothers. The elder of the two appeared to be in charge while the other was soothing him. Elvis Presley crooned in the background.

Tools clanged and clattered in the garage, and amidst the din, I heard low, muted moans punctuated by shuffling and scuffling. The unmistakable scent of blood reached my nostrils, confirming that something nefarious was afoot. I whispered my discovery to Ellena, who maintained her composure, her hand covering mine as my claws threatened to emerge.

"It's a beauty, isn't it?" the fair-haired, medium-built man approached us, mistaking our interest in the Sierra Cosworth.

"Pardon?" I replied, feigning ignorance.

"The car. Only 48,000 miles on the clock," he said, his forced smile betraying his unease. His attempts at deception were transparent.

"That does seem low for a car of this age," Ellena remarked, playing along.

"Aye, one previous owner, I believe," he continued, "primarily used it for motorway driving."

Ellena and I exchanged knowing glances. An economy engine like the Sierra Cosworth, driven extensively on motorways, should have significantly higher mileage. The radio in the office was turned down as a phone call came in, revealing a fragment of the conversation between the two brothers.

"The shipment was light; what else could I do? I had to cut it," one of them said.

"Light fingers more like," the other retorted.

The voice on the phone relayed more unsettling information. The younger brother had been seen selling illicit goods in a bar in Hatton. A cloud of suspicion hung over him. The conversation ended with a cryptic mention of a "little job" that needed to be done at 9 p.m., implying that the blood was already flowing.

The puzzle pieces fell into place, revealing a family deeply entangled in criminal activities. Their involvement in drug trafficking, the disturbing noises and the smell of blood painted a grim picture. The younger brother, it seemed, was a liability, possibly skimming from their operations.

As we continued to eavesdrop, it became evident that the family's endeavours were veering into darker territory. The question remained: What were they planning for 9 p.m.........., and how could we exploit their internal conflicts?

Our undercover mission had taken a chilling turn, with the shadow of criminality looming over McNally and his family. The coming hours would demand strategic thinking and swift action as we navigated this treacherous path to uncover the truth.

Chapter 18

I strained to hear anything beyond the oppressive silence in the air. The muffled sounds from the garage had dwindled into eerie quiet, leaving me with a gnawing sense of dread. We couldn't risk calling the police, not in Cruden, where the line between law and corruption blurred. Duncan's warning echoed in my mind, casting a shadow of doubt over even the authorities' intentions. We were outnumbered and out of our depth.

Before us sat a dilapidated wreck of a car, a Cat-D, a stark reminder of a catastrophic crash; with feigned curiosity, I circled the vehicle, my eyes scrutinizing the twisted chassis. Hints of silver paint clung to the wheel arches, revealing a violent history. It was clear the entire front end had been replaced, leaving no room for doubt about the car's dismal state.

"Are ya sure ya dinnae want it?" The garage owner, Alexander, asked, trying to sway us. "Goes like the clappers on a wee straight."

"We're good, thank you," I replied, "I've always had a soft spot for Cosworth engines, but I can't part with my trusty three series. By the way, I didn't catch your name. Thank you for indulging us."

"Och. Nae bother," Alexander replied. "It's Alexander, and that gommy sod in there is my brother, Nicholas. We run this place. If ya change ya mind, I'm sure we could offer a fair deal for the Beemer."

"Thanks for your time, Alexander. Is there much to do around here?" I asked, feeling slightly out of my depth with the Scottish lingo.

"The port offers trips around the bay coast," Alexander informed me. "My father manages that. Not today, I'm afraid, but if you go tomorrow, tell 'em I sent ya. You might enjoy a good trip, perhaps even some scuba action if you can handle the water."

"Amazing. I'll look into that. Thank you again, Alexander."

Leaving Alexander behind, Ellena and I embarked on a stroll, caught between the moral dilemma of intervening and the uncertainty of biding our time. The harrowing cries for help from the garage still haunted us, but we dared not act hastily. Reporting the incident now would only raise suspicions about our true intentions.

As we walked, I couldn't help but wonder why we had ventured to Scotland in the first place. It was a question that gnawed at me, much like the impenetrable mysteries of Cruden Bay.

Our path led us to a mobile burger stand that also offered coffee. It was a mere hundred feet away, providing the perfect vantage point to observe the garage discreetly. Ellena ordered coffee, and my attention remained fixed on the forecourt, acutely aware of Duncan's presence in the limo, ready to assist if needed.

Just then, a sleek black Range Rover pulled up, adorned with all the opulent trappings. Tinted windows concealed the occupants, but a woman in her mid-fifties emerged when the rear door swung open. Her face bore the veneer of youth, framed by long, brown, and gently curled hair, accentuated by a pretty floral dress.

Yet, her frailty was palpable, and she clung tightly to her driver for support. She moved with the hesitance of one far older than her years. Her appearance hinted at a maternal figure, but her condition was far from well.

"Ya can turn that off now, boy," she stammered as she entered, her words signalling the end of music and the resumption of the painful moans and bone-deep thuds that made me wince. I caught Ellena's gaze, who had quickly grasped the gravity of the situation. The beating continued unabated despite the woman's arrival.

I grappled with the dilemma between immediate action and biding our time. The port beckoned as our next destination, even if Alexander had mentioned it wasn't operational today. The agony emanating from the garage churned my stomach, and the prospect of a protracted waiting game gnawed at my patience.

Amidst my swirling thoughts, I noticed an ominous presence across the road. The enigmatic figure in the pristine black suit returned, his unwavering gaze fixed on Ellena. I watched discreetly, concerned by the man's purpose and the lack of a reaction from my instincts.

"Ellena, it's time we headed to Duncan. He must be growing restless," I finally suggested, hoping to divert her attention from the unsettling presence.

"Okay. Are we going to the port next?" Ellena inquired, sipping her coffee and brushing windblown hair from her face.

"Yes, the port is our next destination. We need to unravel the mysteries of this place. They've subjected someone to a brutal beating there, and the details could jeopardize us. Unless you'd rather leave? We could pack our bags and escape this ordeal. Cruden's troubles existed before we arrived; they needn't become ours," I proposed, concerned for Ellena's safety.

Ellena, however, remained resolute, matching my determination with her own. Our connection, a unique bond that transcended the supernatural mysteries of Cruden Bay, fortified our resolve.

"Remember, Wolfie, my recklessness matches yours. I may not possess your abilities, but I can sense when we're being manipulated. Ruth has her agenda, one that involves me. I may not be a witch, but unravelling the mysteries of this town seems essential. We can't walk away from a fight, especially when it's a fight worth having. I know you worry about me, just as I worry about you. What we have together is special; it's worth it if we can change even one life for the better here. Besides, Locke owes us some explanations when we return," Ellena asserted.

I couldn't deny the inherent dangers in our path. Guns, vampires, witches, and the spectre of my sleepwalking loomed large. It promised a difficult journey that might result in copious amounts of bloodshed.

"But just think, if we survive this ordeal, I could write a book about Cruden Bay," Ellena quipped, her laughter warming my heart.

Our conversation lightened the mood, but I couldn't shake the fear that Ellena might not fully comprehend the dangers we faced. She seemed enchanted by the supernatural elements of Cruden, and the lurking threats continued to shadow our steps.

"Well, that may be," I acknowledged, "but your safety is paramount to me. I can't bear the thought of losing you."

However, Ellena had her ideas that stirred my desires and fears. With a sultry smile and a twinkle in her brilliant blue eyes, she presented a compelling proposition.

"Who would've imagined a little lamb and a werewolf in such harmony? I don't intend to let you go, silly. I want to share a bed with you, Georgie. To keep each other safe and warm, perhaps with sleep being optional," she suggested, her playful demeanour juxtaposed with the eerie presence still lingering across the road.

With coffee in hand, we walked toward an approaching gust of wind, our focus solely on each other. The pub behind us grew rowdier, with hotheads being ejected amidst shattered glass and a weathered wooden door pounding against chairs.

At the same moment, Alexander emerged from the garage, puffing like a chimney, coincidentally timed with the arrival of two distressed individuals. One of them, a dishevelled man in his early thirties with shaggy blonde hair and a ragged appearance, repeatedly pressed a key fob, his sunken eyes betraying the toll of drugs and alcohol. He seemed lost, searching for his vehicle amidst the chaos.

But then, something unexpected happened. The man's head snapped toward Alexander, drawn by a piercing whistle that resonated through the forecourt. Alexander pointed to an old sky-blue, slightly rusted Ford pickup in the far left corner, with an open-backed trailer containing three mysterious crates, each measuring at least two feet by two feet. The men regained their composure and headed toward the pickup, activating the hazard lights with a press of the key fob.

My curiosity piqued, and I took one last deep sniff, trying to decipher the contents of those crates. Amidst the myriad scents in the vicinity – food, coffee, alcohol, grease, and blood – a new aroma emerged, hinting at unfamiliar substances. The implications were unsettling, suggesting the possibility of drugs or other illicit activities.

The decision to follow the enigmatic cargo beckoned, but the port remained our intended destination. I shuddered at the thought of David McNally assuming power and the potential consequences for Cruden Bay and its neighbouring towns. The sinister web we had uncovered, woven with drugs and other mysteries, begged for answers, including the enigmatic role of the caves in this ominous narrative.

Chapter 19

We dared not be seen travelling the town in the mayor's sleek limousine, fortunate that the town hall had spared no expense on its tinted windows. As we sped away from McNally's garage, the anguished moans still echoed in our ears, a haunting reminder of the secrets buried beneath this quiet town. The rugged cliffs stretched towards the eastern quadrant of Cruden, where the vast expanse of the restless sea met the domain of Slain's Castle and the enigmatic Ruth.

Frail, zig-zagging metal steps, which appeared rather precarious, descended the face of the cliff towards the hidden port below. Like many things, the closer we drew, the larger it loomed. A protective thicket of trees concealed us, allowing all three of us to venture forth. Ghostly whistles echoed around us, their eerie freedom sending shivers down our spines. The cliff's edge was still a distance away, yet the clamour of raised voices reached our ears, shattering any illusions of seclusion.

I executed a silent commando crawl across the ground while Ellena and Duncan remained concealed in the shadows, vigilant. Before long, our eyes fell upon the harbour, where two imposing vessels were anchored. One, a grim and imposing behemoth, bore the name 'The Brave and the Bold I,' its robust frame equipped with hoisting arms and abundant deck space for mysterious cargo. The other ship, 'The Brave and the Bold II,' painted in a pristine white, seemed more suited for passengers, capable of accommodating many souls. A small group of men, still donned in scuba gear, emerged from the water, accompanied by an armed sentinel.

Upon the jetty lay crates, relatively smaller than those we had observed during our earlier encounter. The group's dialogue was sparse, making it difficult to glean meaningful information. However, a set of double doors opened, leading below deck, and from within emerged a middle-aged man, his receding ginger hair and burgeoning beer belly betraying his identity—David McNally.

My frustration boiled over as I returned to Ellena and Duncan, my voice dripping with exasperation. "Duncan, what in the bloody hell is this madness?"

Duncan's expression mirrored our confusion as he replied, "That's the question, my friend. How McNally acquired control of the port remains shrouded in darkness. My superiors sanctioned the purchase on a Monday evening, only to discover that the deal had been inexplicably finalized by Tuesday morning. It was justified as a sound financial decision to boost the town's tourist trade. As if our quaint Cruden needed any more legends, considering its centuries-old reputation as 'blood bay,' linked to myths of a virus that drove villagers to crave blood."

Duncan's solemn tone conveyed both seriousness and perplexity, though his casual shrug hinted at his disbelief in the supernatural tales. Little did he know how closely these myths were tied to reality.

I interjected, my voice tinged with scepticism, "But surely rumours are circulating about McNally's clandestine activities? Armed men, scuba diving, soaked crates on the jetty—none of this adds up. McNally's garage is involved in nefarious dealings, the cliffs outside the town are hiding secrets, and there's the matter of a brutal assault earlier today."

The pieces of this enigmatic puzzle continued to elude us, leaving me to wonder why Ruth had led Duncan into our lives, especially considering the looming threat of a supposed vampire pandemic beneath our feet.

Duncan continued, shedding light on yet another layer of mystery. "Indeed, one rumour suggests a pipeline connecting Cruden to the shores of Norway, facilitating the smuggling of heroin and other illicit goods. There are whispers of shipwrecks further out at sea, and David McNally has been zealously scouring these wrecks for reasons known only to him. Yet, the tale that intrigues me the most revolves around the myth of Countess Anna Farrington."

My curiosity piqued at the mention of Countess Anna, and I leaned in, eager to hear more. "Tell us more about Countess Anna," I urged.

Duncan obliged, his storytelling voice tinged with fascination and dread. "The legend speaks of how Countess Anna fell victim to the blood virus. She had already given birth, and as the town descended into chaos, Anna sought refuge on a ship bound for her family in Denmark. It was a time of dread, and the fear that Anna might have contracted the virus prompted her to make a heart-wrenching decision—to send her infant on a separate journey under the care of a nanny in case she succumbed to the disease."

His narrative took a chilling turn, and Ellena couldn't contain her intrigue. "What happened next?" she asked, her voice filled with anticipation.

Duncan continued, weaving a tale that was both horrifying and poignant. "The ship met a grim fate, sinking to prevent the virus from returning to the bay. According to accounts, Anna perished and was placed in a coffin awaiting burial upon her return to shore. However, a macabre twist awaited them. One by one, the dead began to reanimate as ferocious, bloodthirsty creatures. In a desperate act, Count Farrington ordered the ship to be obliterated by the cannons of Slain's Castle. If the story holds, Anna was trapped in her coffin on the ocean floor, enduring a ceaseless cycle of resurrection and suffocation. This unending torment has lasted through the centuries. To this day, her coffin remains undiscovered."

The grim narrative weighed heavily on us. Regardless of the integrity of the vampire myth, the thought of such eternal suffering was a harrowing concept to fathom. It begged the question: Was this what David McNally sought to uncover, or was something more sinister at play?

I pressed further, scepticism still present in my tone. "Surely, nobody believes such a tale?"

Duncan's response carried a weight of certainty. "Oh, you'd be surprised. And David McNally doesn't act without substantial evidence to support his actions."

With every revelation, the intricate puzzle of Cruden's secrets deepened, casting a shadow of uncertainty over our mission. We needed to uncover more about Jean and whether any surviving notes were key to understanding his perspective. Perhaps Montague's house held secrets that were integral to the unfolding mystery.

I redirected the conversation towards our enigmatic companion. "Alright, Duncan, you've shown us the enigma; now tell us your purpose. Especially given your acknowledgement that the local police won't intervene."

Duncan's response was laced with a palpable uncertainty. He knew Cruden faced a dire threat, but the absence of concrete facts left him searching for answers. "Truth be told, I'm not entirely sure. I keep an eye on London's news occasionally, and your recent exploits in the media caught my attention. When I heard of your arrival at the bed and breakfast, I sensed an opportunity for some out-of-the-box thinking. A chance to save our town from descending into chaos once more."

As Duncan's words hung in the air, I couldn't help but scrutinize him more closely. His heart rate, breathing, and perspiration betrayed the turmoil within him. Something about his story didn't add up, particularly regarding Ruth or the caves beneath Cruden.

"However," Duncan added, "I have a confession. I've been following your activities closely. There's something else, something about Ruth and the caves that troubles me."

I watched as Duncan's heart rate spiked, revealing a hidden layer of his motives. It was unclear whether it was Ruth's presence or the secrets of the underground that truly concerned him.

With a cautious nod, I responded, "Thank you for your honesty, Duncan. We'll do our best to unravel the mysteries of Cruden, but it seems like we're dealing with more 'dots' than we anticipated."

The relentless wind's chill prompted me to return to the waiting limousine. As I pivoted, my foot slipped, and Duncan's quick reflexes prevented a fall. However, as his hand brushed mine, a sudden, sharp static shock passed between us, raising the hairs on my arm. It was an unexpected jolt triggered by a gold ring on Duncan's middle finger.

I couldn't help but inspect the ring more closely and made a startling connection as I did. The symbol engraved on it was eerily reminiscent of the one etched on the bridge's pillar and the castle's steps—an arrangement of goat heads encircling a star, a symbol often associated with dark rituals and devil worship. It was another perplexing piece of the puzzle, raising even more questions.

In a matter of seconds, the world around us shifted. The skies darkened, casting an ominous shadow over the landscape. The ground beneath us became eerily silent, devoid of wind or rustling leaves, as if time had frozen. My surroundings transformed into an opulent room adorned with a long mahogany table and ornate chairs, their red velvet seatbacks adorned with brass tacks. The table groaned under the weight of sumptuous dishes, but the aroma that wafted from them was anything but appetizing—the scent of blood.

The pounding of approaching footsteps shattered the room's eerie stillness. I watched as a line of figures in crimson cloaks, their faces concealed by small black masks, entered the room one by one. Each took their place behind a chair, waiting in silence. Only one seat at the head of the table remained unoccupied.

The tension in the room thickened as more footsteps approached. Long, skeletal fingers emerged from beneath a cloak, gripping the backrest of the remaining chair. The fingers, capped with long, sinister nails, caught my eye, but what held my attention was the glint of a gold ring on the wearer's middle finger—the same ring that had sent an electric shock through me moments ago.

The room's atmosphere grew more oppressive as the cloaked figures revealed their faces. Their elongated fingers betrayed a sinister grace, and as they removed their hood and mask, I gasped in disbelief. It was the same man we had seen across the road from McNally's garage, albeit paler, more worn, and infinitely more menacing. Though his eyes seemed to penetrate the depths of my soul, they bore into me with an unsettling intensity.

I was immobile, unable to look away from those bottomless black eyes, and the room began to close around me. The lingering scent of blood filled my nostrils, and the oppressive weight of dread descended upon me.

Then, as suddenly as it had begun, the room crumbled away, and reality rushed back. The sea's salty breeze returned, and the rustling trees and distant voices filled my senses once more. Duncan had not noticed the disconcerting episode; he had been preoccupied with preventing my fall.

Ellena, however, had sensed something amiss. Her eyes held a glimmer of concern as I took one last look at the ominous gold ring before quickly withdrawing my hand, pretending that all was well. My smile masked the turmoil within me, for the image of that menacing vampire remained etched in my mind.

Chapter 20

Cruden Bay had succumbed to the encroaching darkness, a shadowy realm inhabited by vampires; that much was undeniable. Yet, the true nature of their stories and the motives that drove them remained mysterious. It seemed as though the ancient vampire, the one who had inexplicably appeared before me, was attempting to establish a connection, assuming he truly was what he appeared to be. With its aura of unpredictability, the ring had consistently led me to him. The vision only served to confirm that he was indeed a bloodsucker.

But the enigma persisted: why? And how did all the threads of this twisted tapestry intertwine? I dared not ask Ruth for a photograph of the Elder for fear that the legends of vampires and their lack of reflection held. Moreover, what were the rules governing this supernatural realm? The "black widow" case had taught us that the supernatural world adhered to its own rules, and we desperately needed to understand them. Common myths did not mention vampires roaming in daylight; if that were the case, what other deviations from cinematic portrayals existed?

The perplexity deepened when considering McNally's excavation into the cliff. They had taken water levels into account, but the true extent of their plans remained obscure. My mind even entertained the notion that they might be digging beneath the town, planting explosives to level everything underground and constructing anew atop the ruins. However, that appeared excessively laborious and convoluted, leaving far too many gaps to be filled in too many versions of the truth to sift through.

In his characteristic manner, Duncan offered to transport us anywhere we needed to go, allowing us space to ponder and decipher the cryptic occurrences in the town. Ellena proposed visiting the Cruden public library to uncover information, if any, regarding the ancient bloodbath that had occurred centuries ago. While contemplating the golden ring, I thought of the pale figure who had worn it.

"Duncan," I began, shifting in my chair as the remnants of Scotch swirled in my glass, "I couldn't help but notice the ring earlier. It appears distinct from what I've encountered before. A family heirloom, perhaps?"

Taking a hearty sip from his glass, Duncan replied, "This thing? Oh no, I was strolling along the base of the cliffs about a year ago. The tide was gradually encroaching, and each sea rush unearthed various debris. That's when I spotted this gleaming in the sunshine. I saw it as a small stroke of luck, and I've worn it ever since."

"Lucky find," I murmured, trying to contain my scepticism in light of what I had witnessed. "So, why the library?"

Ellena interjected, "What better place to gather our thoughts? Besides, we are strangers here, and it would be advantageous to familiarize ourselves with the town's history."

Duncan, offering his insights, added, "Well, good luck with that. The original library was destroyed by fire twenty years ago. I'm uncertain how much they salvaged everyday books, but I've heard rumours that some old material may have survived in the basement. It might be of interest to you. Just mention my name, and they should grant you full access. Also, if, after your research, you find yourselves available tomorrow at 10 a.m., I'd like to introduce you to someone who might shed further light on these matters."

Duncan presented me with a bottle of his finest Scotch as we stopped outside a building that featured a small flight of stairs leading to a brick-recessed shelter. The front of the building bore brown-framed woodwork, almost stretching from floor to roof. The original structure might have fallen victim to the same fire that had consumed the library. This one, however, had been far from meticulously maintained. Duncan had entrusted us with this lead, and while the temptation to grab our belongings and depart lingered, my conscience compelled me to explore further.

As we stood outside, Ellena turned her attention to me, arching her eyebrows inquisitively. "Georgie, what happened back there? I saw your eyes."

"Turned black again?" I asked.

Ellena nodded. "Indeed."

"We certainly make for an unusual pair, don't we?" I remarked, trying to deflect her concern. Yet Ellena saw through my facade with ease.

"That ring I inquired about with Duncan," I began, "when I touched it after he grabbed my arm to prevent a slip, I had another vision."

Ellena's eyes widened in anticipation. "Oh, dear. What did you see this time?"

"I found myself in a vast room with an old-fashioned fireplace and a lengthy dining table laden with food. But the beverage of choice was blood," I recounted, my voice tinged with dread. "They were imbibing blood like we would savour a cup of coffee. The experience was horrifying, and I yearned for it, just as I do in the real world. However, none of my werewolf abilities were of any use. I was utterly defenceless. Approximately twenty individuals, cloaked in red garments, paraded to the table, raising their goblets for a toast. Then, the figure seated at the head of the table lowered his hood and mask to reveal his skeletal, deathly visage. He was undeniably a vampire."

Ellena processed this revelation, her brow furrowing in concern. "So, all the stories we've heard are true?"

"I'm afraid so," I admitted, my unease deepening. "I spotted him at the gallery earlier today and once again outside McNally's garage."

"You saw a vampire at the gallery?" Ellena exclaimed in disbelief.

"Not precisely," I clarified, struggling to convey the bizarre sequence of events. "In a few hours, I encountered a peculiar individual who appeared uncannily real and seemed to fixate on you. He was as tangible as you or I. Later, I beheld the same figure transformed into a vampire during my vision."

"Focusing on me?" Ellena asked, her voice tinged with bewilderment. "I did hear my name being called, but you heard nothing, and I hadn't seen anyone. This is utterly bewildering. Why me?"

"It appears that Amos also took an interest in you," I noted, my frustration and confusion mounting. "I have no idea what is unfolding or who is telling the truth. This dilemma extends to Ruth as well. However, that vampire and the others in the room seemed remarkably secure during the vision. The room appeared well-preserved, leading me to believe that the castle or Montague House conceals a grandeur far beyond what we perceive. For the most part, Duncan seemed truthful until he mentioned knowing about us through the press."

Ellena posed the question that had been haunting my thoughts. "Do you think this has all been orchestrated to bring us here? Locke included?"

I contemplated the possibility, unwilling to believe that Locke had knowingly betrayed us. His apologetic letter indicated that he had believed something significant lay in Cruden Bay, drawing him here. This thought led me back to Ruth, who might have influenced Duncan with her agenda and informed Locke, subsequently orchestrating this elaborate ruse. However, my suspicions remained unsubstantiated, and I lacked concrete evidence.

"We are missing crucial details needed to unravel this perplexing puzzle," I admitted, my frustration evident. "This town harbours numerous secrets, and none of them bode well. Knowing that it may escalate further, do you want to remain entangled in this enigma?"

"Like I've already told you, Mr. Wolf, if you're in, so am I," Ellena declared, her determination unwavering. With a coy smile and a raised eyebrow, she tugged me along the steps leading to the library. I understood that leaving was not an option, and I also recognized that I couldn't navigate this tumultuous journey without Ellena by my side. Her captivating beauty concealed her formidable intellect, but I had glimpsed her true capabilities, and for now, she was my anchor in this swirling sea of uncertainty.

Dust hung heavy in the air, a musty veil that clung to our lungs, while the dim, flickering light of the basement cast eerie shadows upon the surroundings. I had never been particularly fond of basements, and this one, sealed off from the world above, felt especially ominous. A malfunctioning fluorescent light to the right taunted me, its erratic flicker dancing at the corner of my vision, an unsettling distraction I couldn't ignore.

Unsurprisingly, most items in the basement were aged, for libraries were repositories of history, and history aged like fine wine. But what lay before us now was unlike anything I had ever seen. The bestiary had been unsettling, but the contents of this basement promised an even darker narrative. The librarian, casting an odd look our way, had not anticipated our curiosity, as she had regarded us as though we were mad when Ellena requested access to the oldest books.

Amid this atmospheric gloom, Ellena was undeterred, her focus unwavering as she scanned the shelves. She approached a glass cabinet nestled against the back wall, and from my vantage point, I could glimpse a swath of discoloured parchment or artwork approximately sixty centimetres wide. As I drew nearer, it became evident that two distinct sections adorned with intricate designs bore a haunting, almost tactile quality.

"Duncan, do you know what these are?" I inquired, unable to conceal my curiosity.

He shook his head, the lines on his face etched with intrigue. "No idea. They've been here as long as I can remember."

I turned my attention to the first section, a material resembling aged leather, textured with grooves and lines reminiscent of fingerprints or perhaps the intricate patterns of skin. Ellena had gravitated toward the other section, her keen eyes darting back and forth across the surface as she pored over its contents. The librarian's watchful gaze didn't escape me, and it was clear that we had stumbled upon something significant.

With an ardent focus, I examined the first section, searching for any semblance of an artist's signature or initials. My keen werewolf vision yielded no results; there was nothing to suggest the creator of these enigmatic pieces. Frustration gnawed at me as I continued my investigation, searching for hidden ink or concealed messages, yet I came up empty-handed.

Then, I noticed a small, minuscule detail that could easily elude an untrained eye. A tiny, almost invisible sequence of numbers, etched onto the thighs of the horses depicted in the artwork: seven horses on each side, seven mounted vampires, and twenty-three more charging behind, along with seven humans and thirty more humans in pursuit. A total of one hundred and two bodies lay trampled beneath hooves and feet.

"73.17026," I murmured, recognizing the sequence as a set of coordinates, just like the one we had found on the cross in the graveyard. But this time, there was no arrow indicating a direction. Instead, it was a mere sequence of numbers, a cryptic clue that hinted at something hidden beneath the surface.

As I pondered this revelation, Ellena beckoned me to her side. She had discovered another piece of the puzzle, a portrait dating back to 1726—a year later than we had known. It depicted the Farrington family, their household staff, and others who likely constituted their circle of friends. The scene unfolded in a radiant, bright yellow and white room, exuding an air of affluence and contentment.

Ellena, her eyes bright with discovery, pointed to a specific detail in the painting. "Georgie, look beside Anna," she urged.

I shifted my gaze to the indicated area, and there, seated next to Anna and her mother, were two women dressed entirely in white. The significance of this escaped me, and I puzzled over Ellena's excitement.

"Ruth mentioned she was Anna's handmaiden," I said, searching for clarity.

"That's precisely it," Ellena replied, her voice tinged with conviction. "But take a closer look. That woman there, that's not Ruth. People can change their hair but can't alter their bone structure or eye colour. And did you notice the girl has a wooden leg?"

My focus shifted to the young woman in question, and it became evident that Ellena was correct. The handmaiden depicted in the painting bore no resemblance to the Ruth we had encountered. Something was amiss. The web of deception was unravelling before us, exposing layers of falsehoods and misdirection.

But there was more to discover. Ellena drew my attention to a faint marking on the painting, a detail that required my enhanced werewolf vision to discern fully. It appeared to be a partial circle and a small dash on the right edge of the painting, forming what resembled a compass with a fixed direction—west.

The puzzle pieces were falling into place; cryptic coordinates, a painting contradicting known history, and hidden markings hinted at a grander conspiracy that had ensnared Cruden Bay in its sinister grasp. The town's secrets ran deeper than we imagined, and the trail of blood and lies showed no sign of ending.

Chapter 21

Ellena wasn't giving up. The paintings had barely scratched the surface, making me wonder if anyone else had noticed our same details. McNally was the obvious place to point our claws. I hadn't considered it until now; longitude and latitude could instigate his deep-sea diving excursions.

At least the diving aspect of things. If we weren't going to run away, we might as well analyse our information as if it were another case: no half-measures or second-guessing. We had an inkling that Ruth had been lying to us about much of it being another story. What I was sure of was that we couldn't let Ruth know we suspected anything, at least for the time being. How much of a witch she was could also come under the spotlight. However, my lack of knowledge of those matters disadvantaged us.

Unless, by some miracle, Ellena also became a quick study. The way she tore through the dust-covered pathway between the bookshelves made me think this was a typical slice of heaven for her. I still pictured the towers in Ellena's flat quite vividly. Then I remembered her blood on the staircase. I couldn't let her get taken again as she danced from one row to the next.

Melanie may have controlled a Kanaima demon then, but she was human. What we faced now could be a colony of vampires or just a few, for all we knew. Bloodsuckers. And Ellena had already heard voices. My vision made me think that the guy I'd seen could've been the elder vampire. I still hoped we'd find a picture of Jean and Frederick to know for sure. Much of what we'd heard had become a mess; I didn't know what parts were true.

We were in another dismal basement, looking for answers, which felt surreal. Maybe another holiday to get over this one was on the agenda. Looking around at how old everything was, there had to be a detail among them to help us. I was drawn to a series of maps on the wall. Each showed the Scottish coast over the centuries, particularly around the Cruden Bay area. From school, I remembered lessons on coastal erosion.

The cliff face had changed from the seventeen hundreds to the present. I got to thinking about the two number sequences we had. If they were longitude and latitude, we'd be foolish to plot them against how the coast looked now. Ellena caught me staring and came over. I waited to see if she saw what I had done.

It took all of two minutes before Ellena grabbed her notebook. She had the line, so I let her run with it. After all, we had nothing but time. At least a few more hours before something intriguing was due to happen. Nicholas McNally had mentioned 9 p.m. on the phone. It could be a wasted journey, but I wanted to go back. In my mind, it was about whoever had taken a beating on the garage floor.

Whether David McNally would get his hands dirty by removing a dead body or the victim had only been taken to where the McNallys got what they wanted.

"You think it's at sea?"

"Well, those scuba divers are looking for something. The how, what, and why are a mystery for now. But something has them down there,"

"But you think they could be in the wrong place?" It was a working theory; the numbers could've meant something else entirely, and we didn't know who left them to be found or who else knew about them.

"Honestly, it's a shot in the dark. McNally is looking for something in particular. Those boxes I saw seemed old. But check out the year and tear on the coastline over the years," I pointed before stepping aside for Ellena to get closer.

I continued looking from behind Ellena's shoulder. At first, my curiosity held up. Soon enough, I drifted into a daze, focusing on the back of Ellena's head, just taking it in. I had hoped this would be a week to learn more about Ellena's past life. We'd have a nice relaxing time. I wanted to dig a little into ADI Locke to see how much she knew, especially in light of his storage shop in Forest Gate. Instead, I'm looking at the back of Ellena's head as she works out old maps. If anyone could substantiate my thoughts, she could, and I wouldn't seem like such an irrational idiot.

Lost in my admiring haze, a shock rippled below the dip in my neck. One by one, the hairs sparked to life, quickly shivering down my spine. It came out of nowhere, in a place I least expected danger. Ellena kept looking away while my head bounced to the left. My hackles were going haywire. The room had fallen silent, heightening the trepidation in my mind—enough to cause my claws to shoot forward.

Nothing stood out in the dimly lit room, but the rumble through my neck wasn't letting up. I could hear mine and Ellena's heartbeats like a thunderstorm, with everyone else so quiet. Ellena's had accelerated, and I didn't know why, too distracted by the tormenting of my neck hairs.

'Ah, history. If only it had ever told the real story. I can show you if you wish,'

Ellena's heart kept spiking. In short bursts but enough to have me worried. Her eyes darted as the wrinkles in her forehead gathered in the middle. Ellena was bothered. I strained my ears to listen, catching a few voices and footsteps in the distance. Nothing to have my body reacting or Ellena concerned about.

'Beauty such as yours deserves to be admired, adored, and able to endure eternity. You would be a queen. My queen,'

I caught Ellena shaking her head. Whatever was happening, it was in her head. What I didn't understand was why my hackles reacted. Last time, there hadn't been so much as a flicker. Perhaps the drink Ruth gave us affected us in ways nobody anticipated unless Ruth had.

'Don't be afraid, Ellena. You have nothing to fear from me. You never did. It's taken a lifetime, but you've finally returned. They may call you Ellena, but to me, you'll always be Anna,'

It was getting worse. Ellena shook her head harder. While her body rocked on her heels. Even though I couldn't hear anything or sense an immediate threat, my body still felt in danger. Unless it wasn't me in danger...

'Come to me. Find me. Help me restore balance and embrace immortality. By setting me free, you'd help break the shackles that have plagued this town. Let's rewrite history,'

Ellena's heart suddenly slowed, and the rocking stopped. She stood still, looking up at the coastal ridge of Scotland, particularly Cruden Bay, the port, and Peterhead in the 1700s.

'Count Elias Diminescu - the discovery 1725,'

Dirt and rough stones were our pathways for what seemed like an eternity. When you've been wrongly imprisoned, waiting and hoping that somebody will set you free one day, anything other than that place is euphoria.

Entombed behind mud and rock, in the hope I would be forgotten. The gap in my prison was wide enough for the world to be my tormentor. Unable to move, I watched everything grow, wither, die, and grow again. Time didn't exist. Overgrown and vibrant green trees created a shadow across my tomb. With each change of colour, I could tell what season it was—small pleasures in hell. My body had been abused, tortured, and drained to death. All in the knowledge that I was unable to die.

I had been royalty, serving my country with distinction. Overseeing the fall of tyrants as they came and went. Romania flourished. Markets blossomed, and the people thrived on their freedom and newfound wealth from selling flourishing produce. Unfortunately, I was born differently. Cursed with a virus, I was told, destined to live an eternity but at the cost of watching everyone I loved and held dear die. I couldn't stomach normal food like everyone else. I even pretended to spend hours in my bathroom being sick at lavish dinners and soirees.

My hunger was for something different. Blood. When that lust gripped me, my teeth would grow along with my nails. My thirst was insatiable and had to be appeased before it became necessary to tear through flesh. At first, I used loyal castle staff to bring livestock if I furnished local farmers with gold. I learnt quickly that if I asked someone nicely while looking directly into their eyes, my sincerity would penetrate their soul, and they'd do anything I asked. All because they knew I was being sincere.

They'd act hypnotised, a small drawback that would eventually wear off. I would get to eat, and the remaining meat would be put to good use by my kitchen or handed out to townspeople. Then it got noticed I wasn't ageing... I had eyes focused on me anywhere I went, making life uncomfortable until I became a self-imposed recluse. A fact that was hard while in love. Catalin Albescu was her name. Not quite royalty, but she did important work—as a teacher. In the beginning, it was fun, and we were inseparable.

When I wanted attention, Catalin would sneak through the servant's entrance. Then, one day, Catalin got sick. Nobody knew what had caused it. I'd left it longer than normal without animal blood in my absent-mindedness. In a crazed frenzy, I didn't wait to slice a cow's throat; I sunk my teeth in. I realised I could drink easier. What I hadn't realised was that I would also change the cow.

It had dropped dead as expected. Only to resurrect later and be different. Life had gone but left behind a demonic beast: red eyes and sharp teeth. My mind was a mess; my heart longed for Catalin to improve. Instead, she got worse. I couldn't be without Catalin, so I thought, if my bite could do that to a cow, what would it do to Catalin? With the expectation that she'd live. I travelled by night to her hospital fifty miles away. Just in time to see Catalin's body giving up. I had to try, so I bit her neck.

At that moment, two things happened that would shape my life forever. The taste of Catalin's blood was euphoric. No matter how sick she was, the taste made my body come alive. She was a drug to me. I could suddenly hear far more, move faster, and smell the smallest things outside the hospital. I could also hear Catalin's heartbeat grow stronger. The atrium walls rebuilt themselves as her arteries were on fire. Her body seemed far more vibrant and fuller. Was that an improvement in my vision or just Catalin? I didn't know, only that I had to leave before somebody returned.

I left that night with my eyes opened, and the world changed. Human blood made me feel different down to the molecular level. It was intoxicating. The virus I'd been born with made me different. Human blood made me better, and I needed more. I had saved Catalin's life. Unfortunately, everything has a cost. Catalin's revival had been temporary; I learned she changed just like the cow. The illness was gone, but she died anyway; her heart stopped as she became crazed in search of blood. It took a brave person fighting for their life to stab her with scissors. I never saw Catalin again; I couldn't afford the risk of association and what she became.

'Cruden Bay Library 6th November 1987,'

Those footsteps moved slower as they came closer. The stench of death was quite weak and a little different. Ellena remained steady and still. Her head was a little tilted to her left but seemed to be making up the map's details. I crept to my right and towards the stairs to peer up to the top and catch sight of any feet.

Each step was old, thick timber and creaked enough when we came down without thinking about it. Now, I was hyper-vigilant, and every move stood out. First came a heavy creak... A scuff of a chair across the floor. Then suddenly... The lights flashed off...

Chapter 22

With the lights off, my heart accelerated, but strangely, Ellena hadn't reacted. Not at all. No sudden fear or questioning of what the hell was going on. She stood in the same place, bead still tilted. All I saw were shades of red and black except for the radiator and Ellena's body heat.

The situation was off, not just because of the lights. It was Ellena that bothered me the most. I could still see the paintings enough, and my mind drifted to the battle scene for a second. Wondering how much the rest of the town knew. Were there more numbers to find? With the correct map and assuming it was longitude and latitude. The arrows didn't serve much purpose unless they had a direction from that point.

A board creaked, sending a shiver down my back and dragging my attention back to the moment. One after the other, someone walked down the steps. Ellena finally began to turn to me. Slowly. A trick of the red in the darkness, I thought at first. My eyes honed in, and the wolf in me reacted to danger. I got to see the side side of Ellena's face.

It was different. She looked paler, bonier and, dare I say it, deader. Her body twisted into a lighter shade of red, and I caught another glimpse of what I saw in the caves. It may have been a vision, but it seemed so real. I assumed it could've been a warning of what Ellena could become if it went wrong. Then we learnt of Anna. Since Amos and then Ruth, all the little details have shaped a scary path. That glimpse frightened me the most.

Just as she'd come front-facing, her mouth opened like she was about to speak. Ellena displayed the tips of her fangs... Then, the lights suddenly flashed back on. Ellena looked at me still, and she was normal. My hackles dropped, and the wolf settled down. Those footsteps continued, but my body didn't react at all. It had all been because of that glimpse.

"Oh, sorry. We thought you'd gone, nae noise at all. Apologies for the wee fright," One of the librarians peered through the gap between the rickety wooden railings.

"That's ok," I didn't take my eyes off Ellena, more out of a mixture of elements. Disbelief, surprise, fear and a tinge of sadness that whatever was going on, I'd brought Ellena here—the one place she should never have been exposed to. Yet, again, this begs the question. Did ADI Locke know? If he did, he knowingly put Ellena's life at risk and mine. He would have to answer if we got out of this mess.

"Ellena, are you ok?"

"Of course; why is that?"

"The lights went out, and you didn't flinch,"

"I was deep in thought," Her throat juddered, an octave changed when she said 'deep' and her eyes twitched.

"Did you notice the lights?"

"To be honest, I'm not sure where I went. I was looking at the geography of this place and the 1700s, and I got lost in the moment."

Ellena was only partly telling the truth. I could tell she had been lost in a moment. But not the one she spoke of. I was reading every microexpression and chemo signal Ellena gave off. I feared she'd heard that voice again. And when the lights went out, I saw death. At least what it could look like for Ellena.

This wasn't any battle I was used to. We were up against something that could invade Ellena's mind while Ruth weaved tricks of her own. It seemed the only person who could be an ally so far might be Duncan.

"Did you hear anything? Like the footsteps?" I was hinting at the voice to invoke her memory but disguised by the librarian.

"I guess I was trying to imagine if those numbers meant anything, how far in the sea would the 'X' be marked," This part of Ellena's story was true, even if it had been wrapped in something worse.

"Aye, well, I hate to interrupt your wee history lesson, but we're closing," I checked my watch to see it was 4.30 pm. We'd had more time inhaling dust than we thought.

'8.45 pm,'

Nothing but quiet and the night sky. The stars were brighter, but thankfully, the full moon wasn't for another 24 hours. My reason to be thankful was my being alone. Ellena didn't recover too well from her fixation. A headache, she said and the need to get some sleep. Perhaps her late-night walk to the cliffs was far more taxing than we'd realised.

Ruth didn't appear over dinner, and the golems, Dianne and Mary, didn't speak a word about anything from the morning. They more than likely ordered not to do otherwise. Ellena went to bed soon after, and while I took little comfort from it, at least no vampire could enter.

With Our hosts tasked to ensure Ellena didn't go for another walk, I feared they were the better of a few evils. At the same time, I took my BMW to scope out that pig of an 'R.S... Cosworth, hoping I didn't see a body being carted out.

I was hidden close to a run-down caravan and an old Cortina stranded on stacks of brittle bricks across from the motel. I slumped down in my seat and reclined it back enough that my pale face didn't get caught in the moonlight.

While my stomach rumbled again, it seemed my appetite had grown stronger of late, not that time has allowed many breaks when I'm on a case. Even the smell of beer caused a little stir. The pub 'Wrinkled Ferret'. A peculiar name that seemed to fit nonetheless was even livelier than earlier. Which had been bulging at the seams then. Now, it was a powder keg with Alexander and that drip from earlier right in the thick of it. If Alexander was the family's black sheep, he didn't know how to keep a low profile.

A lamp light could be seen to the back of the garage office, and a slither drifted into the yard. I couldn't see anyone in the office, and there were too many heartbeats around me this far away to tell how many were in there. A part of me thought I might be wasting my time. I had to see who or what I was dealing with.

My radio was on low to keep me entertained and awake. That's the trouble with working alone, doing nothing but watching. The boredom. Not that the local radio was anywhere close to thrilling. I'd landed on 'Bay FM', probably a rag-tag shack in nowhere. A huge radio tower next to a garden shed.

Their music seemed stuck a decade or so ago. Some of which I wasn't sure qualified as songs. My ears steadily adjusted to sound like a gaggle of the banjo, a drum and possibly a flute. An odd mix, I thought to myself. I could've quite easily been wrong. The sound quality crackled a lot. Until a local news bulletin interrupted, it started well if well as an update on who'd grown the 'biggest pumpkin' competition. My I.Q. was dwindling by the moment, and I hadn't been blessed with much as it was. Then it took a dark turn for the worst. The reader's tone changed, and I was given a peek behind the town's dirty curtain.

'The body of a 32-year-old man has been found in Lake McClune, two miles east of the Peterhead border. A local dog walker came across a half-submerged truck approximately two hours ago. His name is yet to be disclosed, but local police can confirm the man was in the passenger seat with no trace of a driver.-

-The news desk awaits an update on the cause of death. It has been confirmed as being treated as suspicious, and police are seeking information or sightings of a blue Ford pickup truck with at least two occupants in around the Lake McClune area before 6.30 pm,'

My throat had dried a little from my mouth hanging open. My eyes went to looking around McNalley Garage forecourt. The rusty Ford pickup from earlier was nowhere to be seen. If I've said it once, I've said it a thousand times. I'm not a fan of coincidences.

My immediate thoughts were the bloke I could see laughing with Alexander had done the deed. He was possibly double-crossing his partner in crime. Perhaps they'd been paid a healthy wedge for whatever they had to deliver, and the driver didn't feel like sharing. Unless the shit hit the fan, the passenger came unstuck another way. And being the callous bastard criminals can be. Instead of the hospital, he chose a watery burial. Like some have a habit of doing, it took longer to sink.

I stared at his smug, drug-riddled face, wondering if he knew what was unfolding while he drank his tits off. More importantly, what was Alexander's role in it all? Just as I sank deeper in my procrastination, I heard two vehicles approaching, quicker than the average but not police about to do a raid. There were big, all-terrain with meaty engines. It had to be at least that Range Rover from earlier and another.

Two black vehicles, gleaming under the moonlight, stopped outside the garage. One was a Range Rover, the other a Mitsubishi. The Rover reversed up to the yard gates. While the other stayed opposite the office. The driver of 'Bishi' got out first, lighting a cigarette. Heavy set, six foot two at least, with a bald head. He opened the rear left passenger door and out strolled a surprise first. It was bloody Amos. Larger than life and looking normal.

The moment he hit the air, I could smell it, blood. It oozed from his pores. The rear right opened next, and the bloke on the boat stepped out earlier. I could recognise the receded ginger hair and beer belly anywhere. David McNally. The stink of cigar smoke clouded as his sparse ginger thatch cut through the grey, almost like a shark navigating the seas. He looked pissed off.

My guess is he'd also heard the news on the radio. Next out was the frail woman I assumed to be the mother. It took David to steady her before she fell. She was hunched over and staggering forward. Her facial expression was a mix of pain and anger. I could feel her pain the most, but it also reeked a slightly acidic tone to her scent.

All the while, I could see Amos; he had a big, cheesy, yet haunting smile. He was playing the role of a puppet master. I'd come across people like that too frequently lately. One of the few street lamps hung over his head gave a glimpse of what I saw in Ellena. Death. It almost fluctuated between normal and vampire as the light bounced in the wind.

What I couldn't understand was the benefit of their arrangement: a partnership or a means to an end.

The question is, for whom? Amos wasn't acting how I'd imagined or the impression at the graveyard when he pranced around Ellena to capture her scent. This version seemed calculated and methodical. By aligning himself and other vampires with David, he had to use them to force another way into the caverns. At what cost, though? There had to be one.

David McNally glared through the pub window and pointed two fingers at Alexander and the drip beside him. David's anger had grown, and he was pacing the pavement, muttering. His free hand kept sliding to the rear of his waistband. I heard the metal rattle first, and then as his coat had slipped out of the way, I saw a black handle. Judging by the grip and base edge of a magazine-loaded butt, it was a Glock of some kind.

"What the hell have you done?" David growled as Alexander and the drip shuffled through the door into the open. Neither had the same jovial bounce of moments ago.

"What's going on, Dad? I haven't done anything," Alexander spoke up. Raising his finger.

"Nae you, boy, ya gommy sod. I'm talking to the wee plank next to ya,"

"What?"

"Ya dinnae hear the news in there dancing around ya wee handbag. Ya boy there has fucked up royally, so he has,"

"What do ya mean? I dinnae have a clue,"

"Where's the wee truck boy?"

"As far I heard, Colin borrowed it after the drop, so I heard," Alexander turned to the drip next to him with a grimace that had his friend like a rabbit in headlights.

"Aye, well, currently, the plods are pulling it from Lake McClune with ya wee pal Colin in the fucking passenger seat,"

Alexander looked to the drip, grabbed him by the scruff and thrust him forward. The drip held his hands up, walking backwards. David pulled the gun and held it at chest height. With his back to the pub, they were shielded from the view. David stepped forward slowly. The drip shook his head 'no' while frantically waving his hands.

I wanted to do something; the copper in me knew I should've been doing something. Yet the supernatural in me knew I had to let it all unfold to get a better sense of the fucked up situation. Besides, I may be a demon wolf; I wasn't an army. David was forcing the drip further and further back and off the pavement. Only, I hadn't heard any 'chambering'. The drip tool took one last step back toward the vehicle's left.

Then in the blink of an eye. A scary, ferocious blur. Amos breezed toward and attacked the drip with savagery. Nails crunched into the top of the drip's head. Amos yanked down hard; I heard the crack, and then in a swift, brutally nightmarish move. Amos tilted his head back, open-mouthed, to reveal his fangs before he plunged hard into the neck of the drip.

Skin, muscle, ligaments and tendons all tore apart with blood gushing, and the grim sound of a vampire ripping into a human echoed painfully around my eardrums. As the drip wailed, he squirmed and flung out his arms in vain. Blood spurted over Amos's face; he gargled down the blood like I would a Whiskey. It was horrifying and had my stomach doing summersaults, even if the scent of blood had me drooling a little

Chapter 23

His body hung limp, and the gruesome sound of Amos retracting his fangs and nails sent shivers down my spine. The lifeless form never reached the cold, unforgiving floor. Amos seized him by the scruff of his neck as the driver popped open the rear door, then flung the lifeless body aside as if it were a mere ragdoll. Eleven stone of wasted space were effortlessly tossed aside with a single hand.

In that brutal moment, I glimpsed the unfathomable strength of a vampire. Though I considered myself strong, I had never truly tested the depths of my power. Witnessing Amos's raw might was a stark reminder of the immense danger looming over me if things went awry. And in the cases I had encountered thus far, something had always gone awry.

The Kanaima job had seen Ellena abducted from her home, leading her and Locke to the warehouse where Michael met a gruesome end, his throat ripped apart. Then there was the enigmatic black widow case, in which Michael had been taken, possibly subjected to experiments that further pushed him down the dark path of the supernatural. That case had been peculiar, almost a test for me, as if someone wanted to determine if I could breach their defences.

In truth, as I contemplated these unsettling events, it was evident that much remained to be unravelled once we escaped this cursed town. The image of that mysterious stone artefact and its purported power brought to mind the cryptic druidic riddles Ruth had shared. Could it be a part of something larger? More importantly, how many such places existed, shrouded in secrets and ancient power?

Amos casually retrieved a handkerchief from his coat pocket, dabbing his mouth clean as if he had just finished a delectable dessert. The expression on his face hinted at a profound satisfaction. The door slammed shut, leaving me with no doubt that the McNallys were aware of vampires and involved with them. Their sinister collaboration was far from over.

"You need to put your house in order, or our arrangement will be null and void," Amos declared, his smirk sending a shiver down my spine. It suddenly dawned on me that Amos could undoubtedly hear my thoughts if I could hear him.

I sank lower into the footwell and switched off the radio, allowing only a slender gap between the steering wheel and dashboard to maintain my watchful gaze. I prayed that the chaos unfolding at the pub would provide enough cover for my racing heartbeats.

"Well, hold on a minute," David interjected. "I didn't know that imbecile would kill his friend over greed."

"True enough," Amos responded, his voice dripping with veiled menace. "But you must understand, I now have a contingency plan. It may take longer, but no one will seek refuge because of sickness. I suggest you expedite the process."

"We struck a deal," David argued. "My wife's life depends on it. We create an entrance to your precious tomb, and you heal her while providing us with the locations of treasure troves. It's a mutually beneficial arrangement."

Amos advanced menacingly, causing David to tense his neck muscles without moving his body—an attempt to maintain his composure before his wife and son. Yet, there was a palpable fear in David, evident in the rapid acceleration of his heart rate.

"All you have to do," Amos continued, "is avoid drawing undue attention while you fret over trivial matters. There's more at stake here than the trinkets you play with. You can have your submerged relics. The grand prize awaits me."

"It's not mere trinkets down there," David retorted. "One of the ships is nearly intact. If we could salvage it, it could be worth a small fortune."

Amos sighed dismissively. "You amuse yourself with your toys. But first, you must open that tunnel. Fail in that, and you may join our dear friend here. And believe me, there will be no return."

Amos's step back was accompanied by a smile, one that countless tales of darkness and power had etched. There was an undeniable connection between David's pursuit and the potential treasures he sought. It raised the question of whether the coordinates aligned with the ship David coveted, a secret potentially hidden from his sons. Perhaps they had never set foot inside a library, and David seemed too engrossed in his web of dealings to delve into history. Another untapped location might have awaited discovery.

The stench of death still hung in the air, exacerbated by the oozing blood from the body in the trunk. It threatened to drive me to madness, and I offered silent gratitude that tonight was not a full moon. But the night's horrors were far from over.

The screech of the yard gate disrupted the eerie silence, followed by the emergence of more burly thugs from a waiting vehicle. Squeaky wheels and the clanking of metal joints heralded the arrival of Nicholas McNally, pushing a trolley constructed of wood and metal. On it lay a man, barely covered by a black sheet and hooded to conceal his identity.

The man's heartbeat echoed faintly, but his breaths were shallow and laboured. The gurgling sounds of blood indicated multiple broken ribs and a punctured lung. He was slowly drowning and choking on his life force. Whoever this unfortunate soul was, his time on this earth was ebbing away. As Amos and David approached the cart, the vehicle's door mostly obscured my view, leaving only snippets of their conversation audible.

I had to rely on my heightened senses and the limited glimpse of David's actions to piece together the unfolding events. Nicholas positioned himself at the forefront of the group, joining his eager mother, and ignited a cigarette with an air of annoyance. I wondered whether he had overheard the news about Michael's fate. David clutched papers in his hand, and the ominous click of a pen signified a significant moment.

"Did you truly believe it wise to brutalize him so?" Amos interjected, his voice a cold reminder. "Remember what I said about putting your house in order? This is another clear warning."

Despite his savage nature, Amos displayed an unsettling intelligence, filling in some gaps in my understanding. Intelligence, superhuman strength, incredible speed, an insatiable thirst for blood—Amos possessed these traits. But he also seemed to harbour a purpose, a mission that begged further exploration.

"In this line of work," David defended, "sometimes one's hands must get dirty. And I don't mean the petty acts of your fledgling vampires, sinking their teeth into necks."

Amos chuckled darkly. "Careful now; it wouldn't take much for me to tear through you. I've been around for centuries and conducted my fair share of business transactions. Your methods are sloppy."

"But you won't, will you?" David challenged. "We have a tunnel to complete. You still haven't divulged the true reasons or significance behind it."

Amos waved off David's concerns, a sinister grin creeping across his face. "Don't trouble your little mind. The significance would turn your pitiful courage to dust. But let's say, if I were to frighten you, what's yet to come would have you soiling your trousers. I suggest you finish the job, and our dealings will be concluded. Remember, you have more to lose, my dear matey."

Amos's reference to the alternative entrance hinted at his ongoing efforts. He had considered Ellena a backup plan, but another vampire was influencing her thoughts. Whether Amos was aware of this was uncertain, and it added another layer of intrigue to the unfolding events. David unravelled the papers and removed the hood, revealing a face soaked in blood.

"Right, now you," David addressed the battered man, "put your signature on this, and you can be on your way."

"I...I need...a...hospital," the man stuttered, his trembling hand barely managing to scribble a few lines. The stench of death clung to him, each heartbeat a faint whisper of life.

David couldn't ignore the palpable changes in the man's condition. The weakening body, the faltering heart, and the tainted blood bore witness to the sinister transformation. Whatever fate awaited him, I knew I had to follow and bear witness to the unfolding horror. Who was this man, and what dark pact was David forcing him to seal?

"They will...know," the man choked out, desperation in his eyes. "The mayor won't let you have it."

David's response was swift, and he spoke with chilling nonchalance. "Your feeble scrawl makes four, and I require just two more signatures from the town committee. Once the public discovers that you and the mayor granted me planning permission, they'll turn against him. I will ascend to the position of mayor, and no one will stand in the way of my vision."

But the man, despite his dire circumstances, clung to a sliver of hope. "Not true," he gasped, each word laborious. "There's a deed...to the house and plot...owned by another...unknown to you."

The rasping sounds of blood-filled gargles reverberated in the night air, an agonizing symphony of impending death. I winced in disgust; the raw reality of mortality laid bare before me. In those fleeting moments, as life slipped away, the man's choked words were a defiant "fuck you" to David McNally. It left me pondering the identity of the deed's true owner, further muddying the waters of this sinister business. With each passing moment, the complexity of their dark dealings became more apparent, and Amos's bloodlust-filled grin painted a grim picture of what was to come.

Amos, seemingly undecided, began to pace, his mind wrestling with a cruel idea that had taken root. I sensed the brewing intent within him, which involved transforming their dying victim into something far more sinister. I couldn't help but feel a morbid curiosity, tainted by guilt, about what might transpire. Films have portrayed such transformations through the bite and sharing of vampire blood. Yet, my moral compass recoiled at the thought of subjecting someone at death's door to an even darker fate, all in pursuing information he may not possess.

Amos paused in his pacing, his eyes darting between David and the near-lifeless figure in the cart. Nicholas appeared increasingly agitated, his adrenaline fueled by the presence of a vampire. The McNallys had made a pact with the devil, and the implications were far graver than they could have imagined.

"It doesn't matter," Amos declared, breaking the tense silence. "I'll find another way. No offence, David, but you possess some semblance of control as vampires go. Turning an almost-dead man into a mindless bloodsucker for mayhem's sake is an indulgence we can do without."

Amos's smile remained, a chilling facade of indifference, and he casually ran a Cuban cigar under his nostrils. At that moment, the complexities of their dark world swirled like shadows in the night, leaving me with the unsettling realization that David was oblivious to the true secrets concealed within the caverns.

Chapter 24

'10 PM.'

I knew I should've gone back to the bed and breakfast. Common sense told me that much. Unfortunately, I let my detective instincts take over. They had muscled alongside my werewolf defence. Which probably relegated my human side to the role of a chicken shit that should be tucked up asleep.

Driving with no lights was no easy task. But that's what I had to do. At least at the moments when traffic thinned out. I didn't have the prerequisite tactical covert driving training for surveillance. I was going off gut instinct, hanging back when I had to, gaining ground when I had the chance. The mission was not to lose sight of either car, even though my brain was busy playing devil's advocate over which car I'd follow if they splintered off in different directions.

I had no idea where we were; I'd hardly seen any road signs, a fair amount of countryside and hills. My car wasn't quite equipped for the terrain; it felt more like dirt tracks than tarmac. All I knew was that we'd already driven twenty minutes north, out of town. At first, it looked like we were going near the port until we looped around. By the thirty-minute mark, I saw small white and black signs. One was for a 'Clacken Forest,' and as I reached the peak of a hill, I saw a dark canvas of tall trees that differed from the surrounding area.

The other sign said, 'Danger quarry ahead,' my hackles immediately lit like a forest fire. McNally had to be planning a body dump of some kind. Far enough away from town to not be questioned and wouldn't draw attention to the McNallys. They already had a potential wildfire on their hands to put out if that truck got linked back to the garage in any way.

Disposing of the battered town committee, bloke was one thing. The drip with fang punctures on his neck and drained of blood was another. Unless he was destined for the forest in the hope that wild animals would turn to pick at his flesh, maybe he would never be found. Or by the time he was, the punctures would be unrecognizable.

I got my answer soon enough as we reached a forked incline in the road. To the right, an arrow for the quarry and left to the forest. I was getting heart palpitations, wondering which way they were going. The Mitsubishi peeled off left, and the Range Rover right. I had hung back far enough for neither to catch a glimpse in their mirrors as they turned. There were no street lamps. Only the moon lit our path. And it was a precarious one.

This fork also represented my choice to stay the course or head back. I decided to follow David McNally and the Mitsubishi. I was intrigued by how they were going to handle the mess. I slowly crawled toward the forest, really wishing I had backup. Then I remembered a stash of Dutch courage in the glove box—a small bottle of whiskey to warm the cockles. I quickly grabbed the fuel for my soul and swigged a little as I swerved one of several midst craters in the road. The surface felt sludgy, and I rued my vehicle options for this tour again. Rear-wheel drive is all well and good for speed and sudden acceleration.

Precarious traction, not so much. I was keeping the engine noise to a minimum and the crappy radio off. I could hear both vehicles with my window down, even if the Range Rover was further away. While the vehicle I'd followed was doing at least twenty miles per hour. I stuck to five. My senses were alive; so many different smells. Even the bad ones are like animal shit. I took another swig of the whiskey, and as the bottle left my lips, I couldn't help but be drawn to the darkness of the trees. Two sets of eyes glowed yellow. Without warning, mine glowed red in return. I felt strange. My werewolf instinct to shift. Not because I felt threatened. This was different. Almost the lure of the wild. Suppose that was even a thing. Wait... Let me check the werewolf handbook...oh that's right, I don't have one.

It wasn't a feeling I understood or had experienced before. The yellow eyes suddenly vanished, and I was back focusing on finding the Mitsubishi without being seen. Its tire tread was unmistakable, and its front left was slightly more worn than the rest. I could hear raised voices a few hundred yards ahead and to the right. Their engine idled.

Meanwhile, any noise around the Range Rover echoed. They were ten minutes in the other direction. There was a dark layby up ahead on the right. With the help of an overgrown bush verge, enough for me to park up and not be seen if the vehicle suddenly raced past.

Now, at a standstill, I got hit by a 'what the hell do I do next?' Yeah, I could sit and listen from afar. But I was fidgety, and in the deep recesses of my reckless mind, I knew I weren't going to stay where I was. With Amos still on the warpath, I couldn't let myself get too close. Working my way up the verge and through the jungle of forestry, I picked up on another weird scent. There was still the lingering aroma of cigars, blood, and death but another, primal, which drew me toward it.

There were chains not in the boot, but they beat against concrete. I seemed to be veering further right as I went and could just about make out a little clearing through the trees to my left. The road had swung right. The clanging chains got louder, and then a sound made me stop in my muddy tracks for a second. A deep growl that seemed to bounce around in a hollow space like a cave.

Weaving between thorns, stinging nettles, and thick bodies of trees, I neared. There was a dampness that felt almost relaxing. The scent of fir trees always did that for me. Until I got another wave of blood and death. More chemo-signals and sounds slowly filtered through. It was a wolf. They had a wolf chained up, and it was pissed. I would go as far as to say hungry and rabid, too. What was David McNally doing with a chained wolf while keeping it in the wild?

Suddenly, I felt emotional sadness and anger at what they were doing. Moreover, I thought they would feed it that bloke who Amos had drained. The wolf seemed hungry enough. While I had an uncontrollable urge to try to set it free. My claws were already out full, and I was shifting. Everything was shades of red and black but a little more natural.

David McNally was riling it up; he had a cooler box. Opening the lid, I smelt different blood: animal and fresher. Without realizing it, I'd been almost walking on tiptoes, moving as stealthily as possible until I could see them through the trees. David tossed slabs of raw steak into a caved space burrowed into a natural wall. Rocks and bushes littered its border and, for the most part, were quite concealed. Set back off the beaten path. They'd gone through a chained 'no entry' sign.

I dropped low, sliding myself through the dirt and plants, hoping to mask my scent a little in case Amos caught a whiff. All I needed was a sudden change in the direction of the wind, and he'd surely smell me. I'd gone as near as I dared, hanging about one hundred and fifty feet away. My enhanced vision was working wonders anyway.

What I couldn't shake was the vibe I was getting from the wolf. It wasn't normal. And if something doesn't feel right, it's generally not right. David stood at an angle of twenty to thirty feet from the cave mouth. He kept smiling smugly to viewing eyes. On the other hand, Amos seemed a little on the back foot, which seemed to have boosted David's confidence. Then I looked to the darkness... I saw its eyes... Blue.

The Skipper tried to tell me before what each colour stood for in a werewolf. Mine were Alpha, Skips, and seemingly Michael's, yellow being Beta's. But Blue meant Omega. A werewolf without a pack. A werewolf that had taken an innocent life. This couldn't be a werewolf, surely.

Chains were being dragged across the concrete floor. Its eyes were low; this wolf was on all fours. First came the snout, then the head. Grey and bigger than I'd associate with a normal wolf. Unless, in Scotland, they were indeed bigger.

That wouldn't account for the strange vibe I was getting. It's too strange for me to rule out it being a werewolf. One that had a huge spiked clamp or trap around its throat. I caught another whiff of blood—this time from the wolf. The clamp was biting into its throat.

Pain and suffering soaked its chemo signals and rabid, hungry anger. It tried to move into the slither of moonlight. The chains halted their progress abruptly. They were deprived of being under the moon if it was a werewolf. I may not be all-knowing. Yet I know how I feel when shifting under the moon, not even the full moon. It's how the Superman movies depict him in the Earth's sun. It enriches him. Fictional, I know.

Then again, I thought of werewolves until the revelations hit home. Now, I live in a world of werewolves, Kanaimas, druids, golems, witches, and vampires—one of the first things I planned to do once or if we escaped this hell hole. Acquaint me with the contents of that bestiary to potentially locate any others that exist out there. Knowledge is power, and I bloody well didn't know enough. It wasn't like I had Ellena at my hip as usual, which made me wonder if she'd stayed in bed. More of a worry. But she was being guarded by the golems Dianne and Mary, even if that left her a little exposed to Ruth's deviousness. At least Amos was here.

Although the other two were somewhere about, I'm sure. So, yeah, as I lay in the mud trying to read whether I was looking at a trapped werewolf or a normal wolf, my head was wanting Ellena with me, and not at the same time. I left her in my bed; hopefully, that's where I'd find her. One thing is for sure: I was leaning toward calling Michael in the morning. It's not like I could howl or roar from Scotland, and he'd hear.

The wolf seemed to glare directly at me, its eyes brightened, which thankfully only served to amuse David McNally further. He was enjoying control over something that, if free, would rip David and anyone else, except Amos, in half—that moment made me edge toward this wonderful, trapped werewolf creature. The way its eyes glowed brighter. I'd never known animals to do that.

It snatched up the steaks and devoured them in one go. Amos seemed to understand what would happen and grabbed the body from the boot. Just as his feet thumped on the floor and Amos still had him by the scruff, I caught a slight murmur of a heartbeat. It was very weak, but it was there, giving me a moral dilemma.

I'd been clear that I was on a fact-finding mission for the bigger picture and wouldn't interfere. That was before I realized they might have an imprisoned werewolf, and now that bloke could still be alive. We were in the middle of nowhere, and being away from the public was swaying me toward trying something. Exactly what? I had no bloody idea. The situation could change rapidly beforehand anyway.

Amos carted the body toward David; surely, he could hear the beating, too. My face rested close to a bundle of fallen fur leaves. I was soothed by its smell once more until I heard a loud crash. A vehicle had gone over the quarry edge. I wondered if it was the scumbag's car or if they had wrecks waiting, which wouldn't have surprised me. They had access. At least I knew the committee guy was dealt with.

I couldn't tell anyone the biggest ballache of all this, official. At least not in town with the cops on their payroll. Every time I caught sight of those blue eyes, they blazed. I wondered if there was a way I could try communicating with them. Or was it too wild after being deprived? Then it dawned on me that if they were a werewolf, how were they being dropped from changing back?

"What the hell are we doing now?" Amos dropped the body at David's feet.

"Well, Ya see, I'm no stranger to the supernatural. Not long after, I learnt of you a lot. I began researching. I may look it, but I'm no gommy sod. I needed to know this world better. In Peterhead, I heard stories of a giant fox raiding livestock. Which seemed bizarre, so being the honourable guy I am and saving the town. We worked the problem and laid a trap to snare the beast,"

"What is it?"

"A fookin werewolf," my heart jumped, confirming my suspicions.

"I sensed it was a different type of animal,"

"Yep. Deprived of moonlight cycles. Teased each day while the collar kept them in pain while rabid and stopped them from changing back to human. Until they forgot what it was like to be normal. I created its need to feed, so it will eat anything, including bodies I really can't have appeared anywhere with vampire bites,"

"Och, Ya canny wee sod. Perhaps I underestimated ya,"

"Aye, Ya, not the first and won't be the last. But know this; I'm well aware of these things,"

"Aye, well, afraid not all things. If did, I stand by my assessment of you messing ya wee pants,"

"Aye, well, I'll take ya word. But I wanted ya to see that I'm not the novice, ya think. Having this killing machine to hand is a blessing,"

"All well and good. But ya beast can't be trusted off its leash, so I feel quite safe,"

Amos made a good point that momentarily wiped the smile from David's face. Yet, Amos was a little pissed off by the show and tell. He'd misread David and wasn't sure how to reel back the momentum. Meanwhile, the werewolf sniffed deeply as small blood trickles oozed from the bloke's neck. It began to get excited

It began to get excited, clawing at the ground as if it would charge at someone.

Amos suddenly tilted his head to the body. He then smiled. He twigged the heartbeat. Breezed quickly up to the body, snatched it off the floor, and easily held it aloft. Amod stared at David; his free hand grabbed the guy's chest in one savage move. Amos ripped the guy's head clean off. Blood spirited through the air, driving mine and the other werewolf's senses nuts.

The head was tossed at David, and the body to the werewolf. Amos smiled, blazing his jet-black eyes toward David. He didn't need to say anything; he'd once again shown his super strength and given David some food for thought.

Chapter 25

I could scratch him off the list. Perhaps my thoughts were too ambitious anyway. Now, having seen Amos despatch that guy's head so easily. I wasn't sure whether I could take him on. Running away wasn't an option either.

This brought me to the other night at the cliffs. I scared the vamps, and he realised who and what I was. This made me question why, in this bizarre yet tragic moment of the brutal show and tell. Amos didn't disclose he knew of another werewolf, me. So far, he hadn't given away whether he knew I was watching or if he had a lock on my scent.

Perhaps that was another card Amos was going to play to piss off David further. Or if David had hunted a werewolf once, would I be next? Amos could put David on my path, try to take me out of the equation and free up Ellena to be picked off. My head was a whirl with possible outcomes tonight, and none of them was good or at least ended favourably for me and the other Werewolf.

Who had its claws sunk deep into the decapitated body. It went to sink its teeth through the flesh but paused. They hung inches away, rows of razor-sharp teeth, bared and scary. Huge fangs that dripped saliva. We locked eyes again. I could read their inner turmoil. It was a female. My presence had stirred something within them. Maybe I'd triggered them to remember who they are or at least an element of their humanity.

The Werewolf didn't sink its fangs in. Instead, they began dragging claws across the floor again while twisting and shaking their head, trying to loosen the collar. It could only happen to me; I followed a vampire and a low-life crime family into a forest and came across a chained-up werewolf. Now I was getting down and dirty, inhaling chunks of mud and bark, wondering what would happen next.

David looked confused, scuffing through the mud. He'd already been shoved onto the backfoot after Amos showed his strength, and then his pet didn't chow down as quickly as he'd expected. His heart sped up with nervous glances at the Werewolf. David looked worried it could break free. A blanket of fog was slowly drifting, which I could use to my advantage. Not that I had figured out what my next move would be.

Watching the tortured soul in chains had me compelled to do something. Even if it was to scare them away and give the wolf some rest bite. Rome wasn't built in a day, and if I couldn't break them free tonight, at least I knew where they were. The setup didn't seem the sort David could move around easily, especially being so hidden in the first place. It did mean I had another job on a growing list.

A minute or so passed, and the wolf gave in to instinct. The first bite was savage; any remaining blood spurted across its scary-looking muzzle. Every chilling tear of flesh and muscle made me cringe, and then came the bone-crunching. Loud snapping and chomping had me closing my eyes. My arms prickled with disgust and lust. As much as it grossed me out, I couldn't help but be drawn to it, whether it was the metallic smell of blood, the ripping of flesh, or just giving into the wolf part of me. I didn't know, but I felt different.

David's pet was stirring something in me that I'd been fighting against. To fully give in. It nearly happened at the warehouse on the blood moon. I nearly fully turned. Ellena stopped me. My body, though, began to feel the need and seemed triggered by the Werewolf. They weren't an alpha, so was that even possible? Or were eyes different once fully formed? Some of the fog had slowly thickened the air, causing a need for me to shuffle a little closer. I'd done my best to keep it off the radar. That was until Amos stopped, about to take another drag of his cigarette. He tilted his head, sniffing the air. His nostrils seemed to flare the size of buckets.

I dug my head into the dirt as far as possible while looking through the top edge of my eyelids. Amos kept sniffing from my direction. The other Werewolf noticed what Amos was doing and had been enough to break the beast's primal intent. Temporarily, at least. Its eyes blazed brighter again. They began thrashing wildly against its chains. Metal thumping on stone echoed in the cave and my ears. David McNally stepped backwards with a thin fog wrapped around his ankles.

Amos slowly stepped in my direction, still sniffing. At least I wore deodorant; I thought with a nervous check for sweat patches as I continued to play dead. I heard a voice. Only faint, and at first, I thought I'd heard one of David McNally's minions. Then I felt the pain—their pain, to be precise. The wolf was trying to communicate with me. How was beyond me; my hearing was enhanced, and Michael heard me whisper from across the canal, but this was different. Almost as if they'd shared a thought.

'You have to run,'

To make matters worse, Amos suddenly wore an expression that meant business. He looked in my direction and slowly shuffled forward. The wolf growled and stomped louder, thrashing the chains around, trying to loosen them. David slunk further away. All the while, I was toying with the idea of speaking back to the wolf in my mind. A notion that seemed crazy, even to me.

'I can't leave you like that,'

'He will try to collect you,'

'Why can't you change?'

'I... I've forgotten how. No moon and the changes are coated in a powerful strand of wolfsbane. Every struggle pierces my flesh and poisons me,'

'I want to help you,'

'Then... Run... I...I...can't hold my humanity too long.'

I didn't understand; they mentioned humanity, and the vibe I felt screamed primal. Perhaps a conflict after being deprived of normality for so long. It didn't explain the sudden urge I had to shift. As for running, I felt it wouldn't be my choice. Not if Amos had anything to do with it.

"Right, now ya wee pet has been fed. We have a problem,"

Amos snarled between chugs of his cigarette.

"What ya mean?" David shuffled over to Amos, looking in the direction he was. It took everything I had to keep still and slow my breathing as far as possible.

"Somebody is watching. Or should I say something," Amos had realised what he'd smelt wasn't normal.

"Ya bumped ya head? Something?" David looked confused. Not that he should act so surprised, considering what he had trapped in the cave.

"Steady on, pal. Those wee chains dinnae stretch over here. Do Ya only have one?"

"One what?"

"Pet?"

"Och. Yeah, why?"

"Then, we have another lurking on these trees,"

David's face turned a sheet of white, glancing toward the cave briefly and then back in my direction. He suddenly seemed a little 'shaken' at the prospect of something he hadn't prepared for—that and how he'd treated the wolf throughout its confinement.

The wolf was becoming volatile; that pain I felt earlier and rapidly enthused with anger. Each claw cutting across concrete rattled my eardrums. The chains were strained. Then I heard something else. It was weakening, whether the chains themselves or where they were attached. I couldn't tell, yet they squealed. A loud growl rumbled before something far more terrifying filled the night.

A roar boomed out. Nothing like what I'd tried before. This was powerful; it rocked me to the core. My claws were thicker and burrowed into the mud. As I flexed my painful fingers, the roar seemed to ring around for an age. David looked scared, and Amos stepped aside, checking what the wolf was doing. Then came a chorus of howls in the distance, followed by a scattering of glowing yellow eyes amongst the trees.

A few seconds passed, and everything had eased until it hit me like a bolt of lightning, just like the night at the warehouse. My body began to feel as though it was breaking apart. Excruciating pain was taking hold; I had to run to escape the Werewolf, at least for now. Finding another werewolf among all the chaos and vampires was remote. Now I had, and I couldn't help them. Not yet.

With my claws raking through the mud, I tried to shuffle backwards without drawing attention. Still, my bones were steadily breaking and moving. My hands snapped loudly, and I clamped my jaw tight, trying not to scream or roar with pain. It was enough to pull Amos back into the game. His pale skin glistened in the moonlight, highlighting those deathly black eyes. Another roar shook the trees.

'Run,' the wolf snarled.

'I will be back,'

'I know. But for now, you need to escape before it's too late. Don't be scared; it will hurt, but it has to happen. I had to show you, or else you will fail,'

'You're doing this to me?'

'Yes. It would be best if you fully shifted to get stronger. To be strong enough for what's to come,' With that comment, the wolf roared. I buckled in a heap, writhing around in the mud. My head turned in time to see Amos dart toward me in a blur.

It took everything I had to pull myself upright; my bones continued to break. First were my arms; they could almost pass as hairy legs. I was running faster and faster. My body was evolving; I was scared beyond belief and being forced onto all fours. Everything became heightened. Far more than anything I'd experienced before. I could see, smell and hear everything on a new euphoric level.

Including a vampire tearing through the air at superhuman speed. I was running on what should've been my hands and feet, yet I was even faster, and my limbs were huge. I'd seen fast dogs before, and this felt like that. My fear slipped into confusion, and then the adrenaline took over. My evolved body was in turmoil and on fire. All I knew was I had to escape, get to safety and regroup before I could take stock and understand what had happened. Raised voices were stampeding through the forest, still a good distance away, but had me concerned that they hadn't given up.

I'd had one run-in with Amos, and now he would surely know who to look for, and that had me worried for Ellena. At a stretch, I hoped he'd remember my roar and the dripping toxin from my claws, which curiously hadn't happened this time. Adding to my confusion over which version was the real me. The breaking bones had slowed, still stung and ached, but had calmed. I couldn't pinpoint any particular moment as being the worst. Except when my ribcage suddenly ballooned and changed shape, that was agony with me half expecting an alien to burst out of my stomach. I ran and ran and ran until that's all I wanted to do.

Suddenly, nothing else mattered; the vampire had made up ground, but not enough. Once I'd fully changed, I left Amos behind. I was pouncing over streams, fallen trees and huge ditches without breaking stride as if I'd done it all my life. I felt free, without a care, as I galloped through the fog. That was until Ellena popped into my mind, causing me to skid to a halt. I nearly forgot what and where I was meant to be heading for a moment.

Was this how that Werewolf felt in the beginning? Before, they were deprived of every connection to their humanity and the moonlight. I had to set them free; tomorrow is the full moon, and It could supercharge them enough to bring them back, but I feared what measures lay in store other than the wolfsbane clamp. Would David McNally watch the caves in case I came back? Tonight was a rude awakening on many levels, not least because McNally was more than I'd anticipated and hunted werewolves. I had a double threat, maybe even a triple, if Ruth fucked us over.

My sense of smell was so good I could pinpoint and track where Ellena was, even while she slept. I was about to change direction and get moving when 'clap, clap,' two loud gunshots ripped through, then, 'whoosh', followed by searing pain. One of the shots tore through my front left leg, what would've been my left shoulder. It knocked me for six and sent me flying across the floor. I lay prone, breathing heavily and struggling. The bullet hole smelt different. It was Wolfsbane...

The forest was alive with supernatural activity, and I was caught in the midst of it.

I pressed on, my thoughts consumed by emotions and uncertainties. My body continued to evolve, and the pain slowly subsided. I became more attuned to my newly acquired abilities with each passing moment.

Then, as I focused on my impending escape, a voice resounded within my mind again, breaking through the night's chaos.

"Run," the Werewolf urged me again, her voice filled with urgency.

I had to heed her advice. The danger was far from over, and I couldn't afford to let my guard down. My senses guided me toward Ellena's location, and I prepared to reunite with her, for the trials and mysteries of this night had only just begun.

Chapter 26

The sensation that gripped me first was the searing hot metal, followed closely by the acrid stench of burning flesh. My flesh, to be exact. I struggled to keep my eyelids from slamming shut again as I lay shrouded in darkness. What little light I managed to discern was an eerie, damp glow emanating from stone walls, accompanied by the flickering dance of candlelight. My shoulder was exposed to a patch of dirty but unharmed skin. The last memory I could conjure was being shot in the forest.

In my weakened and disoriented state, it was a challenge to determine my whereabouts. My body throbbed with aching pain, not limited to the bullet wound. Echoing footsteps reverberated a mere ten feet away, harmonizing with the soft strains of classical music. Whether it was the haunting compositions of Mozart or the majestic crescendos of Beethoven, I couldn't discern amidst my struggle. Classical music had always eluded me, much to the chagrin of Michael, who insisted on subjecting me to it during car rides. A futile attempt, he called it, to refine my tastes. Little did he know I was bound to remain impervious to its charms.

While these dulcet tones sought to soothe my senses, I endeavoured to employ my other faculties, relying on senses beyond sight to piece together my surroundings. One thing I could unequivocally deduce was that I was not in captivity, at least not in the sense of being bound and shackled like the unfortunate werewolf I had witnessed earlier. I lay upon a cold and unyielding surface, unmistakably composed of stone, not a table or any conventional piece of furniture. This implied an underground structure or perhaps a cave, though my state of languor prevented me from experiencing any surge of panic. Instead, my thoughts drifted to Ellena, and I fervently hoped she remained safe.

Gradually, my wound began to mend, and the initial shock and pain began to subside. The haze that had shrouded my vision started dissipating, revealing a familiar sight—a telltale trace of dried blood beneath my fingernails, accompanied by fleeting recollections of my transformation. The experience had been electrifying, albeit agonizing, at its inception. However, as the process unfolded, it had taken on a semblance of naturalness akin to drawing breath. My surroundings, characterized by dampness and mustiness, couldn't quite match up to the exhilaration of that transformation.

But more pressing thoughts occupied my mind—thoughts of the enigmatic figure I had seen earlier interrupted my flight through the forest. If this shadowy presence had played the role of my saviour, then my curiosity regarding their identity was insatiable.

My eyes darted around, searching for any hint of their form, but all I could glean was the faint flicker of a single candle. The room was plunged into obscurity, save for that solitary light source and the ominous glow of a gas flame. Clearly, they had made a concerted effort to remain shrouded in mystery. I strained my ears for any sounds or clues, but their silence only heightened my unease.

The pungent scent of wolfsbane still lingered in the air, mingling with the tang of saltwater and an underlying essence of death. Yet, there was a subtle, almost imperceptible undertone of death, like a whisper concealed behind a cacophony of other scents. My attempts to discern more were thwarted, for it seemed that the very atmosphere had been laced with an array of herbs and spices, temporarily impotent my heightened sense of smell.

I couldn't shake the feeling that my enigmatic host was brewing something, a concoction infused with secrets that eluded me. The tables around the stone walls, some fashioned from wood and others of metal were strewn with test tubes, beakers, and lidded jars containing peculiar substances. Bunsen burners flickered with an eerie glow, casting an unsettling aura over the surroundings. Elaborate diagrams and illustrations adorned the walls, much like the arcane symbols I had encountered in the past.

Then, an unsettling realization gripped me—I couldn't detect a heartbeat. It was an unmistakable marker of a vampire, a fact that had eluded me until now. The puzzle pieces began to fit together, linking this shadowy presence to the vampire who had pursued me through the forest.

As my curiosity mingled with trepidation, I resolved to break our silence. "Who are you?" I ventured cautiously, my voice betraying a hint of uncertainty.

A disembodied voice responded, accompanied by the distinct timbre of an accent that eluded easy identification. "Leaving so soon?" it quipped, revealing an air of wry amusement. The enigmatic figure remained ensconced in darkness, engrossed in some mysterious activity.

As my thoughts whirled, I continued to assess the situation. My enigmatic host's motives and intentions remained veiled in obscurity. Yet, an unspoken understanding passed between us—a sense of mutual awareness. I had to tread carefully, for I knew of my vulnerability in this confined space. But I couldn't suppress my curiosity, nor could I deny the inherent intrigue of the circumstances.

"Your aid is appreciated," I acknowledged, "and I'm aware of my ignorance. I have much to learn, but one question lingers—why help me?"

The response, laced with cryptic wisdom, echoed through the shadows. "Because you are here now," it intoned, "and, whether you realize it or not, you can alter the course of this nightmarish tapestry. Not merely the fate of the elder vampire but something far grander. There are layers to this world that you have only just begun to peel back."

My curiosity burned bright. "Layers?" I inquired, sensing that this cryptic figure held the key to unravelling myriad secrets.

"Indeed," came the response, shrouded in enigma. "It is a world where truths have been obscured by the mists of time and agendas that span centuries. The power beneath the surface, like the telluric currents and the nemeton, can be harnessed for creation and destruction. Resurrection is not a mere myth, but a possibility, albeit one fraught with peril."

"The nemeton," I murmured, realization dawning, "and the elder vampire…"

My mysterious interlocutor filled in the gaps. "The nemeton and the telluric currents can reshape the world, to mend the fabric of reality itself. However, it depends on who wields this power and to what ends. The elder vampire seeks dominion, but others understand the stakes and seek a different path."

The gravity of the situation weighed heavily on my mind. "How many vampires are involved in this?" I inquired, my thoughts flitting to Amos and the unfolding plot in the town.

"I cannot say for certain," came the cryptic reply, "but it is a number sufficient to populate a town."

"Amos and David McNally," I mused, connecting the dots, "they're working together to seize control of the town?"

"Indeed," my enigmatic companion confirmed, "but there are other players on this stage, some with motivations that differ from the rest."

My thoughts then turned to Ruth, the enigmatic figure who had entered our lives benevolently but now stood shrouded in suspicion. "What of Ruth?" I inquired, "Do you know her?"

A knowing chuckle resonated through the shadows. "Ruth, eh? She is not who she claims to be. I do not know her true identity, but I can sense deception. Beware, for she is not one to be underestimated. There may be hidden weaknesses, but they have yet to be unveiled."

"Anna," I whispered, a wave of uncertainty washing over me, "What about Anna? You mentioned her resemblance to someone the elder vampire loved."

The response was tinged with a hint of melancholy. "Anna is not who you believe her to be. Her resemblance to another has stirred memories within the elder vampire; memories tinged with longing and regret."

"Whose memories?" I pressed, my curiosity piqued.

But my enigmatic companion remained elusive. "Some questions are best left unanswered for now. Rest assured, I have no intention of partaking in the bloodletting that permeates the night. I hold no vendetta against a demon wolf."

A bewildering revelation followed as the figure disclosed the existence of a "demon wolf" and its formidable potential. I listened, captivated by the idea of a hidden world that defied all I had known.

The conversation veered toward the captive werewolf, held prisoner by David McNally. My heart ached at the thought of their plight. "I cannot leave them in captivity," I declared, my determination resolute.

In response, my enigmatic companion provided insight into David McNally's calculated actions, painting him as a more formidable adversary than I had initially perceived. "You would do well to remember," they cautioned, "that vampires and werewolves are not typically allies. However, this alliance presents a unique opportunity. When the time comes, I shall require your assistance."

The weight of newfound knowledge pressed upon me, and I realized the extent of my ignorance. "I owe you a debt," I acknowledged, "but I am still learning, grappling with the complexities of this world. I need guidance. How can I find you? Where am I?"

"I have already told you," came the cryptic reply, "that knowing me is of little consequence at this juncture. You must embark on a journey of discovery, uncovering the truths that have been hidden from you. History, the real history, is your key. It is time to peel back the layers of deception and confront the enigma that is this world."

As I sought further clarification, my enigmatic companion chose silence, and for a moment, it seemed our conversation had reached an impasse. The uncertainty weighed heavily on me, and I struggled to make sense of the enigma that enveloped me.

Then, in an unexpected turn of events, my companion's arm darted forward, and a cloud of red powder filled the air. My senses reeled as dizziness washed over me, and I staggered backwards, my world spinning out of control.

"All in good time" were the last words I heard before darkness consumed me again.

Chapter 27

7th November

The world lay shrouded in the twilight hours, with the first delicate tendrils of dawn painting the heavens in soft shades of lavender. I found myself prone; my back pressed against the damp earth, my gaze drawn upward toward a sprawling tapestry of stars that adorned the night sky. The sensation of chilled, dewy leaves and mud beneath my palms and the soles of my bare feet confirmed my return to the haunting embrace of the forest.

My senses gradually emerged from the fog of disorientation despite the lingering agony from the dust that had been cruelly hurled into my eyes by my elusive assailant.

As I sought to reorient myself, the gentle murmur of a nearby stream provided a faint sense of direction. Then, I realized I had unwittingly retraced my steps to where I had been shot. Though my vision remained veiled, an unshakable inkling rooted within me—the enigmatic figure who had intervened he or was inexorably linked to either Jean Cortez or Frederick Lasille. My instincts swayed toward the possibility of Jean's survival.

This cloaked saviour, shadowed and mysterious, had interceded to thwart Ruth and the others from their sinister designs, preventing them from unshackling the elder vampire and gaining access to the sacred nemeton. The unsettling question that gnawed at me was whether Ruth was truly who she purported to be. Who was she, in reality?

Summoning every ounce of my will, I dragged my weary frame from the ground, a sudden pang of anxiety seizing me as I contemplated the possibility of having lost my car keys when I divested myself of my clothing during the transformation. Panic gripped me briefly, but relief surged when I heard the keys jingling in my cloak pocket. The extent of my saviour's vigilance struck me as peculiar.

With a sense of urgency, I retraced my tumultuous path, following the faint vestiges of my passage, each step a painful reminder of the ordeal I had endured. The scars of the wolfsbane bullets had faded, but their debilitating impact lingered. Whether it was the peculiar dust thrown into my face or the wounds from the bullets themselves, my strength was a mere fraction of its former self. It was a disheartening reality to confront.

As I drifted the forest, a gnawing realization settled upon me—the knowledge that other captive werewolves ensnared in David McNally's sinister machinations. The thought of a forest teeming with desperate, feral lycanthropes filled me with trepidation. I couldn't help but wonder if there was any hope of salvaging their lost humanity.

In the intricate web of pack dynamics, I might be deemed an "Alpha," but I felt like anything but a leader who could command the loyalty of his fellow werewolves. I was still grappling with the enigma of my nature, a puzzle yet to be unravelled. I was a novice in lycanthropy in many ways, desperately needing guidance.

Vampires and werewolves were, by nature, adversaries. The "cloak" and the revelations he had imparted to me had thrown my world into disarray. Strangely, I might have encountered a truth for the first time since my arrival in Scotland. As I drew nearer to the cave, the agonized cries of my brethren resonated with chilling clarity in my ears. It was enough to bring tears to my eyes.

Fortuitously, I picked up on the trail of drag marks, remnants of my frantic crawl across the cavern floor. My footprints were etched in the earth, but I wasn't the sole pursuer. At least one other set of prints had haphazardly followed the same path—size Eight's, left-footed, and with an uneven gait.

The trail led me beyond the cave's confines, guiding me along the muddy gravel road. My car remained untouched, its four tires intact, and no immediate signs of tampering in the dimly lit surroundings. Puzzling over the reason for tracking my route, I chanced upon an envelope tucked beneath my car's windscreen wiper.

The envelope yielded to my impatient fingers, revealing a newspaper clipping dating back to 1951. Its headline read, "The Death of a forgotten small town." The article chronicled the demise of Oxley, a once-promising mining town thirty miles north of Peterhead. It had fallen into desolation, consumed by flames that claimed the lives of hundreds, ostensibly attributed to pockets of gas.

The article perplexed me, yet I sensed it was another piece of the intricate puzzle I was slowly assembling. With bated breath, I unfolded a handwritten note that accompanied the aged newspaper clipping.

The message, penned with an elegance befitting a bygone era, bore the unmistakable mark of my cloaked saviour. Its words etched a cryptic narrative before me.

"Visit the town," it urged, "look through your other eyes. You'll find it absent from current maps, a place that exists no more. Then, you shall glimpse the depths of Amos's ambitions and the fate that may befall Cruden Bay if he succeeds. Perhaps elsewhere, too. All set in motion for the elder's return, with David McNally's bid for Mayor as the linchpin. In return, he secures his beloved wife's salvation. The lengths we go for love."

The note concluded, leaving me with foreboding and unanswered questions.

The first rays of daylight filtered through the window, and I realized I had scarcely slept. Rest was elusive, a distant memory. I once again ensconced in the same chair, Ellena slumbering nearby.

As the world outside awakened to the new day, I couldn't help but cast furtive glances around the premises, vigilance compelling me to ensure we remained undetected. Amos must have witnessed my presence, though I had been moving at a swifter pace than ever before, my senses honed on multiple fronts—evading pursuit, tracking my quarry, and succumbing to my beastly transformation.

My vigil extended to McNally's garage, a place of simmering resentment where I had been shot. I had harboured hopes of apprehending one of the assailants, perhaps the elusive Alexander, and instilling a measure of fear. A fleeting moment of retribution to soothe my battered soul.

Yet, my efforts yielded nothing but frustration, and I trudged back to the B & B with a heavy heart. An unsettling dilemma lay before me—one that gnawed at my conscience.

I reluctantly reached for my phone, a torrent of emotions swirling within me. I had been wrestling with this internal conflict, a relentless tug-of-war between heart and mind. And soon, I would have to confront Ellena to disclose the truth about my full transformation. It was a revelation that I feared more than the looming phone call.

There was a pressing need, a summons born of desperation. We needed his expertise, his knowledge. I had no choice but to call Michael despite the cruel hour. My heart ached for the weight I would lay upon his shoulders.

With a heavy heart, I dialled the number, mixed emotions coursing through me. Michael was awakened, his voice laced with weariness and bewilderment as he realized the caller's identity. The revelation he delivered struck me like a blow to the gut.

He had borne the brunt of my pain, unwittingly sharing in the agony of my transformation, believing it to be the result of his adjustment to newfound powers. Guilt coursed through me at the realization of his suffering.

Michael, a faithful friend and ally, had remained true to our cause. He had sensed the impending trouble, but his attempts to reach Skip had been met with silence. Concern gnawed at him, and he had already prepared his "go bag" with the essentials—the tools of our trade and the invaluable bestiary.

The fact that he had anticipated my need for the book underscored our deep bond of understanding. A kinship that transcended words.

Yet, a lingering sense of unease pervaded our conversation. Skip, the enigmatic figure who had been our guide and informant, had fallen silent, his whereabouts unknown. A chill settled upon me as I pondered the implications of his absence.

With my gaze fixed on Ellena, her delicate form swathed in slumber, I contemplated the challenges ahead. I had not rested well, and my mind churned with a litany of concerns, each a pressing matter demanding my attention.

Amos, McNally, vampires, werewolves—each element woven into a tapestry of intrigue and danger. The note and the newspaper clipping under my windshield wiper were cryptic threads that begged to be unravelled.

With her hauntingly beautiful appearance and uncanny resemblance to Anna, Ellena had been thrust into the maelstrom of this supernatural world. Her fate hung in the balance, and I was determined to protect her at any cost.

A peculiar scent had lingered in the room, an olfactory puzzle that had evaded my attention until now. It was not the fragrance of tea or herbs but something altogether different. My curiosity finally led me to investigate further.

With all the stealth of a thief in the night, I approached the side table where a cup sat, the source of the elusive aroma. My senses narrowed in on it, my mind piecing together the puzzle. It was the same drink we had been offered the previous day, and it raised unsettling questions.

I couldn't resist the urge to explore further, my fingers sliding the cup aside to reveal a drawing pad hidden beneath. Curiosity drove my actions, though my voice warned me of the intrusion.

As I opened the pad, a rush of emotions surged within me, a mixture of guilt and compulsion. I was confronted with a revelation that shook me to my core.

In her infinite talent, Ellena had meticulously sketched the figure from the art gallery that had watched her with an unsettling intensity. Tall, menacing, and undoubtedly a vampire—the elder. The vivid portrayal hinted at the possibility that this enigmatic vampire haunted Ellena's dreams.

A palpable fear seized me, the realization that I might lose Ellena before we could fully embark on our difficult journey. I struggled to comprehend the sinister forces that had set our lives on this ominous path.

I grappled with the enigma of our existence, the dark machinations that conspired to trap us. Anger overflowed within me, and I couldn't help but contemplate confronting Locke, the orchestrator of our destiny.

Had Locke been aware of Ellena's uncanny resemblance to Anna? Had he knowingly led us into this treacherous web of intrigue and danger? The possibility that he had placed Ellena in harm's way gnawed at my conscience, a betrayal I could never forgive.

With these troubling thoughts in mind, I couldn't help but revisit the contents of the newspaper article, its chilling details etched in my memory. The sudden conflagration that had consumed an entire town, each home claimed by flames, the synchronicity of it all—something sinister lurked beneath the surface.

Even in a town as small as Cruden, the odds of every home bursting into flames simultaneously were astronomically low unless it had been deliberate. And what of the vampires? What had drawn them to this macabre spectacle?

My thoughts wove a chilling narrative—one where Oxley had been transformed into an undercover blood market or a malevolent blood farm. A hidden wellspring of sustenance, less conspicuous than outright slaughter. No bodies to be discovered, no trace of foul play—only an insidious cycle of lifeblood harvested for the insatiable thirst of the undead.

David McNally was the puppeteer behind this vile charade, his mayoral aspirations serving as the smokescreen that concealed the true horrors beneath. The elder and Amos would reap the rewards of unfettered access to a constant blood supply while maintaining their façade.

Yet, imprisoned and desiccated vampires remained, their plight demanding our intervention. The nemeton, a source of power and peril, teetered on the brink of catastrophe. And, most harrowing, a forest teeming with wolves—creatures enslaved and subjected to unspeakable cruelty, as revealed by the mysterious figure in the cloak.

These were the myriad threads that had ensnared my existence, an intricate tapestry of darkness and intrigue. As the first light of day cast its gentle glow upon the world, I knew I could not escape the challenges ahead.

Beside me, Ellena stirred in her slumber, her face etched with distress. My heart ached for her, and I couldn't shake the ominous feeling that something sinister was transpiring within her. Her vulnerability in this treacherous world weighed heavily on my conscience.

A sudden, chilling disturbance echoed through the house, the sound of a door slamming shut. Footsteps reverberated down the hallway, followed by the abrupt swing of the front door. Silence hung in the air, brief but pregnant with tension, before it was shattered by a blood-curdling scream—an operatic aria of terror.

"It's a head," one of the voices exclaimed, either Dianne or Mary. "A bloody mangled head."

Ellena's eyes snapped open, her expression a mixture of shock and confusion. My stomach twisted into knots—the nightmare that had begun last night was far from over.

Chapter 28

'12.30 PM,'

The phrase "Silence was deafening" had never been more apt. An eerie hush descended like a suffocating shroud, smothering all sound in its oppressive grip. It had begun after the haunting shriek had faded into the void, and my thoughts swirled in a chaotic maelstrom.

The phrase "Silence was deafening" had never been more apt. An eerie hush descended like a suffocating shroud, smothering all sound in its oppressive grip. It had begun after the haunting shriek had faded into the void, and my thoughts swirled in a chaotic maelstrom. I lost myself as Mary and Dianne hastily exited the room, leaving the grotesque head in a box perched on the table, a gruesome centrepiece to our gloomy gathering. Ellena, unsure of how to approach the situation or me, moved about cautiously, her balletic grace belying the turmoil undoubtedly churning within her.

Then, the welcome rumble of a familiar engine broke the stillness and Ellena's face registered surprise. It wasn't a bad surprise but it added another question to her growing list. As for the silence, it was an unfamiliar and uncomfortable companion. In truth, my mind was a whirlwind, desperately attempting to connect the dots and fathom why the McNallys would brazenly deposit a decapitated head on our doorstep.

A head severed by their business partner, no less. Of course, it wasn't the same head I had witnessed being hurled at David McNally; this one was far more gruesome. Its eyes were gouged out, its skull crushed, and its facial features mutilated beyond recognition as if it had been used as a football in some grotesque game.

At first, my eyes sought the telltale vampire claw marks at the top, where Amos had fiercely attacked, followed by a search for werewolf claw imprints, wondering if it had been intended for the creature imprisoned in the cave. But there were no such marks to be found. What I did discern, after meticulous examination, were the puncture wounds, now oozing blood, teeth, and brain matter. A vampire, likely Amos, had turned the head into a grotesque sieve, perhaps to satisfy their unholy thirst.

Yet, the logic or tactical advantage behind delivering this gruesome message to us escaped me. Other than confirming they were aware of their pursuit, why would they assume I had survived a wolfsbane-laced bullet? Were we now unwitting participants in a deadly game, hunted like prey for their amusement? Did David McNally harbour delusions of being a werewolf hunter, collecting trophies to add to his gruesome collection?

In my eyes, this severed head seemed sloppy, a far cry from the calculated menace that Amos had warned McNally about. Despite his physical tremors, part of me suspected that David had a grander scheme in mind, one that required a patient, long-term approach.

David's desperation was evident; he longed for his wife to be free from her ailment, to shed the debilitating posture and frailty that had befallen her, a condition detectable perhaps only to vampires and our kind. I pushed that thought aside for now; it was just another stark reminder of her condition. To witness such a transformation daily would undoubtedly drive any man to extreme measures.

Yet, the elaborate plan to capture a single werewolf, let alone the rumoured many, suggested there was more to the McNally clan than met the eye. We needed to tread carefully, as did our vampire allies.

The previous night's events had prompted me to play one of my cards, which I had kept up my sleeve until now. As bedraggled reinforcements arrived, Michael's displeased expression was palpable as he stepped out of his impeccably maintained Audi Quattro. He immediately filled the Scottish air with cigarette smoke, his irritation evident.

"Oi, you bloody magnet for trouble. Do you have any idea how much fuel I burned racing here? It had better be worth it, making me challenge grannies in Ford Escorts at traffic lights," Michael grumbled.

"Michael? You prat. I genuinely apologize, but desperate times, you know. And just so you know, the excessive fuel consumption is entirely your fault for owning a 3.2-litre beast and having a lead foot," I retorted, a hint of a smile creeping onto Michael's face, mirrored by Ellena as they embraced.

"At least you've finally got him talking. The grumpy sod hasn't said a word all morning," Ellena remarked softly as they separated, her embrace reassuring, conveying no ill intent.

"I had a lot on my mind. While the two of you were enjoying your beauty sleep, I was busy getting shot, discovering that other werewolves were being used as disposable 'pets' to make corpses disappear. Oh, and I fully transformed into a wolf."

Michael and Ellena's expressions were priceless. They could have been forgiven for reacting to either revelation, but deep down, I knew my wild transformation revealed had them truly astonished.

"Holy shit, mate. Besides the agony, how did it feel? What was it like? Do we need to start scheduling you for worming and regular flea treatments?" Michael joked, attempting to whisper, leaning in closer to ensure no one else could overhear.

"Christ, Georgie. I wish I'd witnessed that. How did you get shot, though? Are you okay?" Ellena inquired, her hug tightening, genuine concern in her eyes. I could also detect a hint of excitement, even a subtle blush creeping onto her cheeks, and I felt the stiffening of her nipples through her bra and blouse. The chilly breeze couldn't possibly account for that.

Normally, I would have revelled in her reaction. However, it reminded me of a lingering dilemma: Was she excited because of me or what I had become?

"Yeah, I'm alright now. I owe my survival to another vampire, of all things."

"Who?" Michael interjected.

"I'm unsure, but I suspect it might have been Jean or Frederick. I attempted to extract information about this place and McNally's agreement with Amos from them. This was after they disposed of two bodies, one of whom was a town committee member—a group responsible for making decisions that affected the residents. David McNally has been resorting to heavy-handed tactics, bullying, and even forging signatures to oppose the mayor and gain planning rights for the area, among other things."

"Seriously? Why didn't you contact the local police? Why does he want planning permission so desperately?" Ellena asked.

"One of those 'dots' in this intricate web. I couldn't call the police; they're all in McNally's pocket and have turned a blind eye. It seems corrupt cops are the same no matter where you go. Moreover, I found an old news article on my windshield about a ghost town called Oxley, which no longer exists meaningfully. Once home to a thriving community of over two hundred families, Oxley was reduced to ruins. It was engulfed in flames, claiming the lives of at least two hundred people, perhaps more. Much like Hiroshima, the town was wiped out after the nuclear blast. In my mind, Oxley became a haunting echo of what could occur in this place, which already bore the ominous nickname 'Blood Bay.' I couldn't help but wonder: What could be worse than that?"

"How does the severed head tie into all of this?" Ellena struggled to keep up with myriad issues, a sentiment I couldn't fault her for. The situation was a maelstrom of confusion and danger.

"The what now?!" Michael exclaimed.

"That head was once part of a body I encountered last night. For now, it's resting in a box on the coffee table. It might be best to destroy it when we have the chance."

"For heaven's sake. Nothing is ever straightforward with you two. Why did you wait so long to call? And what do you intend to do about it?"

That was the million-pound question. As I scanned the bustling, chilly town, people going about their daily lives as if vampires and werewolves were mere fables, I couldn't help but wonder why the B&B's door had remained closed, with no sign of Dianne or Mary returning from wherever they had fled. There was no trace of a vampire presence, not even the one who had saved me from the cave. My ears strained for any sign of familiar voices or the familiar scent of death, but the crowd concealed any clues.

My attention shifted to Duncan Campbell, whose influence could rival David McNally's. He was already out and about, engaging with the townsfolk. I wanted to discern if Duncan knew of Oxley's history and the supernatural elements lurking beneath the surface.

"It's not just about that, Michael. There's more. Ruth, who controls our hosts, Dianne and Mary, is not who she appears to be. She knows Locke and might have manipulated him into sending us here. I also learned she's not as old as she pretends to be; she's been using magic to conceal her true age."

Michael's face grew serious, and he began to share his concerns. "George, you remember how I told you I called Andy? When I checked on him, I found his house abandoned, with a pile of unopened mail and no sign of him since the day you left for Scotland. I spoke with our dear old ADI, and they had a heated argument. I couldn't discern the details, but something was amiss. We might have underestimated Locke's involvement in all of this. He seems to believe there's a cure for his supposed blood curse here. There are more secrets at play than we initially thought."

My worry shifted to Ellena's unique abilities, and just as I was about to address them, she looked up at me with a reassuring smile and whispered, "It's okay." For a brief moment, panic gripped me, wondering if Ellena had somehow tapped into my thoughts.

If she could read my mind, I was in deep trouble.

"Locke seems to have orchestrated this entire mission, but I fear he might have been manipulated or is far more sinister than we ever imagined," I confessed. My voice dropped as I glanced over my shoulder, a sensation of being watched haunting my senses. Ellena nudged me gently, Michael smiled in approval, and it became apparent that they perceived our closeness as a shield, something to hide behind.

These two had broken through my defences, and I had allowed them to become essential parts of my life. I needed to keep them safe, knowing that they could both undergo supernatural transformations if Ellena truly possessed witchcraft abilities. They had followed me blindly, making me responsible for their lives on this difficult journey.

Skip had left his home voluntarily with a bag, indicating he had plans to stay out, but the nature of those plans remained a mystery. His heated argument with Locke raised questions about their discussions and what role Skip might play in this unfolding drama. We were over six hundred miles from Michael, but he had come to our aid, showing unwavering support in our time of need. Skip's presence here hinted at something significant, perhaps related to his missing daughter.

As we faced off against the elder vampires, their eerie appearance and chilling voices sent shivers down our spines. Clearly, they possessed powerful mind-control abilities, and we needed to be cautious not to fall into their traps.

I couldn't help but reflect on the unsettling developments regarding Ellena. Her encounter with the mysterious drink and the presence of mind-altering substances in the decanter raised concerns about Ruth's true intentions and the dangers we faced in this seemingly peaceful town.

The elderly couple, possessed by the vampires, exhibited unnatural movements and dead-like features, including ghost-grey eyes. Their synchronized steps and eerie silence only added to the sense of dread. Michael and I prepared ourselves for a confrontation, ready to defend against whatever threat these vampires posed.

However, the vampires' true intentions became clearer as they engaged us in conversation. They seemed to view humans as insignificant and expressed their desire for the countess, who we suspected was Ruth. It was a power struggle between our group and the vampires, and their insistence on acquiring the countess raised more questions about her true identity and significance in this supernatural conflict.

Our exchange with the vampires took an unexpected turn when they suddenly levitated off the ground and attacked us with superhuman strength. The situation grew dire as

Michael and I struggled against their powerful grip. Lightning crackled around Michael, and his eyes glowed yellow, hinting at a potential loss of control.

In a desperate bid to defend ourselves, Michael and I tapped into our supernatural abilities, our claws extending and our instincts taking over. It was a fierce battle, but we managed to gain the upper hand, and the elder vampires went limp in our grasp, their eyes returning to normal.

However, the situation had taken a dangerous turn, as onlookers witnessed two seemingly monstrous individuals attacking elderly civilians. We had fallen into a trap set by the vampires, who had manipulated us into a violent confrontation. It was a chilling reminder of the hidden dangers lurking in Blood Bay and the need for caution in every step we took.

As Ellena beeped the horn to warn us of the shocked onlookers, we realized that the vampires had scored a victory in this encounter, leaving us with a sobering lesson: we needed to stay vigilant and avoid falling into their traps again. The supernatural forces at play in Blood Bay were far more cunning and dangerous than we had initially imagined, and we had to tread carefully if we were to uncover the truth and protect ourselves from further harm.

Skip left his home voluntarily with a bag, so wherever he was heading required a stay out, but what was he up to? And what did he have words with Locke about? We were over six hundred miles from Michael, and he felt my pain. Skip had to, as well. Perhaps he had a lead for his missing daughter, but the argument confused me. Not as much as what was going on with Ellena and how I saw her yesterday and her eyes this morning.

There we were ad Michael'a car, with most of the cards on the table, and yet I was being a chicken shit over something relatively small. With the threat of that vampire that she'd dreamt of. Now, I was scared to push her away. But we had to know before we headed to Oxley. Forewarned is Forearmed.

"Also, Ellena, what did you drink in that up last night?" I chirped up between sips from Michaels's flask.

"I can't remember; I was tired, got a hot drink and crashed out quickly. Why?"

"Because it had the same stuff they gave in the decanter yesterday. I saw traces swirling this morning. We need to be careful. There's a big picture going on here, and I think Ruth could be gearing up to fuck us over,"

"I didn't even think about that. I was dead to the world, and Mary seemed so nice. You know, the warm mothering way that makes you relaxed," I knew what Ellena meant, but that was the point. The way everything is set up here, people drop their guard and don't think.

With another sip of whiskey, we were about to get in Michael's car when I had that feeling again. Eyes burrowing holes in our backs. This time, my tiny neck hairs bounced to life. Michael reached for the back of his neck, too. We both began frantically looking around, but all I saw were normal people. Until amongst the busy streets, an elderly couple that had just been walking hand in wrinkled hands. The guy wore a grey coat, flat cap and tweed trousers. Using a wooden cane to support a limp.

The lady had tightly curled grey hair, a colour fully floral dress and a Burgundy woolly coat; she seemed the more enthusiastic of the two heading toward the main part of town, twenty feet past us, only to stop dead. No laughing or anything; my claws slid forward, and Michael's too. Ellena held mine. Michael dashed his pockets. We looked at each other, confused... Then they turned to face us...

We all got to witness another fucking scary first. Both had ghost-grey eyes. I've seen how blind people occasionally look. These had Michael stepping back; his heart raced, and Ellena's, too. More because this was different to everything so far. Their facial skin looked dead; each step was in unison only without the aid of a cane. It didn't touch the ground. Michael looked left, clicking his key fob to unlock the car. I ushered Ellena to Michael, who guided her to the driver's side to get it going.

They may be old, but if this shit had taught us anything, expect the unexpected. Michael came back beside me; the rest of the world seemed normal. No curtains twitched. I'd say they were possessed if I were reaching in the dark. Then, I finally caught a slight whiff of death. Every movement was precise and far more lively. Michael looked at me for guidance; I daren't say I had no idea. Everything screamed danger with an element of the unknown.

"What are we doing?"

"Stay calm for now; keep them hidden just in case," Both had heartbeats, so I ruled out being dead. Yet no chemo signals either.

"There is nothing you can do. May as well hand the countess over, and you two shall go free unharmed. Your fate is inconsequential, and I have far bigger things to concern myself with," the old guy spoke. I say he spoke, more like a chilling grating of razor blades over the skin. Didn't fit the human meat sack.

"How about you stick your fangs where the sun doesn't shine. You're a parasite that doesn't deserve to see the light of day," I surprised Michael but assumed it was mind control from a vampire, more than likely an elder.

"Do you want to do this? The only blood that needs to be shed is for dinner,"

"How about we save you a journey and have a few rats delivered there. I know a place that delivers has five stars in the Yellow Pages,"

"Such an impudent child. I walked the earth long before you were born and shall long after. Our race is destined to rule once more. Stand in my way, and you shall become pets," it was the lady's turn, and it sounded fucking freaky, all manly. No less scary, though.

"No offence, BDSM is all well and good; my friend here even likes a dungeon or two, but decrepit, desiccated blood suckers aren't our type. So we'll pass,"

"Yeah, I don't like the idea of leather stretched over flaky bone. At least not since the ex-wife," Michael found his balls as they dropped from his stomach once more.

"Well, as you humans like to say, there's more than one way to skin a cat or wolf... Oh, that's right, I'm aware. That's why I offered a chance. Natural enemies, but why waste power? Sadly, you have made up your minds,"

"It seems vampires are much like cockroaches, able to survive being stamped on and like dingy, dark places. Speaking of skin, I highly recommend cocoa butter. Plump's up the skin. Oh wait, you're more like beef jerky, aren't you. Maybe just feed you to a dog. First, could you answer this really important question I've wondered since I heard vampires are real... Any denial will only make me think otherwise...Here goes... Do you fart dust?"

Michael laughed; I hid behind a little banter, looking to provoke while faking we weren't scared, even if everything he'd said had my arse puckering. It's squeaky bum time. They didn't respond and were dead silent momentarily, which was different. Then, both began growling. At least that's the nearest I could describe the strange noises behind their false teeth. We almost dropped our guard, my claws hung by my sides, when suddenly both levitated at least a foot off the floor, causing Michael to look alarmed and me confused by how it was possible. Then again, a few hours ago, I was on all fours.

I held my breath, and both roared towards us in a flash. It was a blur; each clamped onto our jugulars with supernatural strength, and suddenly, we were on the back foot, struggling. Michael gagged and squirmed as lightning began to flicker around him. His eyes glowed yellow, and I feared he'd lose control.

The messengers didn't need to get hurt, but we had no choice. The old guy was crushing my windpipe. My claws flicked out fuller, much like the other night by the cliff, while different to last night. I managed to rock an uppercut through the gap between us; instead of punching, I grabbed at his throat. A fire blew through my veins that filled me with the urge to tear his throat out, sending his artery gushing through the air. Michael followed suit, and the momentum swung our way; I was trying my best to hold back in a dangerously impossible situation. Then things took a drastic turn...

Both went limp... Skin sacks of fragile bones hung mercilessly in our hands. Their eyes had quickly turned normal, and to the public, we were choking the life out of two old people a foot off the floor. Ellena beeped the horn to warn us of the eyes I'd already noticed gawping in shock. We looked like monsters attacking and nearly killing two old people.

Michael and I had played into the elder vampires' decayed hands, and when we took the bait, he relinquished his mind control. We nearly became savage killers. A trap we couldn't afford to fall into again. It would've been so easy to have our hands dripping with blood—one nil to the vampires.

Chapter 29

A shower of gravel sprayed into the air, leaving a cacophonous echo in our wake while our hearts pounded in synchrony with the uneven road beneath us. Michael and Ellena exchanged frantic words as he accelerated, foot firmly pressed to the pedal. My gaze remained locked on the rearview mirror, my senses awash with fear and adrenaline. Fortunately, the elderly couple we had left behind appeared stunned and disoriented, unable to recall the harrowing ordeal, let alone complain.

Carefully, I released the man I had been restraining, watching as trickles of crimson snaked down his neck, the aftermath of a close call. In seconds, our inner beasts had nearly sunk their claws into the flesh of two innocent lives, a nightmarish scenario I could never have fathomed. The line between our humanity and primal instincts had blurred dangerously, pushing us to the brink.

But what troubled me even more was the ease with which the vampire had orchestrated that terrifying episode without being physically present. It left me with an eerie hollowness in the pit of my stomach, my body still trembling in response to the memories. In the distance, the old couple slowly faded from view, and I couldn't help but wonder if there would be consequences or repercussions from this chaotic encounter.

This town, it seemed, was a crucible of madness, and we were mere pawns in some malevolent entity's game. A glimmer of hope teased at the edges of my consciousness as I replayed the words of our enigmatic benefactor. Perhaps, driven by fear or uncertainty, the vampires didn't possess full knowledge of our capabilities. Perhaps, in their quest for control, they had inadvertently revealed more of their hand than they had intended. Michael might be second-guessing his decision to aid us, but we needed him now more than ever.

In that tumultuous moment, when our claws threatened to emerge, and our fates teetered on the precipice, I felt an unexpected surge of strength. Seeing those ethereal, yellow glimmers around Michael ignited a newfound resolve within me. We were a formidable force and could be even more potent with Skip at our side. We had to seize whatever advantages came our way, even if they were as rare as a silver lining in these ominous clouds.

Two versions of the same map rested on my lap, each telling a different story. One depicted a quaint, seemingly insignificant town, a mere blip on the map, situated forty miles west of Peterhead. In the grand scheme of things, it hardly registered. The other map, a stark blank canvas, represented the aftermath of a fire, a place devoid of borders. It struck me as peculiar for the scale of destruction it suggested.

True, it had been a conflagration that had devoured over two hundred homes and countless lives. But in this age of rapid redevelopment, rebuilding a community from the ashes wasn't insurmountable. Yet, an unsettling feeling lingered, hinting at hidden truths lurking beneath the charred remains. I dared not voice my suspicions, for they hinted at a sinister underbelly of this enigma-ridden town. Secrets, I mused, might be buried within those bone-dotted ruins.

Moreover, something else, an unsettling undercurrent, left me with a foreboding sensation. Something loomed on the horizon, something I couldn't quite grasp but could feel deep in my bones. The events of this day had set an ominous tone, and I couldn't shake the unsettling notion that a trap lay ahead, or perhaps a town laid waste, its streets adorned with the charred remains of its inhabitants. It was the stuff of nightmares, yet within those ghastly remnants, secrets might be hidden, which could hold the key to unravelling the mysteries that plagued us.

Amidst my swirling thoughts, the enigma surrounding the mysterious fluid we had encountered lingered. The substance concealed within drinks offered by our hosts had ignited my curiosity, begging for answers. And Ellena, she needed to be more vigilant, her safety paramount. Glancing at her through the rearview mirror only heightened my concerns.

Ellena had undeniably changed. It could be attributed to her transformations, the rapid shifts in her eyes and skin tone that played tricks on my perception. Yet, her demeanour had shifted, her once vibrant self now a mere shadow. She clung to us, tethered like a lifeline. I often spoke of the importance of details, and amid her otherwise radiant blonde hair were strands that had turned an eerie shade of white. Not the natural grey of age but an otherworldly, almost ethereal white.

This peculiar alteration had escaped my notice the previous day. It was a subtle change but one that spoke volumes. It wasn't the only unsettling transformation; fatigue now seemed to plague Ellena. Dark circles adorned her eyes, and her overall appearance showed exhaustion. The pieces of this enigmatic puzzle slowly converged in my mind.

Amid these observations, a forgotten detail resurfaced— the tiny pinprick I had noticed earlier. It could have been an injection or a withdrawal, but both possibilities were disconcerting. Ruth or the Golems, and now, with Michael by our side, Ellena couldn't afford to leave our sight. I contemplated attaching a bell to her ankle at night to ensure her safety. While I had been preoccupied with my gunshot wound, someone had seized an opportunity, and it gnawed at me.

Michael's voice interrupted my thoughts, snapping me back to the present. "So Georgie, what are we expecting here?" he inquired, diverting my attention.

"Answers," I replied with determination. "We need anything to shed light on the mysteries we're facing. Thus far, we've been fed a narrative carefully crafted by others, including Locke."

Michael nodded in agreement, his eyes shifting to Ellena. She was beginning to drift off to sleep again, a puzzling weariness hanging over her. It was a weariness that didn't align with our current situation and raised more questions.

"What if we don't like the answers we find in 'Blood Bay'?" Michael ventured.

I paused, considering his question. "How many towns do you know that vanish from the map, consumed by flames, taking the lives of hundreds? And we're directed there by a vampire," I remarked, my tone laced with urgency.

Michael acknowledged the gravity of the situation, but he raised a valid point. "The vampire might have ulterior motives, just like the others we've encountered. Maybe they're playing their own game." He turned his attention to Ellena, expressing his concern. "Ellena, my dear, you don't leave either of our sides from now on, okay?"

Ellena, sounding sleepy and compliant, responded with a simple, "Huh. Okay."

I seized the opportunity to suggest, "Why don't you nap, Ellena? We still have a while ahead of us."

She closed her eyes, snuggling into her seat. Michael, meanwhile, gave me a curious look, sensing that I had something to share. I divulged my thoughts as we continued to distance ourselves from Cruden Bay.

"As for motive, Michael, consider this," I began, "Imagine a town with two hundred relatively new homes suddenly engulfed in flames, claiming over two hundred lives. Then, inexplicably, the town disappears from the map. What does your detective instinct tell you?"

Michael furrowed his brow, contemplating the details. "Based on our information, my gut tells me that a fire that consumes all two hundred homes is either a natural disaster, which seems unlikely given Scotland's geological stability, or a deliberate cover-up. Fires in residential areas typically raise alarms, allowing people to escape. Even if it were a gas explosion, it's hard to believe it would claim all lives simultaneously. This mass loss of life suggests something far more sinister..."

His voice trailed off as he considered the possibility of supernatural involvement. "Go on," I urged, impatient to hear his thoughts.

Michael continued, "This could result from supernatural forces at play. We're still wrapping our heads around the existence of vampires, but it's becoming increasingly evident that they have a significant role in this. The pieces of the puzzle are slowly falling into place."

While Michael shared his insights, my senses were suddenly alerted. A ripple of unease coursed through me, starting in my forearms and spreading down my back like a sixth sense tingling. Michael, too, seemed affected, his shoulders tensing. We exchanged glances, both aware of the unusual sensation.

"You felt that?" I asked, scanning all the mirrors as we continued down the road.

"Yes, mate," Michael replied, his voice tinged with concern. "But what was it, and where did it come from?"

I didn't have an immediate answer. We had distanced ourselves from the vampires and their mind-controlling abilities. However, I noticed a dark green Land Rover, rugged and coated with dried mud, following us closely. It was a different vehicle from the previous night, but there was no mistaking its intent. It weaved with purpose, maintaining a distance of three cars behind us.

Michael made a decisive move, flooring the accelerator, veering to the middle lane, and deftly navigating past an oil tanker and a coach before slipping between them and another tanker. I watched the mirrors closely, ready for any sign that we might be mistaken. But we weren't. The Land Rover, with the plate 'B729 XLM,' was now within earshot, and I made a quick note of it for future reference.

There were at least two occupants, their faces obscured behind blacked-out windows.

The driver, however, lacked Michael's finesse in tactical driving and found themselves trapped in the middle lane with no escape. It was only a matter of time before they had to drop back, and they did exactly that. Michael maintained our position, and I monitored the Land Rover's engine noise. Its fan belt emitted a distinct squeal while the front left brake pad ground audibly with each press. We now had the upper hand in tracking them.

"It's alright," I informed Michael. "They've fallen back, at least two people inside, but their windows are blacked out. I'd recommend listening for the squeal in the engine and the grinding brakes."

"Got it," Michael acknowledged, eyes scanning the road ahead. "Looks like this little adventure might get interesting. I know you're not a fan, but we didn't obtain those firearms certificates for nothing."

I grimaced at the mention of firearms, a topic I had been trying to avoid. "Oh, Michael?" I reluctantly admitted, knowing that we both held special dispensation to carry firearms, though we had chosen not to do so until now. The events of this new world we inhabited had forced us to reconsider our stance. I had a personal aversion to firearms, especially after the traumatic encounter with the block in my mind. Nevertheless, my proficiency with them had been unnervingly natural, scoring top marks during training, with Michael close behind.

"Well," Michael continued, "when someone wakes you up at dawn by sharing their pain, I figured it might be wise to be prepared. After all, you've already been shot."

He had a valid point, and as much as I detested the idea, it was essential to establish some ground rules. "No shoot-to-kill unless it's a matter of life or death," I emphasized. "Incapacitate only, unless one of us is facing imminent death."

"Agreed," Michael affirmed, his tone firm. "Besides, the mere presence of firearms might make these individuals think twice. Now, let's talk about our princess. What's happening with Ellena?"

My attention shifted back to the rearview mirror, where Ellena began to stir. Her heart rate had dropped to 40 beats per minute, and remained in a deep slumber. "Have you not noticed the changes in her today compared to when you last saw her?" I asked, my voice filled with concern. "Something is happening to her. She's hearing voices, a vampire's call. I've even seen one, a spectral presence watching her. And today's episode of possession... It all adds up."

Michael focused on the road, his gaze unwavering but his mind deep in thought. "I'm still trying to wrap my head around the existence of vampires, let alone one wanting

Ellena. How? Why?"

"According to what we've learned so far," I explained, "an elder vampire lies desiccated within the caverns beneath the town. Ellena resembles or is a descendant of Countess Anna Farrington from the 15th or 16th century, who had a connection with Jean Cortez, some kind of druid. It's a lot to take in, but he went missing, and the town, 'Blood Bay,' became overrun with vampires. However, history isn't always the most reliable source."

Michael mulled over the information, connecting the dots. "How does it all tie together?"

"That, Michael, I don't know," I admitted, my voice heavy with uncertainty. "But consider this: we have a B&B owner who's a witch with two golems, a local family entangled in dark dealings, striking deals with vampires to save a loved one and gain power. Meanwhile, the current mayor is battling these supernatural forces with limited success. And amidst it all, a decrepit vampire yearns to break free from an enforced slumber. In the centre of this web of intrigue lies Ellena."

As we continued, signs indicated we were only ten miles from our destination, and the 4 x 4 remained within earshot. Time was running out to shake our pursuers if that was even possible. Ellena had stirred slightly, her head brushing against the door padding, causing her to mumble in her sleep.

At first, her words were nonsensical, like a stream of consciousness drifting between unrelated thoughts. "Chips dipped in ice cream" and "Locke is a tosser" escaped her lips, eliciting amused chuckles from both Michael and me. But then, her utterances took a disturbing turn, and an unsettling gravitas hung in the air.

"When the sun turns to blood, streets will be paved with bones as blood rains down once more," she whispered in a chilling, gravelly tone. It sent a shiver down my spine, for the voice sounded eerily familiar, a gravelly snarl that invoked an uncanny sense of recognition. Yet, Ellena appeared neither controlled nor awake; she remained in a deep slumber, unaware of the foreboding words that had escaped her.

However, these words were a haunting echo of what we had encountered before, intensifying my internal debate. Should we cut our losses and abandon this dangerous path?

Chapter 30

We lost the 4 x 4 before we hit the country lanes between Rora and Longside—a two-car pile-up just behind a Cortina on its side down a ditch by a farm entrance. Three marked police units had their hands full, and I guess the Landy got spooked and disappeared. We were heading in the right direction, but no signs.

The closer we got, an unsettling sensation churned in the pit of my stomach. Instinct told me trouble awaited us, especially if McNally's nefarious associates attempted to follow, assuming it was them. They probably left the head in a box and waited for us to make our move. We might well be playing into the hands of these wretched scoundrels who fancied themselves as werewolf hunters. Michael remained hyper-focused, but I occasionally caught glimpses of sinister yellow flashes in his eyes. The beast within him was on edge, perhaps sensing what I felt. Nothing boded well.

On the other hand, Ellena remained asleep, her eerie mumblings having ceased. The transition from tarmac to dirt roads could not rouse her from her slumber. It was another uncomfortable mile before the unmistakable scent of charred wood reached us. Finally, we encountered a sign that should have welcomed us to Oxley, but it had been repeatedly sprayed with red paint resembling blood.

"It's not too late to turn back, Georgie," Michael finally broke his concentration as we passed over a cattle grid. Suddenly, the world transformed, revealing how profoundly this town had been forgotten. I appreciate paying homage to the past, as other countries do, but Oxley seemed to have been erased from memory entirely. It resembled the quaint American towns one might see on television, minus the white picket fences—though not anymore.

Oxley had lost its homes, and a parade of shops lined the streets as we drove through. They, too, lay in ruins, all charred and blackened. The houses were burned, but I could still make out some semblance of untouched residences in the distance. Michael slowed, and I rolled down my window to take in the eerie silence. Ellena, meanwhile, had roused from her slumber but appeared disoriented. There was an absence of heartbeats, even wildlife, which was unusual. The sun began its descent, heralding the approach of a full moon night. Michael brought the Land Rover to a stop outside what used to be a 24-hour laundromat, flanked by a cafe and an off-license store. Directly across from us, a partially hidden church loomed, shielded by a wall of semi-burnt trees. We all stepped out of the vehicle, Ellena clutching my arm tightly. The scent of scorched wind and kicked-up dust filled the air. Michael's eyes flickered once more, and my claws instinctively emerged.

This town was saturated with death, and that sickly feeling that had gnawed at me earlier had now taken on a life of its own. I sensed something unsettling around us—no heartbeats, just an overwhelming feeling of pain.

My senses were finely attuned to the pain imprinted on this forsaken place. I didn't think Michael sensed it as keenly as I did. It was excruciating, pervasive, and overwhelming, almost as if the pain had taken on a tangible form. I felt something sinister surrounding us—still, no heartbeats, which was strange and eerie in its own right. It was unlike anything I had encountered before.

As I tried to make sense of this unnerving situation, the first ghostly figure materialized before us, peering through the shattered window of a hardware store. A man in his thirties, adrift aimlessly. I didn't share this with the others, but Michael must have noticed the dread on my face. Ghosts still unsettled me, and I couldn't fathom why. Lately, I had encountered more of them than ever before, and it remained one of the many unsettling aspects of this supernatural world that I struggled to reconcile with.

No sooner had I seen the first apparition than many others began to manifest all around us. They appeared briefly, drifting aimlessly before vanishing once more. This macabre town seemed to be teeming with these ephemeral spectres, and their presence only added to the eerie atmosphere.

"What are we looking for, matey?" Michael inquired, his face reflecting curiosity and disgust at the town's state.

"Michael, I wish I knew. This place is dreadful, and I can see why it's been abandoned. Let's check the houses and leave here as quickly as possible. I imagine we might find something inside that could shed light on what transpired here," I replied.

"But what about these ghosts?" Ellena chimed in, finally showing signs of life.

"Yes," I confirmed. "The whole town is filled with them. They appear and disappear quickly, though."

"Oh great, so now we have Casper to contend with," Michael quipped, injecting humour into the situation.

We shared a momentary laugh, a rare respite amid this grim exploration. However, my senses remained on high alert. I had an unsettling feeling that a twist in our journey was imminent. Call it paranoia or the uncanny way our cases often took unexpected turns, especially after the previous night had spiralled into chaos. This time, we didn't have a vampire to remove a bullet. I wanted to find a haven with Michael before the full moon's influence became overwhelming. Somewhere away from prying eyes, just in case, it affected us more intensely than anticipated.

The first row of houses was just two hundred yards away. As I surveyed the devastation, I couldn't help but notice inconsistencies in the story that had relegated this town to a tragic history. Michael seemed to share my reservations. The typical signs of a fire were present outside the houses—charred remains, blackened walls, and blown-out windows. Yet, upon closer inspection, the scorching patterns didn't add up. The greatest concentration of initial heat appeared to be upstairs, while the downstairs remained mostly intact, albeit cracked and blackened. The roofs were also severely damaged, suggesting the fire had rapidly engulfed the upper floors before spreading downstairs. It all pointed to arson.

Michael's sharp eyes scanned the surroundings as he contemplated the details. Ellena appeared overwhelmed by the devastation. We were on the even-numbered side of the street, and the burn patterns and scorch marks were inconsistent. I understood that fires could create chaos, resulting in diverse patterns, but what I saw here seemed deliberate, almost man-made.

"Michael, do you see what I see?" I asked.

He nodded grimly. "Yes, it looks like arson, but it was meant to cover up something."

"Arson in every single house?" I observed that each house had similar points of origin and ended similarly on both sides of the street and beyond.

"How many ghosts did you sense?" Michael's mind was racing, trying to piece together the puzzle.

"Many," I replied. "But there's something different about them. They appear briefly and then vanish."

"I don't think the people in these houses had the opportunity to leave, even if they wanted to. And remember, you said that vampire wanted you to see this," Michael pointed out.

"Yes, why?" I pondered aloud.

"Think about whether the stories are true or even if the movies are remotely accurate. A vampire's primary sustenance is blood. What if, for a period, they had an unlimited supply?"

My realization struck like a bolt of lightning. The vampires might have established a blood farm with an unending source of nourishment. The sheer scale of it was staggering. I had heard stories of vampires but never encountered one until recently. The idea that Amos, the vampire who had warned us, was the only one of his kind was now in question. Perhaps there were many vampires lurking in this town, following Amos's orders and awaiting the day their master would rise again. Everything we had been told until now needed to be reevaluated.

"That makes sense," I agreed. "But what triggered the cleanup? On the night we arrived, I was almost certain that a member of the public had been abducted near the castle. I saw a trail of blood, clear as day, and then it vanished."

"It's simple math, matey," Michael chimed in. "There are vampires here, all waiting to unite with the riff-raff of this town. They had a constant supply of blood until someone grew suspicious about Oxley. They covered their tracks, but the need to feed persisted. So, these wretches occasionally snatch someone from Cruden or elsewhere, using them like a tap, perhaps even turning them into vampires if possible."

"Turning? I'm not sure how their supernatural rules work. I've heard of an 'Elder,' but the details are sketchy. Maybe it's an age thing," I mused.

"Like Milfs and Gilfs?" Michael quipped with a laugh before lighting a regular cigarette.

"No, you old pervert," I retorted. "But perhaps reaching a certain age or milestone confers some peculiar benefits."

As we continued our discussion, my thoughts drifted to Skip and Locke. Skip's altercation with Locke had seemed out of character, considering they had appeared friendly during our last case. Unless Skip had seen through Locke's actions and realized that he had inadvertently betrayed us. Perhaps Ruth had contacted Locke in some manner. We needed someone to finally speak candidly to uncover the truth, but getting that from anyone involved in this supernatural world was akin to pulling teeth.

My attention returned to the task at hand. We stood at the threshold of the first house, its door barely hanging on. Surprisingly, none of the houses had been boarded up, making them prime targets for squatters, though no sane person would willingly stay in this forsaken place. The stench of charred wood and burnt furnishings permeated the air. My keen senses detected another unsettling scent—the lingering odour of burnt flesh and bone. It was a scent I couldn't forget, a trait I wouldn't wish on anyone: the ability to smell death and see ghosts. These were just two unsettling facets of the supernatural world I grappled with.

As I pushed open the door, my hands gripped the blistered, blackened doorknob. The interior of the house was a nightmarish tableau of destruction. Charred glass crunched beneath my feet as I ventured further into the gloom. The dampness in the air was suffocating, a putrid blend of burnt wood, scorched furniture, and the lingering remnants of burnt flesh and bone. Even after all this time, the stench clung to every corner of the room, a haunting reminder of the tragedy that had befallen this place.

The house's layout revealed a trail, a dreadful path of destruction that seemed to lead to a nightmarish revelation. The downstairs had been relatively spared, except for a few charred patches and cracked walls. The upstairs had borne the brunt of the fire's fury, with blown-out windows and collapsed ceilings. My keen eyes noticed another detail that sent shivers down my spine: streaks and splashes of gasoline, unmistakable marks of deliberate arson. Once I caught the scent of gasoline, I could follow it anywhere, and it seemed that this inferno had been deliberately set.

"Are you okay, Georgie?" Ellena's voice broke through my thoughts, her concern evident in her eyes.

I nodded, my gaze fixed on the burned remnants of this once-happy home. "Yes, Ellena. It's just that this place reeks of malevolence. They destroyed everything here, deliberately."

Michael joined us in the room, his sharp eyes capturing the horrific scene. "This is no ordinary fire. It's arson, calculated and designed to cover up something."

We continued our exploration, moving from one room to another, but they were all empty, devoid of any signs of life. It was becoming increasingly apparent that these houses were not homes but merely facades for a sinister operation that we were only beginning to uncover. No family photo or personal memento remained, just the scorched remnants of lives that had been obliterated.

A faint noise from outside caught my attention as I stood on the top step of the staircase, contemplating the jump back down. It was distant but distinct—a series of beeps followed by a soft sliding sound. The hairs on the back of my neck stood on end. I had heard similar sounds before, during the "Black Widow" case when we discovered the tracker under our car. This, however, was different. It couldn't be a coincidence.

My senses honed in on the source of the sound, and my heart sank as I realized what it was—CCTV. It had never crossed our minds that this abandoned town might still have functioning security cameras. The beeping and sliding had me on edge, and I couldn't help but wonder if someone was watching us. The paranoia that had been building up in me intensified. I didn't mention it to the others; there was no point in adding to the tension unless we could confirm it.

We couldn't afford to linger. Our best action was to investigate a few more houses, perhaps the church, and leave this eerie place behind. Why the church? Because it was ominous, and people with sinister secrets tended to be drawn to such places. It was worth exploring, and it might hold some answers.

"The vampires could be anywhere, waiting for their master to stop whispering sweet nothings to anyone with a pulse and emerge from the caves," I said, my mind racing with possibilities. "For now, let's see what needs to be seen, and maybe we can devise a plan to free any captive werewolves. It might also help us increase our numbers."

Michael, never one to let a moment go without humour, said, "Speaking of numbers, those women you mentioned earlier, are they single?"

I couldn't help but roll my eyes at his jest. "Firstly, you old pervert, Ruth has a three-hundred-year hang-up about an ex, and the other two are golems. I wouldn't even guess if that made them anatomically correct."

Michael chuckled, undeterred. "Okay, so Ruth is out of the picture. The rest, I can work with."

Ellena joined in on the laughter, a welcome respite from the grim surroundings. But beneath the humour, I couldn't shake the growing concern about her. Something was changing within her, something that didn't bode well.

My thoughts returned to the gruesome scene we had just witnessed—the two figures in the bed, the metal stands with fluid bags, and the small square tags. This had been part of a blood farm, a horrific operation that needed to be stopped. The puzzle pieces were coming together, and the vampires behind it all had to be held accountable.

As I stood on the top step, contemplating my descent, my keen hearing caught a faint noise outside. It was distant but distinct—a series of whispers and the faint hum of a vehicle. We had company, and the question lingered: Was it the Land Rover?

Chapter 31

It was not quite the superhero landing upstairs, but it was enough to make Ellena and Michael jump. I didn't need to check where they'd been; Michael would tell me anything important. My main concern was the voices. We hadn't had a chance to see anywhere else yet. Perhaps the sudden visit was the point. It had to be CCTV that I'd heard.

Five sets of footsteps were making their way into town, splitting up. As if it couldn't get any harder, I only picked up three heartbeats. Vampires were in the mix. With time ticking on, the night rapidly slipped in, bringing the moon with it. Even though we hadn't experienced its peak, I could already feel some effects washing over me. Michael, too, kept twitching as the yellow strobes rippled around him.

They weren't moving quickly, giving us a short gap to dash toward the church. Its immense structure had more space to work with, aided by steps leading down to a basement. Something I wasn't in a rush for, but we were sitting ducks in a fragile burnt house. Besides, if needed, we could modulate a howl in that echoing space to make it seem like we had more numbers. I used the warehouse across the canal to give Michael some breathing space after he'd been shot.

First, we had to get there; having vampires with them improved their capabilities—superhuman, like my strength, speed, and senses, just like us. With one difference: they could hear our heartbeats. I turned from the doorway to deliver the bad news. My hands brushed through a thick burnt patch on the wall, a claw flicking through it out of frustration when I heard another sound I wasn't in a rush for since last night.

Guns were being chambered. Was this a hunting party or a kill squad? I couldn't decide.

I stumbled, my eyes lingering on my shoulder, where the bullet would've landed. Yeah, it wasn't the first time I'd been shot recently, but for some reason, this one had a far more significant impact on my weary brain. The two shots at the old family home in Surrey didn't register; it all happened too quickly.

After my miraculous resurrection, I went on to play those murder games. Last night was a real kick in the balls because they knew what to use to hinder, which could've been just chambered wolfsbane bullets. And a vamp to point the way.

That flick of charring was weird, too; a small static shock rippled through my fingers as I laid eyes on Michael and Ellena walking toward me. They began to crumble away before my eyes. It was happening again, and the timing couldn't have been worse. Slowly, the black faded into a bright, clean cream. The home transitioned to sparkly, out-of-the-box new. There were voices different from what I'd heard on the edge of town. Two sets were coming down the clean, floral-carpeted steps. I smelled blood, and it was coming toward me, but also gasoline. I was about to see what happened.

Liquid splashed against the walls and steps as I finally saw their feet. Two pairs of black all-terrain boots. They walked, laughing and spraying the liquid around without a care. One carried a big red cooler box with a white handle. One side of the old was open, allowing me to see stacks of blood bags. Their faces came into view, mottled, deathly pale white skin with fangs on display dripping blood as they supped it from a bag. Neither I'd seen so far, and the town was destroyed years ago so they may have been killed by now. Corny to say, "seen one, seen them all," but both were similar with slight differences to Amos, like his weight. But the dead glaze, drained-of-life appearance didn't distinguish one from the other much. Both had short dark hair, were skinny and at least six feet from gangly death.

They moved through the downstairs rooms, ensuring they left a trail of gasoline in their wake. The brazen, sadistic nature of their actions made me sick to the pit of my stomach. This vision thing needed knocking on the head until I knew exactly what it activated because it was happening at the worst possible time. It wasn't as if time stood still. Every time it happened, watchers said my eyes changed, so that meant while I was enduring a bloodsucker fire fest, those other bastards were moving in, and I hadn't the time to warn Michael or Ellena.

"What a shame we have to start over somewhere else. Good thing plans were already in motion," one of them said.

"You knew it could happen. That's the planned contingencies. We need a haven for when the 'Order of the Elders' is finally resurrected. Then maybe we could finally cement our place at the top of the food chain," the other replied.

They said this as they continued to chuckle through gargled blood. More importantly, what the hell was the Order of the Elders? More than that one in the caverns? That made sense; to believe he was the only one would be naive. Yet an 'order'? We had enough on our plates, and the vision was from a while back, so had they been able to gather more elders and keep them hidden? And what were the contingencies? Surely, that hadn't included Cruden Bay because, so far, they'd relied on the bloodline of the countess arriving. The odds on that would've been astronomical...

Unless a certain ADI knew all along and wanted Ellena ready for when the moment arose, for all those pieces to fall in place would take genius planning, and I didn't see it in him unless he'd been a puppet for longer than we realized. That's where Ruth came in.

The vampires trailed into the hallway; one whooshed upstairs in the blink of an eye. I heard something being thrown and then a sudden roar of flames. The vampire was back at his companion's side in a second. The one that stayed lit a match and threw it to the floor. The flames went like a domino effect in different directions.

"The seeds we sow, the blood will flow, and soon we will rule above and below," both said in unison before turning and walking toward me. The fire grew rapidly, with smoke filling the air. The vamps breezed through me as if I wasn't there. The moment they passed through, the cream walls began to crumble back to the charred, stinking black once more. Those flames dissipated to the crumbled, damp wreck of a house we entered. Everything had returned to normal, or as normal as a torched home could be. Straight away, all the hairs on my body stood on end.

I'd shifted without the need to want it. I was standing, facing the remnants of the lounge again. Only this time, I didn't get the witty comment about my eyes. I didn't get the 'Are you ok, Georgie?' and I sure as hell didn't get Ellena rushing to my side to comfort me because neither was bloody there.

The anxious chemo signals were enough to tell me what had happened... They'd been taken.

At first, the confusion of settling back into the present had me unsure. They could've moved to another room or just disappeared from my eyeline. Finally, my vision returned to its hazy red normal, and my werewolf instincts were on guard. I couldn't hear either of them. No heartbeat, no chatting nonsense as Michael had a habit of doing. I began to panic, struggling to stop my breathing from turning erratic. I spun on the spot, looking around time and time again, waiting with thinly veiled hope that they'd suddenly reappear. It was slightly warped thinking, but what else could I do? I was confused. It didn't seem like I'd been gone long enough.

Then again, in moments like that, we still had no idea how it was possible, let alone time changes: the worst moment for it to happen, all the same. Not being able to see any of the real world while being thrown through a loop had me praying Michael and Ellena would slither from a secret basement door or something. My skin crawled with the full moon itch as it drew closer. My connection to Michael had been temporarily severed, and I couldn't sense Ellena.

Those footsteps had spread through the main street of Oxley Town, scattered past the shop parades, at a three hundred-yard gap between each one. So far, I'd locked onto each pair of heels pounding on concrete, but not the two that mattered. My backside squealed with my mind analyzing the information I'd gathered with each passing coherent moment. First, they picked the right moment to pull us apart with ease. Secondly, I wouldn't hear the vamps coming if they wanted to be all stealthy. And finally, they left me behind for a reason, but what?

It was understandable there'd be a lack of fight. Michael didn't know what to expect or knew much about vampires, much less having to play bodyguard to Ellena. By now, he was probably edgier than a crack whore beaten with the ugly stick, trying to hock her pin cushion body on the corner for another fix. Ellena had been rather tired and seemed far worse for wear than she should've been so that she wouldn't have given much of a fight. To kick me where it hurts; I couldn't smell her coconut shampoo.

There had been no change in the number of feet I'd heard in the beginning, so nobody had left, meaning Michael and Ellena were being held somewhere nearby, and it had to be secure enough to quell Michael's strength. Assuming they knew his secret, he'd have to be somewhere cut off from the outside and moonlight. We hadn't even gotten beyond the first house, let alone see if there was a bank with a thick steel vault or an industrial area with heavy-duty warehousing. Something like that would do the trick and limit my ability to hear or smell where they were.

The idea of the vault was what I feared the most. So far, it seemed the town had no power and that CCTV more than likely ran off a battery unit or something. And if Ellena and Michael were sealed inside, they'd struggle for oxygen and push me against the clock. I wracked my brain for a plan, inhaling the shitty burnt timbers. The situation had the terrifying feeling of one big 'dangerous game,' and I was being set up to be hunted.

McNally's thugs and a couple of vampire stooges wanted to carry on from last night and add me to their arsenal of captive werewolves.

I could only hope Michael was nabbed before that lightning strobe flickered again. If so, he was safe. For how much longer, though? There had to be a way to narrow down where they were. Michael would have the strength needed to get Ellena clear; it was just a matter of giving him that time, leaving me to focus on the rest.

With the front door threshold within a couple of feet, my hand tentatively rested on the burnt wall, bracing myself for round two as I leaned forward as far as I could without making my head the bullseye, trying to get the lay of the land. My heart pounded through my chest; even if to be expected, I needed it to calm the hell down. Otherwise, I might as well have walked outside waving a white flag. The thumping beats would be a bloody, desperate beacon.

Flight or fight had me by the throat, and I couldn't figure out what to do for the best; I looked back to the burnt downstairs at the end room. There had to be a back door and a garden. If I moved quickly, I could make it out and try clearing the fences without making noise. I gradually moved forward until I was just outside the little hunting ring. I'd have a few minutes to devise something better and pick them off individually. With a little luck, I wouldn't encounter a vampire straight away.

My heart finally slowed enough to feel a little safer. However, each step I took was on tiptoes and ever so bloody slow. Probably the slowest attempt at escaping in history. As I moved past the lounge doorway, my red eyes caught a lighter square patch on the floor. At first, I figured it was broken glass or debris from a light fitting. With a quick shuffle closer, I realized the object, no bigger than a purse or pencil case, had been left on purpose.

I'd recognize Ellena's handy work anywhere; it was one of her experimental kit cases—a supernatural mini first aid box. My wonderful little lamb had been present of mind enough to ditch one for me to find. Knowing full well, I wouldn't just go off half-cocked. The 'dots' were important, no matter what they related to. And right then, I found something that could give me an edge. Especially if she'd packed those adrenaline-filled gums, there had to be something inside to help me; otherwise, Ellena wouldn't have taken such a risk in the heat of the moment to leave it behind.

Creak after bloody creak until I stood at a blistered black door, praying to god it opened and led to the garden. Otherwise, I was screwed. My heightened hearing remained focused on the footsteps, some heavier than others, and any words exchanged. Bad guys can be dumb and full of bravado, which made them sloppy, so I'd hoped for a clue, a detail I'd missed in my dazed return from the vision to explain the confusion of suddenly finding myself alone.

Was this the vampire's chess move for Ellena? They'd finally shown their hand, or should I say fangs. A news article guided us toward the town, only for thugs with vamps in tow to find us. The troubling CCTV movement-like noises aside, they had to have known where we were heading.

My hand was on the cold metal handle, poised and listening for changes before opening the door. The wind whistled through any burnt gap it could squeeze through, making me jumpy. I could only hear three sets of footsteps now. The vampires had either suddenly discovered how to be still without the need to be desiccated, or they were moving quickly, and I was at a disadvantage. With a slight squeak, I pulled on the handle while doing my damndest to slow my heart down as far as it would go without having to be dead. Yet the beating had to be almost nonexistent if I were to stand a chance of making it through the gardens.

The sudden lack of vampire signs unnerved me. That had to be how Ellena and Michael were taken. A swift, surprise grab and go before they knew what hit them. My warm breath filled the cold air; the skies had become darker purple, and the moon suddenly seemed brighter. It already had my veins bulging and throbbing beneath my skin; it wouldn't have been farfetched to think my blood was boiling as it flowed around my body. Each garden seemed narrow, no more than twenty feet wide. Some fence panels were already down, making my task a little easier.

I was like a child trying to sneak over to the neighbour's garden to get my football before their dog saw and tore it to shreds. Then it bites a chunk out of my arse. Instead, I had vampires ready to sink their fangs into me and some low-life ready to blast a bullet or two my way. As I did with the steps, I dug deep for that strength again, quickly clearing the first couple of fences and gardens. I hung in the air for barely a second each time, long enough to realize two things. First, I could jump bloody high without trying; secondly, I caught the sound of air in short bursts. Not the wind, no, this was more like taking wild swipes at thin air.

Nobody else would ever have heard it, and it was so faint I nearly missed it. Finally, I had a lock on the vampires moving, and I bloody well needed to get my butt in gear. Those sneaky bastard bloodsuckers were moving in short bursts. If I hadn't gone into the garden first, I would've thought they were trying to bottleneck me in a particular part of town.

Before I knew it, I moved faster than before, without second-guessing or needing to dig deep. It was so weird. I'd barely beaten the first hurdle on track at school without falling over. Now, I was gliding through the air. So were the vamps; with the last fence in sight, there was a chance to throw some confusion into the mix. A gap between another row of buildings and more derelict shops. In that gap were benches and a huge tree; I could fly up the tree and through the window twenty feet up the side of the building.

The tree was easy, and so was the window. The landing, not so much. I landed in a heap, narrowly avoiding a facial collision with the corner of a table. Quick enough to leave the vampires circling the pavement. Neither I'd seen before, having been led to believe only Amos and the two circled me at the cliff's edge. What I saw from the window was younger—perhaps turned in the last one hundred years or so. If we survived the night, I had to look through the bestiary to see if this one had anything on vampires. Sure as shit, the films don't cover everything.

The guy on the left looked like he'd been dug up from the graveyard twice, with patchy brown hair and a gaunt face. He wasn't the poster boy for the undead Fang brigade. The other was slightly fresher, brown hair at least half brushed. Both were dressed in 'army and navy' finest. Still, they made bloodsucking unappealing. Perhaps their liquid diet was short on iron; they make anaemics look vibrantly healthy.

I sat below the window ledge, taking a moment to regroup, trying not to cough or gag on the dust I'd just stirred through the air. Quite a depressing situation I found myself in. Cornered in a shitty town that no longer existed, my Beta-friend and the woman I felt I would do anything for had been taken. All for a supernatural game of 'cat and mouse' that I wasn't sure I'd win.

"Oh, come out, come out, wherever you are. We don't want to hurt you," one of them shouted into the night with a strong Scottish twang. Their words bounced around the crumbling walls with a deathly menace, and I sure as hell didn't believe the 'fang police.'

Chapter 32

The two fucksticks weren't going anywhere anytime soon. Although I had made at least four hundred yards from the house and further into town. I knew I'd be taken down the first opportunity they got. Maybe not dead, but as good as if they wanted to chain me up and stuff me in a cave. And I was no pet. For whatever reason, the vampires were turning in circles, looking up. They didn't have a fix on me. I'd landed in a flame-grilled flat above an unnamed shop.

It stunk, reminding me of the charred silhouette at the house. I couldn't put my finger on it; burnt wood, plastics and foam were among the basics of everyday life. With my situation stupidly precarious, I had to take any advantage possible. While marginally concealed, I didn't want to poke my head above the parapet for the bloodsuckers to come calling. That meant I couldn't breathe or inhale deeply out of fear of being heard.

Instead, I slumped below the window smothered in grey and black, dusty crap. My fingers were busy picking through the charcoal flakes when A Mengey rat dam near made me shit myself. The bloody thing ran past my hand along the skirting board. My hands darted to my mouth to trap an urge to shout, 'What the fuck' and empty my lungs. As the seconds ticked by, paranoia crept in; every swallow, blink or twitch had me worried those fuckers could hear. The trouble was, I didn't have a move. Not one good thought.

'You may as well give up; there's nowhere to run. The end is inevitable,' One of the vampires called out again. I didn't take the bait.

This wasn't a situation I should've been in; we should've been in. We'd made the space and seemed safe enough to see what we needed to and go. How wrong were we? The end did seem Inevitable, much like changing from day to night. I had to man up, or should I say wolf up. Stop holding back and second-guessing myself. I was a werewolf, for Christ's sake.

I listened to the outside; the nearest gunman had positioned themselves three buildings further down and across Oxley High Street: another, two hundred yards to their right, in an abandoned maroon Sierra. The muzzle on their rifle kept tapping on the glass, trying to keep steady. The other had hung back nearer to the town entrance. Then and without trying, I heard the faintest sign of life—an emitter. And suddenly, in an out-of-body moment, my line of sight followed the noise. It was fucking weird.

It was like I was invisible, moving past the vampires first, then to the car and past it. The emitter noise got louder as I moved forward. It led me to the church outside the looming, burnt front. What were once huge oak doors were now charred matchsticks. The beeping was so strong, and I felt right on top of it, yet I was at least twenty feet down the path away from the steps. My sight must have lingered two to three seconds before I yanked backwards on super speed rewind, and I was back in the stinking, crusty room.

I was wondering two things. Where was the smell coming from? How on earth did I do that? I homed in on the sound like I was there. Don't get me wrong that could've been another exciting, evolutionary trait to add to my arsenal. I was getting tired of all these new things happening when I least expected them, in moments of trouble and without any semblance of control. At least I knew where to go. It's only a question of how I would do it without getting bitten, cut or shot.

'Och, ya nae fun. Look, we promise not to harm a hair on the fair lady's head if you surrender. She was always destined for someone else. Ya, wee dogs dinnae hold a match to us. Vampires always have and always be the Apex of predators,'

There was that annoying voice again. Cocky as hell. Apex predators? Really? All skin, bone and weird pointy teeth. The fact they rely on sucking blood to survive was a joke. The only sticking point was Ellena being destined for somebody else, hearing voices and drawing him, the tall and scary bloke I'd seen watching her. Do I surrender without a whimper, or would I go down fighting? Ellena was my chance for happiness that I never saw coming. I couldn't just let her slip through my fingers.

Even worse was the thought this little standoff was only the calm before the storm. If we were to survive this, something else would soon follow. Something bigger, scarier and far more dangerous for the rest of this country. Maybe further. I had to stop thinking, dwelling and second-guessing myself; in the moments I didn't, I was so much better in every way. I had to learn if I were to stand any chance of reaching Ellena and Michael.

First, I wanted to throw them off.

I was working on modulating a roar or a howl if I could speak instead and get them guessing. All I needed was for them to turn their backs and for me to get my arse in gear. The longer I sat in the crappy burnt flat, nothing was getting achieved, and for a while now, there had been a sickening feeling. The bullet to my shoulder confirmed it. Blood would have to be spilt, and I had to do it. Vampires were already dead anyway; they just needed reminding. So it wouldn't be taking a life. The bloodsuckers had taken so many already. Their decimation of Oxley Town was a testament to that.

I wasn't sure about McNalley's crew and any other humans that got involved. After all, I was bringing claws to a gunfight—no time like the present to check out Ellena's kit. My hand was shaking as I unclipped the box. As expected, a line of her special gums, a folded piece of paper and what looked like an Epi-pen.

'Hey, my reckless wolfie, this kit is a little more balanced than the rushed testers for the limo job. I know you have a little trouble getting going and letting go. These will not only flood you with adrenaline and a little added protection for what goes bump in the night. Oh, the other thing is a little something if ever in a tight spot that you couldn't handle with a vampire,'

Well, it looked like little lamb thought of everything. Yet, they had me pegged as a werewolf with... Performance issues. Ellena only pointed out what I'd just been thinking. I grabbed a gum and chucked it down my neck; it was time to embrace the darkness. It only took a few chews; the juices flowed down my neck, hitting me like a brick to the face. Not that I'd ever experienced it; imagine it would hit hard and bloody hurt.

In a matter of seconds, my body was on fire. I saw everything bright red; my claws were full and thick, like at the cliff top. They began secreting that liquid from the tips. Everything sped up, including my heart.

"You know that ladies aren't property, and this one has her mind. One thing is for sure: she is off-limits. How about you take a little trip to the chemist? You both look a little pale. Ever considered some lotion," I modulated without thinking; the gum buzzed me, and I'd thrown my voice across the way. Both looked toward the shops.

'Och, a funny wee fooker. Come on, no need to prolong the inevitable,'

"So, that's a no to the chemist. Seriously, they do great instant tanning options. You'd look less like death warmed up," both looked pissed, making weird hissing noises with fangs bared and their point nail spread wide of their bodies.

There was no reason with the blood bandits. It was them or me. Everything ramped up, and veins bulged. My claws tore across the wooden floor as I flew through the air and out the window without thinking or breaking stride.

I was so fast, a blur cutting through the air; I didn't think; my instincts were in control. I ripped through them.

My claws smashed through their chests, and my fingers ploughed into dead flesh and bone in the blink of an eye. I had a heart in either hand, surprising myself as I crushed them. Blood spurted through the air, with my mouth drooling. I didn't care. The vampires dropped in a bloodied heap to the floor behind me. Blood dripped from my fingers; it finally happened, with the full moon bright and overpowering, embracing me and I it. Strength, speed and primal power flowed through me; those vampires had been premature, with nothing Apex about them.

Realising they'd lost their vampires, I heard guns chamber in the building and car. In a blur, I crashed through the glass window, taking the gunman with me clean out of the other window in a heap on the floor. His jaw vibrated through my knuckles with one punch, and he was out cold. Next up, without breaking stride, I was fuelled with anger and rage I hadn't felt before. It tapped into everything that had been wrong in my life. All the bad things, the fire, being kidnapped by my parents, and Helen being killed with my baby by Ethan.

My pain became my power, whether I liked it or not. No thought came into it. I knew exactly where the gunman was. He didn't even get to reposition. I smashed through the brittle black door, taking it off its fucked hinges. My claws gripped his chest, but I made a mistake. I didn't stop. We went through the window, which was not my finest moment. We'd been two floors above the shop—at least thirty to forty feet.

We crashed hard on concrete; the gunman smashed down first; I was on top, still holding on as glass showered the street around us. I was okay, but the loud sound of snapping wood, only that wood was bone. Then blood began to pool across the pavement, and the back of his skull had caved in.

For a moment, I was brought back from the edge. Only a moment, remorse sucker punched me in the balls; I felt sick at the thought of a human life taken. I hadn't held back; he felt the full force.

Then I remembered what they were here to do, their lofty plans, and what mercilessly happened to those two blokes last night. May not have been the same scumbags involved, but the same agenda was there.

His blood painted the grey stone and had my fangs drooling. I checked the cartridge in his rifle. I don't know why; perhaps the human in me still wanted justification. And I got it. '.22 rounds,' I couldn't be sure Whether he got the memo of not killing, but these seemed normal. I'd recovered from gunshots already. The first two the other month was a rude awakening. Last night with Wolfsbane was different and only winged. The guy beneath was dead, and he had wanted to kill me. So far, I'd killed the vampires, rendered one gunman unconscious and accidentally killed another.

One way or another, I had blood on my hands. I hoped that Ellene and Michael wouldn't see me any differently.

Time wasn't on my side; my hands tore away from me. The dead thug's chest and I powered forward in a rage again. This time was about myself and what just happened as I lost control. I had to do better, to be better. The other thug was already sprinting toward his car; I nearly gave chase until I caught the emitter beep again, stopping me dead at the church.

Wheels spun at the edge of the town, and the Landrover slammed into reverse, grinding gears as the panic-stricken thug struggled to escape. I walked the path towards the noise, claws still dripping blood on each slab. My ears twerked to the beep. Michael and Ellena were underground. There were steps beside flaked white and black metal fencing heading down. I should've packed the wolf away, which would've been hard. Until a dose of second thoughts made me realise if I couldn't hear their heartbeats, I didn't know what was with them. Even though I thought I had everyone accounted for.

Carefully, I descended crumbling brownstone. Only to hit my first obstacle, a thick iron gate with a padlock. My ears bounced to the piercing beeps. I was inches from the rusty grey iron, and I heard something that made me smile for the first time. Ellena was checking on Michael. At least she was lucid enough for that. He murmured something back, not so audible. Yet I finally caught hold of faint heartbeats. Not faint because they were dying, more of where they were.

We sure as hell needed a bottle of whiskey once we were done. Mine would only paper over the sins I felt had tallied up in the back of my mind. The gate had four unusual hinges; ordinarily, I wouldn't have wasted a quid on me in a bet. Not tonight, though; I'd taken claws to a gunfight and surprisingly won. There was a cost I'd pay when I finally got to beat myself up. Until then, I wanted to hold Ellena in my arms.

I gripped the padlock cut out and the left side where the hinges were, took a deep breath and began to pull. The veins in my arms pulsated, and my temple throbbed. The wind brushed my fangs as I watched the blood smear where I held. Metal squealed and yawned; it began to bend in my hands and gave way. A son of a bitch, though. All of a sudden, one by one, rivets popped, then screws before the hinges crashed free. One tore off completely, flying through the air and narrowly missing my face. One final yank, the right side popped next, so goddam loud. I heard Ellena whisper with fear until Michael spoke more audibly.

'It's okay, Georgie is here,' a little cheery spring to his tone; I smiled again. These two were my world and people I held the greatest to me, and saying that about Michael was something I would never have imagined. Then again, my world wasn't only six feet anymore, and it was so fucking dark. If I couldn't trust these, I practically had nobody else.

The gate got thrown to the side, leaving an oak-looking door left to go.

I grabbed at the handle, only to get blasted backwards by another obstacle. The door wasn't oak, bloody mountain ash. I went back at it harder; purple, with sparks, flew. It was already draining me; with a firm grip and one big shove, I figured it would bust open. Another one of Ellena's gums did the trick for an extra boost. A final look at the sky at the brilliant white moon basking in its glow. One... Two... Three...crash... I flew through the door into a terracotta-tiled hall.

Rolling off the door as soon as possible, my body would've been spent without the full moon and the gum. The beeping had grown louder, echoing. It was a tunnel away from the church. Underground with steel supports throughout. It made me wonder what a church would want with such a place. Then again, the town hadn't been normal. A heavy-looking grey door was on the left where the beeping came from. Only two heartbeats began to call out to my ears.

Unless they had a vampire with them, they were alone.

Without wasting time or stopping, I kicked the door through. Dust slapped me in the face; the room was huge and nothing like I expected. Not that I knew what to expect; it sure as hell wasn't some medical-looking facility, floor-to-ceiling reinforced in metal. Michael and Ellen were strapped to shiny metal gurneys almost upright and back to back. Neither could see the other.

"Aren't you a sight for sore eyes, matey. Now can we get the fuck out of here?" Michael looked worse for wear; he struggled to keep the shift in check, eyes turning bright yellow. He was chained but also wrapped in something else, a rope with purple flowers attached. Different to Ellena, who was only chained.

"Georgie, break me first; I will help Michael. You can't do it. Wolfsbane in floral form is so much more potent; it will be too much," Ellena said, smiling. She still looked sickly pale and worried me in the long term, but for now, safety.

Ellena's chains broke away easily, but the Wolfsbane radiated from Michael, explaining why he looked like crap. Seeing Ellena smiling made me realise this second chance was worth fighting for at any cost. No decrepit elder vampire would keep us apart as long as she didn't mind the blood on my hands, metaphorically and physically. Her chains dropped free, and Ellena jumped into my arms as my fangs subsided. Her lips locked on mine, and sparks flew between us.

Soft and sweet, Ellena was everything I had to give. Our kiss was hot and steamy, like we hadn't seen each other in years. Only to get broken by an impatient Michael huffing. We parted, laughing; her eyes hypnotised me. At first, because of her beauty, then because it happens again, brief ripples of bottomless black. Something was wrong with Ellena, but what?

Chapter 33

Ellena froze, not on purpose or anything. It was as we parted, and I stood in awe. Her eyes had flickered, and she'd become a statue at that moment. Somebody had a remote and paused her momentarily, draining her life.

Only seconds with her lips hung open, the lights were on, and nobody was home. Or at least they'd stepped out to move the bins a minute. There was no expression, nothing, almost as if her mind was in a deep conversation with an invasive, sneaky vampire. I hated it. With the superhuman speed, strength and all the other weird crap I'd learnt to do, I suddenly was rendered useless, not for the first time.

This battle was for the body and mind, and I didn't know how to regain the mind. Michael only knew the fraction I'd told him. We faced an impossible task. While I got busy taking down two vampires and a couple of henchmen, Ellena was stranded and that elder may have been whispering all sorts of 'evil nothings'. How could we fight these vampires and god knows what else and watch Ellena? There was nobody else around we could trust.

With that in mind and the Land Rover racing away, we weren't safe yet. That thug may have been going for reinforcements. Ellena still had a hand on my arm, and Michael squirmed on his gurney. I knew all too well his irritation and the feeling of being drained were yoyoing. All because the strobing yellow aura around him had grown. When I had the chance to displace my anger, the moon empowered me. Michael got to briefly bask in the white glow before being trapped. By doing that, Michael acted like a champagne bottle waiting to pop its cork.

If we didn't get him to safety soon, a chance to shift without Wolfsbane messing with his mojo. He could go a little rabid. I hadn't helped Michael enough before we left for

Scotland; he'd been intent on using what he'd seen the skipper and I go through. Now wasn't the time for me to take juggling lesson number two. The first was when I learnt what I was and my best friend, Chris Wells's murder. We barely survived then, and now I have taken a life.

Ellena finally looked more coherent, and when she did, there was no hiding the 'rabbit caught in headlights' expression—even a little shake of her head. Either to fight something from getting through or get rid of what had. I knew where my money was going. Ellena smiled again, a forced, worried one, before darting to Michael and tearing at the ropes. A few flowers pinged off and through the air in my direction. Even just one flower two feet before me had me feeling the effects and forcing me backwards.

Finally, the ropes were off, leaving only chains. Michael's yellow strobes lit up Ellena's pale face. Making those black rings under her eyes look worse, brushed a flashing yellow. Ellena went to grab a hairpin from her golden locks, but Michael, ever the stubborn bastard, shook his head 'No' and flexed his hands as his claws slid forward. His eyes were bright yellow; with a quick shake, his chains broke free easily, dropping in a heap.

Feeling on edge, I didn't wait for Michael to straighten himself up; my ears were already looking for trouble while I walked back to the door. The guy I knocked out was likely coming to about now, depending on how hard I hit him. In the heat of the moment, I couldn't tell other than the pain in my knuckles.

Another chance to take in my surroundings, still with the niggle, why a church would have an underground medically equipped room. Not the standard first aid type either. Something fishy had been going on, but what? More experiments? The last thing we needed was some hybrid vampire-werewolf. The bad guys had access to both. I mean, what the hell would that look like? A vampire that could go from sickly pale, clean-shaven to beard in under two seconds.

I peered past the door frame, hearing crickets, the wind whistling through the streets and a faint heartbeat. That thug must still be out cold; his resting heart rate was between 50 and 60 bpm. Ellena and Michael had trudged to be close behind, and Michael's chemo signals were off the charts. He was struggling for control; now, he was free.

I was about to carry on walking when Ellena's hand brushed mine, sending a sudden shock through my arm. Her hand was cold; I mean, really cold. The strange thing was, the cold sensation was only brief; Ellena shifted her hand again to grab mine, warm again. Adding to the mystery of what could happen to our 'little lamb' after all, it's no coincidence that subtle changes have happened.

One problem at a time; we needed to get out of town first before handling a far more delicate situation. By highlighting the vampire in Ellena's head too much, she may dwell on it and open the door more than it already was. Bad enough, Michael was a ticking time bomb that needed to be on a leash until the night was over. Meanwhile, Skip was fending for himself on a full moon somewhere in the world.

Everything felt eerie, too eerie, as we headed through the tunnel and up the steps. I stopped short of the top, holding the others at bay while I checked the coast was as clear as I'd left it. Blood included. I homed in on the droplets through the pathway, making the drool flood my mouth. One sensation I wished wouldn't keep happening. Perhaps one day, I can get a handle on it. For now, my fangs were on show again. It worsened as the breeze rushed past my face, bringing the scent of a thug with his head caved in.

Followed by the two vampires, only they were smothered by death. A morbid, decayed aroma that made me a little sick.

We edged out onto the pavement and headed to the main road; I listened for the remaining thug's heartbeat again. It had sped up since the last time, and that worried me. Something else had me more on edge, though. Michael was growling, rocking side to side. His anger oozed from his pores, the moon spread its glow across our faces, and I had to fight hard for control, not wanting Ellena to see me how I was earlier. However, she hasn't even commented on the bloody hands yet. Perhaps too deep in a battle of her own. We stood at the entrance to the churchyard, and all I could think about was the night not being over yet. By that, I mean bloodshed.

Metal rattled a hundred yards away. I knew that sound of doom anywhere because straight after came the 'chuh...chuh' as a round got chambered. The problem was, with Michael's chaos going on beside me, I hadn't pinpointed in what direction the one hundred yards was. Ellena's heartbeat was all over the place, Michael looked ready to 'go wild', and I barely hid a lid on my rage, and we were so exposed.

"Georgie, something is wrong, isn't it?" Ellena broke my search with her tired-sounding voice. I had to know what that pinprick was, and there were more. It didn't seem to be a bite, but Ellena wasn't well, that much I knew. Her eyes kept changing, and her vacant expression with her head gone somewhere else. She was being lured from our grasp, and I felt powerless.

Michael's eyes were bright but scowling with anger, and his face had fully shifted to the fox persona with the same yellow animal shape around him, tail and all. His claws were the longest I'd seen since he became different. All I could do was hope I could still get through to him if needed. Surprisingly, this was also the longest I'd seen without a cigarette in his mouth. He didn't even reach for one when he was released, which told me he was already elsewhere.

"Ellena, you don't know the half of it. I... I've had...I've had to...-" I was trying to break it to her while we were in the moment, but I couldn't force the words out. And she stopped me in my tracks, grabbing my blood-covered hands.

"It's OK, Georgie. I know. It's what you had to do. There's so much at stake; this isn't like working a case; these people are bad and very dangerous. Throw in vampires and witches, oh and guns. There would only be one outcome if we were to stand a chance of surviving. Nothing changed between us; you were who I had been waiting for. I realised that the day we nearly lost you in the limousine explosion,"

Ellena smiled; she was struggling, but her words were what I needed to hear. She gripped my claw-clad hands, squelching some of the blood onto hers.

"But I killed someone, well the vampires first but the thug, we went out of the window, and it was an accident," I said, hoping her thoughts didn't change.

"I'd rather it be that way than lose you. And I know it won't be the last one. We have to survive at all costs. My reckless wolfie, I think we have the chance of something special; I know I am not like you. But I would move heaven and earth if I had to if it meant saving you. Like you have done for us countless times. These fuckers don't deserve your pity. You're a good man with a big heart that will never change, not will how I feel for you,"

"I would do anything to keep you safe; you are the second chance I never saw coming. Now it's here. I'm not letting go, even if that means destroying an old fuck of a vampire," I said as Ellena cupped my hairy face.

"That's settled then. Now, can we get out of here? We need to work all the details out and see what we do next, and I need to fill you in on something," Ellena dived in with a kiss that sent sparks through my body and hairs tingled on end.

I didn't want to let go but was cautious of that rattling gun. It made me wonder what Ellena had to update me on, though. If only this were a calm holiday, with the kiss driving me crazy, I would've given anything to take Ellena to bed there and then. If I was reading the situation right, Ellena did too—just a little matter of an extinct town and a gunman to escape from first.

A boot scuffed across a dusty wooden floor, knocking an old aluminium can. Not only did it help shake off the moment, but it also gave a direction. We were sitting ducks again. He'd been left high and dry, so what else would he do? The rattling gun told me the guy was scared, and who could blame home.

A werewolf had blazed through a glass window to take him through another before being knocked out. He could've opened fire at any point since I'd noticed he was awake and we were outside. This seemed a defensive strategy; again, I couldn't blame him. It was about him surviving the night after being left to fend for himself. It's said there's no honour among thieves; that applies to werewolf hunters too.

The trouble was Michael looked to have other ideas. His rage grew by the second, and I wasn't sure I could control him. I was an Alpha with training wheels and could be with an old hand like the skipper to help steer the ship.

"Michael, you OK?" I said, watching him raise his fox snout to the air, sniffing away. He had the remaining thugs' scent. That or he'd locked onto the blood pooling across the pavement down the way. It could've been several things, including the dead vamps and their stinking, crushed hearts.

"Grrrrrrrr...grrrrrr...get out of the way G...g...Georgie," Michael had. Begun foaming at the mouth, his fangs were a sea of bubbles.

What I saw happening with Michael was exactly what I feared on the blood moon. Not that I knew what to expect then, and I didn't know now, but what had slowly unravelled before my eyes, Michael had lost his internal fight, making my neck hairs stand up to do the macarena. Shit was about to go sideways, fast. I barely had the furry genie back in the bottle; all we needed was Michael going all 'Friday the 13th' on the guy, only in Oxly instead of Crystal Lake.

"Michael, you need to breathe. Think happy thoughts. Think about the bottle of Whiskey we're gonna polish off once out of this ghost town," I said, hoping I could break through to him—no such luck.

"Come on, old man; I need to hear more of your crazy adventures rubbing shoulders with East End gangsters. Like the one about your night out in a club that turned into a strip bar, you'd spent the night sticking fivers in strippers' knickers only to find out she was a gangster's sister. Damm, near shit yourself in the club, you said. After they wound you up, pretending they were going to shoot you. Remember? You never did finish that story,"

Ellena tried her luck. That story did make me laugh; it was just one of the many in his seedy repertoire. I swear I had had more lives than a cat. But Ellena's attempt failed.

I thought she'd broken through for a moment until I heard the gun rattle again. The thug's heart was a runaway train. About now, he was probably weighing up whether to stick or twist. Stick and only shoot in self-defence, hoping we'd fuck off. Or twist and go for glory, a false sense of reality that he'd be able to shoot us both before we got to him.

He no doubt wouldn't be factoring in details like his shaky hands would cause his accuracy to be off. Or the recoil from the first shot would delay attempts to line up the next target. There were no street lights; it had gotten dark quickly, and I doubted he had a night scope to hand. So, one shot that could miss, by the time that whistles through the wind, we'd be on him.

"M...move Georgie," Michael stammered, full of anger; the flickering yellow lights were on, but nobody was behind the wheel.

Everything fell silent for a few seconds, aside from me having to hear everyone breathe, sniff or shuffle in surround sound. Nobody spoke or moved with my back toward the hidden thug. I presented a big target, but the two in front of me were more important... That was until it seemed my target was too good an opportunity.

'Claaap,' Somebody rang the death knell bell.

Life suddenly slowed; Ellena's fluttering eyelids resembled flapping wings beating through the wind. I grabbed Ellena by her waist, moving at superhuman speed, powered by full-moon adrenaline. Michael into the space to my left. This was the moment he wanted, and I had my hands full.

Michael's yellow thunder silhouette became a blur through the air. I had to be in two places at once. Two jobs. My foot dug deep into the stone floor before powering forward, carrying Ellena with open-mouthed obviousness. In the blink of an eye, I had Ellena safely back in Michael's car.

Looking at her beauty through the glass, Ellena mouthed, 'Be safe' before I floored it to catch up with Michael.

I caught the tail end of his yellow blur smashing through a shop side door. Its burnt black wood splintered through the air. Showering charcoal dust toward my lungs as I made up ground to latch onto Michael's slipstream.

'Crunch'...A haunting sound that took me back to my journey out the window and that guy's crushed skull. All because Michael had reached the thing first, and I'd heard bone cracking along with a heavy thump against a wall.

"Michael, don't." I caught him with his left claw in the thug's throat with the guy pinned against the wall, three feet off the floor. Michael's right hand gripped and crushed a hand still partially holding the gun.

"Why? He was trying to kill us. They all were. We were tied to a fucking table, all for their benefit. Tell me why I shouldn't rip his throat out and leave him in a bloody heap. That's what he deserves; they all do," Michael had a point, but I was already deep down the rabbit hole of self-pity, struggling with the blood on my hands. I didn't wish that on anyone else.

"And enough blood has been spilt already. Not just today, but the whole goddam town. I made a mistake today… I lost control and now look," I raised my hands, claws gleaming in the moonlight showering through a broken window. Both are covered in dried blood. The smell still got to me and had Michael's nose twitching.

"That was you saving us. This one had the chance to stay quiet and stay away. He chose to take a shot," Another point, well-made, but we didn't need to add to the body pile. I could see enough of the fallout by looking through the window at the ghosts drifting aimlessly. None of it was necessary. And it had to come to an end.

"And we can choose not to repay that in kind. Judging by his face turning blue and your claws buried in his throat, I hope he got the message. Why don't you drop the bastard, and we leave? There'll be plenty of time for payback," Michael was too rabid to listen; there were glimpses that gave hope I was getting through to him, and then he'd squeeze his claws deeper, making blood spurt.

I didn't know what else to say or do; the scumbag deserved this moment; we'd only be drinking from the same pig troth, having sunk that low. To make matters worse, I heard footsteps heading our way, treading carefully up the steps. I spun to the doorway, getting ready to fight, but only to get surprised.

"Ellena? I wanted you safe in the car,"

"I brought the car here. Something told me you needed help. I don't know why, but I felt you needed me," another detail that threw me. Could she sense that?

"I've tried. Nothing gets through,"

"Try being his alpha; make him know you're in charge,"

I turned to Michael, watching blood continue to spray sporadically. How could I show Michael I was the alpha? What Ellena said made sense; it was the how that evaded me. Looking at Michael and the ripples of thunder around him.

The cold and calculated killer gaze behind the 'Beta' eyes. It was like a barrier of anger; I had to break through quickly.

Finally, it dawned on me the only way to be heard was to shout or, in this case, roar. Maybe a mix of both. Bloody weird to think it, I guess, when in Rome, right? I dug deep, and one quick shout…

"Michael..." Somewhere between the shout and a modulating roar, it echoed but was scarily piercing. Michael froze; his eyes blazed brighter than ever before. The full fox head shifted to part human, part creature. The way we look when trouble is sensed, and the supernatural side is on guard. Michael let go; his claws jutted out of the guy's throat, spraying the air with blood one last time.

The reprieved dropped to the dusty floor; their feet gave say from beneath them. Gasping for breath and drained after an adrenaline dump. The guy still had a look of fear on his face. It's not surprising he just had claws in his throat.

Michael turned to me with a solemn look. He hated himself a little, regretting losing control. What else could he do? None of this had been planned. I didn't expect to call Michael for help, and I hadn't the time to coach old Mickey Boy.

"I'm sorry, Georgie,"

"That's OK, Michael; now, can we get the fuck out of here?" Without a care for the thug on the floor oozing blood, limply holding his shattered hand near his chest. We head headed for the stairs.

"They'll cuh...cuh...cuh... Get you. They get what they want. Those who don't learn from past sins are doomed to repeat. Hell is coming, and you're in the way." The guy found some bravery, stopping us dead.

I almost responded, but for whatever reason, I didn't. Nothing that needed saying, his words, as dark as they were. Nothing but the same cycle of nonsense. We'd wasted enough time as it was, and our sins wouldn't drown themselves. So, instead, I ushered Ellena forward to carry on walking.

'Click...Claaap,'

The bastard surprised us; very few have managed to do that lately. He did. Bleeding and struggling on the floor, he somehow found the strength to pull out a 'Glock', and in two seconds, a gunshot rang out. Not for the first time tonight, but the least expected. With a click and then a clap, Ellena spun on the spot before sprinting at us. She jumped into Michael and me, pushing through the doorway. Her scream was deafening...

'Noooooooo,' What happened next opened my eyes even further to the weirdness of this supernatural world, and if I wasn't in the same room, I might not have believed it.

Ellena waved her hand past my face, and a thinly veiled wave of purple suddenly filled the room. Everything seemed to slow down, and the bullet lost all momentum, dropping to the floor. Its metal ricochet against wood bounced in my eardrums. A moment of divine intervention or Ellena was a witch and had, in the heat of the moment, unlocked something special inside her. That purple wave wasn't done. Its next trick brought a little sick into my mouth.

The thug exploded. It exploded like dropping a plate of spaghetti, but all over the wall—a canvas of blood and shattered bone among patches of matted hair. Ellena turned him into a 'bloody' Picasso, and I was in awe. Also, a little disturbed, no doubt, would cause my next nightmare if I ever got to sleep long enough. We now had another problem to deal with, to understand how Ellena just turned a guy into a sheet of pebble dash.

Chapter 34

That image scarred my mind. No amount of whiskey was going to wash it away. Hard to believe, I was missing home and, in particular, London. Even the soul-destroying traffic that polluted the air with smog. At least there, I knew what to expect day in and day out. For the most part, anyway. The bar may have been raised a little lately, but it didn't compare to this.

Scotland has been a hell of a lot more than I'd bargained for. We were finally getting the hell out of Oxly, a town overrun with ghosts, and they weren't even the main event. I had Michael driving; he needed something to focus on in the silence. We all had crosses to bear now, and the cracking red flakes of blood were a testament to that.

For me, having everyone else to focus on, especially Ellena, occupied my thoughts for the time being. The fish that got away would've no doubt been licking McNally's heels and embellishing a story of how dangerous we are and how outnumbered they were. That's another thing I missed about being on home soil. When we work a case, if the shit hits the fan, all we have to do is press an emergency button, and the blue army comes running.

Towns like Oxly, Cruden, Peterbead and the rest had small forces; unfortunately for us, they were all dodgy. According to the mayor, at least. Even his words, I wanted to take with a pinch of salt. The truth was getting harder to find in a forest of lies and misdirection. What I saw in that house, the outline of bodies with metal tags, was another twist in the information and, more than likely, what that mysterious vampire wanted us to find.

If only I knew how to find his cave again. That powdered shit he threw in my face knocked me for six. Somehow, I had a feeling he had more stories to tell. A bit like Ruth, who claimed Ellena was a witch, a purple cloud later and a re-decorated wall, it seemed Ruth was right. As we left the town in our wake, I wondered where we'd be safe to regroup. The bed and breakfast were fortified to a degree, but it wouldn't stop Ellena, who was already asleep, from a late-night walk.

We had two options: get my car and kiss goodbye to the hell hole 'blood bay' or get some rest and devise a plan to start causing McNally and his vampire buddies some problems. The first place I wanted to check was Montague House, hoping we'd understand why it's important to the scumbags. The chances of locating those numbers from the tombstone and painting are less to slim for now. With excavation work and the diving excursions we saw at the port the other day and the beating Macnally's men just took. Their numbers would no doubt be reinforced.

Thugly numbers I was surprised not to see along the muddy trench-laden stretch of road as we neared the slip for the motorway. My head twitched left and right, more than a crackhead gagging for their fix. My money would've been on at least one carload waiting to pick us off. There were plenty of dark spots and farmyard turn-offs with overgrown tree patches along the route that we wouldn't have seen until right on top of them. It didn't seem right; I spent needless energy worrying and second-guessing.

By not doing that, we would've left ourselves open to be screwed over again, caught off guard at every turn so far, and it was beginning to grind my gears. The hard shoulder to my left was clear as we accelerated into the chaos, heading back to more familiar territory, the misery that was Cruden Bay. All we could do now was pray there wasn't a welcome party waiting for us at base camp. Some romantic getaway, this has turned out to be. The only thing going for us now was the blanket of clouds covering the moon enough to ease its effects.

Finally, everything was calm; my body had dumped all its pent-up adrenaline, leaving me shattered, surrounded by never-ending darkness that was surprisingly soothing—a rare moment for a power nap to recharge my batteries before all hell broke loose again. Outstretched in the car with my seat reclined, I'd all but dropped my guard until I felt a squishy wetness between my toes. Not in a sweaty, stinking way; slowly but surely, they were soggy. At first, it seemed a hallucination or an over-tired brain making shit up. My legs kicked out, and I suddenly had to cut through half a foot of rising water.

This wasn't my weird brain doing a number on me, but what was it? Everything pointed to the car was taking on water; I went to move but annoyingly couldn't, barely able to twitch my hands, let alone much else. I'd gone from the comfort of my seat to being restricted and consumed by a throat-drying panic...

Nothing I tried to do to move worked; my arms were agonisingly tight to my side, clamped down by the coldness of thick metal pressed across my wrists and the rest of my torso. This wasn't my idea of tied-up fun. I should've been used to the weird by now, but it still finds a way to surprise me. Every breath I took began to ache as if my chest was trapped in a vice that got tighter and tighter by the second.

Changes kept coming, and the ceiling had closed enough for me to smell old, dirty, damp wood. I mean, we all know that one person who tends to stand too close in our personal space with their overpowering bad breath, this was that. Whatever was happening, none of it was good; I sure as hell wasn't in Kansas anymore, Toto and not in Michael's car. The water had risen quickly, looking likely to be unnecessary bath time. Minus the soap or anything relaxing. Being trapped underwater was one of my biggest fears, so this was a real kick in the balls.

One thing became clear: I was in a box - something my shrink would have a field day with(don't judge). It was a bloody, old, stinking coffin that reeked of death. Soft silk padded lining rubbed against my ear; if I weren't so scared or disgusted, it would've been quite comfortable, aside from the water rapidly travelling up my legs and tingling my fingertips. Bloody ice cold and smelt a mixture of seaweed and salt Damm near took my breath away. Let alone cause a hasty retreat of my testicles. I writhed and squirmed in vain, attempting to find some room or leverage to manoeuvre the chains, but nothing.

No gaps and no werewolf strength. This had to be a dream or vision, and the one constant with either was me losing my supernatural abilities. Steadily, my eyes adjusted amidst the claustrophobia and aching lungs, just about making out patches of my soaked clothing; if it could be called that, the style was at least decades old, probably even centuries. I was useless at history in school, not knowing my Elizabethan from my Edwardian. So, there was no telling what era I was kitted out from; they weren't the clothes I had on earlier.

The situation felt too real and got me thinking; there's always some warped meaning to these scenarios. Wait...salty water and the stink of seaweed. Plus, I was in a coffin, slowly submerging into the sea. Albeit it should be impossible, my head went around in circles, trying to rationalise things that had neither rhyme nor reason. With the water swelling all around, a switch flipped in my brain. Yes, it seemed and very much felt I was on the verge of drowning, but I'd let panic and hysteria cloud my judgment and the old grey matter.

Suppose this was what I thought, even with the icy, salty water pooling over my arms towards my stomach. I had to start looking at the details of the 'dots' and the devil within them. I was first trapped in a coffin slowly sinking in seawater. Secondly, it already stunk of rotten death; from what I could see, the clothing was ancient. But I didn't understand why it was happening. What was the story of this misadventure that had me taking short, sharp breaths with my body temperature dropping. What was I supposed to see?

Don't get me wrong, real or not, I was scared. With the likely outcome, I'd either drown or find the solution to all of life's problems. In this case, the missing 'dot'. The higher the water came, the more I felt a stabbing sensation in my heart; it started from nowhere but soon became apparent. There was a huge bloody spike or stake in my chest. I couldn't tell exactly what material or colour it was with no light, but it glowed light enough to be white ash with an unusual ornate metal binding.

This wasn't me I was seeing. I mean, it was, but it wasn't if that made sense. My body simulated the place of a vampire. What with woody indigestion and old-style clothing. A realisation that did little to ease my frantic, cold gasps from feeding my fear. Heightened enough to have me praying for this crazy dream or situation to be over, I'd wake up.

I was busy wasting energy, fighting against the chains, kicking around the salty sea when I remembered the numbers we'd found and what we thought they were for. Grid coordinates that would, after years of coastal erosion, now be somewhere in the North Sea. Wait...what if this was what they meant to lead to? A coffin and a vampire...an old vampire that had suddenly vanished... And now desiccated. It couldn't be, could it? The staked body of either Frederick or Jean, depending on the one who saved me, patching up my bullet wound in the cave.

The pungent water was finally covering my chest, slapping against my chin, and moving toward my face. Surely, I'd seen enough details already for the craziness to be over. It would've been awful if the vampire had to go through this. Chained and had no way of fighting free. I knew little about the effects of stakes in the heart of vampires other than what we'd already been told. Technically, the vampire would be alive through desiccation and having to drown, come back alive, rinse and repeat. It was nothing less than torture, even for the undead.

The longer the vision went on, the more I realised that that was exactly what had to happen. I had to experience it all, especially the bloody drowning, for the nightmare to end. Worst case, I'd die for real; best, I'd wake in Michael's car, and everyone would be none the wiser. The first little flow went through my nose, making me gag as it stung the back of my throat, with no amount of head twisting or raising off the cushion doing me any good. The last bit of water was about to overflow; I took a deep breath.

Staying underwater wasn't my forte; the longest I'd ever held out for was about 45 seconds. But the pressure on the coffin made my head throb and a little distracting. There was no way I could hold out long. Little by little, my lungs ached as I held the air I had as tight as possible. Until... My head was about to explode, my heart screamed, and I couldn't keep my eyes open any longer. It fell dark. The last bubbles escaped my mouth...

"Huuuuuuhhhhj, cuh...cuh... Oh god, Christ. Quick Michael, I know what we have to do,"
My head flew forward, gasping, with the unreal sensation my lungs were full of water, only to feel everything around me shake. The comfy sporty bucket seating was back, along with the tobacco-staining stink of cigarettes. Yet, I still sensed danger; my hackles rocked to attention as a sheet of goose flesh skated across my arms. Armed with a drowning waft of salt water and death up my nose.

It was an awful experience I never wanted to repeat. I had little control over my life, let alone where these visions took me or how real they were. At least in the real world, there was a tragic, false sense of security; I thought so anyway, until now.

Upright, I shook the bleary haze that was more like a hangover than I cared for or could understand. The car shudders had me unnerved, and the view through the mud-smeared windshield was nothing but an endless, soulless black, much like that bloody vision. Strange, though, as it seemed I was looking out at some weird angle. It took a minute for me to realise it meant one terrifying thing: we were teetering over the cliff's edge.

Being battered by the wind that had cranked up the howling tonight, and every time it chaotically whipped past, our car shook and squealed its undercarriage against the chalky rock edge. My arse puckered while my stomach did somersaults. How the hell could this have happened? I called out to Michael, panicked and too scared to move.

I crumpled on what should've been the safety of my seat, cradling a half-empty bottle of 'Jim Beam' whiskey on my lap and finally clear eyes. I twitched around for inspiration. My brain was a washing machine spin cycle, with rational thinking further over the cliff than we teetered. The stereo light was on, but the volume was down low.

No engine noise and no headlights, almost a blessing because the judder from its throaty 3.2-litre engine may have sent us over by now. It was too dark to see what part of the cliff line we were on but enough to tell we desperately needed a miracle with time running. We needed to act fast.

The last I remembered, we were driving when Michael gave the whiskey from his glove box, which seemed he'd already opened, and he drove toward Cruden, giving him some focus on other than what went on in Oxley town. Ellena had already fallen asleep, and I was dead tired. All the 'beating myself up' I'd done over the dead thug had taken it out of me.

Each creek in the haunting seaside wind rattled my nerves. I turned slowly to the driver's side, fearing any sudden movements or unnecessary weight shifts. Michael was there but out cold, asleep or otherwise. We added more 'dots' to a crazy situation that didn't make sense. We'd survived one nightmare to end up in another.

"Michael, wake the fuck up; we're in trouble," I called out again, shaking him by the shoulder.

His body flopped like a corpse. I did consider smacking him around the face for a reaction until it dawned on me to check his heart rate. With the precarious swaying keeping me on edge, it hadn't even occurred to me to try. Michael had one, less than sixty beats a minute, stimulating a deep sleep; I'd shaken him as firmly as I could, with nervous glances outside. Every see-saw made me a little empty inside. Michael should've woken or at least stirred a little.

Fuck...

In my butt-clenching state, I'd completely forgotten Ellena. Too much else to worry about. After listening to Michael, I was scared to dare look. That and the damming reality of his beats and mine were the only ones I heard. Shuffling further around to see for sure, the car swayed again; this time, it swung lower, causing the metal chassis to yawn before flipping backwards. I'd feared the worst in each instance, us crashing to our doom and

Ellena missing.

With the outline of her perfectly symmetrical backside still cast on the seat and nothing but space, at least part of my fear was true. Ellena was bloody gone, and we hung on by a thread. Michael still didn't stir, even as the car's rear thumped the ground quite hard.

"Michael, bloody wake-up, will you," I shouted at Michael again. We needed to get safe and find Ellena fast.

"Ow...My head. What's happening? We are we?" Michael slowly stirred, his churned-up face in a painful frown as he clutched his head. No coincidence, we both had sore heads; how?

"Michael, don't move too fast or panic, but we're hanging over a cliff, and Ellena is missing,"

"What the fuck, how?"

"I don't know; what's the last you remember?"

"I was driving, pissed off with myself. Ellena was asleep; you'd had a little whiskey and drifted too. So I had a mouthful to wet my whistle. We planned to park near the Bay until you woke, and we decided what was best. But I came over really bloody tired. I remember swerving a lot, trying to brake before I blacked out. Must've stalled as we hit the edge,"

"I don't understand how, though, whiskey?"

"Can't be, was a new bottle,"

"New? It had already been opened. You must be slipping in your old age,"

"No way, matey. Bloody overpriced like the maps,"

"Then we were bloody drugged," Hard to imagine, but I also felt a little lucky to be alive with what Michael said, but how did it happen? What moment could the scumbags have had to spike the drink? Unless it wasn't that it was, it was just the first thing I jumped to.

"So what the hell do we do? I'm way too pretty to die this young,"

"Yeah, right, old man," I looked back, quicker this time, just as the rear end bounced up again.

"Well?"

"Pop the trunk,"

"What?"

"I said, pop the trunk. When I say, you'll be ready to switch the engine on and in reverse. First, I'm going to shift my weight to the back, drop the seat back, and hopefully climb through to the trunk,"

"Well, you are carrying the extra timber to weigh us down,"

"Piss off. You need to be ready; after all, this is all-wheel drive, so you should get enough traction,"

"Traction for what?"

"Reverse,"

"Yeah, but how. In case you didn't notice, we're see-sawing at the minute,"

"It's that, or you try climbing out and kiss goodbye to your car,"

Michael grimaced, his claws sliding forward to bite into the steering wheel. I couldn't blame him. There was no guarantee my plan would work; we had to try something before it was one bounce or whip from the wind too many. The quicker we were safe, the more we could find Ellena.

I gripped the armrest to leverage myself over just as another howl raged past, rocking the car again and lifting it higher off the ground. All I could hear was stone grinding on metal. I dropped into the back seat, hit by a rush of coconut. Ellena had left her mark. The clip was stubborn; I could've easily ripped it down, but every movement had me on edge. We may have super healing, but could we survive a fall off a cliff? I don't want to find out.

"When you're ready, princess, it's not like it's life or death or anything," Michael growled; his face didn't wear the fear well.

"Easy, old man, this ain't no picnic. By all means, if you wanna try, do go ahead...that's what I thought," Michael smirked; even with his front-side view, he didn't want to be climbing and taking the risk.

The back of the seat finally popped free, revealing just how much stuff Michael had brought, like one of those wilderness survivalists. Most of which I doubted he even knew what to do with it; I sure as hell didn't. I could just about squeeze through a gap, shifting bits as I went.

Freedom was near; I could smell the lingering exhaust fumes. Not as strong as I expected, my hands pushed through first to grip the edge of the trunk, shaking, nervously glancing at the lid, flipping up and down. Any minute, I figured I'd lose some fingers. Bad enough, I always have one hand tied behind my back.

I finally had myself ready to clamber over the edge but had to keep it weighed. I slid down the bumper, still gripping, but the car bounced up again as I peeled my legs over; the grinding metal on the stone seemed louder. I clung on for dear life; my heels momentarily dragged forward, and everything was suddenly shifted. Michael was panicking badly.

I glanced at the moon, soaking it in; I part shifted again, tapping into my supernatural strength, slamming the rear of the car down hard. Hard enough to rattle the exhaust, causing something to fall out the end. A thick rag wrapped in that familiar toxic flower. Temporarily making me dizzy until I quickly kicked it away. That's how those bastards got to us. A plan b in case their attempt in the town didn't work.

A part of me thought that scenario had been about seeing what we could do—I realised how the flowers affected Michael and blocked our exhaust as a fail-safe. This means they may now have Ellena.

My heels dug in while I had the car on the floor. With a firm grip and claws biting into the trunk lining, I pulled. The first few attempts had my feet slipping until I finally caught hold of a half-buried big rock—enough for me to lever against. Little by little, I gained momentum toward safety. First, only inches, then a foot, then a couple of feet, yet the wind was still kicking up, and all the hard work could easily be undone.

This was Michael's moment to bloody shine if he was quite done shitting himself. One good news: the whiskey had the all-clear, and I needed some. Michael had already started; I could hear him chugging it down in case our plan failed.

"When you're quite down. Time to do your part," I shouted, taking Michael by surprise, nearly dropping the bottle.

The engine soon roared to life, with the chassis still bouncing as I pulled; when Michael accelerated, there'd be occasional spinning in the air until we got the grip to stick. Slow and steady, we couldn't afford any mistakes, but it worked. Finally, some luck had fallen our way. Rubber ground against the rubble, and we were moving.

"The front wheels are about to touch down," he was right; I could feel the car picking up speed, and I needed less and less force to keep it grounded; then I heard the front grip, too. Michael hit the gas and slowly reversed to safety as I stepped away, looking toward the cliff's edge and sighing in relief.

We had to find Ellena now, and I had no idea where to start. The one true detail I felt was that our night had drastically gone from bad to worse, and it was far from over. No sooner were we safe from the danger of crashing to our doom. I sensed a change in the winds, and it was evil.

Chapter 35

My hand wouldn't stop shaking holding the bottle; I couldn't bring myself to look closer, and it hadn't occurred to me at the time. Too busy climbing to safety. Michael gave the rear of his car a proper once over, hoping there'd be a clue, finding nothing but scrapings of a clay-mud residue along the seat base where legs brush past. We chalked it down to my boots with nothing else to make sense.

"You sure this is wise?" Michael said, snatching the whiskey back.

"Not really; facing up to more bloodsuckers isn't appealing at all. But this house is important, and if Ellena was taken, this has to be checked off as somewhere searched,"

"Weren't you talking about the sea and a dream?"

"Yeah, I think down there is key to stopping the vamp bastards from getting their way, but we need Ellena; her bloodline sets the 'big man' free. If that happens, we could all be fucked,"

We were playing a dangerous game and did not have enough manpower to handle everything that needed solving. It crossed my mind to locate that wolf; with the full moon, I may have stood a chance to return their mind from the wild side. Ellena's di appearance hindered my ability to focus and prioritise. I didn't tell Michael that; he relied upon me leading us, be the 'Alpha', but I couldn't. Ellena was my real weakness, not wolfsbane.

Instead, I chose to play it safe or as can be. The house l clocked far more intimidating up close; I could hear its timbers yawn in the breeze and creak to pile on the trepidation. No lights, and so far, no hint of life. Not that we could use that as a guide like normal. Michael had his face screwed up, whiskey in hand, stalking. His heart had accelerated some since we arrived. Near-death experiences have a habit of doing that. What did I expect to find?

Anything to give me hope; this quest wasn't a lost cause.

My claws were ready with a flick of my hands, followed by part shifting. Michael tentatively followed; I could tell he held back after earlier. So far, nobody was nearby, and my eyes homed in on the steps from the visions I had, half expecting the ghost to appear. In a way, I wished Michael could see them, too, just to know how pant-shitting it can be. When it all began, hearing Chris after the gunman on my doorstep rocked my sense of reality.

"So, run this shit tip by me again; what makes it special?"

"The caverns underneath and god knows what other secrets druids turn vampires had created in there. They housed the older vampire for a while, conducting experiments. All hypothetical, of course,"

"Ah, okay. So we don't expect to walk into a hoard of bloodthirsty bastards? I've had my share of close shaves tonight, and the only person that can legally bleed me dry is the now ex-wife," Michael laughed before swinging and then passing the bottle. Dutch courage was needed.

"I have no idea. Let's hope either is in there, then. This place is fucking weird, though; it looks creepy as shit, Anna's ghost comes here, and everyone else wants it. But nobody will go in there,"

"So, it's the town's dirty secret that everyone knows but doesn't dare do or say anything about it,"

"Exactly,"

"Well, isn't that just fucking great. It looks like we're fucked then,"

"Why do you say that?"

"Oh, come on, matey. The fact no ody will enter means there's bad shit waiting, and I reckon it bloody well leads into those flipping pits below,"

"The catacombs, you mean? Yeah, that's my fear, and we have been misled by so much. Why else did another tunnel if the vamps are sealed magically? No, I think it's more than Ellena's descendant blood is part of a curse that can release the elder. The rest ju t lay in wait for his return, with Amos recruiting an army to swarm the town."

"And that Ruth woman?"

"She is giving off a misconstrued belief that the stones can somehow bring Frederick back. The trouble is, I think his bony corpse has been kept secret in a wreck along the sea bed. That or Jean, depending on who saved me from the gunshot. Whether she knows that or assumes he's desiccated and entombed is another story,"

We were at the base of the steps; I saw shades of red and grey, enough to highlight dirty, old carvings in the area Anna's ghost appeared to focus on. 'Heart and love, always as one' is what I could see; others had decayed over time. No heartbeats anywhere, inside or nearby, but that didn't ease my nerves.

All around was dead quiet, except for a few crickets and the occasional hoot from an owl. Each time made me jump a little as we slowly ascended the steps. Creak after creak with a feeling the wood could give way any moment. Finally sta ding on the porch, I caught wind of what I'd dreaded. - Stink of death. The kind I was getting used to smelling of the vamps. There was no need to ask Michael if he had. He was already screwing up his face and shaking his head in disgust.

The front door had its windows boarded over, varying shades of flaking black, with what I could smell and my eerie feeling. My head couldn't rationalise why Mayor Duncan Campbell would want the place unless we were missing something, which couldn't be discounted with the constant flow of bullshit heading our way.

"You ready?" I looked at Michael, who'd hung back with his heart pounding. Nearer to the door we came, the smell grew.

"Not on your life, and don't get me wrong, I'm game as anyone, but there's a shit load of death in there; why are we bothering?"

"Because of exactly that, so much death and no one bothers. Ain't it best to see the whole table and know all the cards dealt?"

"I guess, to what end? You die? Came close already, and both nearly went over the cliff."

"Look, we can leave now without going in; I can't hear Ellena's heartbeat; what if she has been turned or whatever the creepy fuckers do? She was weird earlier, and something wasn't right; she was visibly different and tired. We may walk into a thousand vampires, think of the stories if we survive this shit," That was the moment that grabbed Michaels's attention the most, not that we'd be able to tell the full story but imagine confirming vampires exist.

Carefully and as quietly as possible, I turned the handle slowly. The door popped open with a slight click. As it yawned wide, a rush of death flew toward us. That and old stale dust, we'd opened into a large hallway with a huge staircase to the right. The place was impressive outside, but inside was a mansion lost to time. In itself, I could see an appeal in restoring it.

Until I clocked the beginning of death, coffins lined around the walls and anywhere they'd fit. Even from where we stood, barely two feet through the doorway, I counted twenty, maybe more. All their lids were closed, so I assumed they had occupants. Michael cupped his mouth in shock. Ordinarily, I would've followed suit; this town has immunised me rather quickly to their crazy.

The floors were solid oak; any step echoed. So we had to shuffle slowly, praying none jumped out on us. I could hear wind whistles, and it wasn't coming from behind us; it sounded like a tunnel, how wind bounced off stone walls. Michael noticed as we pushed forward to the left. It felt like a magnet dragging us toward it.

We moved through a doorway into a large lounge area, old furniture covered in white sheets and cobwebs. Surrounded by more coffins, there are so many coffins. What was weird was that we found where the wknd came from; a large wooden hatch in the floor was open, showing stone steps heading down.

My heart sped up with each step. If any vamp woke now, there'd be no storytelling; we'd be fucked. We crept, lucky to be blessed with superhuman sight and infrared. Reaching the bottom, it seemed we'd landed in a cavern, with the wind sounding louder. Wet walls had more coffins; they'd been preparing for a long time, hoping they'd be free one day.

Not that they couldn't now, but something had to be holding them back. We seemed to be walking for ages; it veered left and right, heading away from the house. I thought we were heading toward the cliff base, as with every turn we took, it sloped lower and lower. Hundreds of dirty, drinking coffins guided our path toward doom. Besides that and the fear of getting caught, little else stood out.

The outside was near; the smell of seawater rushed our way. At the end of a slope, we could see slithers of moonlight spraying the mouth of an exit. We reached the opening, breathing a sigh of relief, not that my hackles settled. We were far from in the clear. A look outside was a little disorientating; we'd ended up at neither part of the cliffs I'd already seen.

There was more to the battle for this town than meets the eye. McNally's excavation work may not have been their first dig. This felt strategic; the other tunnel wasn't to free the elder. If that route was potentially lined with a similar number of coffins and Ellena woke the bastard who seems adept at mind control.

They'd swarm this place like flies on shit. We had to be on guard; where we landed was like a kill box, and we were ripe for picking. Lots of rocks, darkness and the tide was coming in, bringing that slimy sea salt. Nothing else seemed in need of our attention.

"Georgie, do you hear that?" Michael surprised me; I hadn't been listening for anything in particular. I saw no point being as the god-forsaken fanged bastards could evade most of our senses. All except smell. No sooner had he said that than my ears pricked up.

'Pppplease, someone help me,' feint, but I knew the voice anywhere.

"Michael, that's bloody Ellena. Where? How? I couldn't see where. We stood on what barely qualified as a shelf of Stoney Beach. And if the tide maks were anything to go by, the ground would be covered at its peak, but not enough to fill the tunnel.

"Thought so too, but I can't see how,"

"Could it be a trick?" the way the night had gone, and the days before, anything was possible.

We were about fifty or so feet away from the entrance. Baffled, I began looking for wires and speakers or CCTV. Yet I wasn't picking up any static or electronic motion.

"Ssssomebody pleaseeee,' whimpered pleas rang out again; this time, I had more of a lock. It echoed as it got louder in distress. Ellena was either in a cave I couldn't see or... Wait...

"Michael, the ground. Search for holes or anything that looks like a false top," The echo made me think that. There was only one entrance to the cliff I could see. The one we came from. These basta ds had been so sneaky so far, and digging re-enforced prisons in the ground wouldn't be beyond them. The trouble was, we couldn't make any noise. One thing was clear: they may be dead but they also had superhuman abilities.

We scoured the rocks and sand, looking for cracks and gaps that could be a false roof, in our case, floor. It didn't make sense; we heard Ellena's voice, but how could it be snatched from our car and then stuffed in a hole at the bottom of a cliff by 'Montague House' the distress in Ellena's voice smacked of someone worn down and scared. Not only ju t dumped in darkness.

"Georgie, over here, quick," Michael was near the middle of the beach shelf by a large rock. I was at least fifty feet away and just about made out a faint line in the ground.

"Can you see a way in?"

"Not yet,"

'Georgie? Is that you Help, I'm down here,' Ellena croaked, sounding dehydrated. My stomach flipped, wondering how limited her oxygen was down there. It had to be, surely?

"Ellena, yes, it's us. Are you okay? Are you hurt?" I shouted, still searching, but nothing but sandy debris. There was a square outline, ten by ten—just a question of how deep.

"I...I think I'm okay," Ellena had emotion gurgling with her words. It was her breathing that bothered me the most. Her heart rate was up, and every time Ellena spoke, her breathing got shallower.

"Hey, lazy bones, all this resting while we work. How long do ya think you've been down there?" A strange question from Michael: Ellena had been with us when we escaped Oxley Town; the little dangle over the cliff's edge didn't seem that long. Then again, everything else becomes relative when your life hangs by a thread.

"I don't know. Feels like forever,"

"What do you remember last?"

"Erm, sleeping, I guess... Yes, that's right, I was asleep in bed,"

Michael and I stopped and looked at each other in shock. That sure as hell was Ellena with us earlier, right? That's what I tried to convey to Michael telepathically. Because I couldn't formulate the words. Had we been blindsided? What made it worse, neither of us picked up on any deception. Was it possible to have a doppelgänger with us for that long or at all?

That's all I kept thinking as I raked my hands through my hair with the bitter breeze reminding me of the death all around. I was stressed out of my box. All too much, one issue after the other, one 'dot' after the other. I felt we'd come to Scotland to die. Now, I'd dragged Michael into our mess and was riddled with guilt. Oh, what I could do for just one normal day.

The hairs on my neck danced with a fear neither of us had experienced before. What were we to believe, say this was Ellena, and she'd been down there at least a day. Did the vamps have her blood already, or were we being distracted and delayed while they prepared for the real Ellena. We had to test her to be sure. Once we had her safe, that is.

"Any luck Michael? We have to be quick. I don't think Ellena has much oxygen left," I winked at Michael, hoping he was on my wavelength. At first, he scowled, then it twigged; he nodded in approval at my slight deception. The plan was to sense the level of panic in her voice, telltale signs all wasn't right.

"What? Really?" El ena exclaimed, adding more doubt in our minds with Michael shaking his head. 'No.' Our Ellena, my Ellena, would've already been panicking about that detail and worked out roughly how long she had left. Although I didn't want to hide our suspicions, the bigger picture was at stake. All Ellena had to do was scream, and we could have hundreds of vamps after us.

"Yeah, you're probably a little disorientated about now. Don't worry; we'll find a way to get you out soon enough; conserve oxygen and keep the noise down," I dropped the last comment in with the next element of my digging to see if Ellena would be surprised by all the vamps.

"Noise? Whys that? How else would I get help without calling? But you're right, I feel weak, and each breath aches my lungs,"

"You're somewhere precarious, and we don't need to raise alarms; otherwise, a tonne of vampires will be on us in no time," Ellena went silent; her heart fluttered, yet breathing seemed steady. Not the response from someone scared. Yeah, it brought me back to thinking about Ellena's liking of the weird. But this feets off.

Every hoot, click or rumble in the trees played my nerves like a violin. There was no way I could see unless access from underground, but surely Ellena, or whoever she was, would be seen already. Michael grimaced as he scuffed his premium Italian leather shoes through the sandy crud, tapping away carefully at the square line. Metal rattled, and Michael was about to give up when his eyebrows bounced to his hairline. Something surprised him, and for once, it was good.

"It's pressure-loaded, matey. The weight keeps it closed but presses it, and it pops up enough to grab the edge,"

These details added more credence to my worry about how organised MacNally and the vampires were. Perhaps Ruth, too. Right now, I barely knew which way was up. It's hard to tell friends from foes. Only that one was more limited than the other.

Michael and I took a corner each and pressed down. The old boy was right; he had to be at some point. We slid our claws into the gap; it was bloody heavy. At least it would've been if we were normal. Making it hard for anyone inside to push out. The lid came up slowly; it must've been barely two feet before I heard my worst fears coming true. Then we realised why a low beep got activated. It was piercing enough for us to hear, not Ellena. It got the attention of others, though, and it scared me senseless. Michael too.

We flipped it up fully. Straight away, I noticed two things. Ellena wasn't the distressed and aged one earlier. Secondly, there is no coconut. It was her signature hair smell; cooped up would trap her scent. I got nothing. Maybe the trick, grimy slime dripping down the black pit walls, had tainted her.

"What the fuck are we going to do? I thought these fuckers were puppets waiting for the master to shove his pointy fingers up their arse? We can't fight our way out?"

"So did I. Wouldn't have thought they'd risk the bigger plan. Maybe there'll only be the expendable set loose. A test maybe,"

"A fucking test? Seriously, if we survive this place. You'll get your passport and fuck off to the Antarctic for a few days. What's the bloody worst that can happen there? A zombie walrus?"

"I thought your ex-wife was in Spain?"

"You know what, she'd fit in well here. Sleep all day, awake at night and will suck on anyone that crosses her path," Michael struggled to hold his laughter back. We both did "We are on about blood still, right?"

"Well, I guess anywhere with a vein, right?"

"You sick bastard. No wonder she dumped your wrinkled ass,"

"I told you to stop looking when I get changed. Now, who's the sick bastard. Seriously though, you got any tricks up your sleeve, Houdini?"

A million-pound question: was there one trick that could be enough to draw any vampires that came away from Michael and Ellena as they escaped. First, we needed a way out; it wasn't the way we came, and I doubted that Michael could jump to the cliff top even with super strength and speed. Although to the East of us, ledges were jutting out from the cliff face that could take them high enough for a final leap to safety.

Don't get me wrong, it was dangerous; there was no guarantee it would work, but with the full moon still bright. I was going to try fully shifting. Embrace everything I'd fought hard to repress. It was our only choice. If they got to me, Michael and Ellena should be free. Michael made a good point; the Antarctic looked more appealing by the second. The only hurdle was that I hated the bloody idea of flying.

"Michael, come here a second," I called him to whisper the plan in case our fears were right. While I heard thirty to forty slow-moving sets of footsteps, sluggish. Perhaps not fully in control, our chances of escape may have increased if that was the speed they stayed at.

"What's up?"

"You got the same feeling, right?"

"Without a doubt, but how and why?"

"I think we're being fucked, and not in a fun way. When we hit the cliff, I think Ellena got snatched but had already been tampered with. Now somebody has her, and we're being pushed here. Coincidence, we stopped by the house? Some kind of twisted game of fate,"

"We're not fans of coincidences, are we, matey? How's your dots lining up?" My 'dots' is a good question I couldn't answer, just as I thought we had a handle on some, especially from the information at Oxley Town. The shit that happened. Now, these curve balls. It still hadn't sunk in that I'd killed someone; no time to.

Yet, with the hours passing and us being led down the blood-covered garden path, it felt like I would have to do it again to survive intact. Maybe more than once. At least the cloud had cleared enough now, ironic as it was. We were glad of the rest bite earlier, but now I needed every ounce of power I could summon.

"They're not; the game changes just as I think I know an angle. This place has more secrets than those crooked politicians we took down last week," those footsteps were like an army marching through the hallowed halls of death. Still slowly, and boy, did they stink.

"Right, come on, your plan. They're coming. All from on exit bit coming all the same,"

I'd been delaying formulating the words; it was a semi-workable idea. But it happened without me having control or trying. What if I couldn't do it? What if I got werewolf stage fright, you know. That I couldn't rise to the occasion, this wasn't the time to be firing blanks. Can you imagine an impotent shapeshifter? I would need to be fired up; that meant digging back into the bad memories I had locked away for such shitty occasions.

I'd been delaying formulating the words; it was a semi-workable idea. But it happened without me having control or trying. What if I couldn't do it? What if I got werewolf stage fright, you know. That I couldn't rise to the occasion, this wasn't the time to be firing blanks. Can you imagine an impotent shapeshifter? I would need to be fired up; that meant digging back into the bad memories I had locked away for such shitty occasions. After another look across the cliffs, the tide was coming in quickly. No cars could be heard, just those footsteps.

"I will need you to get Ellena by your side; use your speed and head East up the cliff face. There are ledges; don't think; just go on instinct and jump. You'll make it," Michael looked at the cliff with a look of 'Oh for Christ's sake', but I trusted he could do it. Whether this was our Ellena or not, we needed safety first.

"What about you? Not going to try to fight the bloodsuckers on your own? That's suicide,"

"Come now, Michael, you and I know I'm too pretty to die yet. But I will be taking them on, sort of. I will try fully shift again,"

"Full werewolf?"

"Yeah"

"Can you do it?"

"I'm pissing in the wind, so I don't know, but it's the best of what we have,"

Michael gave me a look I hadn't seen before, not from him but toward me. Pity,

Michael felt sorry for my situation. At first, I didn't get it. I never do; it's not my nature; it has always been everyone else and then myself last. This time, It hit home that I could be in serious trouble if I couldn't change; this wasn't even the main event building up. We sure could do with another werewolf or two. After those numbers, we saw this part of the cliffs and Montague House; I knew now more than ever we had to locate as many incarcerated werewolves as we could. To help us, it was so fucking wrong for McNally to use them as pets, disposing of bodies.

That one in the cave helped me change; that was the feeling I needed. I had to tap into that moment. How alive my body became. The fire in my veins and how full my fangs and claws were. That's what we needed to get free from this cauldron of death. Still, why put Ellena in the floor?

Michael jumped down twenty feet, doing his obligatory whinging over the dirt and sludge. He surprised me. I had edged forward to go. Michael had the pity party in full swing. He launched Ellena up to me; I caught her around the waist. My foot slipped off the edge slightly, wobbling, but I had enough balance to hoist us backwards. Ellena's blonde hair whipped across my face in the breeze. Nothing. I couldn't even tell if there was any scent at all. That freaked me out.

What came next... I felt the blood drain from my face. As we got steady, I'd perched Ellena fully on her feet. We made eye contact briefly, enough for me to get shocked. My gut twisted in a knot as my testicles jumped up to hide somewhere between my bladder and kidneys. This alternate version of Ellena's face rippled; I'm talking full-on skin shift. As if they had been wearing a glamour. What showed was horrifying, the stuff of fucking nightmares. If it could be described as that. The face was warped. Scarred through burns, and their nose had all but rotted away. It lasted two seconds but confirmed our worst. My mouth hung open, and I quickly changed it to a false smile. I was pretending to be relieved.

Bad enough, we had vampires heading our way; I now couldn't get that skin-crawling image from my mind. Whoever or whatever they were just moved the bar on us again. After all, it's not like we didn't have enough supernatural shit to worry about. What's a disfigured shapeshifter wearing Ellena's face between friends?

"You okay, George?" Ellena's voice broke a scary train of thought. The real Ellena never called me George. Since he'd heard Michael refer to me as Georgie, that's been her 'go-to' way to talk to me. There was another, as if I didn't have enough proof already.

"Yes, my reckless little lamb. This rescuing lark is becoming a habit; I'm beginning to think you enjoy it," Ellena was taken by surprise, all her chemosignals heightened, with a final heavy gulp of saliva priming the last nail in her coffin. Pun intended.

"Well, what's life without a little risk once in a while, although it doesn't make me some lost sheep wandering around aimlessly looking for trouble,"

Down came the hammer, the lid was set, and all we had to do was bury her and her bloodsucking friends. Ellena's tone was abrupt; a deep frown showed she wasn't amused. Nor was I, while I struggled to see the point—more smoke and mirrors than necessary. Michael heard everything, landing with a thud out of the pit. He knew as well as I did; we couldn't show our hands yet.

The first few vamps came into view; we didn't have long. Even if they appeared to walk like Michael after a heavy night on the tiles, these vamps weren't two sheets to the wind; they weren't the usual either. Not that there's been anything usual about this bloody town. This lot stunk far worse than the two I removed hearts from.

"Michael, you ready?"

"As I'll ever be matey. More to the point, are you?"

Michael took hold of Ellena; I looked to the peaceful moon set amongst the purple sky, praying it didn't fail me now. Michael took a large swig of whiskey from his pocket before handing it to me. 'Soften the pain', he said. Not that much could soften the torture of feeling my body torn apart. I guzzled as much as my throat could, bracing myself for the sickly, burning aftertaste. At least this demon was one we liked.

That hoard of undead was closing us down by the second. I thought back to the moment that made me change. The wild aggression I felt from the other werewolf, the adrenaline, primal rage and untameable power.

'Click...Click,' it began; my body was on fire. The world disappeared into darkness as I lost control of myself and what was happening.

'Crack, snap click,' blood scorched my veins, and claws shot forward full, thick and scary. Michael and Ellena stepped back.

I grew with each torturous snapping of bones; strength, power, anger and unparalleled senses evolved by the second. I wanted to scream in agony, but instead, the only noises coming were a mix of a roar and growling. Blood spurted through the air, nearly hitting Michael. The smell drove him crazy, forcing him to shift again. This time, he seemed more controlled. His big claws wrapped around Ellena's waist, tighter than I imagined on the real Ellena. This pretence wasn't easy to keep up with.

The vampires had spread out, moving a little quicker but not much. I couldn't get my head around what was wrong with them. Almost defective, no less dangerous, though. Unless we were being lulled to drop our guard, one detail I didn't have a problem with was that the full moon-induced evolution had me firmly by the balls. Pain so strong I wanted to stop and find another way. Tears rolled down my cheeks, but there was no turning back. Only excruciating torture until, finally, everything went dark.

Consumed by anger and single-minded drive in search of blood, either to taste or to have dripped from my fingers. The wolf in me had taken over, and my human side, however small, was along for the ride. The last normal image I remembered seeing was Michael's face, a blend of shock and smugness. He saw me as a powerful ally. He was right. With that power came confidence; I revelled in it.

Now I knew what made the other side scared. We had to use this. First, a little matter of forty or so mindless zombie vampires. Whether that was a thing, I don't know. Only, they were nightmarish foot soldiers that had to be stopped.
Wind sailed through my fur, yes, fur. Every bristle was alive with electricity. Every stride was quick and powerful, gliding across the grey and yellow sandy-stone beach menacingly.

'Crunching of bone,'

'Dirty blood gushed through the air with another supple, fleshy organ squelched to exploding point,'

Claws swiped across my chest, stinging like a motherfucker. All that did was add to the fire burning within. One by one, I tore through them. This time. Not an ounce of guilt in sight

.

'Crunch, twist, splurt,'

I ripped a vamp's head off before launching it across the beach into the face of another; the impact caused both to gruesomely cave in on each other, with the body thumping against a large rock, spraying blood over its tough surface.
Sand and stone ran a crimson river, littered with the limbs and guts of the dead as I ploughed through death, fuelled with a list that grew with each body. It grew with each dismembered part strewn on the winter's breeze.

I had become an unstoppable savage, laying to waste anything in my path. Michael and Ellena, we're ascending the face of the cliff. With another arm ripped bloodily from its dead socket, I beat the last, expecting another wave. When I realised, Michael had company making ground on him.

The last body dropped, and I was drenched in dirty blood, carrying its vile stink. The stray had gotten within fifteen feet of Michael, and Ellena appeared to be making their climb more awkward than needed by feigning excessive fear of heights. My Ellena didn't have that problem. They'd slowed down far too much; the gap across the beach from me and the foot of the cliff was nearly two hundred feet.

In under ten seconds, I had to make up two hundred and fifteen feet to put myself in the stray vamp path. We got lucky that these were pale limitations of the real things. The why and how could wait. My claws kicked down in the stone, blood grinding for a springboard. I summoned the remaining strength and powered forward in a blur.

I bypassed the first couple of ledges before pouncing awkwardly between the vamp and Michael. My foot slipped, forcing me toward the vamp. Michael seemed galvanised, using the extra seconds to reach the top.

Meanwhile, I teetered on a narrow, chalky surface, rocking in the wind. The vamp blasted through the air; I did likewise. We collided painfully, falling over eighty feet down and crashing hard. Unlike the fall in Oxley, this time, I felt worse off. Both were flat out; I felt broken. With three ribs, my left arm, shoulder and wrist snapped. However, I could feel them already trying to heal. A perk I was grateful for, now more than ever.

Only that was the least of my worries and pain. Searing heat throbbed from my lower abdomen, and suddenly, I felt drained. Borderline fighting the urge to throw up. Out of nowhere, I coughed; I hardly ever do that. The cough turned to splutter, and a puddle of black fluid sprayed the air, landing beside me.

I looked down, barely able to move or lift my head; the vampire's talon-like fingers were impaled knuckles deep above my left oblique and abbs. Fur slowly subsided, and my veins bulged as black lines spread through my body. I had no strength, fight, or will to push on. I was being poisoned, and there was nothing I could do. My head fell limply as my eyelids finally flapped shut. Everything went dark...

Chapter 36

"Get up, you lazy sod. No time for sleeping,"

My eyelids were heavy; I could hear a voice calling to me. This wasn't the first time, and it sure as hell wouldn't be the last. Although it was a bloody habit, I didn't like that much. My body felt busted while I slowly began to remember what had happened. My hand flew to the wound in my lower stomach; the vampire's fingers had been removed, but I was naked—a downside of a full shift. I remembered feeling sick; a black poison had spread through my veins, and I passed out.

I pulled my arm before my face, checking that all was normal. My vision was still a little blurry, but clear enough to be sure there were no visible signs of whatever toxin the vamp released. Painfully pointy stones dug into my back; I was still where I'd landed. Only a pile of fresh clothes lay beside. I was about to breathe a slight sigh of relief when the real panic struck. If Michael was back with me, bearing gifts and all, where on earth was fake Ellena?

"Is everyone alright?" my throat ached, and I could barely speak. The inner had also started as I relived every punch, rip and shred of flesh—time to beat myself up again. Even if necessary, I wasn't a violent man by nature. Yet, since being in Scotland, I've thrown more punches in a few days than my entire life. And the tally wasn't complete.

"Are you fucking crazy? You've just obliterated over forty vampires, stopped us from becoming the next danger delicacy and then fell practically a hundred feet, Being penetrated by the last of those bloodsuckers. How was that, by the way? It looked like you accommodated well. Oh, and when you're ready, get some bloody clothes on,"

"Piss off, you sick fuck; how can you be so goddam cheery after what you saw?"

Michael was his usual 'sick-minded' self. While I feared how he'd be after seeing me change to a full werewolf and then go on a blood-filled rampage. I bet it looked grim. I'm unsure how my constitution would hold out if the roles were reversed. I know that in the heat of the moment, I was euphoric—a feeling I didn't want to get used to. Otherwise, I'd be no better than the murderers we hunt.

"Matey, it was flipping awesome. Fleas aside, of course. But seriously, if that's what happened when you got shot, it's amazing, and we need all the power we can get right now. Oh, FYI, my abilities felt ramped up when you were like that. I mean, it really ramped, far more than ever. Princess struggled with the heights which hindered our progress," I sat up, peering around, first the blood bath, scattered limbs and then the cave entrance before seeking out fake Ellena.

"Talk of the devil, where is she?" we had to keep her on a leash until we reached the bottom of it all; finding 'little lamb' was our next priority. Even if it meant a lack of sleep, it was already 2 a.m. from what I'd seen, sunrises around 6-6.30 a.m. with skies getting lighter before then. Details that mattered because the later it got, the lighter it got, and the moon would slowly slip away. Reducing our strength slightly. And if we were still on the go, you could bet a bloody year of my salary that McNally's clan were also.

"I locked her in the car, played it cool for her safety. We need to find our girl fast. If the whole blood thing is true. It could already be too late," Michael was right, but it would be like looking for a needle in a giant haystack.

Although the prominent places could be worked through quickly enough, the quarry and other similar rat holes worried me the most. I was busy reminiscing about Ellena's smooth, pale skin, her warming smile and the scent of coconut from her malicious blonde locks. When that image popped into my head. To think I nearly forgot it. Truly horrifying.

"We need to be careful; I caught a glimpse of what lies below her facade, and it bloody scares me—burns, disfigurement and then some. I couldn't even guess whether it was a man or a woman. Whatever this imposter is, they're wearing Ellena's face for a reason. Even to do that would take a lot of power. Surely?"

I didn't know what I was talking about; it was the details. Ruth mentioned the nemeton and its natural power. If someone could call on that and had the know-how. Anything may be possible.

Being the over-thinker, after recalling that, I finally connected some 'dots' until proven otherwise. Michael was busy digesting what I'd said as he fished a crumpled cigarette box from his pocket. The last one, and it barely classes as a whole. I stared at Michael's tired face, looking through him more than anything; the only person capable, seemingly conniving enough, had to be Ruth.

The bitch had quietly manoeuvred her chess pieces to suit her narrative. Ruth needed access to the caves and the nemeton. I couldn't believe I was thinking it, but her goal wasn't some dream of bringing back a lost love. Ruth wanted the ability to look normal, to be whoever or whatever he-she had been before and anything she fancied. Perhaps her plan was far greater than I surmised as Michael joisted me off the floor. It seemed a safe leap to make. The trouble was that we didn't know what Ruth was capable of.

"So we chain the wench up until we're done? Or find some leverage to make Ruth spill her guts," Ruth would be too smart to leave anything to chance. We had to be smarter and think outside the box.

"Speaking of guts, how did you get rid of the poison?" I said, finally almost fully dressed again.

"Our princess had made a load of tricks already. Ground mistletoe, a little wolfsbane and some secret ingredient from what I gather. Worked a treat. Seriously though, what next?"

"Well, we're already in hell; may as well keep going. We're going to head to the pier and check around there for Ellena; while there, I may or may not steal a boat. There's something the water I'm supposed to find that could help us. I'm sure of it. The grid points mark a spot in the sea; may as well find out,"

Feeling more normal, we began climbing the white, chalky face; I moved gingerly. The broken bones had healed, but the vampire clawing to the gut took longer. Everything we'd done so far was chase shadows. We eventually neared the top, and for once, I was the one breathing heavier. A temporary feeling, I told myself while hoping there would be no lingering side effects from the 'battle of blood bay' part two. Or a prequel to a massacre. It's said the second is always worse than the first. In this case, it could mean far greater bloodshed.

What we walked past, through Montague and the grim, leaky tunnels, were pale imitations of the real thing. Credit where credit's due; those fucker were dedicated to the cause. I suspected that was Amos's doing. So far, it's seemed like I'm being tested, as they loomed for weaknesses. This time, making some cannon fodder to keep our limited numbers busy before the main course. One extra large serving of rotten meat dished up with a side of fangs and an Elder to wash it down. None of which appealed; after being up that close, I'm scarred for life. They fucking stunk. No amount of 'Hugo Boss' aftershave would paper over those rancid cracks.

Our hands grabbed at the top; I was still a little and relied on my claws to dig into the ground for grip. Michael hoisted himself up and over with ease and a lack of wounds. My stomach kissed the rubble briefly as I inhaled a grit dust plume, allowing exhausted saliva to drop free. If only the day and I could be done with each other.

"Come, old boy, get to your feet; we still got shit to wade through," Michael grabbed my arm, dragging my tired arse upright. He was right. First, we'd been treading water, but now we were treading tonnes of horse shit with no real idea what the next move would be.

We needed to locate the real Ellena without tipping off the imposter. Easier said than done. Her charade may have fooled anyone else, but we knew Ellena and this bloody well weren't her. I was bothered by the recent vision enough to feel its meaning could push my need for a swim to the top of our to-do list. And before another wave of vampires got sent our way. Up close and personal with 'fanged beef jerky' has its limits. Their blood was still engrained in the grooves of my skin and now smeared by dirt.

Michael was already steps ahead, looking around, being his usual twitchy, curious self. I dusted down, stretching the strange feeling of going from human to wolf and then human again out of my system. Surreal, just how much my body morphed. I only hoped the pain would ease up in time. Until then, paracetamol and whiskey both of which were in short supply.

Ellena, the imposter, stared at us through the car window with the moon's reflection shading her face perfectly. All I did was lock eyes, and every hair on my neck bounced to attention. She looked far too smug and at ease, considering where we'd rescued her from. The alarm bells were ringing loud and clear. Our Ellena would never. Ellena would never have allowed Michael to leave her locked up. That cocky purse-lips look of fake Ellena, adding to the eerie static through my hair, I sensed something amiss other than her. But what?

Michael hadn't been paying attention to the 'dots' not enough anyway. I questioned whether Michael purposely wanted to remain oblivious or just had about the bullshit. He may put on a front, but Michael's tolerance for being given the run around was lower than a whores g-string on a Friday night. Non-existent. Dusted down, I moved to catch up to Michael, who was already a few feet ahead, when I heard a strange noise. Faint, more strange because everything else had gone quiet. Or has it been that way, and I hadn't realised. Too eerily dead, until..,

'Tick...tick...tick...tick,'

That is what I heard. It couldn't be the last bone fragments setting back in place or a small clock. Michael didn't seem fazed at all. Maybe I shouldn't have been, but I was. My foot shuffled forward tentatively while I looked every possible way, seeing nothing except Ellena, who, out of nowhere, stretched a huge grin upon her face. I stopped in my tracks, thinking, 'The nerve of that bitch', trying to understand what has her so buoyant. I went to move...

'Boooooom, Boooooom,'

Two earth-shattering explosions tore into the night sky as a giant, swirling roar of yellow fire filled the air. It shattered free, tearing apart the steel chassis of Michael's car. It snapped, bent and rippled under immense power. I saw a ball of yellow swell torturously from inside to out, engulfing anything in its path, shredding through the skin and bone of fake Ellena, all in slow motion as the shockwave rocked Michael and me off our feet, sending us high through the smoke-filled air.

Michael, being closer, took a harder hit. He shot past me as we spewed across the travelled surface in a painful heap. I could barely move. Feeling broken had become a way of life lately. This was no exception, with my skin turned a shade of amber, stroked by the fire's overwhelming warmth. I smelt scorched flesh, bubbling and cooking under immense heat. Followed by the scent of something different. Something similar to clay.

I rolled onto my side, unable to turn my neck properly, but I needed to move around. The expectation of company very soon meant we had to regroup and get a believable story together. I oozed blood from slices and scrapes while my ribs still felt the blast. I'd rolled over most of the way and nearly laid on my front.

"Help. Help," Michael croaked, faint and distressed. I forced my painful neck up to look behind. All I saw were fingers. They dug deep into the stone, 'shifting' before my eyes. Michael had been propelled toward and over the edge of the cliff. Michael hung on for dear life.

Every move I attempted was a pain-riddled struggle, but I had to. With the last ounce of energy left in storage, I summoned enough to 'shift' and enough to throw myself forward with all the grace of a dying elephant. Reaching the edge just as Michaels's claws tore free from the chalky edge. His hands were outstretched, reaching in vain as he was about to fall to a probable death. My claws clamped into Michael's wrists, and blood spurted up my fingers, but I caught Michael in time. All twelve stones of him dangled in the air; my body was half over, too. Michael may have been saved, but my body began slipping across the loose gravel. We didn't have long.

Chapter 37

'8th November 3 am'

My fingers slid back a little; dripping blood made my grip loosen. I could only hold onto Michael for another thirty seconds or so. Stone cut into my stomach, and we'd landed too far from a bloody ledge. We were short on hope and options while the fire raged behind us. The only move I had left wasn't even guaranteed to work. Clamping into Michael's flesh harder than ever, I clenched before slowly swaying my arms from side to side, gradually
building momentum.

Michael was a helpless kite dancing in the wind, and we needed enough sway to make Michael fly, hopefully landing on the cliff top. Every yank left and right was excruciating, even more so for Michael; he roared with anger each time. Anger was exactly what we needed from both of us. Maybe it would be enough for a final push.

"Michael, I need you to use all of that when the time comes," I said, not being very clear. It was hard to do when I could feel myself inching forward. There was no guarantee both of us would make it. Any momentum from me throwing Michael up could send me down.

"Whatever y...y...you're planning Georgie, you better bloody hurry up,"

"What's the matter? Not having fun hanging around?"

"If you find this fun, you must get laid seriously. Will be having serious words with Ellena when we find her,"

With each swing gained, two more would do it. Right on queue...Sirens, followed by a sea of blue and red lights. It is a rare sighting in the wild of Scotland. Police. Only these wouldn't be any help.

"Get ready, Michael, they're playing our song,"

"What's that? The death March?"

Michael slipped from my grasp a little more, his bloody flesh slooshed through my claws. Now or never. The final swing from right to left had Michael flailing his legs above my head.

"Now, Michael, anger, use it to reach the ledge,"

As Michael reached high enough, I let go. My claws ripped free, sending a spray of blood across my chin while I prayed to god this would work. Michael's arms and legs rode an invisible bicycle; he roared, using everything he had to fight toward the surface. Michael landed hard; I got distracted, losing my upper-body balance to slide forward dangerously over the edge. My right arm clapped against the cliff face, and my left dug in hard. I had neither the strength nor the energy.

I was in free fall, looking down at the death-bringing rocks. You know that phrase people say in situations like this, 'Life flashed before my eyes,' I didn't get any of that as I lurched forward. Disappointing. If I was going to die, at least it could've been seeing something different. Then I felt a dog bite down hard on my leg. It fucking killed me; at least I could have sympathy for postmen now.

I was dragged back up the cliff until I was finally dumped on the floor. My face was buried in stone and dust, blissfully thanking my lucky stars and breathing like a forty-a-day smoker. The pain from the teeth exiting my flesh was far worse than the initial bit. Slower was trying to be careful, but little did they know that their large fangs had already crunched through bone and my calve muscle.

I finally looked around to see Michael half-shifted, dragging his 'bloodied' snout away as he morphed back into a human chambering to his feet on a background of rotating flames. In a minute, we'd somehow saved each other from a tragic ordeal. My leg was already healing, and by the look of it, so were Michael's wrists. Only when we were both upright, facing the flames, did it sink in what had happened.

Ellena or otherwise was blown up in Michael's car: no accident or mistake. Between me mauling vampires and Michael putting fake Ellena to safety, a bomb had been attached to his pride and joy. He bloody loved that thing more than the ex-wife. This would account for her being the 'ex' but as if we hadn't been through enough tonight. My 'dots' were all fucked up; I couldn't see what went where anymore. Just as I thought I had a grasp on the 'Ruth' part, boom, the explosion. Now, we had four police cars throttling our way.

We were frantically looking around us for answers; strangely, most of the resident's house lights had stayed off as if they knew better than you go crawling the streets at night. For something so loud and bright, the only attention we had was from the boys in blue. No other cars, not yet. The closer they drew, my hair rumbled again, so many times over the last few cases. But this, anywhere else, we'd be safe knowing we didn't do it and had to look for the real suspects. Yet, here, I knew the police were coming with one intention: us. Detain, kill, feed us to the vamps; it felt like Russian roulette, only each bullet was loaded with something that screwed us over.

"Cheers for that, Michael,"

"Just returning the favour. Besides, you're the only one with a working car now. So, what's our move?" Michael glared at me, eyes bright yellow. The veins in his arms were bulging. Michael sensed the trouble, too, and we weren't done for the night—only about how much more blood needed to be shed.

Oh, what I would give to be back in Mile End London knocking back a cold pint or two, present company included, of course. Instead, we may have to kiss arse. Unfortunately, I wasn't in the mood to pucker up. We'd been shot, dangled over a cliff twice, kidnapped and in a fight at least twice now. A car blew up, and I was sure I'd missed some. Not bad for a few days away. Heaven help us if we have a whole week or more. I was feeding off Michael's adrenaline-pumped point of shifting.

He was recharging me. I didn't know that was possible, but I could feel my strength restored slowly. The strength we may need. What was the point of the bomb, though? To make us think Ellena was dead? Or to frame us for it? If that was the case, it didn't seem from the vampire's playbook. This was another player. Fake Ellena looked comfortable and smiled so devilishly that she knew. Who or what was that wearing Ellena's face, though?

"Move? At the minute, I'm thinking on my feet. We know we can't trust these, and don't you think it's funny nobody else has come out to see? In London, it would be like a street party," the more I thought about it, looking at the lights, to the fire and back. It felt more like a showdown.

That would explain the hackles. Moreover, I feared they'd exit their vehicles armed to the teeth.

No ordinary ammunition either. No, these bastards would no doubt be up to date with current affairs and that they had two shapeshifters roaming free, terrorising their town. Each car flew through the dirt, spraying it skywards, all movie-like. The skidded to a stop in a semi-circle around us before slowly pressing us back toward the edge.

"So, this little re-visit of the cliff's edge, all part of your thinking? Or is there something else for a rainy day? Because I don't fancy doing all of that again, not so soon. Fuck that; not bloody ever again. Next time you come out with a parachute and deal with the cliffs nonsense yourself," Michael half grimaced, half-smiled. But he wasn't hiding what he was. In light of everything, he didn't care. Who could blame him?

"Less of it, old man; we are in the same sinking boat, remember? It was no picnic for me, either. I reckon they'll be armed, too. If the need comes, charge towards as fast as you can but zig-zag so they can't aim properly. Leap the cars and head to mine, okay?" right on queue, I heard a rifle chamber inside a vehicle, and the rest followed.

"I take it they're not here to take our details so we can file an insurance report? Or even look at the burning body?"

Michael was right; not one branched off to the crime scene. At least it would've been back home. The point is they knew who and where to surround. Response time was pretty good, too, now I think about it. Too quick not to be lying in wait. If we could still see the silhouette of a burned body through the flames, then in all of twenty seconds standing outside their cars, one of them would notice or smell the charred flesh. Unless told not to look for it. I was speculating when nothing made sense; there had to be an end game to this misdirection. We weren't going to find out just yet. This potential firing squad was about surviving. Michael could cry about his 'baby' later.

"Considering they all got rifles that just chambered up. I have a sneaky suspicion they're on the insurance company's side. If we navigate this, we head to the pier, right? The sooner I know what's down there, the better. They want Ellena alive, and this decoy was to throw us off somehow. So Ellena is still of use, and that gives us time,"

My brain fired a hundred miles per hour, analysing our problems, the situation, and the exit strategy. Mostly winging it, surprisingly, what I'd said made sense. They needed Ellena and blew fake one up before disposing of us one way or another. Pale imitation vamps didn't work; why not guns? Always the fucking guns.

Again, we had to bring claws to a gunfight. The last didn't end so well for my emotional well-being. If we did survive, we would need plenty of therapy; I thought as I braced for the crap to come. Soothing music, a leather couch, the whole nine yards.

"Eight of them, two of us. What's not to like? Aside from a torrent of bullets or plummet off the cliff. Maybe the vampires would let us join the dark side after. I reckon I could manage constant nights and a liquid diet," Michael chuckled slightly; he always had a way of injecting humour when we needed it.

"Not all vamps hate sunlight; it is somewhat of a myth. Most look like death but can function in society to a point. At least according to what we've been told. Which could be bullshit. What I will say is they do smell better than you, so that's a win,"

"I have you know these boxers were fresh on... One day last week, not sure which. Seriously though, that zig-zag lark sounds like hard work. We could stand and fight?"

The car fire raged on, painting the purple-black skies full of stars. My lungs were already full of the fumes and the deathly stench. Aside from the different tinge I smelt earlier, it's hard to mistake. Pops and crackles rang out with regularity. Not once were we at ease. Even as expected, they still had us jumping like the woman's husband had just got home and was about to catch us cheating with his wife. That's how skittish we were. Yet, neither police car retreated for safety. With the noise so loud, I was banking on at least one.

The cars torched on the shoddy estates in London would have the kids scattering like cockroaches when they went off. Not these bastards, though. They had a dodgy reputation to live up to. It shows corruption spreads like cancer no matter the 'force' if only there were a way to cut it out. For this place, that may only happen in death—hopefully, theirs and not ours.

I watched each front passenger door open in unison, too dark to distinguish features, something they would be happy about. I glanced at Michael, arms hung wide with claws on show. He was ready while I was busy seeking chinks in our latest obstacle, so it didn't necessarily end in more bloodshed. Unfortunately, all four police officers stood, shielded by their doors and rifles perched on top. Bloodshed was exactly what they wanted.

"We could stand and fight, sure. They know what we are, so what do you think is in their bullets? All it would take is a stray, and either of us would be hitting the deck like a sack of shit," I said, trying to appease my conscience more than Michael.

Their cars continued to roll slowly, narrowing the space with headlights on full beam, impairing our line of sight. Our heels kicked stones and dirt with each shuffle, nearing the edge. We were running out of time to do something.

'Time for a wee jump, or we'll blast ya over. Up to you,'

I jumped out of my skin. One of the drivers used their loud hailer to confirm my fears and scare me senselessly. So wrapped up in the eerie silence and my thoughts, I was surprised. On the other hand, Michael had slipped deeper into his focus, eyes brighter and fangs pronounced. Dejavu of Oxly town earlier.

With a quick look at the stars, I saw why the moon was overhead and beaming down on us. Without realising, my claws were thicker too. In the moments we spent being herded to our doom, those dodgy fuckers had allowed us to recharge even more. Not quite firing on all cylinders, but it would be enough for us to leave another trail of carnage in our wake.

'Claaaap,'

We darted to the left as one of the officers fired a warning shot, sending it smashing through the gravel between us. The clap echoed through the darkness, yet no one dared open the front door.

'Tik Tok - we dinnae need outsiders interfering with business that doesn't concern them. I estimate it's ten feet to freedom, and your problems will disappear. All you have to do is jump,' the officer said again. He wasn't wrong; barely ten or so feet. Each car had at least five five-foot gap between them, and that was it. We were being squeezed.

"Or we could have a civil conversation over a beer or two?"

'Claaap'

Another shot boomed out after Michael made a tongue-in-cheek comment. This time, to our left. Sending dust in the air. My eyes glowed brightly; I ground my feet in the dirt, building momentum with a slight bounce as I prepared to go for it. If we aimed between the lights, our speed would have us blur through the shadows enough to throw their aim off and buy time before vaulting over the bonnet. I gave Michael a hand signal and whispered, 'Between the lights and over. Fast,' he nodded.

"One...Two...Thr-"

I'd begun a countdown to going on three when a rapid series of loud honks on a car horn stopped me dead. First, we saw another set of headlights moving quickly in the distance. Real quick and racing toward us. Its engine was familiar, the one I had a conversation about recently. It wailed with all its might; the driver abused the automatic gearbox as it struggled to keep up with the throttling. The honking, though, was for attention, if we were lucky, and my thought was right a distraction. Two officers remained fixed on us while the other two focused on the stretched beast flying toward us.

I could hear every suspension bounce, brake squeal, and squelch of rubber on the tarmac before it tore across gravel, veering around the cliff line. The police were rattled. Hands began to shake, pulses quickened, and their hearts pounded. They'd had the upper hand until an unknown element entered the game. Boy, was I glad. Michael relaxed as we shuffled forward, regaining space from the edge.

"Relax, it's the fucking mayor,"

"The what now?"

"Mayor, Duncan Campbell. I don't know how, but the timing couldn't be better,"

"Is he a good guy then?"

"To be honest, the jury is still out on that one. Mostly, he seems to want good things for this place. Although he does want control of 'hell house', not sure that would be the same if he saw what we had," Michael's wrinkles flapped upwards, creating a look of surprise—that or constipation. I never could tell with him sometimes.

The Mayor's limousine burst through the shadows past the fire. Still, no gossip seekers dared open their doors as the long metal beast skidded through the dirt. It was putting itself between the fire and the police. Its headlights blazed a grit-smoked path, covering the two with guns to our left. A to yes window rolled down slowly.

"Officers, you stand down right now," Mayor Duncan Campbell's voice hollered through the opening.

Michael and I had moved closer; the two facing away suddenly seemed less up for it. Hands shook, rifles rattled, and their arseholes seemed primed to fall out. Their heart pounded so loud I was surprised neighbours hadn't finally entered the fray. The tow-facing though had 'hair trigger' syndrome, and we were in the cross hairs.

On the balance of things, though, our survival odds had increased. Not much, but we were creeping forward. When fired, their rifles seemed to carry a little 'kick'. Squeezing the distance not only made their shots harder. Any miss would allow us to tear up close, and if blood got spilt...Let's say my hands were still drying.

While I stared down at the one on the left, six-two, broad, with a thick beard, not bothered by his uniform appearance in the slightest, kinda summed up this place, honestly. He had the rifle at my face, steadfast and angry. I could hear the low grinding of teeth while adrenaline surged past the scotch through his veins.

Now and then, the moonlight flickered a line down his face and gun muzzle, causing a little glint. I could've held back, but in the heat of this weird standoff, I didn't care. Besides, a little intimidation could go a long way, right? If I was about to be shot in the face, it might as well be my true face. Not so long ago, the only reveal I needed to worry about was underneath a five O'clock shadow.

My eyes glowed with one fang after the other, slithering out as my face morphed. Less inhibited this time if we're going to die. It may as well be, 'fuck what everyone else thinks, me,' Michael seemed likewise.

"I suggest you listen to the Mayor. After all, do you want to get blood over that little uniform of yours? ... And in case you're wondering... Most definitely yours,"

"Come on, boys, why fuck up your night by bothering with us. Or should I say morning? Either way, let's not start something you can't finish,"

Our weird situation fell silent; everyone's heart rates were through the roof. While I was busy being tortured by my conscience and a whirlwind of emotions, I didn't know how to handle it. Michael and I had to focus on the 'now' so we didn't get 'blown away', and Michael probably would've turned that into an innuendo. My heart, though, ached to find Ellena one way or another. I only hoped she was still alive.

Conversely, the Mayor was another puzzle that didn't fit into this dark and masochistic equation. Yeah, he wanted the house, picket fence, the whole morbid none yards. Doesn't explain the sudden riding-in on a white horse moment. How did he even know to come? A question that needed answering if, by some luck, we escaped. Again. That seemed all we have been doing lately, escaping life-or-death situations. In some cases, 'Death or Death.'

A chill crept up to my shoulders in the silence and rippled across. The feeling that came with it was hard to describe. Other than it was as if all the happiness in the world had been ripped away, leaving behind skin-crawling fear. My hackles were a bed of nails, and Michael's eyes were so bright. Life could be about to go from bad to worse. We needed an 'out'.

A sheet of cold wind whipped past our backs first, dashing to the trees and shaking the branches for all they were worth. If I didn't have the benefit of enhanced vision with infrared, I would've said an invisible beast was using them as toys. With the flames still rippling the air, it cast dancing patterns across the limo, adding to the unshakeable eerie feeling in the pit of my stomach. Then came the sudden, loud and blood-curdling snapping of bones.

Chapter 38

At first, I couldn't see where the horrific noise came from. Then, necks slowly twisted, causing flesh ripples, stretching and warping like rubber. Bloody awful and left me unable to stop a little sick flying into my mouth; ironic that something this strange should freak me out, considering I had fangs and claws. But this looked out of a horror movie.

The party tricks didn't stop there; each officer turned a rifle on the other. Their creepy heads, a mottled white, bounced and sprung on twisted necks. Michael and I stood, staring, mortified. All the while, I hadn't felt fear like it ever before.

"Wise words from someone who barely knows what he is, let alone use such a gift. You say start something that cannot be finished. What if I told you it was already over?"

Each creepy, contorted officer spoke as one. A menacing curdle to a voice that told me who was in the driving seat. The elder vampire had taken control. Deep down, he'd been in control for a while already. The fucker chose his opportune moment to take centre stage. Yet, it was what he said rather than the how. Was it already over? After all, we had no idea where Ellena was or how long ago the switch happened. The Elder had flexed his power to control people again, making me wonder why he had taken so long to be on the cusp of freedom.

The latest example was only seen because he wanted us to see it. Everything had been. The zombie vamps, finding fake Ellena and the explosion and now, us at gunpoint. All to show one hand while the other weaved plans. We had to endure the pantomime so we could use Duncan's hospitality and get a fucking move on.

"Hey, Creepshow. I don't do 'What ifs' but rather the 'what is', and this is you using theatrics to bully and hide behind walls of people because you're scared. You're scared to go fangs to fangs,"

I had to call his bluff, tired of the shows and having guns at our faces. We've been limping around with blinkers on. Michael gave me the death stare for being so bolshy. I was waiting for a slip-up, hoping we'd finally be able to connect a 'dot' and find Ellena. The fire kept kicking up the stink of burnt flesh and death, aggravating me because I missed it. We didn't see the strings moving us like puppets.

"Insolent child in such a rush to die. It would be best to cut your losses and go about your life. Anna was but one woman in an ocean, with plenty more waiting. Now you wish to become a path of bones upon which your kin shall walk, trapped to serve at my 'heel' like all lowly beasts should. Your kind was never 'Apex Predators.' You aren't even the alpha in your pack. You never will be. My kind is destined to rule, and there's nothing you or anyone can do. This battle was lost before it even began,"

The old bastard's words cut deep for someone living in a box. Was he right, though? The battle was already over. That would mean they had Ellena, and the vampires wanted to rule, not just a small town in Scotland either. Looking at what he was able to do, the four police officers without being present. What else could he do? And was there any hope of stopping him?

"You see, that's where bloodfuckers, I mean suckers, have it wrong. We're just in a hurry to make sure you can't drag your beef jerky ass out of your shoe box. I couldn't care less about all the Apex bullshit; it's our job to catch murderers. Coming here was meant to be a break. It seems trouble follows. To me, you're just another type of killer. As for 'Anna', you old fuck, must be going senile; that one is long gone, and it's not polite treading on another man's toes. How about you tell us where she is, and we'll swoop to pick her up? No taxi is needed,"

I tried hiding behind the bravado, even though deep down, I was scared. I couldn't let the vampire know that. We were in a supernatural pissing contest, and I was trying not to do it in my pants. Michael couldn't help a smile as I'd taken a leaf out of his playbook—trash talk to throw them off. Only, I didn't get a response, not straight away. The heads drifted forward a little, hovering under the moonlight.

Their eyes were a ghostly white.

Each one brought their rifle to aim the barrel under their chin—a threat to make them take their own lives. Little consequence to us as they're crooked as anything, but to the town this small, they were more than likely the extent of its force—a detail they'd notice.

Distracted and almost in awe of how this scenario unfolded, I nearly missed the next frightening trick.

'Crack,'

'Pop,'

'Scrrrrttttt,'

'Snap,'

First came the arm, still fully engulfed in flames as chargrilled flesh and brittle bone pried itself from below the window line. Fake Ellena was still alive but shouldn't be or couldn't be. Michael and I had our attention dragged from the puppet police in disbelief. This thing that wore Ellena's face was burnt to a crisp and still lived. What I saw underneath was nightmarish enough, let alone now. Both arms gripped the door and were pulling its burnt shell through the opening, letting loose a screeching groan that sent goose pimples across my arms, another step for us in the world of the scary unknown.

Michael shuffled back and sideways like a chess move to my shoulder with a look of 'what the fuck is happening' I had no idea. The vampire was busy with its hand up the police officers' backsides to bend them to its will. Bringing a burnt corpse back only had me flashing back to the basement in Bow and being pulled free on the brink of death.

This was the parallel I was drawing in a moment that had me wide-eyed and off guard. It took a nudge from Michael to get me back on track. I had to wonder if they were like me more than we thought. Disfigured underneath, but who were they before?

"You like you've seen a ghost," said Michael, wanting me back on task.

"Not recently, no. But that thing, it's alive and burnt, how? Are they?-"

"-let me stop you there. No, nothing alike. Don't be fooled; we both know there's probably a pointy-toothed bastard pulling the strings,"

I couldn't see it; that would require a lot of power to control everything. If the Elder was still trapped, I couldn't imagine them fully fighting fit. So this had to be something else.

"Oh, before you ask, that's not mine," the officers echoed before laughing wrapped in a haunting octave.

At least he put that detail to bed. The burning crustation was now fully out and upright, staggering toward us. Strips of torched skin gristle dropped free with each step, still lit like a Roman candle. The horror behind this ran my blood cold. Far more than the threat of suicidal police officers. My hackles didn't know what to react to the most.

"there was me thinking it was a disgruntled Ex of yours. It must've been bad for you to hide from her in a coffin behind a curse. Wouldn't an injunction have been easier?" I goaded, trying to buy some room for thought.

"Your humour only hides how weak you are. Soon, you'll be on bended knee begging for mercy," I looked to the limo, then to the officers before the walking corpse, working out the space we had to play with. While the Elder continued its bold claims, I had no intention of begging for anything, and Michael looked primed to rip a head off.

"What's the fucking plan, Georgie? I'm all for pissing off these bastards, but we need to prevent a shoot-out, bypass crispy fried chicken there and get in that limo. All without a bloody cigarette, I might add,"

Michael looked worried, a permanent state at the minute. I went to answer when all the rifles chambered up, and one swung free to point at us. Only it kept going side to side—a fifty-fifty choice. We could use our speed to rip the guns away, but even with the 'Michael-Full moon' boost, I was still tapping on the red with little in the tank. Moreover, our emergency supplies had gone up in flames with the car.

All the windows on the limo were dark so I couldn't see the driver or much else, just an outline, but its engine began revving, causing the chassis to bounce forward, trying to create a distraction.

"Yeah, Georgie, what's the plan?" Mocked the four gunmen. Hearing them speak simultaneously was something I couldn't get used to. Although perhaps that could be the vampire's career change. Be a ventriloquist. One soulless dummy controlling another. Yet, both versions of the question had the same blank expression as k looked around in vain.

The chargrilled chicken staggered between two police cars, part of its body stuck to their chasis with small flames in the paintwork. It was fucking gross.

"I could ask you the same: where the hell is Ellena?"

"Oooh, come now, acting all fired up, don't suit you. Don't worry; she's safe...for now...once it's over, Anna will be on cloud 9. And in 24 hours, for you, it will be inconsequential,"

In 24 hours? What could be happening, the next full moon wasn't for another week, and the blood moon had not long passed. And the fanged fucker continued to call Ellena Anna.

"If you're so smart and confident hiding behind puppets, why don't you spill your guts... Or sawdust, whatever's inside now. Either way, you cocky sycophant, do tell,"

I grabbed Michael's arm, edging us backwards and right because that other thing was relentless in its approach, and we were torn between two threats, if they could be called that. The screeching was like Velcro ripped down my spine; I looked behind the cliffs, and for a minute, I was tempted to drag us back down to hell.

"Anna will finally be my queen once the moon meets the sun, and the streets will run red. It will be glorious. I'm keeping you alive long enough to watch Anna by my side as we make all Bow before us,"

It sounded like the Elder was describing a lunar eclipse or similar. I'd barely grasped our full moon cycles, let alone these other things. A situation like that had to be rare, but why that particular phase? We were so underprepared for this battle, and I was sick to my fangs of 'Jerky' calling Ellena Anna. Like hell, was he gonna be walking arm-in-arm with her. Talking as if we were in 'end of days' territory, the shrivelled old bastard couldn't get himself out of bed without help.

"Well, I'm gonna have to pass, and a side note, I'm looking forward to crushing your fragile bony ass,"

I must've struck a nerve; all four guns were back on us, and we ran for the nearest gap away from the corpse. All four let rip, first blazed across my front, clipping a car bonnet. We leapt backwards, landing in a heap as bullets wrapped the stones around us. The officers quickly reloaded; just the burning body stepped in front screaming, pounding our eardrums.

We'd just got to our feet to go again when something crazy happened. Well, on the scale of weirdness that's happened so far. This was Oxly Town again—the wall-splattering kind.

'Walking burnt dead' raised a fried chicken arm in time as bullets flew through the air. They were stopped dead. They were hitting an invisible wall. Another flick and all four exploded, spraying blood everywhere with showers of skin, guts and limbs raining down on us. We were drenched in the stuff, my face dripped red, and I cleared my eyes in time to see the flame-grilled saviour melt away. Dropping in a pile of slop.

We stared in confusion, wrapped in a disbelief blanket.

Surrounded by blood and the pile in front was fucking clay. One big puddle of clay. And it was still burning. This was a 'Twilight Zone' moment. One I had no words for, Michael even less as he shook the empty whiskey bottle in his mouth, hoping there was one more miracle for the night.

Chapter 39

Something was mesmerising about the clay puddle, smoking with a little blood flowing toward it and a stray hand lying at the edge. My head had trouble understanding how it could end that way on so many sickening levels. Michael paced back and forth through the stones attempting to skip around the blood and body parts. Until he finally gave up.

His Italian leather shoes bit the dust; hands raked through his hair, greyer by the day because all our rubbish had him stressed out of his mind. So deep in individual hells, we'd forgotten the patient limo. I crouched beside the puddle, feeling a peculiar sensation. Hard to say what or why but even in this sludgy state, I felt power or similar. Whatever it was, the vibe was off. Then I put two and two together. - A fucking golem. Another one.

"Michael, come here and breathe it in,"

"Piss off, no offence, but the only wet thing I want to sniff isn't on the menu here," Michael relaxed a moment, walking towards regardless. He was like that, though, on the one hand complaining; on the other, he'd still do it.

"If you can get your head out of the gutter for one minute and use your deeper senses. I want you to close your eyes, inhale deeply and visualise what you think it is, ok?" Michael crouched beside me, giving me daggers, but I knew he'd get it soon enough.

"Fuck... That's mud. I mean clay but also human; I can almost sense traces of its essence. It's thoughts,"

"Exactly, like a remnant, right? And yes, clay. Come on, maths time, what's two plus two?"

"Well, I would say an exciting foursome, but this sounds how you described that golem thing. How though? Shit, the mud in the car?"

Michael jogged my memory, the traces of leg height in the car; it may have been the real Ellena at one point until we hit the cliff. Then Ellena got snatched, and the golem hid the bomb then. The bomb only got armed when Michael put her in the car for safety. Then she decided to detonate it. After all, we'd been told Ellena was a witch, so her escaping the exploding car to make the police officers shower us in blood wasn't as farfetched as it sounded.

"The sleight of hand blinded us. It was put there when Ellena disappeared. You shut her back in the car for safety, and she finished the job. Every detail that's happened was designed to have us chasing shadows,"

"That's why the vamps were like zombies, controlled or some weird shit like that. Enough to occupy us while seeing what you're made of. George, this old fucker is far smarter than we gave credit for. Imagine what he'll be like once set free,"

Michael was right, the Elder had them all dancing a merry little tune, and me having to fight through them. All to make me think that's how they were. Mindless and easily beatable. I fell for it hook, line and sinker, fully 'shifting' showing my hand. No wonder when he strung up those officers, he sounded so confident.

We stood with a final look around at the mess we'd left behind, including the bloodbath at the foot of the cliff—still, no residents paying attention. We'd been taken for fools. Ellena was now hidden somewhere, and I dreaded to think what they'd done to her. The Elder wanted 'Anna', as he called her, to be his partner in crime. We had twenty-four hours to stop his plan from happening. A part of me realised I would have to spill more blood.

The event got me, described a lot like a lunar eclipse, and the elder vampire wanted them aligned for whatever reason. A strange detail that Ruth failed to divulge. Not to mention the haunting vision of me drowning in a coffin or whoever I was supposed to be in place of.

Although, one thing I'm certain of, what's in there will either help us or end us. Why else would I see these scenarios? The one I hoped not to come true was Ellena, all broken 'fanged' up. The 'dots' were there, a case of which ones connected.

All the papers Ruth showed, the stories, even Locke's input. I didn't know what to believe, and looking at Michael's haggard face, I felt guilty. With us surrounded by destroyed vampires, four exploded police officers, and a puddle of fake Ellena, I had to inspire us to carry on. After all, that's what 'Alpha' is meant to do, right? The Elder had me second-guessing; what was it? He said, oh, that's right.

'*Insolent child in such a rush to die. It would be best to cut your losses and go about your life. Anna was but one woman in an ocean, with plenty more waiting. Now you wish to become a path of bones upon which your kin shall walk, trapped to serve at my 'heel' like all lowly beasts should. Your kind was never 'Apex Predators' You aren't even the alpha in your pack. You never will be. My kind is destined to rule, and there's nothing you or anyone can do. This battle was lost before it even began*.'

How could I inspire Michael to fight on, going up against something that, so far, had us by the balls without even getting out of its crusty bed? If only Skip were here, he'd know what to do; he'd be the 'Alpha' I'm not. Instead, the planning was on me. Two schools of thought were going through my head as I watched the limo door open and a bottle of Scotch get waved over the top. As if Duncan was a mind reader.

I had to go diving, knowing surrounding the pier, there would more than likely be a circus of McNally's thug's guarding. The other thought was to seek out reinforcements. Find a way to make them listen and bring them back from the wild. Perhaps a little inspiration along the way. Michael included. I could see it buried within the wrinkles of his tired face. What Michael says and what I sense are two entirely different things. His chemo signals were off in so many ways. Not even flight or fight. If I were to bet, he was 'all run', unlike Michael, but the rules had changed again.

The 'bar had changed considerably since the 'Kanaima' affair, and now vampires were miles ahead of us. There is a niggle buried deep in my subconscious trying to break free that tells me one of us may not escape this hell hole. The close shaves were adding up, calling me a cynic, but perhaps Michael would've rather I hadn't saved him. Only to end up here on the wrong end of some fuckers fangs. At least, that was my reading of him while he was in a trance state, wide-eyed, looking into the blood and guts.

Or my emotions were muddled without Ellena. The last few moments had no rationality to them, and no matter the way I tried to spin an explanation, taking in the vamp pieces and what was left of the Cruden Bay police force. How on earth that thing could make it to us and still throw some magic shit in the air while all but 'Kentucky Fried Chicken' was the hardest to explain. As far as I knew, Ruth was the only person capable of creating golems. I couldn't figure out her true skin in the game.

I walked around the cars, suddenly realising each car had a driver and hadn't given them a single thought. So much blood on the windshields that it concealed much of the insides until I neared an open door. 'Fake Ellena' destroyed them too. Now, the size of their police force, I wasn't sure, but suddenly eight had bit the dust. The elder vampire hadn't given them a thought in his control, but if this was Ruth, she could do that much carnage. As I soaked up the intestines swinging from the rearview mirror, why hadn't she acted sooner?

With the sky purple edging lighter, we had to move sooner rather than later. We may not have had an audience, but the fingers would undoubtedly be forced on us. Michael crouched quickly to pick something up before glancing at his hand and then at me with a pissed-off face.

"Michael, you ok?" Michael's mouth hung open about to speak while his eyes twitched and lips twirled between his fangs.

"His name was 'McCree'," Michael spoke softer than I expected, more full of sadness.

"Sorry, what?"

"This pool of blood and entrails has, I mean, had a name," Michael hoisted a name tag for me to see. Half covered in blood soaked into a black and white embroidered velcro material that gave me chills.

"Yeah, so did all those that got turned to vamps down there,"

"I know, but look at all this and what's left. How fucking easy it was for both sides to play with them like toys,"

"Michael, I would understand if it's too much. I didn't expect any of this, and it's so far out of our wheelhouse I don't know where to begin,"

"Are you kidding me? Except for me to walk away? After all of this?"

"Like I said, I couldn't and wouldn't blame you,"

"No fucking chance, matey. It hit home how bad it is here—the stuff of nightmares. I don't know if there are any normal people in these towns, but if there are, they deserve the chance to live. For some, it may well be their first experience being free from the horror that lurks all around,"

"So, you're staying?"

"Matey, through thick and thin, we're in this together. We must end this and get our girl back. Get your girl back—time for you to taste happiness for a change. Make no mistake, though, there will be more blood spilt. I know you don't like it deep down, but this is our world now. Nobody else knows the real thing that goes on, and sometimes it becomes a necessary evil. It's not like we can sit on fluffy cushions and ask nicely, is it?"

"I get that, I do. The feeling earlier was awful. Then I came round to realise it was them or us. One thing, though, no innocents. We must try if they've done nothing and we can prevent collateral damage. Ok?"

"Agreed... So are we going to put these fuckers in their place or what?"

What place was that? I thought as I smiled at Michael, glad he was all in. At least one doubt eased from my mind; the drenched image of the 'McCree' badge told me the only place they'd fit was dead. In this case, it turned to dust. So the fuckers stood no chance of coming back. The 'how' was the stumbling block.

"Are you ladies gonna keep gossiping to the wee hours, or are we gonna crack open the bottle and hatch a plan that leaves me with some town to be mayor of?"

I heard the enticing brown liquid swirl in the bottle; this time, Duncan Campbell stood out of the limo, propped against the door. Surreal to see him dressed so casually, in navy joggers and a grey hoodie under a black bomber jacket. Not the sort I'd associate with the suit brigade. Dare I say it? Duncan looked dressed to get his hands dirty.

"Don't suppose you got any cigarettes in your stores there, Mr Mayor," Michael chirped up cheekily. He had been gagging for a while now, surprised he hadn't rolled some flaky vamp skin and tried smoking that.

"Afraid you're shit out of luck. Will a wee cigar do? It's Cuban. Aside from that, the pantry is bare, I'm afraid," judging by Michael's face and quickness in his walk, he was happier. I was too distracted, wondering where Ellena could be. Not being able to sense her or smell her 'coconut' shampoo had me fearing the worst. Knowing how far we could reach and track would be better.

As I thought earlier about the rules changing, we still needed an instruction manual for our shit. 'Shapeshifter guide for dummies' kind of thing. One surety, my body ached so badly, and I was looking forward to a scotch to take the edge off.

The area around the pier was dead, nothing at all. I'm talking desiccated vampire in a coffin dead, which surprised us. Michael hung back with Funcan, still smoking, Scotch in hand. I limited myself to one, and reluctantly I might add. But no matter what, I was going in. The waters seemed quite calm, meaning at least one thing may go our way tonight, the current.

If the twenty hours were true, we had much less now, and I couldn't shake the pull toward whatever was down there. McNally had been searching for something too. Whether he knew what the numbers meant remained to be seen. The sequence in the painting was hard, even for my enhanced vision. I guess they had at least half the information to be in that area. A question of which snake fed it to them. More than likely Amos. I still wasn't sure where I stood in the elder stakes. If he was old in centuries' terms but not the same as the Elder, was he born or turned?

If I was putting the pieces together right, and anything like us werewolves or shapeshifters, pure born are stronger. The story around the Elder describes him as born different, with a need to live on animal blood until tasted human. He'd given us a peek behind the curtain, and Amos at the cave showed strength and speed. Could we stop him easier than the Elder, though? Take out a general and make them weaker? Would that work? We're stronger as a pack from what we've learned as shapeshifters. Would the Elder get strength from his minions? That's what we didn't know, and had us blinded.

I scoured the cliff's face, looking for hiding places, dreading any bloodsuckers jumping out. The jetty path had a solitary boat moored. A small one that looked likely to sink and could only carry a couple. I had a clear plan in my head, at least. Michael and Duncan to keep watch while I went looking. We hadn't escaped the smell of death, even from being half a mile further around the chalky edge. Every rush of wind carried the rancid musk of decayed flesh and showers of blood. We didn't need a second wave just yet. I only wished it would carry 'coconut' instead.

Even though the coast seemed clear, a little dark lingered in my hackles, telling me there would still be a sting in the tail. I Could probably count on one clawed hand the number of times they hadn't been on guard. But this seemed strange. Like earlier, almost lulling us toward another 'fall, made worse, being unable to sense anything. The air was too polluted, and no other heartbeats. A detail the vampires realised as soon as they knew what I was and worked it in their favour.

Michael and Dunca were busy chatting, and all the staring into the dark waters wasn't doing my anxiety any good. With the sound of frothy waves crashing against white rocks, I threw caution to the wind and ran for it. I didn't have the energy without shifting, but I tapped into the supernatural enough to use my speed. Everything became a blur.

I pictured a smiling Ellena in the distance, her blonde hair flowing in the wind; she was wearing a white rippling dress scattered with small blue flowers and a thin, light brown belt. Open-armed sat in the boat waiting. Ellena made me stronger in so many ways. Ellena made me a better person and drove me to heights I never knew possible, and now I didn't have her. But seeing her in the boat pushed me past the red line, and I was so fast.

There were recesses and rickety steps similar to the other side we came from but in a moment of insanity. I just let go. I jumped. The world suddenly slowed as I leapt through the air. The thick wind cut across the hairs on my arms; adrenaline tore through my veins, and I felt free for ten or so seconds. I was a kite dancing through a jet stream as I cleared the cliff edge by twenty feet. I should've been freefalling, but this was another foolish superhero moment, even if I was anything but.

My feet drove down hard as it hit the stone beach shelf. Sea-salty dust sprayed the air, leaving me shocked to be in one piece. I looked up to see Michael and Duncan with hands cupping their mouths. Ellena was waiting for me in the boat. And I had a 'dot' that needed answering.

I crept toward the jetty, not liking the silence; even the slight rumble from my stomach made me jumpy. Although it served as a reminder if this would be life from now on, I had to eat more. Maybe I wouldn't have been so zapped.

I reached for the little lawnmower-like engine strapped to the rear of the boat. Ellena probably had more powerful hairdryers. The whole bobbing and rocking on the waves already had my stomach churning.

Just as I was un-gracefully stepping aboard the leaky, rag-tad strips of plywood, I witnessed the second coming of Christ. Or whoever it was that walked on water. Only this one looked like 'Anna'. She walked through the air, a cloud drifting effortlessly toward the water and kept going for at least half a mile from shore, stopping near a lighthouse-shaped bouy. A small white light shone through 'Anna'; she was different than before.

It was her face, the one I saw in the cave before we arrived. Vampirism had a hold, 'Anna' just stood looking out to the murky, ink-black waters that rocked beneath, spraying ice cream froth all around looked bloody freaky.

This is the thing, why did I have to keep getting the crazy ghosts? Or see dead people at all. I swear, one day, that'll be a film. Someone spends their life seeing the dead. Maybe I could be the 'star' and make real money for my troubles. Why couldn't I get the cool ones like a visit from 'Elvis' or 'Abe Lincoln'? Instead, I get a woman with a sharp-tooth fetish.

Michael would've been in his element back then. Who knows, the way our shit dice have rolled so far, we'd get 'snake testicles' or 'eyes', whatever the saying, we'd get it, and vampire Anna would rock up. Flaunting her ancient ass, there'd be 'bats in the belfry' and then some.

I daren't picture the dust and cobwebs, sure enough, to make a grown man cry. I watched as Anna's ghost was still for twenty seconds; it felt like a lifetime.

My ears were busy searching for the slightest noise because I couldn't take my eyes off the action. The positioning had to be another clue. Until Anna suddenly vanished; I can't say if in the water or anything like that. But in the blink of an eye.

Finally, I had all of me in the boat and immediately regretted my impulsiveness. Rocking side to side, I latched onto the engine starter cord, doubting whether it would get going. Ellena was long gone, leaving me to my thoughts and fears. There had already been enough surprises tonight.

Chapter 40

First, pull...nothing. Second pull...nothing.

If any vamps popped up, I was a sitting duck, and the Damm motor wasn't budging. I still had a lock on where I saw Anna; the little map and compass were still in my pocket, waiting to be checked if I ever got going. From memory, where Anna stood wasn't the coordinates but not a million miles off. Who was I to argue when our plotting was guesswork around maps a few hundred years apart. McNally had been even further off than we had, by almost a mile.

Third pull...

A little life in the old dog as it coughed and wheezed, like Michael, after a day on the cigarettes.

Fourth pull...

Finally, the little whisk stirred to life, kicking froth through the waters. All I had to do was unmoor the rope to set off. It was now or never, but for a second, I had doubts. A part of me still thought it could be a fool's errand. Then why the hints, the ghost and the vision? Who left the numbers?

Off came the rope, and the boat chugged slowly through the cold and away from safety, one hand steering the other grabbing for the map. It didn't take long before I was at Anna's point. Suppose I had the bearings right with the cutting wind picking up, serving a chill to my bones and bouncing the boat around. Where we'd guessed was at least twenty feet to my right. Maybe a little more. The ins and outs of coastal erosion weren't my forte; a few hundred years was a long time for things to change.

Judging by Anna's ghost, the pier location had been different. The more I thought about her drifting through the air. Were her movements forced if I looked past the surreal hover over water? She seemed to stagger; maybe she was frantic, but she Had me curious. The details mattered; I couldn't imagine a vampire countess, let alone Anna's ghost, walking toward the sea. Whose trail had I been following?

My head hung over the edge, just about making out my reflection; with each blink, I swear I could see flashes of Anna again, between her and Ellena; their image was constantly on my mind. The grey, almost see-through face rippling up at me. I knew that was impossible. My mind was playing tricks. Everything around was too calm. Michael and Duncan were two little toy figures in the distance, and I sensed nothing else.

I suddenly went blank. That's the trouble with 'spur-of-the-moment actions; I hadn't thought everything through. What was I to do, dive in and hope for the best? The boat had a bundle of sheets, flippers and a life jacket. Were werewolves good in water? Could I hold my breath longer? I had no idea. I kicked through the sheets and found a crusty regulator with a mask and air tank. The gauge read twenty minutes left. I sat holding it for a moment, realising I didn't have the first idea about scuba diving or the kind of pressure under water could be involved.

I've seen it in plenty of movies, if that helps. A particular one caught my attention; I couldn't quite think why, perhaps the big fucking shark-eating people, 'Jaws', so, of course, I looked to the sea, hoping not to see a big grey triangle cutting through the waves. Were they even in this part of Scotland? So many unanswered questions. This was a bad move. It was also the only one we had. I needed to know and see what was down there. Every time I caught sight of the water, I saw her. 'Anna'. While inside, I was terrified we might never see Ellena again, at least the version of her we knew.

Cloudy black and brown as far as my eyes could see. Even using my red eyes, the water was tough going. It seemed clearer the deeper I went, but the current dragged me around like a rag doll. I could feel the pressure building around my head the deeper I pushed, and I began to regret my choices.

Breaking through a wall of weeds and other green shit, I finally saw that my irrational moment wasn't a lost cause. Ship wreckage and broken barrels were embedded amongst rocks.

Dead centre of that wreck was long heavy chains; they appeared connected to large boulders, at least four, anywhere from half a tonne or more.

It was like wading through mud, and I couldn't guess how deep I was when I caught the first line of links. Black dirt kept swirling across my path, with me rocking side to side. Ten feet along the line before my heart jumped, and that horrible drowning sensation took me back in my vision, the tightening of my lungs and throat before my head needed to explode. That's how bad that experience was. Immersed amongst the sludge and debris was an old coffin wrapped in chains. Was it the coffin I was in? Why was it buried at sea and held down by so much weight?

Ornate craftsmanship for something discarded in such a way had me wondering if this could be what McNally was searching for or if I had been fortunate to find it, maybe unfortunate, depending on its contents. This seemed to be what I was being guided to; I couldn't figure out how Anna's ghost fitted in. We'd seen her at the gravestone, the steps of Montague house, and even the cliff top when we arrived. Now, the water.

A quick check on the gauge gave me another problem to worry about. The needle hadn't moved; it had already been at least ten minutes. My claw tapped the glass; it spun left and right before stopping at the eight-minute mark. I didn't have long or any idea what to do next, but as I pulled along the chains to keep myself grounded, my eyes wouldn't leave the algae-encased corners of the lid. Ellena's face flashed before me, rippling in the current; this time, it was Ellena.

I'm unsure why I felt it, but the coffin was key and drew me in. I reached the edge of the coffin soon enough. The chains looked tough, covered in shells, encrustations and flaking patches of rust. I still had a little power left in my tank; whether it would be enough was another story. I gripped tight where the chains intersected; underwater made it harder to use my strength, but one of the links slowly began to stretch and flex, and it finally popped free. In a hurry, I did the same three more times. After a quick check on the gauge, three minutes were left. With the final one dropping slowly, grot and a few shells drifted across my path.

My claws clipped the surface of the coffin lid; sparks flashed in my mind. It's happened before, but not for a while now. Short bursts of images, yet darkness is all I could see. Metal, and the lid looked fused shut. I ran my claw over the metal again; the flashes came, lasting longer. This time, I saw glimpses of a person dressed old-fashioned, like I was in the vision. Each flash threw me off balance; my bead became a little disorientated. I went to touch it again.

Two minutes…

Time had ebbed away. Instead, I went for the handle at the end. This time, nothing, no flash images. Surprisingly, I could move it. At first, I was a little reluctant as it pushed more dirt into my view, making it harder to see through the clouds. My werewolf strength came good; whether it was right, only time would tell, but first, I had to get above water. I could feel my throat tightening as a little red light flashed on the gauge.

The coffin was towing along in my grip; I fought hard to swim upwards. I was cutting it close. A loud beeping echoed… My lungs ached. A dim light bounced on the surface, growing the closer I got. My body was tired; the coffin dragged heavier, slipping a little. Claws gripped tighter; the last thing we needed was a wasted journey. I wished I'd dragged Michael along to at least be in the boat waiting. It's bloody hard trying to swim one-handed with an alarm screaming how stupid I'd been.

That free hand punched through the surface, cold air greeted by claws. My lungs felt as they had in the coffin. Yeah, that was only a vision; it didn't make the ache less real. My head broke through next as I aimed for the oval shadow and past the little propellers. I grabbed the side, spitting out the regulator and gasping for air.

So, there I was, barely treading water, spewing my lungs out amidst another blank moment because I hadn't thought this part through either. After all, the hints were there; even after I broke the chains, it hadn't occurred to me how I and it would get into the boat, let alone back to the jetty. Then I noticed the mooring rope hanging over the side.

The coffin came as close to the surface as I could get it, too tired, while I tugged on the rope and looped it around the handle. Tieing off as tight as I could. Its weight had the boat tilted far too much for my liking. With the last ounce of battery I had left, I flipped myself out of the water to safety, damm near, putting my foot through the floor. I wasn't safe; my hackles were on fire, and I couldn't see Michael or Duncan on the cliff top.

My stomach was in knots, full of worry, panicking over what to do for the best while hoping it was over nothing and would soon be greeted by the pair. The boat tipped and bobbed uncomfortably at an angle, feeling the weight of the coffin bound to its mooring. I didn't have any more air to double-check where I'd marked on the map just in case there was another 'dot' waiting in this cluster fuck of a town. My hackles were relentless, sending wave upon wave of static through my body. More trouble brewing and I couldn't see a damm thing.

Even with my red. This reminded me I was exhausted beyond my limits now, an empty tank and still having so much to do. I needed a quick fix, but Michael's car and supplies disappeared. I quickly got dressed again, pulled up my jeans, and my warrant card fell out.

Brought back a mixture of memories, good and bad. With a flip open, I was faced with my Detective I.D., remembering when Michael handed them across the pub table. We weren't the cohesive double we are now; it's amazing how much we'd been through in a short time. Now, we're connected in ways that only the supernatural could understand.

Then, the limo explosion and what Ellena hid for emergencies. I was flapping it shut when I noticed it seemed chunkier than I remembered. A solid square outline protruded from behind the metal badge, causing a crease, which seemed impossible because the leather was sealed shut. My U.V. flashed across the leather lining, 'Break Glass' is what it said. Invisible ink or something, Ellena's ingenuity struck again.

Those words are normally plastered on emergency fire alarms. It looked like I had a present in case I needed it—another reason I wanted her back so badly. We were meant to be. At least, that's how it's felt for me since I finally got my head from up my arse to realise life goes on. My claw shredded under the leather while I listened for the trouble my hackles were warning me of. Out slipped a carbon fibre box, different from the last one; this had a catch to open, a switch, and a little bulb.

I checked from the box to the cliffs, hoping this had useful tricks. Sure enough, what looked like gums. Also different. With it, a note and twist in the form of glowing red capsules.

'*Georgie. Trouble seems to follow; sometimes, glass needs breaking. You've been full tilt for weeks now; don't think I hadn't noticed. So, I tinkered a little. The gum is slightly different based on your complex DNA, demon included. It will give you a boost, and the capsules are supercharged, restoring your levels and boosting healing... You're welcome... Love Ellena*'

'*P.S., I have no sense of direction; if a need, flip the switch,*'

I quickly flipped the switch, and the light slowly flashed red; a faint beep pricked my ears, but it was far and echoed toward the southwest of Cruden Bay. Pointing the box in that direction, the light flashed a little quicker, and I finally had the rub of the green. I've never been a fan of tablets or capsules, but I guess when in Rome, right? And needs must. Besides, my body was wasted; supercharging sounded intriguing.

The sooner I was back on dry land, the better, especially with my senses going wild. The motor started at the first time asking, if it sounded feeble before, now was nothing more than a wheezing old man blowing bubbles in the water. Progress was slow but gave me time to scout around, delaying the pill drop.

For the first time in a while, I picked up on heartbeats, at least two. No, four. The numbers grew, but I couldn't see or narrow down a direction. That worried me all the more. With the pill rolling between my thumb and forefinger glowing, I dreaded the unknown. 'Bottoms up.' I tossed the capsule in my mouth, threw my head back and swallowed. A few seconds later...

'Searing heat tore through the pit of my stomach,'

'My veins pulsed and swelled until they bulged under my skin. Forearms, hands, everything,'

'My claws grew too, thicker and longer,'

This was merely the appetiser; the main course quickly followed. A euphoric high spread through my body encased in a heart-pounding adrenaline rush that made my eyeballs swell from their sockets, and the red haze became a blazing forest fire. So, so bright. Ellena came up clutch again; not only did my tank feel full, but my body rejuvenated. The fatigue had gone in the nick of time, too. Hopefully, it would last long enough to find the others and proper safety.

Before that, it was something I never imagined myself doing. Crack open an ancient coffin; maybe there'd be leverage to get Ellena back. That's how I had to think, that I would get her back. If I were to stand any chance, my emotions needed burying for the time being, which was easier said than done for a guy who lets his heart rule his head. The mere thought of me being cold and methodical didn't fit, well, perhaps methodical but not cold. The last thing we could afford me to do was to give up. There was more than our survival at stake. This town, any others nearby and god knows what after.

With the red so much brighter, showing a crazy depth of detail, I picked up four heat signatures moving on top of the cliffs to the northeast, the same numbers northwest where Michael and Duncan should've been. With each, I caught sight of a metallic glint, 'fuck' more guns. I chugged along regardless; I could not do much in a small boat that had begun to take on water behind me.

With every glance to check how big the puddle had grown, the bobbing shadow trying to pierce the sea had me in a trance. No rhyme nor reason to it; I felt a pull. There was no way of knowing whether it was because of the visions or Anna's ghost, and it had become distracting enough that I nearly missed further signatures approaching from the right cliff foot. I've never been a fan of coincidences; that's exactly how the situations developed. I went into the water with no one else around, and by the time I'd retrieved the coffin, there was company. Not the friendly kind.

Finally, within a few feet of the jetty, watching those signatures stand guard like the 'beefeaters' at Bucks Palace. I was more than on edge and getting psyched up for another fight. Although, more guns added a wrinkle to my adrenaline surge. Yeah, I could run fast and dodge, but with the men stationed where they were, most angles were covered aside from returning to sea.

As willing as the next guy to be daring, I'd jumped down a cliff, for Christ's sake. A boat leaking like a sieve didn't fill me with the joys of spring. That left the jetty and prayed that the gods were on my side. With the rope in use, I had to take it to shallow waters, not that I was getting far with the dead weight. Stone began to scuff and drag across the bottom of an already fragile underside.

I grabbed hold of a damp beam to pull closer. No sooner had I raised an arm than a cluster of red dots lit up my chest like a Christmas tree. 'Heart in mouth' time again. I spun forward with the grace of a drunk ballerina, holding my arms at chest height.

"Och, aren't ya just a wee obliging twat," A voice echoed through the shadows. We were in the early hours with the skies lighter, but the bay still held enough darkness to hide the scumbags eerily.

"I'm afraid you have me mistaken; I'm just an over-enthusiastic nautical explorer,"

"Oh, are ya now. I dunnae think so, Detective,"

"Detective? Me? Honestly, who doesn't like a bit of diving in the dark? It's fun. You should try it sometime," So far, I counted the same eight heartbeats above and now four at ground level and mostly calm, but two were different from the rest. One reeked of fear, which had to be Michael; the other was strange, almost adrenaline-filled. Could it be Duncan, or was it the guy speaking and enjoying the moment too much?

"Oh, aye, Detective George Reynolds, I'm well aware of you, been sharp as a tack, and we would never have got to this monumental moment without you,"

My mouth hung open, catching flies; them knowing me wasn't the surprising part. It was the 'monumental moment' comment that threw me. I didn't see anything special in having guns pointed at me; it's been quite the theme lately, especially since we'd been in Scotland.

"Monumental? That's what you call it? There's me thinking, having all those laser scopes on me a little excessive,"

"Can't have you running away now, can we, not with a job still to do,"

All four continued forward; I attempted to step out of the boat. That's as far it got, an attempt. I'd barely lifted a leg toward the edge when a laser-lit up my forehead—the red-blazed between my eyes. A shower of moonlight painted the beach shelf set back from the water, a reluctant scuff across the gravel and the unusual foursome finally showed themselves. Sure enough, Michael and Duncan were there. It wasn't long before I realised who had the adrenaline-fueled heart and why. Duncan had a black Glock held to Michael's temple.

Chapter 41

All the possibilities could've happened coming out of the bloody water. I had to admit I didn't see that coming. Stunned was an understatement. He hadn't given anything away and seemed on the right side of the darkness, if there's such a thing.

Then again, maybe I should've. It was bound to happen. We'd been fucked over left, right and centre throughout. Half the time, I haven't known whether I'm coming or going. The only solace we've had was the one person we could've trusted in this god-forsaken place was the mayor. Why didn't I question how else Duncan Campbell would know to be our saviour earlier?

We didn't think about it; too much had happened and was happening. My hands and claws were dripping blood and had just torn through a tonne of vampires—Zombie ones, but bloodsuckers all the same. And yet again, guns were pointed at us by the police.

In the calm after, the scotch helped, but Duncan made us feel okay with him. So, I left Michael alone to find a way to Ellena and the truth. We've been blindsided, and I didn't know what to do for the best. Michael had another gun to his head, and I was lit up, waiting to have my chest blown to pieces.

Yet, while I wrestled with my flight or fight, I looked for a way out and wondered if my body weight kept the boat from being dragged back by the coffin. There was enough rope for it. I got slapped in the face because we weren't dead already. My arse had fallen out, but I clung to the one saving grace from this mess. This dysfunctional group of bad guys seemed to need us for a purpose. At first, I had it pegged that it was and still is all about Ellena.

Yet, I'd made the shitlist somewhere along the chaos and fitted into the equation. Or had I been the one all along? My head spun, overloaded with the second-guessing I was doing. I may be loaded with supernatural steroids, but I didn't see any good options other than surrender. If there was a hail mary out there, we needed it. You know, the kind where each gun backfires or that all eleven scumbags hadn't loaded their guns. Not too much to ask, right?

My biggest bugbear of all this how did we get mixed up in a fucked up town dodgier than a second-hand car salesman riddled with more bloodsuckers than the tax office. Our beloved Locke had a role in it, but I suspected unwittingly. It's who set the ball rolling and where the 'dots' fell in line. Ruth felt key; all the golem stuff was crazy in the how and why. Her motives were about as clear as the mud puddle left by fake Ellena.

Then there's the mystery guy who saved me in the forest, or did he? That's how bad my mind was with all the red lights on me; I cycled through each thing that had happened. I got shot, but if they knew me, was that the ploy, and I got saved? Was I being tracked? As conspiracy theories go, it was feasible beyond the smoke and mirrors of CCTV bullshit. The bad guys have had us in the crosshairs through, pun intended.

Every jigsaw piece was pissing me off, with a horrible picture forming. Boy, it was making me sick to the pit of my stomach. An almost night-and-day moment, the moon falls, and the sun rises to start a new day. Blinkers were being removed.

As I always say, the details and the devil behind them matter. It wasn't my inquisitive need to follow the 'dots' and find how they connected. The Graveyard numbers were a detail anyone with a few brain cells could've seen and thought weird; the painting was the unknown I couldn't account for...yet. McNally was searching the water too, and now more than ever, I think there was something else down there, but I'd been mind fucked the wrong way.

Not that there's a right way to mind fuck someone, I guess. Each time I felt the boat shift beneath because of the incoming tide, I stared at the thing I'd realised they needed me for. To retrieve the coffin. It's the why that I couldn't find an answer for. It had to be so. Nothing else. Otherwise, we wouldn't be at gunpoint. It wasn't for my or Michael's sparkling personalities or astonishing IQs. Granted, we aren't stupid, but how this scenario played out would say differently.

The vampires could do what I'd just done. They had just as much supernatural strength as me or Michael, maybe more so. I didn't know if this was the blinker's moment with the coffin. They had to have known where and could've retrieved it. What was I missing? Because with the real urge to lurch over the flimsy boat and spew my guts into the sea, it dawned on me why it was so monumental. I'd just recovered the coffin containing the 'Elder' vampire. All the smoke and mirrors nonsense was exactly that.

Ruth may need the caverns, and more vamps could be waiting, but their master had just been salvaged from his watery grave. I'd been pulled, pushed and manipulated in their desired direction, playing on my emotions and feelings for Ellena. Looking at Michael with the barrel rubbing up and down his temple, he didn't need to be a telepath to understand the conclusion I'd made in my head. My screwed-up face, full of fear, painted a big enough picture for anyone to read. What did Duncan Campbell gain from it, though?

"So, this is the big prize then? Why all the theatrics? Oh, Duncan, is this part of your mayoral campaign? As far as I'm aware, I heard of ballots being filled out with names from gravestones. A thousand 'Mr Vampire' slips don't count," There was no point in beating around the bush any longer. Michael's heart was going so fast it could explode with how unsteady the gun seemed. Dincan's hand wasn't steady at all.

"Ding ding ding, give the wee twat a prize," stepped forward Amos and McNally; surprisingly, it wasn't Amos being bolshy. His moment would no doubt come.

"What do I get? Timeshares in this fucked up new town you lot intend to throw together. You do realise this isn't a monopoly, right?" While we were back and forth with the new regulations, I had had half a mind to get out and hope the coffin sunk back. Then, I didn't fancy having more holes than the ones I was born with.

"Ya, think ya slick with all the answers trying to guess our game. Dinnae, worry about my counterpart there; the bigger picture is beyond your comprehension," McNally fired back. It wasn't him I watched, though. I looked for any micro expressions from Amos. I couldn't read his heart, but even in the limited light, I had the measure of his body language.

I'd been a little standoffish for someone with so many guns on him. I couldn't tell them just how scared I was, mindful of the beeping from Ellena's location that the vampires could no doubt hear now—scared for Michael, too. When McNally mentioned the bigger picture, Amos smirked, giving side glances to the back of McNally's head. There was a bigger picture, and little did McNally know, it may not feature him. The circus could yet take another fucking twist, and we had to be ready. If only I could get gum to Michael, him a little while getting the necessary boost.

My feet slid wider and angled, carefully to as not to draw attention. I had to be ready for the right moment to dive out of the way. There was one small option that I just noticed as the boat creaked beneath. It would take some doing, and I'd have to be accurate, but the crusty wooden supports to my right had big enough gaps for a person to dive through and get covered by the platform above. I would get banged up to don't, but it was an option. My fear was leaving Michael vulnerable. Those lasers could easily be switched to him.

"My comprehension has never been great; just ask my friend there. It's not my cup of tea. More than happy for you to have the boat in exchange for my friends, and we can get the hell out of here," I knew they wouldn't bite, but the boat lurched back a little as the waves rocked forward. The coffin had slipped. In my estimation, there was a shelf difference underwater; with the tide coming in, it would get deeper, and a drop would be sudden if I let it.

A black line across the stones ten feet in front gave me a gauge for where it would come in. A matter of how quickly. Perhaps they'd be to frantic trying to save it. We could use the chaos to shield and dash for it. As crazy a thought it sounded in my head, the B & B may still be a safe bet temporarily. Protection against the vampires, and if the exploding bodies were anything to go by, Ruth still had some skin on the game to want to guard us. For now, at least. We could not trust her role in Ellena's capture or the body swap. Suppose everyone had a price; if Duncan were on their side, he would gain well. Why would Ruth be any different?

"Afraid not, pal. You're all integral to the main event. Well, most of you. The rest can bear witness to divine intervention, one that will change this place and the world," Amos finally spoke up with a confident gruffness that ground my gears. There was something about him I hated; aside from being a murderous bloodsucker, he was a smug twat. More so after the cave situation.

Michael was finally brewing a temper; his fists balled, and his claws pierced his palms. I smelt the blood spray down through the cracks of his fingers. He looked out the corner of his eye and picked certain moments when Duncan was lax and created space. Only an inch or two, the barrel wasn't pressed, which made enough room for Michael to fire a punch or claw to the chest if needed.

"No offence, I'm not into watching or any dogging scenario you fuckers have in mind. How about we get a pass on that? Look at all the willing sycophants you have at your disposal. I'm quite sure they'd do the job,"

"No, no, no. See, behind all your bravado, I know you've concluded, and now you're scratching for the how. Ya see nobody other than someone of your unique state could see the prize. All it took was some coaching. What's the phrase? That's it, 'to walk a mile in another man's shoes. The next step has two parts that require some sacrifice. Make no mistake; this is happening. It just depends on what side of history you intend to fall. There's a place in the master's kingdom."

Amos told me everything I didn't want to hear, making me shift uncomfortably. Some I'd guessed, no matter how many times I'd said it already, they still couldn't take 'fuck off' as an answer. I had no interest in a vampire kingdom; Michael did neither. These were beyond deluded; the scary part was the 'Elder' and the danger he'd bring.

"History is exactly that, the past and belongs there. I'm more about the future, and I want to be standing at a bar with a nice cold point, if it needs, to wash down the taste of blood,"

McNally was pissed off with my front and kept looking sheepishly at Amos, waiting for direction. Wondering what the hold-up was, his impatience worked in our favour. All the while, Amos was the real one in control. That's the problem with different agendas trying to work together.

Everything went silent except the crash of bouncing waves that had the boat dancing forward and had grown shakier by the minute. Then Amos stole the authoritative thunder and raised both hands to flick them in my direction. Two gunmen began moving toward with enthusiasm. Neither stood out as anything spectacular, the run-of-the-mill bearded thug dressed in black, army surplus.

The one on the left had curly brown hair, a matching beard, and a larger build than his sidekick. He jabbed the tip of his scope-clad rifle in the base of my skull and shoved me forward. The other grabbed some black rope strapped to his hip and tied it to the front of the boat before pulling forward as I was shoved onto the beach.

We left a series of groans in our wake and many stones grinding. Then, my eyes rolled to the sound of the coffin breaching the water's surface. Amos raised his arms again. This time to the men on the cliffs and directed them to come down.

Amos approached, smiling, his fangs showcased proudly; my reaction was to shift. That made him smile all the more. Almost as if I were playing into his pale hands. Michael also shifted, looking for an excuse to fight, but this wasn't the moment. Or if one would come. The gun remained firm at my head; Duncan looked awkward, refusing to meet my gaze. Amos pulled a machete blade from inside his blue Parker coat.

My heart skipped a beat as he pointed it at me, moving closer. I knew he wouldn't kill me. Otherwise, I would've been shot already. The shiny blade didn't inspire confidence.

My heart skipped a beat as he pointed it at me, moving closer. I knew his intent wasn't to kill me. Otherwise, I would've been shot already. The shiny blade looked too menacing as it twinkled under the moonlight to inspire confidence.

The other heartbeats had joined us quickly; a quick nod and a few branched off, strapping their rifles over their backs before helping the guy, still pulling on the rope. Before long, I heard scraping across gravel, then reluctant groaning as it took a few to clear the coffin, carrying it over beside us.
Out of the water, it looked far scarier and intimidating. The detailing was elegant and unique; considering a knife pointed at me, I couldn't take my eyes off the seal. I couldn't see how it would be opened. Almost seamless except for a small cutout, maybe two inches long. It appeared like a spirit-level gauge.

"Has the brain caught up yet?" Amos broke my stare, pulling me back to the knife as he moved closer. Far too close, his death stench wafted up my nose.

"What did you mean by my unique state?"

"All them years ago, our master was improved, and such was the cunning of the druid, he concocted a unique curse to make it almost impossible to break,"

"Was that Countess Anna's ghost? A curse? So that bit was true then?" I said, attempting to filter the fact from fiction. We'd been told so much; I had to know how it all connected.

"Oh, aye. The lass wanders around. She is still searching for her true love. The stupid wench had escaped only to come back. The master used her ghost and the likeness of your girl there against you. He's seen inside your head and knows what makes you tick. Fate is curious; a descendant of 'Anna' gets with the one thing capable of bringing forth the second coming. Curses are all too real; this bastard is called 'the curse of blood bay', and mark my words, once you break the curse, the bay will be painted with blood once more,"

"Jean? That's who she was looking for? Do you know all the blood stuff is a bit outdated? I mean, it didn't work out too well last time. Do you think the second time is the charm? The old fuck may have been in my head, but that doesn't mean he knows what makes me tick; if he likes it there so much, maybe I should be charging rent,"

"You shut up right now... He was never her true love. She belonged to the master and always will be. Carnage is the only way to bring the world in line and make them bow;

you all will. The master knew enough to pull on your heartstrings and make you follow the breadcrumbs," Amos shot aggressively up to my face, blade pressed under my chin; I couldn't help but chuckle at his reaction.

It brought a new meaning to 'wingman', figuring bats and vampires go hand in hand, but Amos trying to suck up to the contents of a coffin was laughable. The anger on his face was pathetic. But I'd also struck a nerve.

"Did anyone tell Anna? Because clearly, it's not your master she's looking for,"

"Why worry about Anna when he can have the next best thing? After all, they say blood is thicker than water. It's her blood that gives life, and your blood will open the door,"

Before I could respond, Amos had his skinny vampire fingers gripping my wrist, and he tore the blade through my veins. Blood gushed, and I dropped to my knees. Several spurts shot in the air, hitting the coffin. It dripped steadily until it ran into that small gauge. I could feel the energy being zapped again as I fell to my back. I'm a heap.

"Noooo, you bastards," Michael screamed out, his eyes went bright yellow.

Amos crouched beside me, smiling. His long fangs glistened in the moonlight as he alternated glances between the coffin and me. My veins throbbed, and I was too weak to do anything, especially as these red dots remained on me.

"Oh, yes, wolfsbane-coated blade ruins you furry bastards over, doesn't it? But don't fall asleep now. You'll miss the best part. Did you think we wouldn't search her for trackers? Your girl has been closer than you think the whole time. In all the chaos and confusion, you couldn't tell she was tucked safely in our mayor's car boot. To think you had her all along, and now you can bear witness,"

I was too weak to stand; my eyes kept going blurry. First, I heard the faint screams from a woman who'd been gagged; then, I heard feet dragging. I just about make out the figure of a woman dressed in white being dragged across the beach. It was Ellena; a rush of wind sent me her familiar coconut scent. Two men in black dumped her on the floor by the coffin.

Ellena's eyes bulged with tears streaming as she endured a white cloth gag in her mouth while her wrists were bound behind her back. There was nothing I could do, blood was still pissing out of my wrist, and I wasn't healing quickly enough. The trickles of blood continued. Suddenly, a bright red line whipped around the coffin's sides, followed by a loud click. A gap steadily appeared, releasing waves of pent-up death. I needed to be sick but couldn't; I had no strength for it. Loud cheers roared around as Amos returned to me.

"Ya see, wise guy, only someone with demon blood coursing their veins could find the master and release him from prison. Don't ask how it was done; in the grand scheme of things, it doesn't matter. But somebody with a mutual interest remembered the news about a small boy in a London house fire over twenty years ago. And the people involved. Well, I'll let you dwell on the missing blanks of what led you here. I have a master to awake,"

The coffin lid opened slowly, and Amos gripped Ellena by her throat. I tried to move and find the strength to fight back, but I couldn't with the wolfsbane working its way through me; instead, I had to watch Ellena flail around, choking under Amos's grip. His long fingernails slowly pierced her neck, causing enticing blood trickles. Michael broke free, stepping forward with an ear-shaking roar; a gunshot blazed through the air, hitting the floor by his feet.

The guy beside him smashed the butt of his rifle into Michael's stomach, taking the wind out of his sails and making Michael buckle to his knees. We both looked on helplessly as Amos tore the restraints free before slicing the palm of her hand and holding it over the coffin, squeezing. Her blood smelt strong and even had me drooling, let alone what it would do to the vampires.

Everything went quiet, almost ant-climactic. Then came the rumbles within the coffin. I nearly chalked it down to delirium before a high-pitched screeching ripped through the air. The sky suddenly turned blood red as everything around us turned black. Sheets of crows and bats came out of nowhere, squeaking and squeaking through the air. I was scared senseless. Michael too.

My eyes had gotten blurry, and all I wanted to do was let them close. I had no fight left in the tank. I could hear bones crackling; it didn't need a genius to work out what I was hearing. Ellena's blood was bringing the vampire back, and its body was slowly rebuilding bone by bone—tissue by tissue. The sounds twisted a chill through my already weak body. My head was dropping lower as I could barely hold it up.

'Flaaap…Flaaap'

Something began smashing against the inside of the coffin before a huge shadow whipped against the red sky overhead. I could just about see a tall, looming presence with a large wingspan, bat-like.

'Mwahhhh ha ha ha,'

A sinister chuckle echoed chillingly as a vampire's arm ripped Ellena from Amos's clutches.

I attempted to use the last of my strength to push up, lunging forward. 'Clap...clap...clap...clap,' whistles through the air before one, two, three and four bullets tore through my body mid-lunge, searing, excruciating heat. Everything became slow; Michael attempted again, clap...clap...clap. Three more bullets ripped out through Michael's stomach, chest and arm. I crashed to the floor. First, Michael dropped screaming, facing me as our blood painted the stones.

That flipping gathered pace, whipping dirt into the air and my beleaguered face as Michael and I lay lifeless. Was this the end? Was this the way we were destined to go out?

"You had your chance to join my kingdom; now you'll be a historical footnote. My new era will right the wrongs of a world forgotten. Thank you for making it all happen," The elder vampire taunted; my blood flowed under my outstretched arm, still trying valiantly to move. We'd lost...

Chapter 42

I found myself surrounded by an endless darkness. Nothing but black as far as the eyes could see. There are no rocks or stone beaches. No coffin or a lifeless Michael was lying nearby. I sat on what seemed to be the floor but was so black everything blended.

There were no bullet holes or dried blood under my fingernails. I was alive but normal. I felt like the person I was when I got married to Helen, the oblivious person I was back then. During that time, I did not know about the supernatural, had no nightmares and very little memory of my childhood. Almost as though I'd travelled back in time. The darkness threw me, though. Was I in hell?

I remembered everything until I got shot and watched Michael fall before the elder vampire taunted me, clutching Ellena. The moment I was in didn't make sense. Perhaps, being what I was meant, I belonged in limbo, having to remember everything that had happened, the knowledge of what had been set loose, and I was now doomed to dwell on it in an endless emptiness.

I slumped back, looking up, thinking through my life, especially the more recent stuff with the supernatural. I even questioned whether I would've wanted a do-over. If it meant Helen remained dead, I had no idea what I was, and that part of me never woke up. Hand on heart, I would do it all again. I thought as my hand rested on my chest. Realising I had a heartbeat, another 'dot' that didn't make sense like most that added up since our arrival in Scotland, plenty of 'dots' with no particular connection.

The more I thought about it, the more I wanted to be alive. After all, how could vampires be allowed to take over the world? First, Cruden Bay, then Peterhead and the surrounding towns before engulfing Scotland. They wouldn't stop there; the vampire numbers would grow in England and beyond.

Count Elias Diminescu would rule with 'Anna' reincarnation, Ellena, by his side. To think, all the nonsense we were told initially, caves and telluric currents, viruses and curses. Not to mention the handmaiden that wasn't; Ruth should've been straight with us; why say the vampires were in the caves if the Elder was buried at sea, and only someone of demon blood could find the coffin and break the seal? Was that the work of Jean Francis all of them years ago?

The whole dynamic and story around him and Frederick LaSalle were odd. While Ruth claimed to be a witch who could make golems into people, the mysterious guy in the cave was anomalies that...that... Holy shit.

Too little too late, I put two and two together, coming up with four and for once, the math worked. Barring the theory and reasons why. But as I lay in darkness, I concluded that neither Frederick nor Jean was dead. Jean strived to fix, cure and keep the town safe after they brought the vampire to town in 1725. He fell in love with a countess(Anna), and she got pregnant. With the town going to shit, Jean wanted Anma to travail somewhere safe with their impending.

Meanwhile, Jean had turned bad, helping Count Diminescu rise again. The count formed a fixation on Anna but had to get through Jean first, so he turned Frederick against Jean, who attempted to kill him. By then, Frederick may have been turned and bit Jean, but he didn't die. Instead vanished.

Why did I have to work this out after I was dead? At least the 'empty' was good for one thing: thinking. While Frederick embraced it, Jean must have been working in the shadows, looking for ways to stop Diminescu. Jean couldn't risk exposure, and when Anna came back looking, they used secret ways to communicate until one day, Anna never came. Fearing her death, Jean sought to kill Diminescu and succeeded in using his druid powers to desiccate and imprison the Elder vampire, not before the town was painted with blood.

I couldn't believe I was thinking it, but Frederick Lasille, armed with the same ability and turned, was Ruth. I mean, Frederick assumed the identity of a woman named Ruth to hide away until he found a way to bring Count Diminescu back.
A lot of good conjecture was doing me; now I was dead. At least I was working through some of the 'dots' that had hindered us.

The caves were details I don't see a way around unless there were telluric currents and a down there, buried. So Ruth concocted another way, enlisting local scumbags to dig tunnels, some being escape routes and places to hide bodies, whilst making a way in. Amos and the others were loyal to the count also and had looked at ways to make a sustainable food source pending the count's rebirth. That's what happened to the town of Oxley.

With all this information working out, it made me wish we'd figured it out sooner, but they had us on strings, bouncing from one problem to another, all to do their dirty work. There were more 'dots' to understand, but I had an eternity. Why spoil the fun ahead? I stood up to walk around, half chuckling to myself, thinking how Frederick has had to be a woman; I mean, would that even work?

Anatomically, I mean. I am, or should I say, as open-minded as anyone. No doubt, at some point in the future, there will be men born and want to be women and vice versa, with their thoughts, feelings and very essence meant to have been born in an opposite body to what they got. No doubt science would help put that right. But the notion of magically changing a man into a woman was crazy.

My main regrets as I wandered the never-ending prison were that I had got others killed, the vampire took Ellena, and we never got to see what we could be together. If I was in limbo, where the hell was the old git? Surely he never passed over? Lucky bastard. Imagine him following me around and lecturing me on our latest mess. Defied thinking about it.

'Georgie, Georgie lad, time to get up now,'

I heard a voice echoing and faint in the distance but couldn't see how or recognise it. It was almost familiar and was on the tip of my tongue, but I couldn't remember. Was I beginning to forget? Oh, and another thing, that double-crossing bastard, what's his name... Harold or something, the bloody mayor of all people.

'Oi, Georgie, come on. Your job isn't done yet, lad,'

It came again. I swore blind I could recognise it; what did they mean my job wasn't done yet? I was bloody dead, for Christ's sake. Doesn't get more done than that.

'Georgie. You have to wake up. You have to roar; you need to roar,'

Nice try, arsehole; I can't. I thought as the voice sounded off again. There was no element of a werewolf or demon in me. I tried. Looking at my hands, I concentrated hard, straining until my head felt it would burst, trying to force flaws to come, but nothing came.

'Get the fuck up. Too much to do,'

The voice was sterner and closer. I couldn't shake the feeling; I knew whose voice it was. The whole situation was bizarre. Like I was in a black goldfish bowl, and some giant was starting at its plaything. Kind of how we'd been treated throughout the trip to Scotland, playthings for the vampires to manipulate and move around like chess pieces.

'Georgie, you're bleeding to death; you must wake, dig deep and roar to trigger your healing. Come on, Georgie, it's time to come back, lad. Too many people are relying on you. I'm relying on you, and most of all, that lovely lady of yours, Ellena, is relying on you,'

Ellena...my heart sank. I hated that I had to leave her. She didn't deserve to be a vampire's bitch; how could I be stuck in limbo while her life got taken against her will. Ellena liked the supernatural and embraced me as a werewolf, but I was alive then. Now, she was with the dead and would be dead once turned. The more I thought about her, the angrier I became. Why did it have to go down like that?

We'd been outnumbered in a town that should've been the one wiped off the map. Now, it would be the hell mouth for all the evil in the world. After all, once the outside world learns of how dark it is, what's stopping other supernatural creatures from seeking somewhere dark and dangerous?

The bestiary gave me a glimpse of what existed, and that was just a fraction of one book. By all accounts, many exist. All those powerful creatures, who would be the 'Apex' then? The Elder claimed that's where they belonged and would assume that mantle. Not once had I considered to be anything 'Apex', especially a predator, and after seeing that trapped werewolf in the cave, there was an argument to say we never were.

It was wrong to have vampires killing at their leisure, just to feed. When I was shifting, I lusted for flesh and blood; you tore through it and let the blood drip for my skin. After biting Michael, I remember not liking the taste in the wake of it. But in the heat of the moment, 'chicken', that's all it was to me.

That werewolf was rabid and crunched through that guy like nothing and was being used to dispose of bodies for McNally; were we any different? In that state, I mean. If werewolves were kept rabid somehow, the count could have an army of werewolves at his mercy if McNally was being rueful by how many he caught. Let alone how many there could be.

Deep in my limbo procrastination, a lightbulb moment occurred. Thinking back to the 'Black Widow' case, I say 'back' like it was an eternity ago. Where, in fact, less than a week. The point is, in the tunnels, we found the papers Michael took, showing the ancient relic of the serpent and the 'Devil's circle ' symbol.

That relic is said to be able to tap into the supernatural and the power it has. Fuck, what if the vampires could use an object like that and the telluric current with the negation?

What could he do or create?

Was all of those factors together able to make a hybrid? Vampire/werewolf and then some? With me in limbo, my body was vulnerable, and they would have my blood mixed with someone like a vampire witch; they could be unstoppable. All the strengths, no weaknesses. They'd be able to control the need for blood, be so much stronger and almost be normal like werewolves out of their 'shift.'

Did the people behind the politicians, Warren Whitlock and his scumbag cronies, know of this? I couldn't believe Whitlock and the rest of the devil's circle wouldn't want to be involved for one minute. Imagine, though, a hybrid elder; what have I done?...

'Georgie, bloody wake-up and roar. You can't go down like this,'

The voice was closer this time, and suddenly, I felt a dampness around my chest, a weird cold feeling. In the middle of a pitch-black limbo, I felt a chill run through me. How was that possible? Should I have been able to feel anything? I looked down, and a small wet circle started to seep through my white shirt. I hadn't noticed before, but I was dressed differently. White shirt, black jeans and shiny black shoes. It is not my ideal style; being dead has drawbacks.

A sharp breathlessness gripped my balls; blood was seeping through, and it hurt—searing pain. The bloody patch grew, and then the other three came one by one. Four bullet holes were leaking blood; it was pure, unadulterated agony. My head spun with confusion. My body felt different again. Weaker, yet not normal, either.

A look at my hand again, one after the other, the claws slid forward without trying—Fuller and thicker, like the night on the clifftop when I scared Amos and his friends away. Then I let more of my demon side in, and now they were leaking that fluid. What the fuck was happening. The pain was getting too much, and I dropped to my knees.

My breathing was getting shallower, and I could taste blood in my throat. Wheezy and struggling, I flooded down, arm outstretched. I couldn't move, too weak to try. Was this limbo?

'Open your blooming eyes, Georgie; we have much to do. Come on, lad. The world still needs George Reynolds'

My body was heavy, and the voice sounded right above me. My brain finally twigged who it was. Andy! Skip was calling out to me. My eyes closed, and I had no strength to move or respond as my blood flowed across the blackness, soaking under my outstretched arm.

'Smaaaaaack,'

'Rooooooaaaaaaaaaarrrrrr,'

The cliffs shook, and a swarm of starlings whipped from behind the trees as the jetty rumbled deep into its foundations. All the stones beneath my body trembled as I sprung upright, emptying a roar brewed in the bowels of hell. In my case, limbo.

One by one, I felt each bullet slither from my body; my eyes blazed bright, blood red, while my claws pounded deep with the stones. I was alive and pissed. I'd never felt anything like it before, not the time at my parent's home when I got shot, not the exploring limo, not when I got shot in the woods and not from taking Ellena's emergency gums or pills.

I jumped to my feet, seeking a target for my anger. My claws wanted to shred through the flesh; a look down, I saw they were full and thick like I saw in the empty. They dripped that toxin, too. I'd tapped into my demon side, which wasn't going away soon. My head bounced right to the left in a frenzy until I felt hands grip my head.

"Skip? It was you, I heard," I said, feeling my eyes focus better.

"Yes, lad, in the nick of time too. Now bloody heal," he said, looking toward the bullet holes through my blood-soaked t-shirt. The feeling was weird, I can't deny it, but I could feel each wound close from deep within, layer by layer, until only the skin was left. My hand gripped my t-shirt to shake the bullets free, and then I changed my mind and simply ripped it off.

I should've been cold, but I wasn't; I stood bare-chested. My blood was on fire, and the anger wasn't going anytime soon. Everything was surreal, still mentally lingering in the empty; I couldn't be sure this was happening until the reverberation in my cheek finally made its way to my senses. Skip had smacked me around the face to wake me finally. If that's what I was, asleep.

"Shit, Michael," I said, remembering the rest of the ordeal.

"Down here, Georgina. Thanks for the beastly alarm call,"

"What do you mean,"

"I was in darkness, edging towards a bright white light, when I heard and felt you roar. Every cell in my body woke up. In that place, I was normal, and I didn't like it. It shows what can be missed in a short space of time. Your roar dialled everything up to eleven and felt far more than I ever had before,"

Skip gripped Michael's hand and pulled him to his feet before embracing him with a hug. I got a smack to the face, and Michael got a cuddle. Suppose it's what I deserve.

"Skip, I've fucked up. I've screwed up big time," I looked him deep in the eyes, feeling a tide of sadness rip through as Ellena sprung to mind.

A single tear rolled down my cheek; I was partly shifted, fangs bigger than normal, and yet tears were about to flow. So many emotions swam around in my body, being pushed down by anger; I didn't know how to deal with them.

"Oi, you stupid sod. None of this is on you, none of you. There's one person, and I think even he has been led down the garden path by his testicles," Skip chucked me a bottle of whiskey from a black holdall that looked fit to burst.

Skip had ADI Locke in the crosshairs, much like we'd been before rocked to our core. There were questions in need of answering, but with what we've been told so far, he'd also got screwed over. Skip wasn't one to stroke the ego, so if he was saying something, it should be taken with the intent it was made. Unfortunately, I was better at beating myself up than anyone ever could.

"Erm Georgie, since when did you grow them," Michael said towards my chest; I figured there were scars from the other bullets. I looked down, and I was bloody ripped. No joke. Muscles stacked on muscles, I'd always been quite lean. A look at my arms, hair aside, a lot bigger. It had to be me cutting loose with the demon part.

"God knows, but no good at the minute, is it," the lid came off the whiskey, and I inhaled for all it was worth. Not every day I come back from being dead. It burned my throat, but I deserved that; Karma had earned the right to some payback, and the suffering was warranted regardless of what anyone said.

Until Ellena was in my arms or the vampire's head pinned to my claws. Then that's what I deserved. Maybe they could happen at the same time. Rip a head and get a cuddle. It would trump Michael's from Skip.

"Will you stop it? All of this is new to you and all of us. You came for a holiday and got screwed over. Now, it is about righting the scales. Come hell or high water, we must get your girl back and stop these bastards from escaping this town. If that happens, then the domino effect is in play,"

Michael appeared confused as he snatched the bottle. I knew what Skip meant. No university degree is needed to fill in those blanks. That is exactly what I concluded in limbo. They spread from here; we're fucked. Be like breeding rats. Or every town becomes another Oxley; only it will work because nobody would be around to care.

Chapter 43

The night was gone, and the clock was ticking down to whatever eclipse was to come. The sky still covered us in a blanket of blood red. More details beyond what I thought was possible. Much like being stranded in limbo, only to be yanked back with the bullets forcing their way out.

It took a while, but I managed to find the road taken when I followed the two SUVs the other night. It wasn't long before I encountered those signs again as we reached that forked incline in the road. To the right was the arrow for the quarry; the sound of the car crashing over the edge and exploding rocked through my eardrums. On the left was the forest. Along came the heart palpitations like before. Panic sweat began setting in as I veered right sharply, recognising where I'd parked at the last second.

Skip and Michael flew sideways, grimacing in my direction before Michael showed his confusion. Skip, on the other hand, wasn't so shocked as if he knew more of what was happening. The 'how' seemed impossible. Then again, his demeanour had been quite calm; lucky for us, he came when he did. The timing was too spot on, and I'm not a fan of coincidences.

"Care to share, Georgie?" Michael lurched forward, his hand stretched for the Whiskey perched beside Skip. We would need much more before we were done with this hell hole.

"This was where I followed the McNally family. They were with Amos. They came here to dispose of two bodies, one over the cliffs; the other got fed to an imprisoned werewolf,"

"Oh, said something about that,"

"Yeah, starved of moonlight and prevented from changing back from a part 'shift' weirdly, it was able to help me fully turn. It had blue eyes, though,"

Skip tilted his head back, eyes rolled to the ceiling of my car. He was deep in thought. Before the lightbulb flicked on. I didn't know much about the eye stuff besides what Skip had told me; I gathered it from research to help him understand what he was long before that side of me was unlocked.

"Then lad, if they're blue and could nudge you into your first evolution, that's a 'fallen one.'"

"Fallen one?" I said; hearing that term for the first time intrigued and scared me.

"According to some folklore I dug up in the beginning when I was navigating this world solo. A werewolf can rise and fall through the pecking order through integrity, valour or sheer act of will. They can also fall if, in one way or another, if they take the life of an innocent. They captured a seasoned 'Alpha' and forced them to kill. Costing their red eyes and the strength that came with it. But enough to point you to what you needed,"

"So, what you're saying is, they will have the knowledge and wherewithal to help us,"

"If they can be brought back. Some don't make it back from the wild. I read that many years ago, one in South America was described as a bigfoot or a long-lost caveman thawed out; it tore through a small village with no relent until hunted down and shot dead. Only then did they turn back to human form. This may not be easy, lad; it could go wrong for us. Their eyes aside, imagine an Apex killing machine with a lobotomy. You're trying to plug his brain and humanity back in. So it's going to depend on how long you have been deprived. The upside is they may have a pack here too,"

I took the Whiskey and sat weighing up the situation; the blood-red sky added a haunting haze across and through the trees. Skip made a point I hadn't considered, adding to the many details. The assumption of other captive werewolves being strays McNally had hunted down to use as toys; it hadn't occurred to me that McNally may have caught a pack. Once the 'Alpha' went missing, others went looking and got caught, which made me wonder how big the pack could be. We needed all the help we could get. I was under no illusions about how big the task was.

If we didn't act now, all would be lost. McNally, being the human element, needed to be removed permanently, too. The trouble was, how? So far, they'd used the wolves to dispose of dead bodies. Short of killing them, I didn't see how we'd stop the rot. In a hypothetical situation, we remove the key vampires, stop Ruth and cut the head off the snake. How would we stop it all from starting over? There's so much out there we didn't know, like what could we do? I mean completely. Ruth passed the buck while highlighting its power connected to the currents.

When you strip the details and gossip down, what the hell was it really for? There was still another move waiting to be played; I could sense it but couldn't see where it may come from. Our brush with death may have been brief, but it gave me a new perspective on how much danger we faced.

The only advantage we had at the moment was we were considered dead or as near as. If Ruth and my mystery saviour were who I thought, then they could be the sting in the tail. Each had an agenda we weren't sure of. Ruth needed unmasking to be sure; was her power endless? Had both been turned in 1725 as suggested?

Would they die if the elder vampire was destroyed? Instead of giving the fucker a watery burial if we obliterated the body, were any contingent on him? It could be a good and a bad thing. Perhaps why the count was only buried meant his sire stayed alive. Suppose they could be classed as that. The fact I was thinking 'sire' and things like that was bloody weird; that's the situation, though, nothing but weird.

"How would I even reach someone or something that far gone?"

My ears twerked to movement deep in the forest, a slight rattle. Oddly, my hearing was far more tuned to the little things. Previously, I could hear a lot and at great distances but would have to filter through. This time, it homed in instantly. Having a six-pack now, I got some perks from this 'hell' hole. That wolf was having it far worse than us, and if the rattle was anything to go by, it was agitated.

As Skip pondered my question, I used my hearing to scan around that rattle, assuming I was on target and that was the cave. In case McNally had anyone guarding. They shouldn't be for us if we'd been left for dead; he was far shrewder than I gave credit. Would've realised that the wolf was powerful and couldn't be left alone if it broke free. Imagine a bull on the loose looking for a red cape; only everything appeared red.

Anyone that got in his way would be torn apart. There were two, approximately two hundred feet from each other and one hundred back from the cave. No doubt with scoped rifles. Their heartbeats were steady at that distance, but we'd have to take them out first. Both had walkie-talkies but had the volume low. The chatter seemed active but hard to understand.

"Georgie, you would need to dig deep. Similar to the roar that forced your healing. This time, you want to rock the very foundations of a person. Michael and I will feel it, too. But if done right, you will tear down the barriers and wake their humanity up. Perhaps even give them a burst of power to break themselves free. If it works, once unchained, they should be forced to 'shift' back to human again. Know this, lad; it's not going to be easy. Use any pent-up pain and leave it all out on the gravel,"

Pent-up pain I had in abundance and the fear of not seeing Ellena again. At least, Ellena, we knew. The vision before we'd arrived was far too telling. I could only hope she never became that.

"What if I can't? I've hardly been on the ball through all of this. Let alone play the 'Alpha.' I'm still surprised you two are still willing to be in the fight,"

"Oi, you idiot. One in all in. None of this could've been accounted for, matey. Fuck, I can't imagine seeing the crap you have, let alone having that vampire mind fuck you into following its trail. It's high time we burnt their kingdom and sent them back to hell. Hopefully, that satan fucker could do with some pointy-toothed batches to play with,"

"Noted. Question though, why does your mind always involve women, bitches, bondage and playthings, Michael?"

I smiled, joking. It was nice to lighten the mood before phase one of Mission Impossible. In truth, I was lucky to have Skip and Michael in my corner. The fact Skip came to our aid was beyond priceless. Not the first time either. It's like he's chosen to watch over me or us from afar.

I downed a mouthful of Whiskey, causing my face to screw up in a bitter lemon disgust. I handed it to Skip before flicking my claws out in a part shift. A look in the rearview, one of the few times I'd dared, I noticed my wolf features had changed slightly.

My cheekbones were more pronounced and menacing. Fangs were longer and wider while my skin tone had darkened, almost aged. Not in a decrepit Michael way. The wolf side seemed less like a pup version. Crazy to say, and based on no knowledge, if I were to draw a demic fucking werewolf, I wouldn't be far off. I caught Skip looking at me from the corner of my eye; he smiled. An almost fatherly approval that I'd grown up now. Perhaps the death scare was a shock to my supernatural system.

I even scared myself; I sure as hell wouldn't want to come across doppelganger me. That had to be on the list of possible weird shit. Which made me think as I stared, were dragons real? It might sound strange considering what we were about to do, but my head wandered a little, and the idea of dragons roaming free came up. If vampires and werewolves could be, why not them? If we had one, we'd end this in no time. Until then, claws and fangs to a gunfight, yet again.

"I take it you both heard what I have?" I said as a little toxin dripped from a claw onto my leg.

"Two? Yeah. What's happening there, matey? A little premature problem?" Michael said with a smirk, pointing to my claws.

"Funny twat. Yes, two. Remember, vamps don't have a beat, so key in you're sense of smell for 'death.' That's the best we can aim for, considering how sneaky they could be," I said, swinging my door open to signal it was time to move.

A deep breath once outside didn't give away anything like that—some blood and minor traces, but nothing that drinks blood and stinks. The trace was probably a leftover meal for the werewolf. That thought made me shudder; how nonchalant to think of a person as a main course.

Nothing was said; we were all equipped with the same skills and senses. Skip blazed left, Michael went right, and I headed straight as we ploughed through the forest as quickly and stealthily as possible. Our speed was no match for the unsuspecting gunman.

The one Skip got to went down first; he gargled; the surprise rang out, the minimum of struggle, a broken bone, maybe two, but Skip had him out cold and rushed to my side as I came to a stop near where I had before, getting an eerie sense of Dejavu. Michael's gunman fell next, again, minimum fight, only Michael sounded more aggressive, going a step or two further than needed. The gunman had been subdued; the first bone snap saw to that. But several blows pounded the guy's body. Their squeals told all. The jaw was next, teeth smashed together, followed by the next break. Then, at least three ribs and another unknown. Michael had anger I could relate to but was walking a fine line.

I worried about That part of him, not just in Scotland if we made it back to London. What would happen if he lost control in an investigation? We couldn't afford to lose him or draw attention to us. The normal world wasn't prepared for that, not yet. Some may believe in things like ghosts and the afterlife. It's the shit they don't know that would haunt them.

Michael joined us, and all crouched amongst the damp dirt, waiting. Chains rattled against stone with an echo. They'd heard the gunman getting taken out as the werewolf shuffled forward to the edge of the cave's limits. Their blue eyes pierced in our direction.

He knew we were there, with nothing else sensing we stood to approach. I held out my arms to stop the other two from following. This was for me to do alone; I had to be what Skip suggested and didn't want the wolf to feel threatened. They'd endured enough already. The closer I got, the stronger the blood stink grew stronger. It had the mouth watering a little, and I saw no point in fighting it back—far more important things to worry about.

Moving slowly to within ten feet, I dropped my arms, opening my body as I tried to be unthreatening, but they were already on guard and seemed not to recognise me. They were far worse than the other night. My arm hairs bounced with trepidation while my stomach churned. This could go horribly wrong quickly. Another first and another out-of-my-comfort-zone moment. This whole mess had been that way.

The wolf began pacing; they gripped their chains aggressively and thrashed them around. Its collar buzzed, and I could feel the pain from where I stood as its body writhed with agony. They didn't give up, continuing to pull at their shackles. One screech looser, making me step back. 'I can do this,' I muttered before stepping forward again. I was still a wolf, so they could tell what I was; they just didn't connect the dots.

They rode through the constant shocks and pain, emboldened by the lack of guards or McNally. Our presence was tiling them up, and they felt far too gone. I closed my eyes and attempted to lock into their chemo signals. Nothing but immense rage and bloodlust that scared me. Remembering how they spoke almost telepathically, I tried the same.

'We're here to help; no harm will come to you,' I said. They just glared, widening their stance far more aggressively. I repeated that phrase; their blue eyes dimmed slightly like I was getting through. They were followed by shaking their head, confusion and my words. That moment told me there was still a spark within that wolf. Now, I had to break down the wall and set them free. It would either work, or they'd break free and try to tear me apart.

"Now, Georgie. Do it now while that spark of humanity lingers," Skip shouted from the forest's edge.

The werewolf looked at me, pacing side to side, shaking its head with agitation as its eyes switched from bright to dim and back again. My heart pounded out of my chest, hearing the chains weaken. This was a mere blip on the horizon in the grand scheme of things. Yet, if it worked, we'd remove an element of the vampire's bigger picture. At least what I'd surmised it to be.

I blazed a blood-red gripped all the pain and anger stored deep down. Ellena's smiling face appeared beside the wolf; she gave a little nod, enough to drive me on, pulling a loud, soul-rattling roar tearing through my lungs. Trees shook, and stones vibrated beneath our feet. A look over my shoulder, Michael and Skip's eyes were bright yellow. Their faces seemed to evolve more beastly, and I felt stronger. A lot stronger.

The wolf's eyes narrowed; they'd stopped pacing. For a moment, nothing happened. Then the wolf gripped its collar, and electricity sparked. They didn't let go; with teeth bared, they fought through the pain. I watched as the spiked metal collar began to stretch. It creaked and squealed with more sparks firing off. Until, after a final yank, the collar smashed apart in the wolf's grasp, dropping to the floor in scary slow motion. Followed by one shackle and then the next. The wolf was free and looked hungry, with bright blue eyes; I feared that spark had gone.

The wolf slowly stepped forward, and I stumbled back. My hackles were on fire; all I'd done was set free an unparalleled killing machine, which had me in its sights. As I stepped, a thought flashed across my mind: I couldn't keep bending. That's all this town has made me do since we'd been here: bend to its will. If I were to have any chance of winning our greatest battle yet, it had to begin now.

I stopped, my feet ground into the rubble, bracing myself. I had to prove myself to a stranger. If they had been an 'Alpha' once, I had to earn it to get them to help. The wolf let out a roar, which gave me chills. I refused to waver, and neither Skip nor Michael budged. The wolf sprinted powerfully toward me; I leant into my footing. Its claws clamped ferociously around my throat in the blink of an eye. The tips pierced my flesh, but I didn't budge. They were strong, but so was my willpower. Ellena lingered in the background; I powered back every time the wolf tried to take me off my feet. This to and throw happened repeatedly until I felt it weaken.

His piercing bright blue slowly dimmed. I stood firm for the next onslaught; this time, my claws met its chest and instead of riding out, its bone-jarring thump into my body. I met it head-on, roaring through my anger and drive with everything I had to get to the image of Ellena even though she wasn't there. As we collided, I couldn't honestly say what caused it or if it was my imagination enacting a shift of power and dominance. It seemed we made a small sonic boom echo around us; stones bounced as a wave of wind circled us, pushing out. With the wolf's claws pulled from my flesh, I had him back on its heels, and suddenly, the dynamic changed.

That powerful roar broke him free physically, but embracing my strength and sheer force of will tipped the scales in my favour. His blue eyes dimmed and didn't stop. We let go of each other and watched this intimidating, rabid killing machine slowly claw back its humanity. Those blue eyes became human brown; his body phased back to normal.

A little dirty, but nothing a long shower couldn't fix. He stood at six foot one, with shaggy brown hair and an athletic build. The poor guy looked traumatised and lost. With his eyes widened, I couldn't be sure he wouldn't burst into tears, but his emotions were going haywire; he didn't know whether to run or stay.

I was simply relieved that we could bring him back; his right arm dropped limply to his side. It was brief, but there was a flash of a symbol on his wrist. Like how mine reacted, his did, only different. A cluster of pine trees in a circle with a path of flames underneath. It flashed green and red, confirming suspicions of a pack in the area. Could we save them, too?

Chapter 44

The guy was stunned and kept checking his hands to see if this was happening. If he was truly free. I sensed he wasn't sure whether he could trust us, and I didn't blame him. Being used as body disposal would leave a sour taste behind. I chose not to push; we stood in silence, and luckily, Michael had the good sense to bring the whiskey.

His grubby hands grabbed it like he hadn't seen a drink before. Then again, chewing down on human bone for however long needed washing away. Unfortunately, the cost had already taken its toll. His hands couldn't stop shaking. The bottle was in the middle or circulating for round two; we all felt it. We shuddered as though somebody was dancing on our graves while our hackles rumbled to attention.

"We got company," I said, trying to sense what direction. There were no heartbeats, but that 'death stink' was strong, and every so often, there'd be cracking or rustling through the trees and bushes.

"How many?" Michael spun around looking, but there was no way of telling.

"Vampires, I take it," He and Michael shielded our new friend.

"Yeah, these are far quicker. We need to split up. You two get him to the car. If I'm not there in five, leave," I threw Skip the keys, bracing myself as I felt short bursts of air rush around us.

"No matey, we can't,"

"Go. It's the only way. Besides, I've already taken down a load of these fuckers. What's a few more to the tally,"

Our friend was weak and confused, so Skip and Michael grabbed each side and ran for it. Surreal to watch how fast we could move; they were gone In a blur while I counted the movements around me. At least four, maybe a little more.

"Ya just couldn't let sleeping dogs lay; I knew you weren't done. So I watched and waited until you came here," a voice, much like Amos, whooshed past. Confident as ever.

"Where would be the fun in that?"

"The end is inevitable; why stand in our way."

"Nothing is certain; how about you cut the theatrics and just face me? You've been dying for your pound of flesh. Or has your boss for your dead nuts in a vice,"

"Who, David? He's another that sees the end soon enough,"

"I was talking about the old bastard that just got free, but now you mentioned it. What's it like being only 3rf or 4th in charge,"

The whooshing quickly stopped; my goading had the reaction I wanted. After all, it's easier to hit a target that isn't moving. That's exactly what I braced to do. Clinging to what he did to me, I anticipated that Amos would be the one to confront me. My ears focused on the tiny wafts of air that circled, counting seconds as they neared, waiting for the right moment to strike...

'Thump,'

My knuckles felt his bony face connect. His jaw flapped as I sent Amos flying helplessly against the side of the cave, landing in a battered heap. Vampires may be supernatural, but so was I, and I unloaded another wave of pain that seemed bottomless. I raced forward; my claws crunched into Amos's throat. All I had was revenge on my mind as his mouth hung open, choking. This would've been the moment anyone else would turn red. Not Amos; he stayed mottled, deathly white.

Four other vampires stopped behind us; I gripped tighter before picking Amos up one-handed to shield myself from attack, using Amos as leverage. I could've ended him right then, but I figured I would at least try for answers. Mindful of being overrun, I ensured his throat wasn't getting away.

They postured and bounced toward us, hissing. I was scared beyond belief, but that had to stop if I were to stand a chance of ending the bloodshed and get Ellena back alive.

"Come closer, and he will only be the first to fall," I said, attempting bravado, a little let down by the croaking voice but did enough. Amos's skin was brittle, and my claws had pierced easily; if it could be called that, only his blood was black, stank and spurted over my claws.

"Cuh, cuh. Go on, do it; I dare you. I can smell the hatred seeping from your pores. As long as you're happy not seeing ya wee lass ever again,"

"Eager to die, are we...again? I could easily do it. I want to do it; how did you even know to come here?"

"Death is nothing to be in the presence of a god in the world of man,"

"Your master isn't a god, not even a human; he's just a disgruntled bloodsucker pissed off that he was trapped underwater for so long,"

"God's shape worlds in their image, vampires will take over, and all will buckle under our heel. Supernatural included" What Amos said struck a cord. If they got access to the caves, would its power attract more from the shadows or cause a greater battle for control? Surely, it wasn't the only one in Great Britain or the rest of the world.

"Why, though? What's the point?"

"Because we're sick of hiding and being deprived of food. Aren't you fed up with having to hide your true nature?"

"There's no hiding here, and you've hardly done the same; now, where is she?"

Amos squirmed; the four in front didn't know whether to attack or stay. Dancing around us. I was in a tight spot; I could manoeuvre us for me to run, but the vamps were equally fast. I may have evolved a little physically; my energy levels after being shot still weren't at their peak. Or I could rip out his throat and hope the others have second thoughts.

"Just because a few can walk in daylight doesn't mean all is a bed of roses. We have to use fancy witch magic and talismans while you stroll around freely. Not for much longer. The master will see to that,"

Amos surprised me while confirming Ruth or someone of her ability was helping the vampires. After our first meeting, I was stunned to find out Amos was a vampire. All the stories showed them as creatures of the night, while Ruth fed us some cock and bull information that they're weaker in the day. Instead, she was more than likely helping them. I couldn't see how that would change, though.

"If you wanted to enjoy the daylight, why become a vampire? What do you mean much longer?" I asked no sooner than my senses picked up on another presence, moving slowly. There is no heartbeat but another tinge of death, only slightly different, and some strange spices. It had to be the guy in the cave. Now wasn't the time for more distractions.

"Who said it was a choice? Death was already coming. It was that or live but be something else, something powerful, and soon we'll be back at the top of the food chain,"

"That's wishful thinking,"

"Like the thinking that had you searching the water to retrieve his coffin for us. I will admit we got a little lucky. After all, the cliffs and caves used to be that far out, and it had been in one, but none of us could see it until blessed with the touch of a demon. What are the odds, eh? All it took was the master to make you see what you'd been chasing,"

Amos managed to gargle a chuckle; my reaction was to pinch my grip further until my claw tips almost met around his windpipe. I thought it wouldn't take much as I toyed with it a little. Amos needed to understand his bony existence was in my hands. It also made me think of those numbers; if that area used to be all cliffs and caves, there could've been another entrance at the grid point, only now it's moved back.

The cliffs seemed full of caves and tunnels; never know what else could lurk in one. As much as I didn't like the idea, we may have to venture down there at least one more time to be sure. I couldn't shake the feeling there was something important waiting to be found, and it could help us.

"Where is she?"

"There's no point. If she's not turned already, she soon will be. Every Count should have a countess, after all," Amos laughed again as anger tore through me; I was a centimetre or two away from ending him.

"If you're an all-knowing blood bandit. What happened to the original Countess, Anna Farrington?"

"That one is a mystery that torments you and is so easy to use. Stories say she returned from safety. Believed that Jean Cortez fella was dead, and she died of a broken heart. Well, the fall killed her, but that's the reason,"

"So she did jump?"

"Yeah, I dinnae want to scare off the fresh food on their first day, now did I?"

"Fresh food? You do realise I have your throat in my claws. What happened to her body?"

"Nae bother, what will be will be as, for her body. It disappeared. Happened around the time the master got imprisoned,"

My head was suddenly in a whirl with thoughts. What if those coordinates led to where Anna was buried? Locke claimed in his letter about being distantly related to Jean Cortez, truthfully I couldn't see it, but how else did he have a blood curse? Unless that part was true, we were told a story that wasn't. That Anna's burial site could hold the key to stopping Count Diminescu. Who would've moved her, though?

A shuffle near some bushes to our right grabbed our attention momentarily, enough for Amos to attempt to break free. He drove an elbow into my stomach, catching me off guard; I was a little winded but still clung on. The four in front were frenzied, not knowing what to do before a hooded stranger appeared from the shadows. Only they appeared like the person who saved me from the first gunshot. To think about it, I'd been shot five times since being here and twice the other month. I didn't want another any time soon.

"You have to destroy the heart, or he will heal," the cloak spoke. Amos and I looked at each other, and Amos smiled. Another 'dot' I hadn't known. That's why Amos was acting so 'matter of fact' he figured I'd drop his body, he'd play dead, and I would leave him. Then Amos could heal in time for the main event.

Everything in front blurred, and a series of whooshes whipped around. Whatever was happening, I hadn't factored in, and as I was getting caught up in trying to tell who was who, one flew toward knocking me backwards; my grip on Amos's throat released, but I still had him as we hit the cave wall. Amos swiped at my face with his long, talon-like nails. I dodged, but he tore across my chest.

They ripped deep into my flesh and began to burn; the cuts were on fire and agony. Amos tried to push off, but I couldn't let him escape.

I was amidst another moral dilemma; having already taken a load of vampires out, it shouldn't have been a problem. It was the whole walking and talking bit. A crazy conversation made it feel like murder. Then again, I remembered what I witnessed Amos do the other night and thought about how many others he'd slain in search of 'food' he had to be stopped.

With my claws still gripped to his right arm, Amos spun around to swipe at me again; this time, I didn't think I got him before he got to me. As Amos threw himself down to swing his arm, I punched up. My claws tore through his bony chest, clutching his stinking black heart and out of his back. Amos went limp, impaled on my arm.

The blurs suddenly stopped. I stood up, dropping the body of Amos to the floor while still clutching his heart as I held it aloft like it was a trophy. It was crushed between my claws with one quick squeeze, spraying black blood everywhere. Leaving me with a feeling of redemption. It didn't feel nice, but we'd taken a big chess piece off the board.

The other vampires froze a quick look at each other before disappearing in a blur. A huge sigh of relief until I dropped to my knees in agony. My chest was on fire and had progressed. Those nail slices in my skin were now black, vein track marks spreading as sweat pooled over my forehead.

The cloak breezed toward me; I finally saw his face. High cheekbones, lean face with a carefully crafted goatee, mottled pale. If I were a betting man, this was Jean Cortez. I'm not one for assumptions, but he had that vibe.

"You're being poisoned; vampire's nails have venom, particularly harmful to werewolves. This is where this will be your friend," he pulled a handful of herbs from a small black pouch on his waist next to a very old-looking curved blade. The way sickles are but only the tip, its handle was carved out of oak and lined with gold and black leather. He began crushing and rolling the herbs in his hands.

"Firstly, who are you? And secondly, what is it?"

"I'm Jean, and I'm sure you've heard all the stories about me. Very little of it's true. This is mistletoe. Now brace yourself because it will hurt," At least I was right; I did as suggested and braced. His skinny hands ground the crushed mistletoe into the wound. It hurt so bad I couldn't help but roar, shaking the trees. My eyes glowed blood red.

"Christ, you weren't wrong. As for the stories, yes, I fear we need your help, and I need to understand what happened here them years ago and what happened to you,"

"Well, the short version. My friend Frederick Lasille and I discovered an old body with long fangs in Romania. I found it quite remarkable how someone could have animal-like teeth and brought with us to our next destination in Scotland; by the time we got settled there, Frederick kept poking around with the body, especially when I wasn't present. Suddenly, Frederick got sick, and then dead cattle began appearing through the town and eventually dead people. By this point, I had grown close to Countess Anna.-

-Frederick got sicker; he had the same long fangs and craved blood. We tried hiding him chained up in Montague house, but he escaped. He accidentally cut himself, poking around the dead body's fangs. That blood miraculously revived what we later discovered to be an ancient vampire. Frederick was its puppet, feeding it to make it stronger until we were at the point of no return. With the dead body count rising, the town turned on us; only the dead soon rose, becoming vampires. Count Diminescu was his name; he tore through the town, bathing the streets in blood. Frederick became his loyal servant as the Count destroyed Anna's family to take over the castle; he had designs on Anna, too. He wanted her to be his broke and was relentless.-

-Anna had fallen pregnant as the months passed; for the most part, I kept us safe in Montague house, but the Count's numbers grew. I had been busy mixing herbs and using every druid trick in the book to test against early vampire samples to see how they reacted. A mix of mountain ash and white oak causes cells to desiccate. We finally had a weapon. I rounded up as many willing villagers as possible and sent Anna away for her and our baby's safety as the Count came close to grabbing her on more than one occasion.-

-the Count had developed a cult following, with huge lavish meetings with his most loyal minions who'd die for him. A high battle ensued on the grounds near the castle; so much blood was spilt that it sometimes seeped through the soil. I'd managed to use a tunnel from Montague to the castle to sneak through the carnage. Little had I known, amidst the melee, I'd been bitten. Feeling the vampire venom spreading, changing every fibre of my being, I summoned the last ounce of fight before the darkness took over.

I'd forged a spear crafted with a blend of white oak and mountain ash so I wouldn't have to get within his deadly reach. If the Count locks eyes with you, there's no escape. When I found the Count in the grand hall, he was crouched over another victim draped in blood. From the shadows, I launched the spear with all my might, sending it straight and true as it tore through the Count's chest after he'd turned my way at the last second. Otherwise, it would've gone through his back. The spear impedes the Count through his heart. -

-I watched his pale skin slowly turn grey as he gradually desiccated. Frederick rushed in as the dropped to the floor, looking like a dehydrated corpse. Frederick, in a fit of rage, cast a curse upon me that I would be forever bound to this village, and if I came within a hundred feet of Anna, she would die in excruciating agony; what's more, my bloodline would forever crave to feed on blood, so my pain as the vampirism slowly took over could be felt for centuries to come. With the battle won, I had no choice but to go into hiding. My blood lust took hold, ravaging my body, until I managed to subdue it with a spell of my making. That didn't stop me being a creature of the night, imprisoned in this god-forsaken town. Unable to see Anna or be together as a family. I did the only thing I thought would be for the best and made it seem to others that I was dead.-

-Word reached Anna; I assumed she'd take the news badly but would stay away. She didn't. Knowing I couldn't see her, I had to stay away. Then I found her dead at the bottom of the cliffs. So, being as I was cursed to stay here, I arranged for the townspeople to entomb the Count and cursed that he could only be retrieved by something demonic from the bowels of hell. Never did I imagine a demon wolf being in existence. As extra security, after spending hours cradling my Anna, I added that he could only be revived by her blood or bloodline. Two details that I never imagined were possible, and the two would be safe. Frederick disappeared along with a few stray vampires; I'd known over the centuries that they'd been quietly amassing numbers for when the time came.-

-It seems they never gave up hope on the Count's revival. I kept a watch from afar, overseeing various incarnations. Whilst taking safety measures that should the time come, secrets could be uncovered to send the Count back to whence it came. As I say, I never imagined a demon werewolf would be used to revive him but could also be the saviour,'

That was supposed to be the short version, but his story blew my mind and sounded genuine. It was a trap I'd fallen into so many times since being here, but the emotion Jean conveyed was too painfully heartbreaking not to be true. In that, I could see a parallel between Ellena and me. Our story wouldn't end that way if I could help it. Jean had me curious about the 'secrets' as safety measures.

"What's the secret?"

"Well, you were almost on track to where a cave entrance would've been; through that is a tunnel that led to a tomb where my Anna is laid to rest. It's amongst her bones that the secret is hidden. One that appears will be needed,"

Jean's black eyes sunk to the floor. Disturbing his loved one would be hard, but that could be the only way we stood a chance. The only way we may get Ellena back is to stop what's planned.

"Why tonight, though? Why has he chosen an eclipse?" I said, not expecting Jean to know but wondering because that was a huge 'dot' not lining up.

"Then. Offer it some kind of blood token on a lunar eclipse and some enchantment I do not know of but exists. The skies will stay permanently blood red, making it easier for vampires to be free. Some do it with little bewitched trinkets. While others, like me, can use magic without that. But that leaves the ordinary level or newly turned vampire. What better way to signify the Count's return than a permanent blood-red sky? Vampires can rule, and what's more, it may affect the lunar potency for werewolves. Dare I say it, deprive them,"

"So, let's say someone has imprisoned a horde of werewolves and had been driving of moonlight or the ability to change back. Take the moon away permanently; then the Count would have an army of enslaved werewolves, not just for here but wherever they decided to go,"

"It appears so. The only way to stop this is to kill him,"

"What would happen to the other vampires?"

"I don't know, but it has to end,"

"Where do I get white oak and mountain ash?"

"You already have the information; just picture the shift over time to the right. You'll have to use your other eyes,"

"Why are you helping us?"

"I lost my world; watching that happen to someone else wouldn't be right. Not to mention the trouble it spells for the rest of the world," Jean looked serious; that idea of a vampire helping us was weird; Duncan seemed on the up and up; look what happened.

It was hard to believe what I'd heard and the dangerously world-changing 'dots' I was assembling. My heart wanted me to be wrong, but my head knew otherwise. What's more, a sickly feeling brewed in the pit of my stomach over who the sacrifice could be…Ellena.

Chapter 45

'9th November 5 am'

Their faces were a picture as I slowly approached the car. The headlights were on full; damn near blinded me as I walked in the beamline with my arm three-quarters covered with dried blood. Jean vanished as mysteriously as he'd arrived but had given me plenty to digest, and none of it was good. He made it clear he'd join the fight when the time came; this was one battle he couldn't afford to miss.

Jean's help aside, and mostly he'd been sincere, a tiny element of doubt crept into my mind. He may have another motive at play. That could well be freedom. If Ruth was who I thought, and the curse got broken, Jean would be free to leave; with talk of Locke being connected, he could be too—two birds with one stake.

What if the Count was killed, and that ended his sire line? Surely, I wasn't the only one to think it, except Jean and perhaps Ruth. This means that not only did we have to worry about vampires coming at us from all angles, a low-life crime family, a dodgy mayor and a supposed vampire witch. We had to be weary of contingencies in motion. A luxury we didn't have the numbers to afford.

"I see that went well," Michael rolled down his window to hand over the whiskey. His eyes fixed on the blood.

Straightaway, my brain flashed the image of me holding Amos's aloft before crushing it in my claws. That alone rapped a chill across my shoulders that made me shudder. It was all well and good in the heat of the moment, but once sober from the adrenaline, I feel a tinge of shame; maybe over time, that will ease. The way life keeps handing our arses to us, I'm going to need to get good with it, fast.

"You could say that not before the bastard clawed my chest up. Look," I pulled open the shredded clothing, but nothing. It was completely gone.

I was used to speed healing; normally, there is a little reddening left behind that takes longer. Considering how much it burnt, it appeared as though it never happened. Don't get me wrong; I'm all for that. A little consistency would be nice.

"What did they have, rubber nails?" Michael laughed.

"Christ no, burnt so bad, but I have another story for reasons why,"

"So, what happened, lad? Scare them off or something?" Skip piped up as I downed a large mouthful of whiskey. Throat-burning music to my ears.

"Let's just say Amos didn't have the heart for it in the end," Skip smiled a huge cheesy grin.

"Thank fuck for that. After that shit fest by the pier, he deserved what came his way. Question though, is there any way he could still come back?" Michael enquired genuinely, and I'd say no if this place has taught me anything except the unexpected.

"Not unless he somehow could superglue all the pieces back together or regrow a new one. Being as he's dead, I mean dead, dead; he wouldn't even be able to try,"

"What if one of his bloodsucking friends got a shovel and scooped it back into his chest?"

"No, Michael,"

"But if they did, and say, the big boss decides to give him a decrepit 'golden shower', could he then? I mean, they're all sorts of fucking weird, aren't they?" Michael smiled; he knew what he was doing.

"Firstly, I highly bloody doubt it. I'm not even sure vampires can go to the bathroom. Secondly, Michael? Again? What's the matter, Michael, missing dressing up as your alter ego 'Sharon' and taking a trip to SOHO? Or is it your weekend gimp fests?"

I couldn't help but laugh; Michael could see I wasn't comfortable with what I had to do to Amos and his heart, so he turned it into a joke. The sick bastard has a twisted sense of humour, but it is exactly what we needed.

"Right, wise guy, leave Sharon out; she's done nothing to you. Now, what the heck are we going to do next to get our girl back and send the wrinkly bastard to hell,"

"Oi... less of the wrinkly bastard," Skip butted, chuckling to himself.

I paused momentarily as a sudden brisk rustle through the bushes grabbed my attention; I felt jumpy and didn't like it. Not being able to hear the bloodsuckers had me on the back foot; we had to be careful. My class flicked out reluctantly, ready and still with dried blood under the tips. What's a little more before we move on? I saw a pathway through the bushes whipping side to side and heading straight toward us. No meandering, almost arrow and the more I looked, I noticed how quickly it was moving.

"Guys, look," Skip and Michael stared. The newly released werewolf was still a little shell-shocked. Oddly enough, my hackles hadn't moved. Then a rush of wind rampaged through the towering trees, getting tormented in the breeze and bringing an all too familiar scent...blood.

"What the heck?" Skip shoved his door open, a looming presence waiting beside me; his forehead wrinkles all puddle together in his confusion.

"Whatever is coming is bleeding or recently devoured some," I said, stopping Michael from getting out; the last we needed was to spook our new companion. He was teetering on the edge of insanity as it was.

The scent of blood grew stronger, with the bushes thinning out, and the last tall stems parted ways with a final whoosh. A cannonball-like shape shot toward me; its appearance was unmistakable: a bloody head. Quite literally, somebody's very bloodied head. I also recognised who it once belonged to, and I couldn't believe my eyes. Mayor Duncan Campbell had served his purpose.

I caught his rounded bonce with more blood squelching across my hands. Duncan's eyes were rolled backwards, and his jaw fixed open, almost like a morbid Picasso abstract art piece. Why, in God's name, did this have to happen? He'd already switched sides after all, or had he? Yes, he handed us over to Amos and Co. Could he have been coerced?

"This shit is getting weirder," Michael caught my attention; I couldn't take my eyes off Duncan's decapitated face.

It wasn't long before the details jumped out, oil. Finger smears around the flayed neck skin. Mostly, the head appeared to have been cut cleanly, especially the vertebrae. My red eyes scanned closer at the smear, no long nail-tip impressions, normal fingers covered in engine oil; I could almost see prints, too. This had to be the work of McNally.

"Skip, in the boot; there's an empty ice box,"

"Why, lad?"

"Because this here is a straightforward, brutal murder. Yeah, somebody with supernatural strength launched it at us. But this was chopped off by a human hand. A vampire could tear the head off, leaving gristle skin and bone flapping loose. This is different, but they've been sloppy; we have a print, possibly DNA. Mine will be in the system and can be eliminated. That oil will likely be from McNally's garage,"

"Not to piss on your cornflakes, matey, but why?"

"Because we're better than this," I said, showing my blood-covered arm.

"What do you mean?" Michael wasn't getting what I meant.

"We may be supernatural creatures, but we're also human first and still are. There's demon in me, too, but that doesn't mean I have to be demonic. When the last trickle of blood stops falling, the vampires have been sent packing. There are still elements that could recycle the mess over and over, especially if a certain someone takes the mayoral seat unopposed now. David McNally is too dangerous for a position of power, and chopping off the head of his competition is proof. It may not directly involve local police, but if we go to a main office or CID equivalent in Glasgow at the end, maybe they'll be taken down for murder," I stared at both, getting the seal of approval.

No sooner had I finished my soapbox moment, and Duncan's head was safely stowed in the cooler. That rustling noise began again. Far brisker this time, with the same pattern and speed. Surely it couldn't be, I thought, using my wolf eyes to look as far forward as I could, seeing no one. One is an incident, two is a coincidence, right?

Sure enough, breaking through the thinned green, another bowling ball shape, only this had longish Auburn hair. It whistled toward us, spraying blood droplets along the way. This time, Skip grabbed hold. This time, the eyes and mouth were closed, and her face had substantial bruising around her cheekbones and further traces of oil. She must have been Duncan's wife and the reason for switching sides.

"This is bloody sick, lad," Skip didn't waste time showing; I already saw the details I needed. He simply added it to the cooler.

Instead, I was searching the distance, praying we weren't about to be hit by decapitated head number three. Even worse, neither of us suspected a thing. All I saw was endless green and red due to the sky; I was lost in my thoughts while Michael and Skip debriefed between themselves in their usual hate-the-world way.

I took out Amos, and they took out Duncan and his wife; this was quite the warped game of chess we'd caught up in. Each took pieces off the board, and I wondered which side was the better for it.

Amos was quite old compared to other vampires and could've been one of the strongest in their ranks aside from the Count, Frederick or Jean, maybe even the older women that we knew little of and seemed more on the periphery so far. Whereas Duncan had been on the outskirts, he saved us but also carted around Ellena to hand over her and Michael.

To me, it seemed we won these moves. Little did David know of their mistakes. What

I'd told Michael and Skip about being better was true; somebody had to take the fall, and we may have the evidence to do it. The harder part would be keeping it safe in light of Michael's car blowing up.

I looked at Skip again, wondering how much he'd seen this week. How long had he been watching and why?

He may have argued with Locke, but that could've been about anything. Our beloved ADI wasn't the sort to tell a different story to what he wrote in the letter unless Skip has had his doubts over Locke for longer. After all, he mentioned Locke had the druid symbol and followed him to that closed-down shop in Forest Gate. The more I analysed the reasons and what-ifs, I began questioning just how fine a line Locke was treading to the bad side.

While we still had to get the Whitlock family back home to rear their heads. They wouldn't just take a back seat, not with the 'Black Widow' information knocking around and that ancient relic that could be connected to this and telluric current nonsense. As sad as it sounds, I was looking forward to returning to London and an investigation's surreal normality—no doubt wrapped in the supernatural.

At least we wouldn't fumble so blind, and Ellena would be safe. It wasn't just the mysteriousness of Skip turning up, though; it's been the sudden departure and consultancy stuff like he has an agenda elsewhere, which worried me. If there was anything I knew the best about Skip, he liked playing cards close to his chest, and we'd only see them when he wanted us to.

'Georgie, you there?'

A blood-chilling echo of a voice I longed to hear with my heart aching skated its icy words through my head. I shuddered, darting my head around; my body trembled as if it had been touched by death. The voice was Ellena's

Chapter 46

This dangerous, bloodthirsty chess game was driving me crazy, enough to have me hearing all manner of bizarre things. I was about to get in the car and head towards the next quest in our never-ending sleepless nightmare. Instead, I couldn't stop twisting and searching. This time, not for freshly severed heads being laughed at us. Those words couldn't be hers; they just couldn't. Could they? I wanted Ellena back with us so badly my mind was tormenting me. I still blamed myself, and this was the result. I was finally cracking up. God knows how I hadn't already, but perhaps all of the vampire mind fucking and then holding Duncan's head was the straw that broke the werewolf's back.

'Georgie, Don't be scared, it's me,'

Ellena came again; I could feel my blood draining to my feet as I walked into a misty freezer; that's how cold each word made me feel. Even my hackles didn't know what to do. They didn't jump because of danger; they were shocked with fear. That was the underlying sensation I was trying to grasp. I was bloody afraid.

The elder, Count Diminescu, had done a number on me; now, I couldn't trust my instincts, senses, or sanity. Was this another chess move? Throw us off with the heads, then mess with me by getting in my head like he had to guide me to the coffin. My heart was going to explode; pain began shooting down my arm as I struggled for breath and composure. My erratic behaviour had gotten attention, but not from the likeliest sources.

Our newly freed werewolf friend, whom we hadn't even the time to find out their name, saw me acting weird and jumped to my side. All it took was one hand on my wrist, the one with the symbol which surprisingly suddenly glowed, and so did his. He didn't talk, not out loud anyway. My head got crowded very quickly.

'It's ok, breathe. Alpha uses this old technique; it's normally used to bring pack Beta's back from being rabid during a full moon, among other things. I saw you spiralling and know the vampire's tricks all too well. How else did you think I was kept at bay for so long? I can now hear what you can for now, at least. Relax and wait,'

'How is this possible? There's so many things I don't know and questions I want to ask; we don't even know your name,'

'All in good time. Seeing as I owe you my life, and I think it's it's Logan,'

'Georgie, it's Ellena, please don't be scared,' it came again. This time, I didn't get the same chill. I looked at Logan, who nodded to say he could also hear. The hard part was controlling, only talking in my head. Meanwhile, we were getting strange looks from Skip and Michael.

'Ellena, is that you?'

'Yes, what Ruth said seems true. Wherever I am is dark, damp and stony. So I fell asleep thinking of you to see if I could reach you. Georgie, I'm so scared. I need you,'

Logan signalled to keep talking by rolling his hand forward in the air.

'That happened quickly?' it seemed too good to be true; what did I know? Perhaps that stuff worked; imagine your target and Bob's your uncle.

'All I can think about to keep me calm is you and that you're out there trying to find a way to end this,'

Ellena had me thinking, mainly because of our experience with the Golem version in the ground. I wondered if Ellena saw us getting shot; how would she expect me to be still looking if I was dead? Let alone get in my head.

'What do you remember about the beach?'

'I was dragged to a coffin; my hand got cut. All sorts of horrifying happened that I won't forget in a hurry. You know I'm good with creepy, but watching a body form back together little by little until the bastard jumped up and grabbed me by the throat, I passed out,'

Everything Ellena or her voice said sounded truthful. Still, in this awkward moment of another werewolf gripping my symbol, a fallen Alpha to boot, I couldn't wrap my fragile brain around Ellena using telepathy. Assuming that's what it was, I'm a sceptic at the best of times, especially around psychics and holding events in pubs.

I've lost count of the number of times I've driven past an advertising board 'psychic night with Gina from 8'O'Clock' and joked if she knew could see or know how many would turn up. I mean, they had to, right?

This is another ballpark; we didn't even know how far away she was being kept. Let's say it's in the castle, damp and stony, she said, that's ten miles as the crow flies. So, how could she zero in on me? Unless we were far more connected and in sync than I'd realised. Ellena had been giving the right signals, but a couple of passionate kisses aside, we'd yet to get going as we wanted. Unless I was missing how much she cared for me. There was a test I could ask to prove it, though.

'Ellena, do you remember the limo in Trafalgar Square and what happened?'

There was silence; I looked at Logan, who gestured to wait. My heart hoped this was her and she'd answer right, while my head still didn't know which way was up and was still a little freaked out about having a conference call. Skip and Michael leaned halfway out the windows as if watching a movie. Then Ellena finally spoke.

'Sorry, Georgie, this isn't easy to control. As for that day, oh god, yes. It was awful. With me stuck in the office, you and Michael went to a call to a limo covered in bloody writing. Being the brave arse, you are searched inside while Michael waits outside. Then you got locked in with a time bomb in a corpse. When you said it was too late, I realised I'd fallen for you; I couldn't understand how so soon or why, but I felt you were where I was meant to be, and my heart was breaking. You used that adrenaline gum, and all I could do was pray... after what felt like an excruciating wait, I finally heard you'd made it. Bloody scared me senseless,'

It was Ellena; it had to be. Only she or Michael would know all of that. Unless the Count somehow sees her memories. It had to be her, though if we had any good luck left in the pot, then Ellena really could 'mind walk' or use telepathy. Either way, it was a sign of her being alive or the greatest game of smoke and mirrors.

Yet, it's always about the details, and there were two within that heartfelt speech that raised 'red flags' - the fancy gum and time bomb. I never heard Ellena refer to her creation as fancy; she'd always go way beyond my scope of knowledge with fancy words about what each part did and was proud of it.

Our radio channel was open when I told Michael what I'd found and where while I inspected one of the Black Widow girl's dead fathers.

'Ellena, that was a scary day I never want to repeat. So many things were going on; crazy to think they lined the seats with Semtex, waiting for pressure to trigger. Given me nightmares about sitting down anywhere new since.'

'I know the worst moments in my life, waiting. Georgie, please find me quickly. I'm scared of what they have in store. The idea of being a vampire pincushion, well... not on my to-do list,'

My hackles rumbled, Logan's too. His grip over the symbol shuddered. The alarm bells were like St Paul's Cathedral, ringing loud and clear. This wasn't Ellena. Logan tore his grip from my symbol, maybe a little PTSD over what he'd been through; he looked worried, dragging dirty fingers through scruffy black and grey hair. I had no choice but to play along, even flying solo.

'Ellena, what did you see when awake, smell or touched,'

'Once the surreal smothering of Death eased, there was blood and decay, then sea salt, perhaps seawater. Every step echoed as air vacuums blazed around, carrying sprinkles of pent-up dust. Not the usual, more of ground rocks. Does that help?'

I was doing my best to remain calm as the anger crept up. At first, I was so excited that it could be Ellena. Whilst an abnormal blood-painted sky glazes over us. I sought a silver lining in the bloodshed; with the remains of Amos's crushed heart engrained in my skin with no respite to wash another sin away, I longed for normality. I longed for the golden-haired goddess. Then, my mind was rattled by unexpected words; being hot on the heels of those launched heads, I should have known it was too good to be true.

This had to be the Count, and if I read this tight, I was being lured to a point somewhere important to the vampires. No doubt, where they'd surround me with no escape. He knew I wouldn't have died that easy; much like Logan, he knew more about me and what I could do than I did. The only reason for something unique and powerful in its own right to reach out to me was because I still had a purpose. More likely, my blood did.

Maybe, if he'd woken a while back and made connections with the scum of London or my dear old former foster brother, he'd have it already. That pint hasn't resurfaced yet, and I assume it's been sold to the highest bidder. The Count will attempt to bleed me dry; I hoped I was wrong with my guesswork. Earlier, I thought the sacrifice could be Ellena; what better way to break her resolve than to have her watch me die being sacrificed to the?

Using the mix of my blood to change the vampire's ability to survive in daylight without using magic, trinkets or any other fancy bullshit I'm unaware of. He's now been in her head, seen what she knows; once she's broken, he'd bend her to be the bride he couldn't have in Anna Farrington.

The trouble was, no matter what we did or needed to do, the culmination would lead to one result. A face-off. Or another battle. One that wouldn't last long because we didn't have the numbers. We were almost a punch line to a very bad joke. 'Three shapeshifters walked into a vampire-riddled town looking for a bar; one says to the other, shall we try somewhere else? It's a bit dead around here,' Unfortunately, the joke is on me.

If I could at least make it so that Skip, Michael and Ellena went free, then so be it. I came from nothing and was a nobody; Skip lost his family because of me. Michael had nearly died twice being my mentor sidekick, and Ellena had already tasted far too much of the darkness than she'd bargained for and had so much better to offer the world.
In that moment of madness amidst another vampire mind fucking, that was my decision.

Suppose we got to the point where there was no chance we'd win. I planned to offer myself up in exchange for their freedom. Looking at Logan and the shell he'd become and how easily I had already been manipulated. This could be one supernatural battle, too many. Until then, I had to pretend I knew nothing and play along.

'I don't know; the obvious would've been the castle. Unless you can give me more. Anything else, any slither, may well be the detail we need,'

Again, there was an eerie silence, more to put me on tenterhooks and have me worry while buying into the notion Ellena didn't have control of this power.

'Waves... that's it, I heard waves, and when awake, they seemed loud, echoing. Is that any better?'

The last few words were far more relaxed and almost mischievous—the right amount of detail to tell me where they'd likely be. The cave pathway was open; why else rush to release the elder immediately if all the 'dots' hadn't lined up for the vampires? I'd been so stupid not to realise sooner.

'I will find you, Ellena; we will end this with that vampire's heart impaled on my claws,'

My mouth had to go and do it without showing my cards; the glutton for punishment that I am couldn't let the bloodsucking bastard jump out of my head Scott free. Call it food for thought, besides 'B negative', the moment I finished the sentence, I'd realised I was pissing on the wrong coffin dodger. Screw it; I was going to hell anyway.

'Be careful, George, he's not as easy as Amos,'

My mouth dropped, but nothing came. I felt it leave, though; my mind felt lighter, but it had been left scarred by that comment. He already knew I'd despatched with Amos. I turned to Logan, who'd calmed a little while Michael and Skip still hung out the windows.

"What that bloody hell is going on with you, Georgie," Skip spoke first, slapping back to the present.

"You wouldn't believe me if I told you," my throat shrivelled as I tried to digest the weirdness, taking another joy ride on the crazy train that showed no sign of stopping.

We had to find Anna's tomb urgently.

"Come on, spill the beans so we can get a move on,"

"Let's just say my head was a little crowded. Our newly awakened vampire decided to cross-dress as Ellena, pretending to give clues for us to find her,"

"Are you sure it wasn't her? Without even trying to understand the how,"

"Oh, at first it was convincing, then I asked some questions. I didn't get the right answers, unfortunately,"

"Shit. So, what do we do?"

"We need to find Anna's tomb first; then it looks like we have a date wherever it is supposed to be. It's going to be a trap,"

Logan was looking to the sky, listening. I could tell his ears kept twitching. As I finished telling them what we had to do, he slowly turned to face us, walking forward; first came his claws and bright blue eyes. With each step, he slowly phased, and it was amazing. Scary but bloody amazing to see. Without breaking stride, Logan had phased into a fully formed wolf by the time he was beside me.

It's much bigger than the typical I'd seen on TV. He was bloody huge. This time, Skip and Michael were left speechless, a nice change for Michael; he always had something to say. I was confused about why, though.

'You three handle the tomb; I will seek out the other werewolves. It will be easier for me to bring them back from the wild. When the time comes, we'll be ready. You need to be, too; stop holding back and second-guessing. Embrace what you are; otherwise, you will get yourself killed; too many rely on you. Let it all in; you may surprise yourself,'

Logan spoke in my head like he had the first time we met, and with that, he glided through bushes and trees, becoming a blur on the breeze. It made me wonder if that's how I was when I changed; it happened easily. Logan was right, though, about it all. Fear held me back, and I couldn't shake it free so far. As his shadow faded, the size of his task ahead hadn't. We didn't know how many werewolves had been captured or where they were held. To do all that and be ready to face the evil at this blood-dripping rainbow felt a huge ask of someone who'd barely had their head unscrambled from a vampire's head fuck. I only had a glimpse, which was bad enough, while our next mission wouldn't be easy either.

Chapter 47

With the ominous red sky still smothering everything in its path, my fear level was at its peak. Roars from the crashing waves pounding against the white and black rocky cliff front made my fragile heart jump. Froth kept looping overhead while the cutting winds made my precarious climb dangerous. Michael and Skip had the good sense to listen and stay back to keep watch while I dared to brave another coffin; using my werewolf eyes allowed me to see the concealed recess and what Jean meant by a hidden entrance.

What's more, it was three-quarters up the jagged cliff at the end of a slim rocky path that was past the face curve and hung over choppy, deep-looking waters with the high tide battering its way fully in. Jean intimated our grid findings were near the mark, but coastal erosion had been far worse than we'd realised.

Skip wouldn't manage the route too easily, and with what's happened so far, I felt better knowing they would be safer together. At least then, the surprises would be limited to what's inside the cliffs. I dreaded to think just how many daunting tunnels had been dug by McNally's clan and to what end. Why would they be needed unless what we saw in Montague House and the route out to the beach, we're going to be more of the same? My vision on the way here, which feels like a lifetime ago, could be where and how I find Ellena, hopefully without her being a vampire.

It hadn't even occurred to me that caves could've been used or how deep they went before time slowly changed the coastal landscape. It was probably the giddy explorer in me that got excited by the prospect those numbers could've been to something exhilarating like artefacts or treasure. Something worth hiding. Fooling myself that nobody else could've figured it out already. After all, those digits in the artwork were hard for anyone to see without enhanced vision.

I know it was a fail-safe laid out by Jean before he went into hiding. His story was believable, but the trust issues I've inherited since being in this bloody town have left me doubting whether Jean had fed me what he thought I wanted to hear. He could've been in my head, and I hadn't noticed. This brings me back to the elder, Count Diminescu; how long had he been there before he spoke as Ellena, It was a neat trick, I might add.

Was it while those severed heads were being launched at us, listening to what we said and how we took the shock of it all? Then sucker-punched me.

I couldn't get over that last sentence while pretending to be Ellena. 'Be careful, George, he's not as easy as Amos,' Ellena wouldn't have known that, being a prisoner. Like our entire stay in this town, we were prisoners from the off. All the talk of Ellena being a witch, I now believe that was a ploy to get her interested in discovering more while accounting for any weird goings on with her.

Ellena looked sick on the way to Oxley Town, and the tiny pinprick had to be the cause. Unless Ruth simply drew some more blood to be sure, for what exactly is a 'dot', I can't figure out yet.

There are too many 'little details' drifting around the wilderness of my mind without a connection yet. Unless they were nothing more than theatrics and misdirection, each seawater shower made my footing slippery, no more than two -three feet wide. With each step along, I could feel a chill crawling up my spine; there was something eerie about this section of the cliffs. Whether it was the prospect of finding Anna's tomb or whenever I looked out to sea, I pictured where I was manipulated to go.

Keeping my chest close to the wet stone face, I gripped anything I could to pull myself in. Even with my claws, it was hard as the surface crumbled with each move. They say slow and steady wins the race; this was torture with little margin for error the higher I got. I stopped for a minute to regain my composure as my fear grew.

My senses were going haywire; something was off; I was picking up on pain, sadness, and hatred, but most of all, evil. Overwhelming darkness came hot on the heels of that chill. It could be a precaution to put people off, scare them to go no further. And it was getting to me, breathing deeply, pushing dust out the cracks. It may have been a trick red shade from the sky, but as the dust clipped my claws, I could've sworn it was blood. Not just red, but actual blood.

I got moving again. Every time I grabbed a stone, it happened again. It had to be tiredness, fatigue gripping my balls and making me see all sorts of weird shit. Sheer panic caused me to speed up, and as I did, more sprayed out. Blood began running across my claws and down my hands. A trickle became a small stream, which became a 'bloody' waterfall smothering the rocky face and my arms. My heart screamed with pain, a bass drum beating out of my chest. I tried shaking my head and closing my eyes, but it was still there when I opened them again. I was finally cracking up. How could a cliff bleed? All the while, I still felt that evil in the air.

'Ohhhhh George,' Flicking the blood from my claws, I was struggling, my chest tightened with anxiety taking over my body. I was caught in two minds about whether to turn back when a sharp breeze whipped past carrying a chilling man's voice. I was already scared, but hearing my name called made me jump, stumbling close to the edge. I looked but saw nothing, and it wasn't someone I recognised. Was this the next step to madness?

'Awww, the big bad werewolf is afraid; how does it feel to be powerless,' His icy tone cut deep, my head bounced around, and the world became a blur without me taking anything in. Blood continued to flow, covering the narrow ledge and raining down. I daren't move either way, scared I may slip.

'Don't look down, George,' his voice whipped up from below the ledge.

'Who are you? '

'One, two, vampires are coming to gut you,'

There was no pinning it down; each time, it flew toward me from a different direction. I was pinned to the wall, showered by blood and scared out of my mind.

'Three, four, we will rule once more,'

"Fuck off, leave me alone,"

'Five, six, I will end Ellena with a kiss,'

My body shook relentlessly, and I couldn't take a step at all; I tried. He was right; his constant torment paralysed me. The elder toying with me again was another move to make me believe it was Ellena earlier. Should we give up? I kept thinking.

"You leave her alone,"

'Seven, Eight, it may already be too late,' this time, he flew at my ear, and my stomach flipped at the thought it was already too late.

"She doesn't deserve this. Leave her be,"

'Nine, ten. Poor little George will never be with Ellena again,' Helpless, powerless and enduring an onslaught of torment from someone I couldn't see. A small part of me wanted him to end me now instead of all the games. Ellena was my weakness, and things the Count said were breaking me.

"Eleven, twelve, how about you go fuck yourself," I barely managed the strength to growl back as blood painted my body.

'Oooh, it has some bite, after all. Will do you no good; what I find fascinating is your inability to grasp how close to death you are and how easy it would be to snatch your last breath, even now. I know your innermost fears and your darkest secrets. You're a killer, George, a savage beast pretending to be normal; there's no escaping the past,'

Could he know? Or was it part of this sick torment he'd executed at my expense? It seems to be a common trait with vampires, grandstanding and liking the sound of their voice. My answer soon came, with the flowing blood easing to a trickle and nothing. I watched all traces fade away as if it hadn't happened, listening to the biting cold howls carrying menacing laughter between the taunts.

The last to disappear was the dark red puddles across the ledge; with my back against the wall, I checked my arms again to ensure. Normal didn't last long; I get seeing is believing, but if it weren't happening to me, I would've found what happened next hard to digest. First came the thick, heavy metal shackles clamped deep into my skin.

Then, the terrifying chains wrapped in the potent smell of burning and bubbling burnt flesh. A tear rolled down my cheek; I remembered the last time I wore these. As a child, I'd been left for dead in the basement of a house in East London.

The shackles were hot, melting into my flesh as blisters spread throughout my arms, riding on the agony of my body boiling. My blood boiled. Looking at the sea, everything in front began to change. Water became scorched walls with demonic symbols etched deep or painted in blood. Pillars rumbled up from beyond the ledge, and in between, I see the symbol for the 'devil's circle,' dripping blood. My arms yanked up and forward, leaving me suspended in chains. I couldn't see how, but the chains pulled tighter, disappearing within the burnt brickwork holding me captive.

There was no fighting against it; I had no strength as I edged forward. My world catapulted me back to my nightmare childhood. Then came the dead bodies. They appeared from nowhere, burnt to a crisp, flesh peeling free. The tears flowed quicker now; I felt lost in every way imaginable, wondering what was real and how the elder vampire could make me experience all the horrors I'd long since hidden all over again.

My brain had blocked it out the first time for a reason, and since my memories came back, I hadn't wanted to embrace them. Now, I had no choice. A distraction or torture, neither worked in my favour.

'Look at what you did, George. I told you you're a killer. Look at the family you destroyed. Why should you be happy?'

"I was just a kid; they trapped and experimented on me. It wasn't my fault,"

'Oh, but it was. So will be what's to come. Their blood will be on your hands too, and there's nothing you can do,'

His words were terrorising me to the core. Being tapped in chains represented my life in more ways than one, and I didn't know how to break free. The burnt walls and pillars slowly became sheets of rippled metal. I could smell sawdust, lots of it. The chains faded along with the pain and burnt dead bodies. One detail lingered, though the smell of blood.

Moreover, I was back in Billingsgate market and the warehouse where we took on the Kanaima demon. Blood flowed like a fast-moving river, swarming everything in its path and turning the sawdust to mounds of clumpy crimson; dead centre was Michael. His throat was shredded just like that night. The bloodsucker was forcing me to relive all the bad moments in my life so far.

'If you needed more proof, look what you did, George. More blood in your hands,'

I couldn't take my eyes off Michael's throat; I could hear his heart slowing as blood continued to pour. I remember everything from that night. This wasn't my fault, was it?

"None of what you have said is on me; I was a child without knowledge or control. I grew up unaware of what I was until somebody made me remember everything, including the pain. You can't hurt me anymore than I have endured already. I was broken before I was given a chance and should've died at just six years old. Then my wife and child were killed because of that house fire and the deaths of those people. So, I think the scales may be in my favour there. As for Michael, I saved his life. Aside from slaying innocents, what have you done in all your years on this planet?"

The longer I saw Michael bleeding out, the more I realised that he would've died without me, and at the time, ADI Locke and Ellena were strapped to tables with a paralytic toxin going into their organs. A lot happened at once, and there were only so many places I could be at once, even with my speed. Count Diminescu peeked behind the curtain of my mind and thought he could turn it against me.

I'd allowed him to siphon an advantage, but each story he'd highlighted had a silver lining. Skip saved me that night and helped me become the man I am today. This stalling tactic had to end. I needed in that tomb but had a bad feeling that the pain and evil I sensed were more than the Count, and I may already be too late for what we needed.

'The difference between us, George, I know what I am. All you are is a sack of meat and juicy blood with a name. Too afraid...Too ashamed and weak to be what the devil created you to be. I may have slayed all before me, but I was born different, too, unable to eat normally. Imagine surviving on nothing but cattle to realise the blood makes me tick. Was that my fault? If you want to play the blame game, Daddy didn't buy that race car or bike; we can all do that, only I embraced what I needed to live. Why shouldn't I live? What makes you decide who lives and who doesn't? I needed blood, so I took it, and then the world decided it was evil; my right to live was evil. So, I ask you, what makes your need to live any greater than mine or others like me?-

-All because they named my rare condition vampirism? Did you know werewolves naturally lean to the wild? They want to run free and hunt, eat meat and tear through flesh, no matter what kind. When a wolf is wild, they don't care; when instinct takes over, the beast embraces its primal urges and need to survive. How are your urges, George? Ever felt the adrenaline rush of the 'wild hunt'? The winter solstice? No, because you scare yourself; once the genie is out of the bottle, the world will know what you're really like. A savage beast forged in the bowels of hell. So, please don't pretend to be all high and mighty; we are the same. I offered you the chance to join us. One last chance because your gift is a waste, I could help you become the real you.-

-We could shape the world and make a new race of supernatural beings with no fears or weaknesses. We could give everyone the choice to be different, to enjoy the power that comes with such a divine blessing. Those who resist will be food.'

I couldn't figure out this demented vamp just when I thought they would sacrifice me for my blood and craft a different entity. I'm thrown in another direction, even if some of the details were on the money. His offer sounded more like a 'join us', or they will steamroll us. He wanted a unique army, and I was key one way or another. Neither was on the menu for me, but I had no way of coming out on top, not if he found it so easy to torment me to the brink of giving up. Every savage card pulled from my fragile mind pushed me closer to the edge.

Then I realised it was all guesswork; the crusty bastard mistook parts of my troubled life for tools to use against me. They were building blocks and moments that helped me get back to a different kind of family. Michael didn't die, and his earlier speech on the clifftop told me he has no regrets over what he's become. Now, I had to dispel this illusion he'd created around me.

"Let me stop you there, my decrepit friend. As much as I should really be all aboard what you're selling, I'm not enjoying the vibes you're giving off. I mean bloody hell, you're like a crazy stalker Ex, who doesn't understand the word 'no'. Did all that seawater fuck you up? This mind fucking thing you got going, it's not for me, so I'm afraid it's time to turn your hearing aid up or get one of your 'blood bitches' to listen In. I am going to rip your rotten heart from your bony chest, then tear your head from that shrivelled neck and mount it to the door of that bloody castle for the whole town to see,"

His voice remained silent. Instead, the wind tore around and through me, throwing my body like a rag doll and smothering my senses with the overwhelming intoxication of blood. My head spun, blurring my vision until I didn't know whether I was coming or going. After a few seconds, I settled, too little too late as I had the rug ripped from beneath me, taking the traumatic illusion with it. The throwback to Michael's watershed moment dissipated quickly. Confused, I stumbled. My foot slipped at the edge of the ledge, a sharp shock, my stomach jumped into my throat, and...

'Aaarrrrggghhhh,'

Chapter 48

"Arrgh, for fuck sake. Why do you always get yourself in a mess,"

I skidded over the edge, about to drop, when something sharp clamped onto my forearm. Blood ran down; I was twisting in the wind with my chest bouncing into the cliff's face. Thankfully, it wasn't from another illusion. With the wind carving across my face, I see Michael with his claws gripping me. My stomach was finally settling, and I was more than done with this place—first, a little matter of some bloodsuckers.

Michael yanked my arm up a bit before clamping his other hand on. I latched onto the biggest rock I could reach before kicking into any crack I could to hold steady. Michael's claws dragged painfully through my flesh, enough to make my eyes water. A small price to pay to stop from dropping into the choppy waters. Each roll away revealed some nasty-looking rocks that I didn't fancy meeting.

"Urghh. Not to sound ungrateful, but why are you up here?" I said as Michael dragged me to my stomach, scraping across the edge. I managed to grip a jagged slither in the floor to help.

"Maybe because you were bugging out and looking a little frantic. As you danced too close to the edge, I figured it was my turn to be the saviour," Michael's timing was perfect and not the first time I could say that. With a final look at the crashing waves, I got to my feet, relieved.

The trouble was, the worst was yet to come. We were facing the pathway to move forward again, no more voices travelling on the wind to torment me; the rest was. The pain mixed with sadness and, most of all, evil. How could this be so if the elder had disappeared as quickly as he came?

He was in my head and knew what I was going to do. With all those emotions I was picking up on, we could be heading into a trap. What else made sense when my senses were being ravaged, and now Michael was being roped into it, leaving Skip vulnerable, keeping watch.

"With good reason. A certain pointy-toothed bastard won't take no for an answer,"

"Hey…I only asked you once to have a night with Ellena. There's still life in this old dog, yet you know," Michael joked; the most I could manage was a brief smile. I didn't have the energy, even though the old sod eased my tension a little.

"Less of it, you twat. I mean the other pointy-toothed bastard. He still thinks that I could join his army of supernatural misfits. That and use my blood to help the vampires stick a bandaid over their weaknesses,"

"Sooo, you're thinking about it?" Michael continued taking the piss as we carefully moved through the path.

"I may have made things worse. I told him when this was all over, I would've ripped his rotten heart from his bony chest, torn his head from that shrivelled neck and mounted it to the door of that bloody castle for the whole town to see,"

"I bet he took that well," Michael said, and I was quickly overcome with guilt. My flippancy may have poked the bear too much. Especially with the ease at which the elder pulled my strings.

"Well, he said, '*What makes you decide who lives and who doesn't? I needed blood, so I took it, and then the world decided it was evil; my right to live was evil. So, I ask you, what makes your need to live any greater than mine or others like me?-*

-All because they named my rare condition vampirism? Did you know werewolves naturally lean to the wild, they want to run free and hunt, eat meat and tear through flesh, no matter what kind. When a wolf is wild, they don't care; when instinct takes over, the beast embraces its primal urges and need to survive. How are your urges, George? Have you ever felt the adrenaline rush of the 'wild hunt'? The winter solstice? No, because you scare yourself; once the genie is out of the bottle, the world will know what you're like. A savage beast forged in the bowels of hell. So, don't pretend to be all high and mighty; we are the same. I offered you the chance to join us. One last chance because your gift is a waste, I could help you become the real you.-

-We could shape the world and make a new race of supernatural beings with no fears or weaknesses. We could give everyone the choice to be different, to enjoy the power that comes

with such a divine blessing. Those who resist will be food.' Those were his exact words; as sales pitches go, the old…I mean, older bastard went all out and even made me relive fucking nightmares I'd rather bloody forget, saying it was all my fault, and I was a killer,"

My mind was rattled; everything the vampire showed me was real, triggering all my senses and emotions. What else could he do once we're finally at the witching hour?

"Fuck me, isn't it nice to be wanted? Seriously though, what the bloody hell? He has it bad for you, doesn't he? I take it that's where the heart tearing out came into things? Nice save with the 'older bastard', by the way,"

"Yep, that's when the illusion got whipped away, and I damn near slipped at the edge. Looks like I owe you again,"

If anyone had been keeping score, we were probably in double figures on both sides, not to mention Slip's timely interventions lately. Our pathway was getting higher and higher and seemed narrower, too. Michael shimmied as close to the wall as if his life depended on it. We were thirty feet from the concealed entrance, and my nerves were shot to pieces, made worse by the 'evil' growing too.

If anyone had been keeping score, we were probably in double figures on both sides, not to mention Skip's timely interventions lately. Our pathway was getting higher and higher and seemed narrower, too. Michael shimmied as close to the wall as if his life depended on it. We were thirty feet from the concealed entrance, and my nerves were shot to pieces, made worse by the 'evil' growing too.

"I trust what we're sensing; isn't part of the illusion?"

"Afraid not,"

"Well, that's just bloody perfect,"

We'd reached the rocky entrance front; typical of our luck, the ledge around its base had crumbled away or made that way, so it would be harder for anyone normal to navigate their way. Assuming they found the cave. I could see two small rocks three feet apart to grip a hold of, and one cut out for footing. I knew how to get across, but it wouldn't be easy.

Michael's wingspan and all-around preference to keep his feet firmly on the ground meant he wouldn't attempt it. After hanging off the ledge, I was probably due some clean underwear; what choice did we have?

"Michael-"

"-Let me stop you there; I know you must do it alone. No matter my strength, I can't get that grip, and you know my fears. But if the shit hits the fan…again! Just shout, and I will come. I may need a shit tonne of therapy after, but I will come,"

"Thank you. As for the therapy, I think we will all need a shed load,"

I slowly scooted at Michael, and my right leg began shaking. Everything I'd done so far had been wrapped in fear, and now was no exception. My leg went light, almost numb, and I needed to knock it on the head to get across. Ironically, this was the easy bit.

My fingers barely brushed the bumpy surface, with the wind rocking back and forth; I looked down the gap to see waves battering the cliffs, lining the watery black border with a curtain of white foam. Every bounce unnervingly twisted through my eardrums. Anxiety was steadily building again; I could feel my chest tightening. For Christ's sake, I was a bloody werewolf; I should be braver than this.

Then why couldn't I dare to grab the rocks properly? That lingering evil in the air played a part; my hackles didn't know whether to bounce or rest. There was no escaping fate or the horrible feeling this could either be a wasted journey or something was waiting for me that I didn't want to find.

'Fuck it,' I muttered, letting my claws come forward, phasing a little.

Shuffling my foot toward the crumbled edge, I pushed up on tiptoes with my other foot as I stretched toward the first of the two rock bumps. First swipe...missed, and I nearly lost my footing in the process. Another heart-in-the-mouth moment, a deep breath, and I went again. Second swipe... Sparks flew, and electricity rumbled through my body; everything went black.

I could see flashes of rocks buzzing before my eyes inside a cave. My heart thumped through my chest; it looked much like the vision on the way here. Only, no Ellena. I could smell death, which was so strong it burned my nostrils. I looked around, and ever was the same, including the big pointy rocks and the...coffins. Lots of them stacked. One, in particular, grabbed my attention. Ornate and spooky, with the only slither of light drifting across its crusty body.

Again, the same. The only difference is that this one is closed with no bony fingers dropping out of the crack. The flashes sped up, and with each one, I was closer and closer. I tried my werewolf eyes to scan better, but again, I had no powers, just like the first. All the hairs on my body were on fire. This rubbish was getting older than the 'beef jerky' doing the tormenting. Another sparked, and I stood up close—a rustic, rotten grey with an old-fashioned floral border around the lid. The stink of death was all too consuming. I wanted to run, but I couldn't. I wanted to turn away, but I couldn't. Most of all, I wanted to be sick but couldn't.

The lid slowly creaked open, rocking a chill down my spine. Short and sharp bursts at two-second intervals until what I dreaded came true.

Again, unlike the first scenario. This felt worse. Ellena was inside. I needed to cry but couldn't; she looked normal, with no sign of vampirism. With no super hearing, I couldn't read her heart; Ellena looked at peace, and I hated it. Why was I being shown this? Another torture? A glimmer of what to expect? It was hard to work anything out because each flash played havoc with my vision and seemed disjointed. So far, nothing else grabbed my attention; if there was a message to be had, I wasn't getting it.

Watching Ellena lay so peacefully was hypnotising, even through the flashes. The crazy situation was bloody haunting, and I hated not having control or use of my werewolf abilities. Yet I could feel and smell every rancid detail; maybe not as intense, but I had the sickly pleasure while getting whipped by rushes of salty wind. Ellena's flesh smelt dead and seemed all too devastatingly real.

'Raaaaaaghhhhhhh... They're in the bones... The secrets you seek rest within the bones. - The bloody secrets are in the bones,'

In the blink of an eye, Ellena bolted upright, ghost-white eyes stretched fully, her mouth flying wide open. Ellena let rip with a piercing screech that tore through my eardrums, rocking me on my heels. It beat a ferocious echo around the cave walls. Ellena appeared as a soulless puppet; the screeching stopped, and Ellena curdled that sentence. Not the first a message had been given that way; the last time, it was '*Secrets and the dead are imprisoned amongst the rocks. A key will set them free, and the dead will rule once more,'* ominous and true the word, setting us on this path and me deep in another moment that I couldn't label.

My arms were covered in a sheet of goose pimples, and my brain replayed every second of those words as I saw the flashing black space interrupting another nightmare. My throat tightened as I attempted to brace myself for the next twist, as has been the pattern.

Everything sparked into darkness before echoing back. I didn't return to stretching for a rock to grip and climb this time. I was still in a cave: disbelief, surprise and the feeling of having no idea what was happening other than standing in the middle of the same cave, Deja Vu, or some weird obscure horror loop because I was again facing rocks and the...coffins. Especially the ornate and spooky one. This time, no images flashed, my claws were out, and I, god, used my werewolf eyes; I had no recollection of climbing the gap.

The same triggers tormented my senses, only this time, the pain felt etched into the cave walls, trapped with the coffin. Whistles of wind swooped and looped around the rough, grey dampness on either side; my red eyes highlighted detail to clear a 'dot' in my mind, linking to the beginning. 'Only the dead rests' was carved into the far left wall. A tiny part of me was glad not to be going mad, although if that was real, what about the rest? Especially Ellena.

I walked forward slowly and carefully; the clapping of my heels against the stone floor epitomised the horror movie moment where you shout at the screen telling the character to 'go no further,' or 'turn around you, idiot,' things like that, knowing full well nobody could hear. The coffin was still closed, but I felt I wasn't the first person to come looking; that death stink may be because the seal had been broken. Yet those words were burnt into my mind, 'the bloody secrets are in the bones'. Fear was eating away at me the closer I got. I listened for Michael; he was still standing where I had left him when I first grabbed the rock. His heart was slightly elevated but steady. He kept stepping two paces back and forth.

I got to within a few feet; my hackles flapped relentlessly; I had to be cracking up because I felt the darkness close in on me, like a huge invisible cuddle. I sensed the air suddenly cut off near me while the whooshing through the cave continued. Perhaps paranoia that I was being watched, so much had happened without warning, I doubted everything I sensed. Count Duminescu's mind tricks worked, and I didn't know how to break the pattern. I nervously checked over my shoulder, but nothing. My red eyes scanned every corner, but still, nothing and all I heard was my heart pounding to break out of my chest and the persistent dripping down a wall.

My claws hovered over the edge of the coffin. The image of Ellena popped into my mind, and that's all I saw, looking at the lid. Her smiling face and how I saw her moments ago lay there dead. It couldn't have been Anna Farrington, could it? I thought as I went to grab the lid. That notion hadn't crossed my mind, so I was sure it was Ellena after the head torment. I should've realised that Jean could've concocted some fancy magic bullshit. The how? I had no idea, considering I still pictured magic as guys in black tuxedos pulling a poor rabbit out of a hat after some sap shoved it up a hidden hatch. Not this crazy herb rubbish and nemeton's. If this week had taught me anything, on the one hand, I needed to be more open-minded; on the other, I needed to be careful who I opened it up to. That was one crazy magic trick that even Houdini couldn't figure out.

Three claws on each hand jammed into the coffin's crevice; surprisingly, it wasn't budging. I had it set in my fragile mind that it would fly open because I was again second best. There was no give; opening the lid would take some werewolf strength. Whether it was also magic acting as further protection or I was simply weak, there was no time to second guess.

If the coffin's contents were Anna Farrington, there had to be something in or on her bones that could help us. Boy, did we need it; time was short, and so was my patience. Ellena aside, the fate of the village and beyond was at stake. Even that's ironic. 'Fate at stake' would take a special kind of 'stake' to end that bastard. My hackles continued bouncing, and there was an eerie darkness surrounding me. My only hope was Michael being true to his word if I called and didn't bottle out of the short jump or climb. Also, another bloody 'dot' for me to work out, but that could wait until my tired ass was out of the caves.

I took a deep breath, inhaling more death dust and other crap; I gripped the lid tighter, pulling harder. My eyes glowed bright red with veins pulsating throughout my body; I dragged all the horror we'd endured from the pit of my stomach and used it to fuel my strength...

'Rooaaaaarrrrrr,'

With fangs out full, I let rip with a roar that shook the cave; stone and other debris rattled free from any crack that would allow it. The echo was quite something; it even made the tiny hairs on my balls tingle. Just like the Kanaima case, it felt so good. With a loud creak yawn, the lid flew open, breaking out a thin cloud of purple that had to be magic. Hot on the heels of that cloud came a shower of death—more a curtain of putrid particles powering into the salty sea breeze.

There she was, in a crusty white dress, the mummified skeletal remains of a woman who had to be Anna Farrington. Traces of leather-like skin stretched over several visible bony areas, truly sad and horrific. I didn't want to be trashing her final resting place, but there was no other choice.

Anna's skull was. Still, In good condition, considering cobwebs spun from eye sockets to the coffin's corner. As far as I could tell, she wasn't a vampire or hadn't been one. All her teeth seemed normal if there could be such a thing. She looked like 'Jason Voorhies' mum's decapitated head from Friday the 13th, part two. So goddam creepy.

Fighting the urge to spew my guts, I scanned through Anna's crusty bones; her hands were laid across each other on her stomach. That's when I noticed another detail nobody had shared. An elaborate, diamond-topped wedding ring. Had Anna and Jean married without anyone knowing? Perhaps that's what turned her father against Jean. Unless that was the plan and Jean buried her with it after being too late. So sad how their lives played out, a fate I didn't want for Ellena and me.

I couldn't take my eyes off the size of the rock, imagining the value it would have now. Not that k would take it, but it would surely be worth a fortune. My eyes finally broke their gaze when I noticed the odd positioning of the fingers on her right hand. More importantly, the forefinger appeared buried within Anna. I moved closer; the stink swamped my nostrils, and no mistake, the finger was buried through the dress. The curious wolf in me kept whispering to try pulling it out. Common sense slapped me in the face, telling me to leave it.

'Fuck it, in for a penny...'

I muttered, teasing a claw through the gap underneath, trying to be careful yet scared shitless. It's moments like this that I was glad Michael was outside. He would've been scaring me by now. Although just being so close, did the job well enough. My claw looked huge compared to the bone; I was worried it could snap off if I pulled too hard. Then, I would be condemned to hell. How on earth had I got myself into this position? I kept thinking as I slowly brought the claw to meet the cringy bone.

'Click,' the finger released a trigger inside.

'Mwaaaaaashhhhhhhh,'

A loud, blood-curdling screech tore through the darkness, making me jump out of my skin. A bony hand swiftly crunched into my arm; blood spurted; I tried to run, slipping amongst the dirt as my legs turned to jelly. Anna latched on and wasn't letting go as she suddenly sat upright, fingers tearing into my flesh as life drained. No scream would come. Her head chillingly twisted slowly to face me, sparse wiry strands of hair encased her eyeless sockets with her fragile jaw creepily chattering.

I could've sworn a little pee had leaked out; I was that scared. The floor had become a magnet, keeping me stuck in one place. I had to be dreaming, right? Or another illusion? There was no way a three-hundred-year-old skeleton could come back to life, right? Anna was not letting go for love nor money, displaying strength I'd only experienced from the living or vampires.

Chapter 49

'Are you destined for the secrets that lay in wait? Or is a 'bloody' pool going to be your fate. Only a person whose intentions are pure. Could wield what's made to help the world endure.'

Did I hear right? Too busy squirming against the grip. I should've been able to rip the arm clean off Anna's skeleton, but somehow, I couldn't lift my arm an inch as I dangled amongst the dirty cave floor. In a daze, my throat shrivelled without the strength to shout. I was in the middle of another setback on my road to hell when Anna's skeleton suddenly smashed through the eerie silence and sent me another wave of chills. It was like a 'Creepshow' story, and the voice was equally terrifying. Did not sound like a woman at all.

I couldn't believe I was even contemplating it; for the second time this early morning, my arm was being torn to shreds and having a skeleton do it was a new level of crazy that not even Michael would believe. But I was about to talk to the dead, suppose was a change from ghosts, no less strange. With every wiggle or flinch in my attempt to at least get onto my knees, Anna's fingers squeezed deeper; my blood flowed down my forearm, sending my tastebuds crazy.

Another element I was trying to hide from since ripping through the vampires so far, especially Amos, my blood lust and to shred flesh had grown. Harking back to the count's comment, *'When a wolf is wild, they don't care; when instinct takes over, the beast embraces its primal urges and need to survive. How are your urges, George? Have you ever felt the adrenaline rush of the 'wild hunt'? The winter solstice? No, because you scare yourself; once the genie is out of the bottle, the world will know what you're like.'* I may not have liked it; I'm scared he may be right.

I looked at Anna, freaked out by her skull and chattering teeth, with my mouth primed to speak when an 'I wonder if she could see me without her eyes' thought crossed my mind. With every move I made side to side, Anna's head followed, but the eye sockets were empty, barring a few slimy worms and stray maggots slithering their way free.
I know a stupid thought at that moment; some of me still didn't believe this week was happening. Or didn't want to. So, in peak fear, my brain wanders elsewhere.

"I…I erm…I'm looking for something to help end the bloodshed and prevent the world from being overrun with vampires," I said, barely able to get my words through my raspy throat while trying not to feel or sound insane.

'Ah, the demon werewolf who struggles to believe what they are, who'd rather stay out of the way and watch from afar. Yet you find yourself on this path to save someone whose name you find too painful to mention. Fearing the end is near for someone you hold so dear. I ask you this: what makes you any different from the rest? What makes you so sure you can prevent a blood fest?'

Every word had my goose pimples jumping; we didn't have the time for twenty questions; was I any different from the rest? After all, I was another supernatural being capable of doing terrifying things. That's not what I wanted, though; as a pack, our abilities could do great rather than bad, and we had to strive for that. Far too much evil in the world; decks needed clearing.

"I don't know if I'm any different from the rest. I only know I don't want innocents killed or put in harm's way. This world balances good and bad, but evil could be about to tip the scales. We want to stop that, at least for now, until the next monster escapes from the shadows,"

'You talk of balance and scales; there's no assurity over who prevails. As you so fondly say, 'the devil is in the details'. You have until midnight to write the wrongs of the past and present or become another sad footnote in history's irrelevance. I strongly urge you to make peace with a preference over whose fate may be dire as a consequence,'

A sudden feeling of doom swept through me; for a while, I thought at least one of us might not survive, even resigned to the fact it could be me while praying it wasn't Ellena. Anna's words rocked my core; there was no way I could make peace with anyone's fate being anything other than safe. With all that's gone on, I should take the comment with a pinch of salt; I couldn't see the gain from dead Anna's remains playing games. That consuming, sick feeling was rising again; every move we made had ended with a kick in the balls. Now, I had to take the word of talking bones. Oh, how far my sanity had fallen to the depths of hell. Meanwhile, the old git Michael remained outside, patiently oblivious.

My arm hung limply from bony clutches; I looked out at the blanket of red smothering the cave's entrance, dwelling on the canvas that echoed our failings. We'd endured so much already; the battle to come would be the making or breaking of this village and beyond. Three hundred years in the making, the vampires seemed to have all their pieces in place for victory. Was there any point? If we were doomed anyway, was there a final seedy thread we could pull on to bring down the decrepit, bloodsucking house of cards? We'd taken Amos off the board, like the hydra, no doubt cut off one head, two grow back in place.

Yet he was one of the oldest and seemingly the strongest; when push came to shove, I despatched with him quite easily, much like the rest.

The more I thought about that, a warmth grew deep inside; the sum of all parts might be a force to be reckoned with, but separate them, and suddenly, weaknesses show through. They had our strength speed and were far stealthier. They didn't have hearts, I don't mean in the physical sense, but their vulnerability made them lack the desire to overcome. Whereas that's all we've done, endure and overcome. Together, we were stronger. If we could survive being shot several times and all other attempts on us, I had to believe we could survive this.

I turned back to the bones, eyes glowing brightly, and slowly, I pushed upwards, first to my knees. The grip tightened, but my claws grew bolder as I finally forced my way back onto my feet. Anna's skull chillingly freaked and tilted to meet my blood-red stare.

"Nobody dies that doesn't deserve it. That goes for now and the future. Just because I'm part beast or killing machine doesn't mean I have to be. Power doesn't maketh man; it's what he does with it that counts. Now, I say again, I'm looking for something that could help end this goddam bloodshed and prevent the world from being overrun with those cockroach excuses for vampires," I said, finally feeling empowered, being in my conviction.

'Finally, his true face is revealed; like a coin with two sides, you finally stand on the one you chose. Fortune favours the brave and your efforts to stave off an early grave. You've overcome torture to realise you don't fight alone; it's time for you to grasp the 'secrets in the bones'. Now, wash away the blood with water, prevail and prevent the slaughter,'

Pain shot through my arm as Anna's grip crunched free from my arm, and her skeleton dropped back into the coffin, landing in a dusty heap. Then came a loud 'click' and an odd key popped up from the crevice a bony finger once rested. It, too, appeared to be made from bone, an off-yellow in colour, its end carved to shape a skull. This couldn't be what we needed to end the vampires, could it? How? Where did it go to? What did it unlock? All those questions were blazing through my mind as I hastily grabbed it. 'Secrets in the bones' indeed.

Pain shot through my arm as Anna's grip crunched free from my arm, and her skeleton dropped back into the coffin, landing in a dusty heap. Then came a loud 'click' and an odd key popped up from the crevice a bony finger once rested. It, too, appeared to be made from bone, an off-yellow in colour, its end carved to shape a skull. This couldn't be what we needed to end the vampires, could it? How? Where did it go to? What did it unlock? All those questions were blazing through my mind as I hastily grabbed it. 'Secrets in the bones' indeed.

It fits in the palm of my hand, with the dirt and dust from a dead body's decay cleared away. I got to see just how detailed it was, especially the skull. Floral patterning throughout the body, and a little surprise when I flipped it over. Only one side was the skull; the other was Anna. It had been hand-carved from bone with love and dedication; my instincts told me, human.

The nagging question teasing my little pea for a brain, why? All the effort, cloak-and-dagger games and the way I got to the cave in the first place. Where did it fit? There was no door I could see; my gaze wandered throughout—nothing but a decayed cave stone structure steeped in death. We needed to find those secrets urgently; I couldn't help but feel the midnight warning carry an ominous sting, waiting for us to fail.

'Wait,' I exasperated loudly, realising I hadn't been thinking out of the box.

I'd been looking for the obvious, too caught up in the notion it was a physical door. Instead, there had to be an inconspicuous space; otherwise, no key would be needed. Any Tom, dick or Harry would've found it, and every time I caught sight of Anna's coffin, it made me shudder. I closed my eyes to focus, picking up on Michael outside. Wind ripples ran amock throughout the cave; sea waters crashed against the cliffs. My eyes opened, blazing blood red again, searching for the glimmer of hope we desperately needed.

I was looking everywhere, spinning on the spot, getting frantic and dizzy, which gradually led to confusion. I had a fucking key made of bone, hidden in a three-hundred-year-old bony dead countess. The fact it spoke, I needed alcohol to finest that mentally scarring segment. I'd been serious earlier with Michael; we were too g to need therapy after this shit storm of a holiday.

After a final spin, stumbling on the uneven rocks, I finally caught a promising glimpse. At first, I thought it could be a trick of my red haze, the way it was covered in shades of red and kind of grey. It was small, then again, and so was a keyhole. It was where I saw it that caused a mouthful of bile to surge from my stomach. The side of Anna's skull, behind the wisps of dead hair and above where the earlobe would've been. The key was in her stomach. I shouldn't have been surprised, and yet the shocks kept coming.

After Anna sprung to life the last time, I trod carefully towards tensing my body in case it happened again. The wounds on my arm had healed, but the blood stains still lingered. My hands hovered near her head, shaking, like when I was sixteen trying to unclip my girlfriend's bra for the first time—all thumbs. I daren't breathe too hard up that close to Anna's wretched skeleton. Why on earth didn't I send Michael over to do it, I thought as the key drifted near to a jagged slither that could pass as wear and tear of decay; only coincidences weren't my friend, and as sickly morbid it would be to shove a key in a skull, there was little else that rung possible.

The scraping of bone-on bone echoed in my ears in surround sound, jarring me deep enough to rattle my tired skin sack-covered matchsticks. Another click made me jump; I first checked the cave entrance, but nothing but that red curtain. It's funny how that was my natural response, considering what Anna had done already. The rough off-yellow pushed far deeper than I'd imagined or wanted. Another click...

'Oh my god,' I shrieked, darting to the nearest part of the wall I could and covering it in a shower of clear vomit. My stomach had been empty for a while, and I had nothing else to give. I wretched and wretched until nothing else came, damm near tore my abdominals. The top of Anna's skull popped open like a jewellery box; only no bloody musical ballerina was waiting to twirl a calming tune.

After a minute or so and the drop had been wiped from my chin, I was finally ready to go again. Thank god Ellena wasn't around to see the aftermath. If I was lucky, the nursing and butt-wiping stage wasn't for at least another forty-odd years. Then again, Michael has been a dribbling mess on many occasions, a typical night out, he calls it that, and a desperate attempt to cling to some semblance of youth.

Back at Anna's convertible skull, I was a little underwhelmed initially. I couldn't see anything until I reluctantly peered over the top—a greyish-black stone shaped like a heart. I grimaced, stooping with the weight of the world on my shoulders, and this bloody search kept getting weirder and annoyingly frustrating. I get that if it were too easy, I probably wouldn't have been standing with Anna now, and we'd already be screwed, but I'd had enough; my patience was spent along with my sanity. All of which left the station when I redecorated the wall fifty shades of puke.

With all the enthusiasm of a probationary constable standing on a cold crime scene, I fetched the stone and began my search again. This was way beyond Dejavu and had far too much rocky space; the stone could fit. Until I figured that just maybe Jean had kept it close to Anna, like he had with the key and where it slotted.

Sure enough, I'd all but stood over it a dozen times as I moved around. A dark cutout on the floor at the foot of the coffin only appeared different in shades of red. I hurriedly jammed it km, praying to god and Lucifer, whoever deemed it necessary to listen, that it wasn't going to be another clue or weird-shaped object to stick somewhere other than a fucking stake to shove where the sun doesn't shine on our blood munching friend. With a quick press and fake stone, the hatch flipped open, spewing more dust into the air.

Finally, we were getting somewhere; within a gloomy hole lay a velvet bundle, at least a foot long and thick as my arm, which may not say much. I was like a giddy kid on Christmas day; I wanted out of the cave and move on as soon as possible. I tore off the dark leather cord keeping it together; the velvet bundle unfurled like a new carpet, without the fresh scent.

Six ornately carved stakes, their potent, fruity smell was unmistakable, white oak Ash mixed with mountain and some other substance. Each was inscribed with wording I had no idea what meant, possibly Latin. A leather cord grip, the tips, though, gripped my attention. I couldn't help but admire how tantalisingly dangerous they looked. Sharp enough to pierce hearts forged in the bowels of hell. Over the points was a black metal sheet blending with the points; the butt looked like it could be pressed. Every inhale picked another scent...garlic and mistletoe. Fuck it's an injection tip.

Jean was covering all bases; the stakes meant I would have to engage in close-quarters combat, and having to inject would keep me in one place too long, making me vulnerable to a vampire's fangs. A price I was happy to pay if it ended the chaos. Now we had elder vampire-killing tools; it was time to ring that fuckers bell. I was rolling the stakes away when I noticed a small black leather puch slid under the stakes. I could hear glass against glass rattle as I slid it out. As the thick leather rolled between my fingers, they felt like capsules or vials.

I hurriedly reached in to ease my curiosity; what I saw did little to do that. Each contained a shimmering reddish-purple liquid that gave me the uneasy feeling of adapted blood. The longer I stared, the more I could picture. What would Jean do with six small bottles of it hidden with the stakes? Just when I thought this week couldn't get any weirder, now this. All as we're at the crossroads of hell. Armed with the 'Secrets in the Bones,' I had to pray it would be enough as I dragged myself from the floor, closed Anna's coffin and headed for the cave's exit.

Nearing the cave mouth, a rush of sobering seawater shook the tired suitcases under my eyes. With it, I caught the scent of fresh blood. My hackles were razor sharp, and the predictable slither of my claws. It was human. I darted to the corner, fearing for Michael. No heartbeat was picked up, and my worst fear was realised by the moment I clutched the wall curve. Michael was gone...Again. Right on queue, and to emphasise the impending darkest hour further.

Lightening cracked across the red sky, and my heart jumped into my mouth, bringing emotion. This time, another piece had been removed from the board from my side. My numbers were stretched already; to make matters worse, I wasn't confident I could get them back. Alive, at least.

'See how easy it is, my furry friend. To tear down your house brick by brick and watch the foundations crumble like decaying bones. Something I'm sure you know all about now. All, to hit another 'dead end' pun intended,'
The count's voice made me shudder, but he thought I came up with nothing, and clearly, the vampires had tried already.

"Enjoy your moment to fill those shrivelled lungs of yours while you can; by the time I'm done; you will be flakes of ash scattered to the winds and all your little blood fuckers too,"

'Is that so? TikTok and another pawn down. You're almost out of moves and time, much like the people of this village. Soon, we'll bask in your blood and savour the freedom it brings. I believe I shall celebrate by awakening my bride-to-be to our world,'

The cracking and our sparring stopped, leaving me with a bloodied mouth and still chasing shadows.

Chapter 50

I found him out cold, in a battered heap among the stones. The strong scent of his seeping blood had me dripping with worry and shaking when I reached the ground. Panic was already rife after finding splatters of Michael's blood painting the ledge where he'd waited. Then I couldn't see Skip; I just heard a faint heartbeat. I'd been so wrapped up in finding the secrets I wasn't listening to make sure they were okay.

Vampires are sneaky bastards at the best of times, but now they were toying with us. Their elder seemed to get kicks from the mind games, but why take Michael and leave Skip? Don't get me wrong, I was relieved that both weren't gone, but the state of Skip was unsettling. Being a big guy, he could hold his own; it would've taken a few and real quick, too.

Skip's back was littered with scratches shredding through his clothes and flesh. His bald head was covered in blood to the back, and a load ran down his neck. I dropped beside him carefully, not knowing the extent of his trauma, and if I startled him, Skip could lash out. It was only up close my hackles livened up again. My head rocked from side to side, searching every nook or cavern I could find; early morning made it easier, even if every surface was a shade of red. No vampires in sight.

Even inhaling deeply, I wasn't picking up the usual 'Eau de death'; there was something else, though, something pungent, and it came from Skip. Whatever it was, it had been enough for my claws to arm my fingers as I went to tip back his 'polo' collar from the blood. Using the tip of one, it peeled back a little, enough to raise my worry a little further. Skip had been bitten.

Not just once either, two sets of punctures on either side of the corroded artery and, from what I could see, another on the back of his neck below his remaining hair fuzz. The smell was a slimy, tar-like black liquid oozing from the fang holes. Those bastard vampires used Skip for a pin cushion, and I hadn't examined anywhere else yet. Judging by the blood, there could be more.

"Skip? Skip? Can you hear me!" I nudged him hard; his body rolled forward and flopped onto his back. Black trackmarks spread from his right ear, neck and down his arm that had been squashed beneath him. The vampire venom was spreading through his bloodstream fast, and I didn't know what it would do to a werewolf - perhaps kill him. Or worse, he becomes a killer.

"Skip, can you hear me? I need you to wake up. We don't have time for you to be sleeping on the job," This time, I whacked his shoulder, getting a grumble back.

"Wwwhats happening? Fuck I feel like I've been run over by a truck," Skip's eyes eventually slid open. His pupils were different. Being up close, I got to notice little changes.

The brown had become black with time tracks web-like branching off.

A thin yellow ring circled the black, making me think Skip may be changing. Perhaps my being a demon werewolf forced him that way rather than death. A fight I didn't know how to win. Actually, 'another fight' like the many I seem to be facing at once. Now I knew why they left him; Skip would distract me by watching him instead of relying on him to do his job. In one move, the count and his 'blood bitches' inhibited my two strongest pieces on the board.

"Skip, do you remember what happened? They messed you up good," I asked, hoping for something while torn between tending to him and watching for more of the bastards. It's funny how the stone beaches seem to be their favoured hunting ground. Perhaps it's the caves. My ears searched the village, mindful it was nearly 8:30 a.m., and soon, the cattle would start their days. Yet, nothing. No door opened. No one was going to work or about their daily routines. Instead, I began sensing something else. With Skip's blood and the vampire venom occupying my scent finding, I shifted gears.

The silence amplified my fears, so I began looking for confirmation. I had an inkling the vampire's sick fun was well underway, and I was right. Blood slowly tainted the air. Then came the screams. One, then two, then each time multiplying, they were loud and full of pain, fighting for their lives. Skip looked at me as he heard it; worry and fear blended with the blood smears across his face. I dragged Skip's sweaty carcass to his feet to see the big lump stumble forward. He wasn't healing like we usually do. I tried not to show my worry, but he'd already seen my face. The black track marks spread the web through both arms and the top of his chest. His skin was steadily turning a clammy pale.

"It happened so fast; I was busy watching Michael and got a little stunned. One minute, you gripped the wall; the next, you'd vanished. Too sidetracked, I didn't hear them coming. No flipping heartbeats or anything. I felt a tush of wind and thought nothing of it until it kept coming. Different directions, relentless, and then it started hurting. I tried lashing out, but nothing stuck except my feet to the blooming floor. One bite after the other, I lost strength and crashed out. My eyes flapped shut at the sight of Michael going through what I did. I hate to be all doom and gloom, but I don't think we have a chance,"

Skip only said the obvious; he and Michael were easily taken out. Now, Skip is slot getting poisoned, which leaves little old me. It looks like I'm bringing claws and stakes to a 'fang fight'; the blood bitches outnumber me a thousand to one or something damm close. We needed to get somewhere safe to figure out a plan and see if there was any way to stem the poison. An idea could be to head back to the B & B. Whatever their damm guise, Ruth or Frederick would no doubt be kissing wrinkled ass about now so we could have the place to ourselves and a chance for me to snoop. Unless those fucking golems were house-sitting still.

"Right, well, whatever happened to me up there felt like a drug-fuelled 'trip', no idea how I got in the cave; I had a crazy vision before getting tormented by the skeleton of Countess Anna Farrington. Check this out. *'You talk of balance and scales; there's no assurity over who prevails. I guess, as you so fondly say, 'the devil is in the details'. You have until midnight to write the wrongs of the past and present or become another sad footnote in history's irrelevance. I strongly urge you to make peace with a preference over whose fate may be dire as a consequence'* Was only a small part of her decayed repertoire."

Watching Skip's face as we returned to the cliff line. He wasn't well; I was propping him up to get us moving, and repeating that sentence had me fearing Skip's odds.

"Well, lad. Maybe you should've asked the skinny wench who wins the national next if she's so good at seeing the future. I might be having a beer with the Reaper; he ain't carting me off to the knacker's yard yet, you know," Skip had a way with words; he even attempted a smile. All that did was mask the truth.

Nearing a pathway to head up, I finally got the scent of death. They were swarming the village, given licence to kill. We weren't fit enough to fight yet, assuming Skip would at all. Sweat dripped down my back as I bore his weight; stealth would be hard to manage.

We made it to the cliff edge. Michael's car still smouldering in the distance behind the abandoned police cars sprayed with those officers' blood and guts—another mental scar of this horrific holiday.

"Fuck, they're everywhere."

"Yeah, I can smell the bastards now. There's so much blood, too,"

"We need to get into the B & B; from what we were told, it's secure against vampires. Unless that was rubbish, too. Definitely an adapted mountain ash mix,"

"Mountain ash isn't our friend, though," Skip was, of course, right, and I'd usually agree. But it seems the supernatural rules for this place are different. It had to be druids, the only ones I'd heard of who could use herbs to an advantage. If Frederick was part vampire, how was he not affected?

Perhaps it's the chain his alter ego, Ruth, wore. He or she kept toying with it; perhaps she could feel the effects and clung to the little charm. This was, of course, all guesswork. It's not like the truth has been free-flowing in this place. Once safe, I wanted to know what was in the vials. It seems an odd choice to have hidden with stakes unless...

"Fuck...I may be carrying a cure for you," I said, trying to convince myself it was possible.

"You have what?" Skip's search was laboured; his face worsened by the minute. Death warmed up wouldn't be far wrong.

"I found stakes in the cave that seemed specific to killing the elder vampire, but with them was a small pouch of vials that contained a strange liquid. A lot like...wait..." My brain suddenly spun into high gear; surprised smoke wasn't firing from my ears. I thought back to the moment Ruth did that weird blood test and the drink that seemed different. What's in the vials wasn't dissimilar; did I have it all wrong? Did I have our allies wrong? Blindsided by impromptu help, I suddenly felt the ones who started this all years ago were playing far different roles this week than we were led to believe.

"What's up, lad?"

"I think we have been manipulated again; I have been. But I need to check things out first,"

"Your gut telling you something?"

"Other than it's empty, yeah, a whole lot of wrong and now I'm not sure who might be who,"

While I was busy navigating this cluster fuck in my brain, we were watching four vampires strolling through the cobbled streets wiping blood from their chins. All enjoying their freedom under the red sky. We had to cut across a field before that wooden bridge Ellena and I first crossed when we arrived. The field would have us exposed for too long. We would have to drop into the stream and use its bank as cover before moving again. Once across the next field, which was shorter, we would have brief cover from a line of parked cars, that judging by the screams earlier, they wouldn't need them anymore.

We saw the vamps in action; they smashed through the front door of another home. Screams ripped through the air in a matter of seconds. Gargled cries for help that made us shudder. Further afield, too, the vampires were off their leash. I could smell them, many spreading out from the surrounding caves. Those arseholes, the McNallys, made perfect turns for them to swarm from. Yet, to our right, the looming castle appeared untouched and vacant. I figured Count beef jerky would've been all nostalgic and gone there straight away.

"Skip, you feeling up for a sprint to that bridge? We will drop into the stream for cover before going again.

"Speaking of, lad, where are we going? I need to rest a minute," Skip nodded to go on, but he was fading fast. A bigger question lingered, like a bad smell or vamps: what would I do about it? No amount of whiskey was going to was the venom away. It can cure many things, but sadly, not that.

"Just over there, to the B & B. I will warn you, though: it's run by two golems and a witch that could be a vampire. And well... Let's just say the rest is messy,"

Skip grimaced. I grabbed the back of his t-shirt, and my claws tore through as I gripped hard; his heavy arm slapped across my shoulder. I was dragging both of us as quickly as we could. The grass still had the early morning crunch, and every step made me nervous that the fuckers would hear us. We'd made a few feet from the slope by the bridge; my ears strained to focus on the nearest vamps I saw go in that house; the screams had stopped. We crouched and braced for them to leave; a leg appeared first, followed by laughter. I gripped Skip and launched us as hard as I could across the ground.

We skidded through the frosty grass and down the slope, tumbling into the stream at least a foot and a half deep. Skip splashed through the loudest and was about to let loose with a gruff pain, riddled yell. I leapt at his head, my claws cupping his mouth, barely avoiding his eyes. Skip grumbled and squealed against my palms; I tried to tell him why, but he was in too much pain to care.

"Ssshhh, the vamps," I whispered, slowly releasing my grip. I heard all four come out laughing; my head tipped above the slope enough to see one tossing a head to another.

Then they stopped dead. A tall, skinny vampire on the group's left tilted his head, sniffing. Their sense of smell was as good as ours, with us sweating buckets; no doubt we were giving off some odours. I was busy watching when I heard a heavy thud behind me. Skip flopped back against the muddy slope; the black tracks now had a veiny blue glow outline, and his eyes barely remained open. The one sniffing the air stopped, turned and began walking in our direction, again sniffing.

"Skip, you need to keep your fucking eyes open; there's one coming our way,"

"I...I can't, lad; just leave me and get in the house,"

"Respectfully, fuck off. This mess ends today, one way or another. Now, wake up. ,"

"Cuh...cuh...family eh, well you've always been like a son to me lad, ever seen I rescued you from that fire. Does that make Michael the grumpy grandfather? What about Ellena?" I could picture Michael like that; it reminds me of 'Alf Garnett' the grumpy TV character. As for Ellena, I wish to get her back alive, minus the fangs. The rest will matter once the dust settles, especially if that dust belonged to a staked vampire turned to ash blowing in the breeze.

"Ellena, that's in the wait-and-see box; get her back safe first, which is where we need to get to. That vamp is moving slowly; I'll take him out if needed. That should grab the other's attention, but you need to use your remaking strength to run for the B & B. Okay?"

Blood dripped from the vampire's fingers, his pale skin coated by the red sky as he tilted his head, fangs bared and smothered in blood. We had thirty seconds; I shuffled toward the other bank, keeping low through the water. The vamp stink was getting up my nose, making it easy to sense the right moment. I turned to Skip to make sure he was ready to go; the last thing I needed was to be checking my shoulder when the shit hit the fan.

'Mmmm, fresh meat. Come out, come out, wherever you are. Or don't. The fear in your blood will taste all the sweeter,' The vampire tackled. The other three tossed away the head and quickly joined their friend. It was going to be four against one. I kept still, trying to slow my heart down enough to blend in with any surviving residents. Skip, on the other hand, was all over the place and was on the verge of giving us away. I couldn't drown him to keep quiet or stem his erratic breathing.

'Oh, come on now, we will make it quick,' the vampire squealed. He was about four or five feet away.

"Fuck it. Get ready," I whispered.

'Ooh, there's two of you. Aw, and one of you is sick. Don't worry; soon enough, we'll put you out of your misery. I will gut you, then separate your head from your body to use it like a cup. How does that sound?' The gall of him was shredding through my last nerves.

His black boots came into view, scuffing through the white gravel bordering the slope to stop. I was pressed flat to the slope, looking up at the tread of his boots. Blood and pieces of intestines dripped from grooves, with smears painted across the ball of toes. With my claws ready, I leapt forward, swiping at the vampire's legs. My claws tore through his jeans, and tracing-paper-like does. He let loose a scream; his legs buckled over the edge. I yanked him down; his body flew forward, and instinct took over.

I punched through his chest as he tumbled down. His heart flew out the back, landing at the feet of his onrushing vamp friends. He desiccated as I pulled my claws free. I watched the body drop, looking at his surprised grey face with his mouth fixed open. I didn't wait; I couldn't. The other three steamed forward; I spun a look at Skip. He staggered his way up the slope, nearly cartwheeling forward. His groans caught attention.

I figured I was going to hell anyway; I may as well send some vamps there first. I didn't like the feel of punching through their brittle flesh or their squishy, cold hearts. - At least the human part of me didn't, but it was them or us. With Michael and Ellena taken, Skip was used as a vampire teething ring. The vamps became a blur; my claws connected with a head, and my claws crunched through piercing bowling ball holes. In a rage, I tore it clean off his shoulders, sending it into the stream.

The other two turned tail and ran. Two blurs in the distance. Skip crumbled to his knees, dragging his hefty frame across the gravel until he face-planted on the B & B steps. I was covered in blood and a werewolf frenzy of wanting to rip more flesh. Then I saw Skip's face, mottled with blue lips. He looked dead. I rushed to his side, clumsily checking for a pulse, but nothing. No heartbeat either. Skip was dead.

Chapter 51

Blood, sweat and tears. Three words I never imagined using in the same sentence. Skip's skin was on fire; considering there was no heartbeat and how clammy he looked, it didn't sit right. I had Skip by the scruff with blood falling from my claws, adding to what Skip was losing as I dragged him through the doorway. My head was busy shedding tears, boiling with anger that I may have lost the only consistent and good father figure in my life. While looking for any sign of those vampire bastards coming back with reinforcements.

I could still see a headless, desiccated body on the floor. I watched Grey Flakes slowly crumble into the wind for the first time. Embers of death shredding away. A bittersweet moment. Now, I had to get us safe and fast. I hoisted Skip on the sofa in front of the fire before securing the front door. The fire was soon on, but Skip's condition spooked me; his chest suddenly started bouncing more like thumping rapidly. Still, he had no heartbeat or sign of breath, with his eyes clamped shut.

His fingers were next; the claws slithered forward and became sets of skinny talon-like nails, then phased back to normal again. I was frantic; nothing made sense in my frazzled mind. I kept dashing to the window, checking for unwanted company—each time, painted by the ominous red sky of doom. Time was quickly ticking away with us far more fucked, and now I had another no-win situation to add to my list. At first, Skip looked dead. Or as good as, now, his body was becoming something else.

Becoming one of them. I damm well couldn't afford that; how could I let my surrogate father, friend, and beta become a bloodsucker? Could I even bring myself to end him? My family. My options weren't looking good.

Nothing around us stood out, no fancy herbs or wonder drugs I could jam down the big guy's throat. The place was quiet, far too, so I only realised when I stood still to get the hamster spinning in its wheel and think. My ears scanned everywhere, still hearing some blood fuckers in the distance; no other heartbeats. Ruth, or whoever they were, was probably polishing the count's coffin or whatever he demanded while I watched Skip die or become one of them.

It was eating me up that the week had come to this, and I felt broken; I hated being so helpless. Bad enough, I nearly gave into temptation; the alcohol cabinet was calling, 'Georgie, come to me and drown your sorrows,' and I nearly fell for it when I saw that decanter on the mirrored shelf. Half full or half empty, depending on how you look at it, with a shimmering brownish purple-red liquid, reminding me that we still didn't know what Ruth had put in it. Only Ellena seemed to get sick.

I was mesmerised by the liquid shimmers when I had a light bulb moment, the 'secrets' and the six vials. Which, in itself, was a strange number to make. There was no way of knowing what it could be or what it was for. It had to be important, though, right? As I picked the velvet bundle off the floor, I kept saying that to myself. I mean, what reason would a bunch of vials be doing hidden with modified stakes?

With a quick tug on the crusty leather tie and, the smooth velvet bundle rolled open across the coffee table. The fire's warm yellow glow made the vials shimmer like the drink I now badly wanted. Each had tiny black stoppers. I rolled a vial between my fingers with a sickly, uneasy feeling in my stomach. I was so bloody out of my depth, and this piece of glass was nothing but a hail mary. A shot in the dark. Like a blind man playing darts.

It was time to either take a risk by tipping it down Skip's throat or watch our slim hopes fade with him turning during our final hours. The little devil and angel were back on my shoulders whispering sweet nothings, one saying don't and the other saying why the hell not; Skip was all but dead anyway. He would die now, or I would have to find the courage to impale his heart with a stake.

The devil won again. As I say, I'm going to hell anyway. I shook the vial; why? I had no idea. A force of habit, perhaps. It's what we do with medicines bottles, right? Another clueless example of me winging it. No time like the present.

'Fuck it,'

I flicked the stopper off, kneeling by Skip's side, shaking slightly. His bulky chest was still bouncing like a bloody trampoline; his skin was far greyer and deader. My hackles buzzed with fear when my hand hovered near his chubby jaw. The wolf in me wasn't happy. I 'shifted'. My claws cradled Skip's clammy chin, gently pulling on his jaw.

'Holy shit,' I gasped.

Skip had fucking fangs, not like a werewolf. No, these were scarily thinner piranha teeth but longer, with two big ones on top and bottom. He was changing alright; was that even possible? It had to be my blood-like, I thought. I shuddered at what version he'd become If I allowed it. There was no guarantee the liquid would work, but it's all I had. 'Here goes nothing.' I held the vial and my breath, ready to pour. Braced for the worst, like our situation wasn't bad enough.

'Oh my God,'

The first drop trickled forward when I was rocked back by the hear-pounding, sudden opening of Skip's eyes, and I nearly jumped out of my skin. They'd turned a spooky black that gave me chills, with a thick yellow outline that thickened by the minute—rippling with blood-red veins that were truly scary looking. Skip's hand ferociously gripped my arm in the blink of an eye. Brandishing razor-sharp Vampire talons that bit into my flesh, causing the same black tracks to painfully throb and spread through my arm. I still had his jaw locked open; I flung the liquid down his throat before he became too lucid and jammed his jaw shut, praying with the last ounce of grace hidden in my hell-bound soul.

"This better work, you mean old bastard. Don't make me kill you; besides, I still need you in my life. You're one of the few good things in it, and I'll be dammed if I'm going to watch you become a blood fucker," I grimaced through gritted fangs as the venom from his talons seeped into my bloodstream.

Skip's eyelids slowly slid closed; his rapidly bouncing chest began to slow. Everything calmed until his body heated up. Skip's skin drifted to a shade of red; those black track marks suddenly glowed and pulsed, growing to bulge under his skin. I quickly let go of Skip's jaw, breaking my arm free from his talons and shuffled backwards, feeling the fire's warmth against my back. I feared those tracks exploding if that was possible. A statement I'd said a lot lately because everything I'd seen shouldn't be possible. Much like me phasing to a wolf.

Holding my breath again, I waited for a sign, anything good or bad, to tell me what was happening. Amazingly, the bouncing chest stopped, and the bulging black track marks began to shrink and fade. They receded throughout the visible areas of skin along with that redness, which disappeared as quickly as it came. I stared at my blood dripping from those razor-sharp tips, only to see them fade next. Skip was returning to normal if he could ever be called that. Dead looking but normal.

His mouth was still a morbid blue, and everything about his was lifeless—no beats, pulse or breathing. I may have stopped him from turning, but I could've put the final nail in his coffin. I slumped against the ornate fire surrounding, holding my head in my hands, finally admitting defeat. Wondering, 'What the hell was the point,' what good were the vials if they only stopped the vampire transition? So much for praying; my mind was blank; I couldn't scrape together a single idea or the energy to move.

I had the supernatural abilities of a werewolf and a demon, yet I was useless. Was there any use in fangs and claws if all I could do was make life worse? By coming here, I made the village worse. We may not have intended the outcome or knew we were being manipulated until it was too late. I still did it. I still brought the elder vampire back to Cruden Bay to reap destruction all over again.

Self-pity is quite a deep pit to wallow in, and I was so busy trying to dig deeper that I nearly missed it. Only ain't at first, almost untraceable. My head slipped from my palms, dripping sweat and tears, wondering if I was hearing what I wanted or if it was real. I'd heard a heartbeat that wasn't mine and couldn't be anyone other than...Skip.

Had it worked? I waited on bated breath to hear it again. I'm straining my eyes, watching his chest—desperately searching for a silver lining. Otherwise, I saw no other way forward that didn't involve my surrender. Skip may only be one person, but he made me stronger. And if the vials worked, there was a way to save Ellena and Michael, even if they were 'turning'.

'Der-dum,' I heard it again.

'Der...Dum...Der...dum,'

'Der-Dum, Der-Dum, Der-Dum,'

'Derdum derdum derdum derdum derdum der dum,'

Each wave got quicker, and each beat sounded stronger until his heart was purring away between 50 and 60 bpm. I noticed his burgeoning chest's steady rise and fall, filling mine with hope. I pulled myself from the floor and pit of self-pity, brushing off the dirt and lingering doubt. Whatever was going on seemed to bring Skip back from death's clutches.

Everything was moving in reverse of the vampire transition. His claws came out fuller and thicker than I'd ever seen, and I sure as hell wouldn't want a slashing from them. This time, they didn't disappear. Skip lay still, but he was phasing into a werewolf. It's quite something to see on the opposite side of the looking glass and not in the middle of a shit storm. This was bloody weird, though; he wasn't shifting back. Skip was, for all intents and purposes, alive. Why wasn't he awake?

I hung my head close, checking my senses hadn't deceived me. Too much of that has happened lately. Warm breath drifted at my face while I still held mine.

'Rooooaaaaarrrr,'

Skip's eyes shook open, revealing bright yellow werewolf eyes glowing. Skip jumped upright, roaring, throwing me backwards across the room with my heart in my mouth, beating one hundred a minute. I couldn't keep my feet, heels skidding out for grip. Which only sent me back quicker, landing in a shocked heap. My eyes blazed bright red, adrenaline ran rampant, and my veins bulged. Blood pumped through them faster than ever. It was like a domino effect from Skip, and I now had a full tank of energy and strength.

Skip sat, panting heavily with fangs bared; all the vampire punctures were healing, and within a few seconds, he phased back to human, wearing a startled 'dear in headlights' expression. Before patting his body down, checking the moment was real.

"Crikey, I could murder a cuppa," Skipbfinally spoke, his eyes the last to change as they slowly dimmed.

"Are...are you ok?" I said, with a throat full of sawdust.

"I...er, think so, lad. How? The last I remember, I'd been ravaged by a bunch of fanged bastards. We ended up in the stream, and another group of vampires who'd just finished butchering a household caught hold of my struggle. You took them on while I tried to get on here. I think I made it halfway, then it goes blank," He'd been lucid enough for most of it with a great recall, even if he looked anything but with it.

"Great memory. The how? Let's just say for once, we got lucky. Just as you looked to be changing to one of them. I tried what I had recovered from the cave. And it bloody worked...left me touching cloth for a while, but here we are,"

"Ha, that would be amusing, you shitting yourself. Whatever you dad lad, I'm grateful. I didn't see any limbo or white lights like you or Michael. What I saw What I endured was blood, lots of blood and screams. Never-ending screams. It scared me and still does,"

Skip completed the trifecta of near-death experiences. Michael was heading to the light.

I was in limbo, and Skip's was more akin to hell. Or some vampire version of it. I wasn't in the tea-making mood, but the liquor cabinet looked good. Not the decanter either. I spied a wide, oval-based brandy bottle tucked on the bottom shelf.

I grabbed two glasses and slid the dusty bottle forward. A key dropped to the floor just as I pulled it off the edge. It was old, dark grey, probably silver at one point. Not the typical looking, short with a wide looped head. The kind is normally seen on internal doors to a basement or cupboard. From where I stood, I could see into the kitchen. There's another brown wooden door with a black handle and a keyhole.

"What you got there, lad?" Skip hollered gruffly, spinning his lower body from the sofa to hoist himself upright. He stumbled to the left and right before finally getting his bearings. Just seeing him standing there brought a smile to my face. Relieved that I didn't need to kill him.

"It was under this. Who hides a key under a brandy bottle? A dusty one at that," I said, showing Skip the bottle after I smeared a finger through a thick sheet of dust.

"Someone with secrets," Skip grabbed the glasses, making it easier for me to pour. My free hand was busy toying with the key, causing glances at the door in the kitchen.

"Drink up then; I want to see what's behind door number one. If you're up to it, of course,"

Both downed our drinks in one; I checked the window first after a brief shadow cut across the red shade, making me paranoid. Thankfully, the vamps were still busy elsewhere. Surprisingly, not every house was an 'all-they-could-eat buffet,' with doors appearing reinforced. Seeing that reminded me of old films and vampires having to be invited in. Perhaps not all rules are as rigid, at least when it comes to these fuckers.

"Ready when you are, we ain't got long, and we need a plan, lad. Hopefully, there's something else we can use, or if that 'Doris' is who you think, they've left a clue as to where the wrinkly bastard could be held up,"

"Don't let Michael hear you say that; you know he's a bit touchy about the wear and tear," I said, making us both laugh. Skip's boomed around the room as always. For a second, I forgot our troubles. Then I heard another piercing wave of screams, peppering my skin with goosebumps and a chill rampaging through me.

"Well, once we get them back, Michael can moan all he likes. But the old git will have to suck it up because we would've saved his arse," I nodded, barely able to produce a smile after picturing Ellena tied up at the mercy of Count Duminescu.

I chugged another mouthful to calm my nerves before sliding the key in. It Didn't stop my hand from shaking, though; too much had gone wrong, and this door was another unknown. The key rattled because of it, prompting a reassuring hand on my shoulder from Skip, which did the trick almost immediately. It was only when my hand was still that I heard the whistles.

Faint and high-pitched whistles of wind cut through the crack under and to the side of the door. Whatever was on the other side had to be large enough to cause a vacuum of air needing escape where it could. Judging by the pitch, it had a slight echo caused by stone walls, just like the cave earlier.

Chapter 52

'Click...Clunk,'

A well-oiled or well-used look for sure - it unlocked with ease. With a quick twist of the handle, the door sprung free - barely an inch or so, enough to mess with our sense of smell. It stunk of many things I had trouble dissecting, except for one very prominent scent: blood.

"Seems like there's no escaping it, eh?" I gave Skip an almost apologetic smile.

"Dammed if we do, dammed if we don't, lad, no time to waste," He was right as always. It just wasn't the most appetising of aromas to welcome us.

The door swung open with a creak. Immediately in front were wooden steps descending; the walls were rough stone with a flimsy handrail on the left. I used my werewolf eyes to navigate as I couldn't find a light switch or cord. Our path was a steep one that seemed to plunge into never-ending darkness. I lost count of how many, at least fifty, maybe more. The stench grew with the darkness as narrow stone walls widened to almost cavern-sized space, with the roughness of a cave. Except with the position of the house, that wasn't possible.

Skip stayed close; we bumped shoulders several times as we walked. This was no ordinary basement, a winding stone walkway that would've taken us under several houses at least. We moved slowly, with no sound except our heels and heartbeats pounding between our ears. The walls were full of dampness tinged with sea salt, and the whooshes of wind were gathering speed. The first real sign of any purpose was a vent with ducting running from the ceiling along the wall that suddenly veered left. I was busy following the ducting when...

'Boom. Boom. Boom. Boom,'

A loud series of booms echoed through the space as a big fluorescent light rocked on one by one. Illuminating just how big and disgusting the place was. We found ourselves in a huge underground home-type layout. Except that ducting led into a wall next to black cell bars that formed a gated door. Beyond where we stood were a patch of darkness and another walkway by the looks of things.

These walls, though, were littered with tables, some wood and others metal. Test tubes, beakers, lidded jars of strange-looking ingredients and Bunson burners. That reminded me of the cave I was taken to when I got shot. Who I believed to be Jean Cortez had saved me. Like that place, the same Articles and pictures hung on the walls.

I moved around slowly; several diagrams caught my eye. First, they appeared to be experiments—a body on a table with electric conductors. Then I got to the juicy stuff and more on what I'd already heard. The nemeton. So many variations, including a tree, but one titled 'Cruden Bay' looked fucking crazy, a throwback to the pyramids. Made out of stone, only smaller, a flight of steps leading up to a stone chair with clamps on the wrists, ankles and head. Scribbles mentioned 'sacrifice' with two narrow cutouts running to a large, elevated pit. 'Blood' and 'Lazarus Pit' were written beside them.

A picture was forming in my head, and I didn't like it one bit. Other diagrams showed lunar events like the blood moon not so long ago. 'Winter Solstice and Unholy One,' scribbled in places. The image of the huge pit played in my mind with what Anna's skeleton said, 'Or will a bloody pool be your fate,' Everything pointed to Ruth trying to resurrect someone, but who?

There were many jars of herbs and books, even skeletal remains, all with vampire fangs. Even a multifunctional gurney with leather straps. Ruth had been delving into some dangerous stuff. Anything that speaks of resurrection makes me think of zombies. Nobody wanted that. Skip seemed in awe at what he saw. He walked with eyes fixed on the walls; another step forward, I heard...

'Click'

It came from the floor. Skip was standing on 'zero', and there were others too. It was laid out to resemble a game kids played at school. A series of stone floor tiles stopped at the wall, zero through to nine, going one tile, then two, one, two, one, two and then one. If that tile could be pressed down, it had to utilise a code, possibly one that opened the prison-like gate.

"What are you thinking, lad?"

"Erm, this is bloody weird,"

"Besides that?"

"Erm, a code for the gate, maybe,"

"Okay, wiseguy, what the heck is the code?" I was already looking around, but nothing.

It wasn't like we knew Ruth's date of birth or the other two, either. Not Jean's or Frederick's. Wait a goddam minute, I muttered, scanning around us once more. If we assumed Ruth was one of the two, the code had to be specific to them. Then there were the documents Ruth showed us, their travel log for the day of their arrival in town.

"What's your jumping skills like?" I said, waiting for him to tell me to piss off.

"Really? You know I was recently dead, right?" Skip smirked, thinking I'd go easy on him.

"Exactly, now you have a new lease on life. Besides, by my Count, I've died twice here, Michael once while here and once in London. That's you outnumbered and for a change in pulling rank," I said, waiting for the penny to drop; I was messing around to a point but intended to play the Alpha card, as I was thinking for both of us.

"I'm quite sure even a semi-retired Sargent is senior, you cheeky sod,"

"But not over the Alpha. Now, pull up your big boy pants. I'm trying to remember what I read. Can you try one, seven, two, five, please,"

"Blooming hell, now you owe me. Jokes aside, I trust your weird little brain. Let's get this done; I want to see behind door number two,"

Skip with all the grace as though he'd had one too many. I listened closely, the stones pressed, but nothing happened after landing back on the five. It was a shot in the dark, and I shouldn't have thought it would be that easy. That was the year they arrived after uncovering the Count. It was August, too.

"Skip, same again, but try, Zero, Eight, one, seven two five. Okay?"

"Sure, boss, anything you say, boss," he chuckled before starting over. Meanwhile, my mind was split in two. The current puzzle and the diagrams for the nemeton. Leaving me reeling at the confirmation of why I hadn't been killed yet. I may have been shot; the second time was more out of the Count's control. Once woken, the game board changed. There were two opposing sides involved, other than us. Both want to use what's in the diagrams. The vampires walk among people without their afflictions.

Ruth's purpose remained unknown but could become clearer if we made sense of the underground hideout we found ourselves in.

Each tile Skip hit moved; nothing else happened, though. We were back to the drawing board, and I ran out of numbers. There was one other we could use; I distinctly remember the day of the month being on the documents, but I was torn between two combinations.

"Fuck, there are two others to try, Skip, after that I'm stuck,"

"Right, let's do this,"

"What do you want to try first? The twelve or sixteen?" I raised my eyes at him, waiting for a decision.

"Let's the number Michael claims he lost his virginity,"

"What's that? Forty?"

"Twelve allegedly, some camping trip by all accounts. Just another fanciful story, but let's do twelve,"

Skip had us laughing, and for a change, I didn't feel worried about being caught or heard. Even my hackles were resting. Skip was beside zero this time, bouncing on tiptoes with a tinge of apprehension. His heart had sped up and not from the jumping. My guess was he had been thinking about what may get revealed. Our luck hadn't been great with surprises, and for Ruth to go to all this effort, she wasn't hiding the family silverware or an antique vase. No, this could be far more impactful today than we thought.

"Here goes, lad. One...two...zero...Eight....one...seven...two. Time for the last one, I'm telling you, there better be no spikes shooting at us, or I fall down a hole...Five... wooaah, what the heck,"

Skip landed on the five, and the floor shook; a low rumble echoed around us, dust filling the air. Skip stumbled to the side, the wall the numbers led to shifted and a seam carved creepily through the stone to form the outline of a door. Skip wanted to see behind number two. This was number three. I wasn't sure whether to be excited like a kid in a sweatshop or scared out of my mind because I smelt death through the slithers in the stone. Not in a fresh corpse kind of way or a vampire. This stench reminded me of Anna and her coffin in all its vibrant pungency.

"Are we doing this?" I said, running my fingers along the groove. My hackles stayed down, which was one plus side, meaning no danger yet.

I followed the line to the floor; there were rainbow-shaped scrape marks through the stone floor as the stone door pivoted open. The tips of my fingers ran across the scraps, thick and deep recesses from the wear and tear of repeated opening and closing.

"You know there's death behind there, right?" Skip said, wiping a few beads of sweat from his brow after his little stint of exercise.

"Of course, it's the who or what that concerns me. And some element of truth behind the manipulation to get us here. It's only seeing this now and a million details spinning through my head. But Locke isn't a fool; would he have bought into a story without checking? Yeah, he was underhanded in getting us here, but he must believe there's some truth in it,"

"Meaning?"

"We've been told so many things, but the more I look at the diagrams and everything Ruth has done, not said. Done. Please bear with me because the 'dots' are moving around, and my brain is pulling them in line. Whoever Ruth is doesn't want us dead, not yet. She has moved Ellena around to make me work. Even in a position with the elder vampire, she wants the nemeton and plans to resurrect someone. To do that required it to be today, my blood and perhaps something from the Elder vampire. I have fallen for massive misdirection and lies, even illusions. Possibly chemically induced from the moment we stepped foot in the B & B. Judging by all those herbs, the pinprick in Ellena was to subdue her. Giving us something to worry about while nullifying her ability to help us. Which made it easy for her to be grabbed-"

"-This is going to get worse, isn't it?"

"Well, the elder wants my blood to make hybrids, him included. Ruth wants to pit us against each other so she can scrape up the pieces to get what she wants, and hardly anything has been as it seems. There was a murder all those years ago, and Anna doesn't know who did it and wants him back. She will do anything to make it happen. Uncovering who committed it may set Locke free, but there's a huge chess board to manoeuvre,"

"You on drugs, lad? You talk of that Anna like she's alive," Her coffin gave the first hint the bones were under a spell. Why such a manly voice? And as much as the supernatural may predict the future, the words 'bloody pool' spoke to someone of knowledge.

"Because I think she could be. You may call me crazy, but I'm finally seeing clearer. If what's on the other side of this differs from what I think, I'll hold my hands up and admit it. Besides, the handwritten notes with the pictures don't match the logs I read,"

Skip nodded with a puzzled expression as he weighed everything up. We both pushed to the left of the stone, making it flip inwards. The opposite swung towards us, grinding loudly across the stone floor, making my teeth itch. As a precaution, we both 'shifted'; the door was now fully open, revealing soul-sucking darkness, made no brighter by my werewolf eyes.

Crusty bones were the first scent I picked up on. Stale and cooped up with a smothering of dust. Candles, too, ones that had not long been snuffed out. Seeing our claws in front of our faces was a struggle, and neither wanted to breathe too loudly. My stomach was doing somersaults at the thought of what we may find.

'Click,'

With a shrug, Skip unleashed a small torch from his pocket to say, 'What? We don't normally need it,' and he would've been right. This was the next level of darkness. While breathable air was far thicker, giving a claustrophobic feeling. Skip did a few casual swishes across the floor to see where we were walking before lashing it forward.

I jumped backwards, leaving my heart behind. We were in a horror movie, much like most of this week, but what he found so abruptly had me jumping out of my skin. Skip wasn't much better. He may not have jumped, but his heart rate was sky-high.

We were in a smaller room, dressed to appear like a bedroom. Right in front was a dusty, dirty bed. A neatly laid body was tucked in that bed as if they were sleeping. It was an adult male body judging by the initial glance of the skeletal structure and still dressed in clothing dated at least two hundred years. Black or navy velvet top with a light top underneath that elegant ruffled cuffs.

"Blooming heck lad, who?" Skip's voice croaked huskily, reeling from another body. In reality, it was probably the manner of the body and what it meant. That it was likely my thinking was right. Not that I dared say it yet because there had been so many twists and turns. There could yet be another.

"Well, it's down to two now, and I have a sickly hunch. For now, I'll spare you. What's that he's holding?"

"It's a note lad. Quite fresh compared to Skeletor here,"

A folded piece of paper rested within crusty finger bones. I leaned forward, scared he would suddenly jump upright like Anna did. Even as a skeleton, his skull with sparse decayed black curls still managed to look quite judgmental as I pinched hold of the note. At least, that's what I thought with each nervous glance.

'Read me,' in a fancy swirling handwriting I haven't seen often.

'Congratulations on your survival so far. By the time you discover this note, the eclipse will be upon us, and the Count will no doubt have been revived and their plans in motion. I ask that you uncover poor Jean's murderer, and I will lift the curse that plagues your friend. Whether you survive the night to see him again is another story. Good luck,'

"Skip, shine the torch over him. Start through the head slowly. We have a murder to solve after all,"

The light flickered through the dead black curls, down the curve of the skull brow. A slight two-inch crevice poked out from a patch of four curls. The skull was over two hundred years old and in reasonable condition, but the dirty grey highlighted every crack from wear and tear. The light drifted down to the next detail that shocked me: his teeth were normal. No hint of vampirism. Which dispelled further details from the stories we'd heard.

The torch blazed across his neck next. The first glance caused a sharp flash of memory to flicker into my mind's eye. The hooded figure that intervened after I'd chopped down Amos. He introduced himself as the missing and elusive Jean Martin Cortez. He stopped the vampire poison with herbs. I kept seeing what was tucked into the waistband next to the pouch.

I remembered what I thought at the time: it had a slight sickle curve at the end. The oak handle was encrusted with gold and bound in leather. It appeared very old, which suited the person carrying it. The corpse we were viewing had a wound across his neck that's weathered over time, but with the aid of the torch and my werewolf eyes, I could see where it began and ended. It would've been fatal. Judging by the pattern, depth and angle, the attacker approaches from behind, no doubt taking this man... wait... fuck it, go with my gut.

The attacker took 'Jean Martin Cortez' by surprise from behind. In a swift move, a curved-tipped blade pierced the left of his throat. The curve cut an angle before tearing through Jean's jugular to the right and through the carotid artery. Being human, Jean would've bled out within thirty seconds. I turned to Skip; his expression was of disgust and dreading what I may say.

"Right, Skip, I need you to move the body around for me, lift each limb so I can examine and be sure," I said with a slight smile, wondering if he would believe me or realise I was joking.

"You want me to do what?"

"Nothing. I think I know how and possibly who already,"
"Care to share with the class?"

"We are looking for someone with a small curve-tipped blade. Cause of death: he bled out after having his jugular and carotid arteries cut through. Dead in thirty seconds, didn't hear the attacker, may have seen him in his final moments, but that's all,"

"Bloody heck. Now for your 'A+' grade, who?" I paused, having a final look over the body, wanting to be sure. A gold ring on his right hand had the initials 'J.C', which could be a ploy much like everything we'd encountered when we thought we had it cracked. We get fucked over. The room, though, was a shrine hidden away—a bedside table with a vase with flowers smelling two days old. A rocking chair beside the bed told me Ruth spent much time there with a knitting basket and some books. This was love. This was the care of one person.

"The killer is someone you won't believe is still alive. Not the only one either,"

"Fuck me, who? Elvis?"

"Not quite. The murderer was Frederick Lasille, hard to believe but most definitely alive still and has played us like a fiddle."

"Okay, now the other shoe?"

"This shoe drops harder, I'm afraid. I'm still finding it hard to believe, especially after what I went through to get the stakes. Countess Anna Farrington. Who is also Ruth. She has manipulated us to this point and to solve this murder. With an agenda to bring this guy back. Which may not go so well for me,"

Skip stared at Jean's corpse open-mouthed. The game board is reaching the end—a game rigged against us from the beginning. From the moment the sweet golems, Diane and Mary welcomed us with warm drinks. And we needed a divine move to swing victory our way. Asking how Anna and Frederick survived, living this long, would be futile; we'd never get the truth.

I suspect Ruth learnt from Jean the ways of the Druid; perhaps he saw the 'witch' in her before she did. Druids are connected to the earth and nature, particularly the telluric currents. Anna has found a way to use them to keep her alive. As for Frederick, that's easier; he's part vampire, part Druid. Why he had helped me so far is confusing, but I feared everyone's motives were about to come for our throats.

"Bloody hell. Well, we should take the note and get out of here. That way, the wench will know we've been and are on the case?" Skip said clumsily, lurching forward to grab the note,"

"No, wait," I shouted quickly as I saw the glint of a thin wire leading to the note at the last minute. Which usually spelt nothing good. Too late…

First, it sounded like a rush of wind, then came the dejavu from the Black Widow case and the tunnels. The stone door grated shut while the room very quickly filled with yellow clouds, smothering everything in its path. When I thought to hold my breath, I had already inhaled a lung full. My airways were on fire; Skip was bright red with bulging eyes. My windpipe was closing by the second as the room began to spin. Waving my hand around was a slow-motion blur. Skip stumbled; his heart slowed to a snail's pace. My body was far too heavy, much like my eyelids. We both dropped hard; everything went dark.

Chapter 53

My wrists wouldn't budge. Nor my legs. A hard surface pressed against my back - stone. I was seated wearing a blindfold; my head was locked in one position. A sickly taste swam through my lungs and mouth.

Many have spoken about the surreal feeling of having their life flash before their eyes, that scary final moment by certain doom. This was me, and it was one of those crazy moments. The heavy realisation of rock hitting bottom, playing a movie about my life. The stark contrast between before and after turning the dreaded thirty.

For most, that's supposed to be when life begins; to some extent, that's been true or, could say, my awakening, what I had with Helen and my nativity around Ethan. I had lost so much so quickly. Then, the weirdness started. The nightmares, the waking up covered in blood, the memories of horrible things I couldn't imagine being true but were.

Then my eyes opened to this uniquely horrifying supernatural world and what I was—adjusting to being a werewolf. Understanding the crazy shit around us is caused by people who are anything but normal. When I had given up on love, Ellena came into our lives; I tried to fight it, not wanting someone so beautiful and seemingly pure of heart to be entangled with the cold, hard and bloody horrible truth, knowing what I was.

Ellena embraced me, werewolf and all. Now, I can't be without her. I don't want to be without her. To have this chance within my claws and get it ripped away is torture. Unable to sense her or know if she was still alive, even human, has me conflicted and unfocused. Without telling Skip, I can't see a way forward if Ellena is killed.

In that same breath, I rest a certain amount of blame squarely at one person's feet. Locke selfishly tricked us into this holiday location so he could finally be free of his blood lust and curse. He knew what evil might be here, and now that evil may cost me everything good. It appeared a quiet-looking village when we arrived - not any longer. Especially after those screams earlier, it's doubtful any residents are left alive or unturned.

Now, I find myself helpless in the fight. With every twist or struggle, something sharp grated against my flesh, a warm sensation trickled underneath, and if I didn't know better, judging by the stinging, I was bleeding. That much I picked up quickly. Then, the rancid stink of death, lots of overwhelming death. Not a single heartbeat besides mine. Lazy scuffs across the floor echoed, spraying stone dust in the air, telling me I was in caves. Strapped to the nemeton, exactly how I saw in the diagrams.

It wasn't long before waves of panic finally took over. Not just for me. I'd forgotten about Skip, not knowing if he was dead or held elsewhere if I had no other heartbeat reading.

'No use in squirming unless you want to speed up the inevitable,' a voice not to be mistaken, the beef jerky elder himself, Count Duminescu. With it echoing, too, told me he had to be nearby.

"So you had someone do the dirty work for you? Too scared to face me,"

'That's what great leaders do when deals are to be made that suit everyone involved except you. Why waste energy?'

"That just proves you're a really old chicken shit,"

'For someone in your position, you have a big mouth. That will get you killed sooner rather than later,'

"Spoken like a true arsehole. As soon as you don't like what you hear, kill them," I was trying to provoke a reaction, one to get the bloody blindfold off. Two to help me gauge if I had any scope to escape. Not that getting out of the restraints would be easy; that yellow cloud had me weaker, made worse by leaking blood. However, I must say the smell of it was intoxicating. Considering it was mine, that said a lot.

"Big mouth, come on, you're doing all the Jedi mind tricks and talking. Time to share the limelight,"

'Don't worry yourself. You had your chance to join us; now you will serve the only purpose we need,'

"What deal did you make?"

'That they'd be spared. Gracious of me, right? Let the human live out their life is good enough,'

Would Ruth, or should I say Anna, make that kind of deal? Considering everything else that's been her benchmark, it seemed unlikely unless she had an ulterior motive. Handing me over without knowing the killer of Jean wasn't good business.

"How about taking this blind off? At least do me that courtesy,"

He didn't respond; I felt a whoosh of air whip towards me. He wouldn't do it himself, would he? I thought. Whoever it was, curdled my stomach with its stink; my hackles gave them a little wave as the blindfold flew off. The sudden burst of light made me screw up my face. Slowly adjusting confirmed it was the nemeton.

The space was huge, and many holes littered the side walls, big enough for coffins. Perhaps vampires hiding places. It could account for the smell. Twenty or so surrounded the elevated stone pool. Watching their smug faces, smiling and laughing with their pointy teeth showing, was pissing me off. I wanted to rip their heads off.

A few blinks, and my sight was normal. Only for me to wish it wasn't. Perched beside me was the weird cloaked figure who helped me after Amos. The person we had just established could be Frederick Lasille—a shadow cast over his pale, bony face. Deathly black eyes with a thick, luminous yellow ring, much like Skip's had turned to briefly.

A thin sheet of stubble added to the menace of his presence. One I wished to escape from, but the bindings had other tormenting ideas; I'd forgotten the bleeding briefly until my squirms caused another stream.

My blood ran through thin cutouts in the stone slope on either side towards the pool. Another detail that's the same as the diagrams. This prompted me to wonder how much time Anna or Ruth had spent around it. After all, there wasn't much else to do. My anger had risen quickly with nowhere to displace it other than wish to ram a stake through the chest of Frederick or whoever he says is.

Yet, no sign of the Count. His voice gave every indication he was close by. He wasn't in my head this time, nor was it like when I was headed to Anna's coffin. So far, he has been full of party tricks. A few I wouldn't mind having. For now, he'd chosen not to show himself, only added fuel to my words. He was a chicken shit.

"What's it like?"

"What?" Frederick answered, slightly surprised and unsure what I meant.

"What's it like having to kiss such dry, beef jerky ass that's been desiccated for so long,"

"You know nothing of which you speak. It would be wise not to leap to wild accusations," I checked his waistband; the knife was there. The thing with blood, you can rinse it off, but it leaves traces beyond the naked eye. Good thing I can see more. A quick flash of red showed me enough to paint a blood-spraying picture. It is scattered across the hilt—rippled stains on the blade, darker across its edge.

"Check you out. What's the matter, got a stick up your arse? 'you know nothing of which you speak' That's some real stuck-up stuff," I goaded, redirecting my anger to push some buttons. He wasn't biting.

"Oh come on, Freddie, can I call you Freddie, or do you prefer wound tighter than a cork, Frederick?" I said bullishly; watching the startled expression was priceless. The penny dropped with this one, and he had no idea what to do.

"How do you know?" He whispered; I caught a glimpse of his fangs.

"Call it dumb luck, or I'm a bloody good detective. For your sake, you'd be wise to cut me loose,"

"I can't even if I wanted to," Just as he stopped speaking, my attention was grabbed by a dragging noise by the pool. Vampires were hauling a large, heavy-duty hose. They dropped it into the pool, a flick of a lever, a tide of red fluid burst out of the end. It was blood, that much I could tell by smell: human blood and lots of it.

"What the fuck is that for?"

"The main event. Our baptism into the light. It's a chance to enjoy all the vampire perks and none of its weaknesses. All thanks to you,"

"What good is a main event if you're turned to ash?"

"Such bravado; I can see why he wanted you to join us. I'm afraid you won't be leaving here alive,"

"I wouldn't count on that. I intend on walking out of here with my friends, watching the wind carry you away in little pieces," I said, scanning the area again, looking for escape routes if the opportunity came.

"Your death will be our rebirth,"

"What, like Jean Martin Cortez, you mean? Because he wants to be reborn, too. By the way, he sends his regards. Hopes you don't mind if he holds a grudge over the sliced throat incident,"

"What? How did you find out? How did he tell you? I mean, he can't; I made sure,"

"Oh, he told me so much. Loves how you double-crossed him in pursuit of power and to get him out of the way so your boss could remove his hand from your arse long enough to pursue Anna," Frederick was rattled. I didn't need him to have a heartbeat to tell his flight or fight had him wanting to run. I got under his dead skin.

"You think you're so smart, and yet you're trapped,"

"Ask yourself this: Which one of us is really trapped? Perhaps I'm where I need to be.

For now," Anna handed us over in a deal the Count called it. I can't help but believe it was to make it easier; she wanted to know things and for us to remove obstacles. A rescue had to be on the cards. Or at least a distraction. If that were to happen, I wanted a direct route to the Count and to know where the stakes were being kept.

"You're where we need you to be. Nothing else,"

"Where's my friend then? The big guy? Slightly annoying, northern with a red face?"

"There was only you. Dropped on our doorstep like a parcel. A present in light of the impending celebration,"

"Listen up you fanged fuckwit. What makes you so sure I'm a present? I mean, ask my friends they'd say I'm more of a curse or a shit magnet. So, saddle up Buttercup, you're in for a bumpy ride,"

Frederick looked over my restraints; the bats in his belfry were working overtime with his morbid eyes checking they were secure. Unfortunately, I could attest they painfully were. More worrying, there was a chance Anna would use Skip as leverage against me.

But I had something she wanted, too. The name of Jean's killer. That note asked us to solve the murder and rigged a trap. It's a huge kick in the balls if ever there's been one. 'Dots' that didn't make sense. If Jean was resurrected, surely he could wake up and say, 'It was him; that bastard cut my throat,' unless she didn't want all her eggs in one basket. Who would I be to suggest otherwise? I'm more of a fly-by-the-seat-of-my-pants kind of guy.

"Well, judging by your position. There's nothing to crow about,"

"If that's so. Where's the organ grinder? I'm tired of speaking to the monkey," A part of me thought he could be listening in.

Frederick's gaunt face suddenly dropped; an eerie gust swept hauntingly through, frenziedly whipping past. The other vamps were becoming rowdy, cheering and rejoicing—bloodsucking arseholes. My hackles shook to a level ten on a rictor scale. I asked, and it was being delivered. The Count decided to flex his fangs, finally making an appearance. The whooshing stopped. Then came the loud thunderclaps sweeping dust throughout, coating the parts of my face still uncovered.

The shadow of huge bat wings spread imposingly across the cavern walls, rattling loose shingle slowly beating down until I finally came face to face with our tormentor. I locked eyes with something I'd never imagined possible: evil incarnate. Yes, so far, I had tangled with other vampires, but this was a powerful elder, far older than the stories we'd heard so far. Much like the strange flashes in the gallery and outside the garage, he was tall, with black hair and neat side parting.

He was smartly dressed in a black suit with a purple pocket square, topped off by a finely groomed goatee. His devilish smile made my skin crawl; goosebumps grew on top of goosebumps, and my blood ran cold, watching those wings phase into his back.

"I hear you wanted to meet. I must say, seeing you caught so easily, I'm disappointed. I expected a little fight, at least. Sssmmmmm," he said, breezing close; his long bony fingers dragged a talon through the blood-trickling from my arm, scooping droplets under his nose. The Count took a deep sniff before creepily scraping it against a fang.

"Don't breathe too deeply; you might choke on your stench," I said, firing back. The Count glared; his deep black eyes glowed red before his stretched, pale skin rippled.

Morphing to something horrifying. The best I could come up with was a monster. Features that were almost bat-like and yet different. Certainly another first. It only lasts a few seconds before going back to menacing normal.

"Oh, I can't wait to silence that impudent bravado once and for all. Your blood is exquisite, and as one life ends, it shall usher in a new era for the repressed. Vampires will be free of their shackles once and for all,"

I strained against the shackles, wanting to break free and tear my claws through his throat. The smug bastard was far too confident for my liking.

"I get that you need a bath, but in blood?"

"The sinful Christians use holy water to welcome new ones into their light. Blood is power, and that's what we are, powerful, and we need to bask in its glory. While you whither and fade, we will evolve and grow. History will be rewritten tonight, wrongs set right and mistakes corrected. Until then, don't go anywhere,"

The Count snarled before disappearing in a blur. In my struggles, I'd created slight gaps in the wrist restraints, the others not so much. I had no idea the time or how long I'd been unconscious. But the pool was filling rapidly; I needed help.

'Stay awake,'

'Wake up, George,'

My eyes kept dropping. As they dropped, I heard a little voice whisper in the back of my head. I assumed I'd weaken from blood loss, but this felt different and swept in quickly. Whatever caused me to bleed had to be laced with wolfsbane. I could barely stay lucid for a few seconds; the voice rattled me at the right time. Only I feared hallucinations, and that fear doubled when I caught glimpses of the cavern walls.

They were glittering bright red; surely it wasn't real, right? I had to be delirious. The longer I could keep my eyes open, the more I noticed the glittering appeared localised to around the now full blood pool, or Lazarus pit, according to Ruth's notes, through the stones and up the path to where I was. I couldn't see how or why. Tiredness had me by the balls, and I may have been slipping for minutes or hours.

'George, you need to dig deep and wake up,'

The voice came again. This time, it lit a spark under me enough to see clearer. The vampire numbers had grown, and their earlier rowdy behaviour had gone up a notch. They were gearing up for something, and my hackles were trying to wake up, but it appeared I was having...performance issues. It's ironic, considering they'd spent most of the time here waving for anything reassembling trouble.

'George, can you hear me? It's Logan,'

This time, my attention was grabbed; no hallucination. Logan was connecting like he had when we first met. Being more awake made my fear worse because more and more vampires were drifting in, and some had begun whooshing around me, trying to intimidate and make me nervous. It was fucking working.

"How? Where are you?" I attempted the weird mind-talking, which made me feel like a crazy person.

'Hang in there; you may feel as though you were gift-wrapped. All isn't as it seems. Our numbers have grown, but the timing must be spot on when the Count is most distracted. But you need to gather what strength you can and listen for my signal,'

"Wolfsbane...whatever cut me is laced with it,"

'That's to weaken you. They will come at you to make a point when the main event begins. You can't let them win. Remember everything I told you before,'

"Do you have any idea where the others are?"

'Sadly, my friend, no. You need to focus, we will find them,'

How could I focus? I was bleeding, poisoned by wolfsbane and surrounded by vampires who looked ready to party. The glittering rocks glowed brighter now, making the blood shimmer through the swirls. Its scent was so strong, and it was driving me mad.

Logan was gone, but the crowd was stirring, and the waves parted. A rush of wind cut through with another sobering stink of death. It wasn't long before the man of the hour strolled in dressed in some red silk gown he probably ripped from the corpse of some granny down the road. With the hood up, it hung open, displaying an anaemic bare chest. He raised his arms to a chorus of cheers from his blood fucking morons. The Count revelled in the attention. Suppose, being underwater for so long, he needed the attention. Poor decided sap.

"Are you all ready for redemption," he roared, sending an echo that gave me chills. He stepped forward smugly, dropping the gown as he stepped into the blood. The Count strolled around with all the time in the world; something felt off. I'm not sure what I was expecting, but nothing special happened.

There was time, a chance to stop whatever this process was before it happened. Logan said to wait for a sign, but I kept thinking, what if it's too late? What is the right time? The Count was on display for all to see, his minions waiting for a miracle. I couldn't leave it to chance that, for the first time, our 'dots' would miraculously connect. Logan said to dig deep; that's exactly what I did. Remembering what he said when we met, I embraced the wolf. Half-phasing brought just enough strength to tear through the restraints.

Without thinking, I blazed a path with one target on my mind, clinging to the anger of everything bad that's happened. I ground to a halt in the blood face-to-face. My claws ploughed into his chest, punching out the other side, spraying blood and fragments of ribs. My free claw crunched into his shoulder, holding the Count in my eyeline. I didn't want to miss his expression as the end washed over.

For twenty seconds, I wasn't disappointed. The smugness was gone, replaced by a gaunt, shocked, dropped jaw. The Count began turning grey, and it looked like I'd crashed the party. Until my twenty seconds ran out. Shock slowly drifted into a stomach-churning smile. I was stunned, at a loss for what was happening. The Count's face began morphing.

"How could you do this to me, Georgie? I thought you loved me,"

"Ellena?" My eyes deceived me, or my mind was playing tricks. Either way, I felt sick as Ellena slid further onto my arm.

"Georgie, why did you kill me? You killed me by bringing me here; why? Why did we have to come?" Ellena squealed, coughing up blood.

"You're not Ellena. She was more than happy to come. What the hell is going on?" Ellena began laughing. Hysterical cackling that grew louder and darker until whoever this was began morphing again - an ordinary-looking vampire, if there could be such a thing. My heart tumbled into the pit of my stomach. I took my shot, and I'd been played.

The laughing was relentless; I let go of their greying body in a daze. My hand slid through their chest, leaving me staring in shock at the gooey debris covering my arm.

'Clap, clap, clap, clap, clap,'

Someone began clapping; it was so loud and seemed to bounce around the cavern. The vampire's body sparked to ash and slowly shredded into tiny embers, like the one outside the B & B earlier.

"Did you think it would be that easy? I may have been reborn at night, but wasn't born last night. I'd already told you I was moves ahead of you; this was one of them. Now the real fun begins,"

It was the Count landing a sucker punch. His words faded into white noise. While I froze, I stood in a pool of blood, and my body locked up. I gambled everything on a chance to grab the cocky 'beef jerky' bastard, and it backfired.

'Claaap,' One last clap shook the fanged masses into a fresh; the cavern got hit by an uncontrollable whirlwind.

At least that's how it felt with a series of terrorising whooshes whipping around me. Dizzying to the point, I stumbled, wading through the overwhelming intoxicating blood. 'Left, right, back, front, left,' so many at once I was punch drunk. I couldn't figure out what the vampire's plan was: intimidation or making me so unsteady I'd fall flat on my face and end up taking a swim.

'Fffttt,'

A low fizzing noise to my left, almost like a tearing of clothing. Then, a stinging, painful throb ripped up my calf. It burned so bad I could barely stand on it. Poison was cutting into my bloodstream, and while dwelling on how to manage it, another came. A slash to my right across my bicep. Another ripped across the back of my neck; all the while, all I could see was a dark spinning wall becoming a tunnel around me.

I tried to dart forward, feeling the toxins rampage through me, only to hit that wall, getting thumped backwards. The slashes came thick and fast, sending me reeling. The wolf couldn't come; I was too dizzy, poisoned, and muddled with the wooshes turning to deafening thunder. I was under siege with no way out or power to fight back. Not that I could lay a claw on any particular target.

This vampire pack assault was terrifyingly coordinated and savage. The cuts felt deeper each time; that burning became a blowtorch tracing my veins toward my heart.

'Cuh, cuh,'

Fluid had steadily seeped into my airways. I could hardly breathe or swallow with my windpipe closing. Before long, I'd lost Count of how many slashes shredded through my flesh. Taunting cackles and screeches pierced my tormented soul until I could no longer stand. Both legs went numb, giving way. I plummeted forward into four feet of blood.

; My right hand tried to prop me up, but the motor function and any sense of coordination had gone. A heavy cloud smothered my brain; the tank was empty. I played down hard, and the vampires descended. My eyes were heavy; my body went limp and lifeless until I was stranded in darkness.

Chapter 54

'Rrrrrooooooooaaaaaaarrrrrrrrrr,'

A thunderbolt lit the dark like Guy Fawkes's night or the 4th of July. An earth-shattering roar rattled my bones. I bounced upright, lungs clawing as much oxygen in as they could, and my eyelids tore open to a screen of bright red. That roar set off a chorus of them bouncing everywhere, shaking the stone beneath me.

"Was I dead? Had I been dead?"

Questions swam around my mind. I'd been in too many close calls like this, and it had become harder to tell real from reality each time. One thing for certain: Werewolves were calling, dragging me off the canvas. This time felt different; I felt different. Another part of me was unlocked. My claws were huge; I stood up feeling taller and far more powerful. Every cut healed in the blink of an eye; my veins burnt, but not poison or pain this time. It was like anything the vampires did had burnt out of my system.

'Shit, the vamps, the elder,' I finally remembered what I was supposed to do. Not one could be seen. The cave still glittered, their luminescence rippled through the blood. Which strangely, I now saw in fifty shades of red. I waded quickly to get out, head on the swivel. My ears were small satellites searching the darkness. The roars continued, and I had the uncontrollable urge to respond.

'Roooaaaarrrr,'

I emptied everything I had, feeling lighter, sending rumbles around the walls. Death didn't smell far away; I followed its stink through a dark, narrow tunnel, moving fast. I sought a way out with no time to hang around and smell the roses. I was finally breaking out into the open, a beach. Immediately faced with a vampire wall ready to fight, so was I.

There was no breaking stride; I was trying to find my friends and end the nightmare. Many questions remained unanswered; most would more than likely end in bloodshed. The first vampire lashed out, 'Too slow.' I was moving far quicker; my claws shredded the first throat. I ploughed into the next, and blood sprayed through the air and over me. One by one until six fell. I dropped the last one's heart to the light stones. The night sky was still red but layered in darkness, littered with screams.

I made my way toward the mainland atop the cliffs. The path seemed clear now, and I was breaking into the grass before long. A part of Cruden I hadn't explored, but in the distance, I could see the graveyard and the side of Montague house to my right. To the left, a series of large barns, far behind, ventured into the main part of town, where we found the library and art gallery. Everything could be a vantage point for the blood fuckers. I wanted to head to the B & B first, hoping Ruth had left Skip safe and well. If the Vamps didn't have him, someone did.

I kept close to places I could shield by; the roars had trailed off, and there was no way of telling how many there were, but I was grateful for the alarm call. One glaring detail I had to digest was the likelihood the vampire plan had worked, at least for the elder. While I was out searching, the nemeton was vulnerable, details I couldn't get bogged down by. There were only so many problems I could handle at once, and a worse evil could be waiting in the 'bat wings' once I finally despatched the crusty old bastard and his minions.

I owed him, I fucking owed them all. No 'ifs or buts. I was going to spill a lot of blood. None of it, mine. That's been done enough already; with the sickly feeling, it was exactly the mix needed in that pool. That was on me and my impatience, thinking I had the elder in my sights, only to be traumatised by the morphing. First to Ellena and then an average Jo vampire. The elder was smart, and I took the bait.

There were footsteps ahead but no heartbeat. I dashed to a short stack of hay next to a barn. I say short, but at least ten feet high and gave enough for me to hide on if I lay down and waited.

It was uncomfortable but safe and a small price compared to what I'd just been through. Those footsteps slowly came into view; I knew time was limited, so I went for it. A quick spring, enjoying my new lease on not giving a dam, I flew into a cloaked figure. We crashed along the ground, tumbling over. I went to grab hold, but they disappeared.

Vanished without a trace. How was that even possible?

There was no cloak or trace of anyone even being there. Had I imagined it? Their footsteps sounded real enough, the cloak too; traces of its roughness lingered on my fingertips. My arse got handed to me earlier, surely this wasn't fallout from that. The last thing I needed was a mental breakdown. I dusted myself and had a quick look around while screaming continued.

'Awe, poor little werewolf, second best again. I thought you were tough; you Don't know when you're beat. Don't worry, the end is coming,'

The count's voice travelled on the window, making me shiver. This was real. He created an illusion, and I fell for it. I didn't think vampires could do that; then again, there was no knowing what he'd become. A part of me wanted to block him out, but the mocking lilt in his voice was too much for me to bear.

"I must admit, that was clever; I saw a chance and went for it. Well played. A quick FYI, though, I did piss in the pool then. Everyone does it. So, if you had a little bath and you smell a little Pissy, that's about ten per cent me,"

'So reckless considering you are but one twig in a rainforest. Will soon be snapped beneath my heel along with any that stand in my way,'

"That watery grave will be least of it for you; I will pluck out your cold dead heart and flush it down the toilet," Of all things I could say to fire back, that was the first thing that popped into my head but appeared to be enough to make him sod off.

Keeping in the shadows, I moved forward again, praying the others were okay. I'd reached within a hundred feet when I saw a welcoming committee. The vampires hedged their bets. I would seek sanctuary first. The cobbled streets were littered with the blood-hungry bastards. I tried counting, but they kept moving, at least fifteen, maybe twenty. But I needed in there, hoping I'd at least recover the stakes and vials. Ruth wouldn't be that heartless, would she? Looks like I was going to get more bloody.

Just as I went to phase, I caught the glimmer of eyes beyond the vampires. Mainly yellow, but one had blue. Followed by the black outline of pointed ears and a large head. So, I figured I would get the vamp's attention by playing a hunch they were about to become a decrepit lunch.

"Hey, which one of you fanged fuckwits is willing to tell me where to find your boss," I shouted, echoing through the cold, wet streets. They all stopped and faced me. They went to charge; the werewolves pounced through the darkness. Leaving me to be a watching bystander as the street got painted with dirty, dead blood and ash. It was carnage; I didn't have to do anything for a change.

It didn't last long. The werewolf pack were savage, precise and well-drilled. Soon enough, Logan phased into a human before my eyes; the rest ducked into the shadows, waiting. I asked Logan if he'd seen the others when the B & B door swung open to Skip staggering forward.

"Georgie? What the hell is happening?"

"Skip, you're okay? What do you remember?"

"Sod all got woken by the racket to find this on my chest and a little velvet bundle," Skip had another note; we didn't need more distractions or misdirections. A good sign was the bundle of stakes and the fact Skip's was safe, Finally some comfort. Unfortunately, another glaring detail came to mind: Ruth got what she wanted, too. It didn't involve the elder; I leaked enough blood. We need to bring the game to an end now. Skip handed me the note, a rough folded piece of paper, unlike the one on Jean's corpse.

'I meant what I asked; I need you to solve a murder. I needed something else to happen. First, I couldn't afford any slip-ups; you're the key to finally being reunited. What happens after is up to you,'

"Fuck, the bitch screwed us,"

"Jesus lad, what do we do now," A good question. Having already picked up one plan, I wasn't confident enough to make another. If I'd waited, perhaps we wouldn't be playing catch up. Logan wasn't best pleased either.

"Why didn't you wait?" Logan bulldozed over.

"He was there; I saw red and went for it. They anticipated the move. I fucked up, I get it."

"Of course, you don't live as long as some of these do by being stupid; chalk it up to a lesson learned. Now, let's get this done. I have support waiting but won't have them run around blind, risking being killed. We have to be strategic,"

"Can you scout the area looking for places that could be over-guarded? That's where any one of my friends could be,"

Logan nodded, seeming much calmer as he left. There were only so many places Michael and Ellena could be hidden. We may stand a chance if Logan and his pack could narrow the field.

'2 am,'

One of Logan's scouts found another route to the west of the castle; almost hidden behind some rocks at the base of the cliff was another man-made tunnel. The money was on it leading to under the castle. So much for Amos saying it was out of use. We followed behind Logan and a few of his pack, despatched with two vampire guards easily. The tunnel was narrow and winding.

Eventually, we were headed to a wide room; it stunk of death and was damp. I could hear a heartbeat, which excited me, and I wished it was Ellena. Only, it felt too easy so far; three other vampires lay in wait. I heard muffled squirms through another corridor. I moved on my own toward a single heavy-duty door. The muffles seemed male; again, I was surprised no guard was outside the door. It squealed open easily, dingey and damp, with a single candle providing the only light.

It flickered, casting across the corner to the right. Michael was crouched in the shadows with arms hooked to chains above his head. My hackles fired up; something was off. His muffles were low. I approached slowly, not understanding why my tackles were acting up. Michael had his knees tucked to his chest; he'd been through the wringer with a dirty rag tied in his mouth. I carefully flicked a claw through the side of his gag; he seemed groggy.

The chains were flimsy and only took one yank to fall apart. Michael was free for all intents and purposes, yet he wasn't moving. His heart fluctuated all over the place; I could smell his chemo signals so strongly. Suddenly, a low growl pierced that dark; I shuffled wearily back, scuffing across the uneven, dirty stone, nearly buckling to my backside.

'Skkkkhhhhh,'

Out of nowhere, Michael flew at me hissing. His face had changed; he was changing. Sharp vampire fangs; dead black eyes kept fluctuating as his skin shimmered the Skip's had. Michael was rabid; he'd knocked me off balance. I didn't want to hurt him, but he was strong and didn't know what he was doing. The same moment that Skip crunched into my arm. This and then were the same. Michael had his claws out, sliding to talons and back again.

Michael had me pinned, my claws wrapped around his wrists, but his head kept firing at my face and neck. He had one goal, and that was to bite me. I called him but nothing. The only way without killing him was to knock him out. Looking at the wall, if I aimed him right and threw him harder enough head-first, it should knock him out cold. Michael thrashed and lunged like a fish out of the water. I just shuffled my body around to the right angle. I heard footsteps pounding forward. It was Skip. He came toward like a freight train.

'Thump,' it was so loud. Skip's fist smashed into Michael's face. I'd like to claim I assisted with the momentum. It was all Skip, sending Michael theatrically flying across the room. His face smashed against the rocky walls hard. That was going to leave a mark. More concerning, though, Michael was turning. I carefully tilted his head left and right, two fang punctures to the lower of his carotid artery. The question now is, how long ago had he been bitten? I didn't want to have to put him down. Judging by the sadness painted on Skip's face, he didn't either.

"You got the bundle?"

"Yeah, why?" He said, fishing it out from inside his coat. "We must try what saved you, but I don't know how long he's transitioned. It could be touch and go." I said, holding back that I feared the worst. I flipped open the bundle to grab a vial. Michael was laid out; I knocked open his jaw and tipped the bottle between his fangs.

"What now?"

"We get him back to the B & B, have someone guard him while we carry on." Skip was worried, but for now, I was trying to push my emotions to one side. That's been my undoing, letting it lead me instead of using my brain. The only silver lining was that we had Michael back.

'3.30 am,'

'3.30 am,'

Michael took Skip's place on the sofa; he remained out cold since Skip's punch. But that wasn't what kept him out. My use of a second vial may have been too late. What I saw and the rage I felt, Michael wouldn't want that. He may have embraced the supernatural world as a shapeshifter and a detective. At least he was alive. Suppose he became a vampire, a bloodsucker needing human blood to exist. That's not living. The B & B was secure, as far as I could tell.

Sadly, the kitchen was locked, the key was gone, and we could not know if Ruth had already removed Jean Cortez.

Logan had his pack moving swiftly, evading detection even if they were up for some payback. For now, silence was key. Tip-off one fanged bastard, and they'd flap their lifeless gums to anyone who'd listen. Something was drawing me back to Montague house; that was where Frederick, Jean and Anna started all those years ago. Was it too far-fetched to think they'd be nostalgic?

Skip and I did our best to follow Logan's example. Unfortunately, Skip's heavy feet could wake the dead of the undead, as the case may be. I had a hood pulled as far over my head as possible, and Skip stole a spare black cap lying around the B&B, which, in my opinion, made him stand out more than anything. We weren't far from the graveyard, and our hackles were already high giving each other. Our disadvantage was not being able to hide our heartbeats.

Chapter 55

We lurked under the cover of that huge tree not far from the house; a new day would break in a few hours, and by the time it did, I wanted the elder blistering into the breeze while I held Ellena.

"Your Journey ends here, little wolf,"

It came from the steps of Montague House. This time, it was no illusion; a cloaked figure waited, anticipating our arrival. Frederick Lasille decided he would take matters into his own dead hands. I was sick of dying, no, my fanged friend, my journey would not end.

"Freddie, I'm afraid you're mistaken. Do you want to do this? You may be older than me, but I've never been good at listening to my elders, or any elders for that matter,"

"You can say that again," Skip whispered.

"We can't have you interfering. I don't know why you didn't die, but it's an easily rectified mistake. Will your tubby Friend be joining us?" Frederick tackled with confidence.

"Bloody cheek, I have him know, a lot of money has gone into this shape,"

"Mostly to the bars that helped you, right? Why don't you carry on looking while I deal with him,"

"No chance, strength in numbers, remember,"

Again, Skip was right. I hated him being right, and I very much wanted to end Frederick, but there was the small matter of Locke's curse needing lifting. For that, Ruth needed to know, maybe even see. Skip hung back, watching; I strode forward, shifting as Frederick glided down the steps before launching at me like he could fly. Both feet off the ground, talons and fangs bared.

All Happened within a few seconds; instead of meeting him head-on, I dropped low at the very last moment as his long fingers went for my face. He hissed wildly, a trait I hadn't understood. I launched my claws into an uppercut, smashing his money jaw and sending him crashing twenty feet back into the steps, busting the middle few, with strips of wood spraying apart to either side.

Frederick was rocked, and for once, I realised not everything needed to be met head-on. My claws crunched into the back of his neck and skull, lifting him off the ground; my other fist was ready to punch through his chest to rip out his heart. "Cuh…cuh…do it, and you won't find your girl," Frederick coughed, spluttered and squirmed against my claws as they dug deeper.

All I saw was revenge, sick and tired of the games and not knowing if Michael or Ellena would survive. I thought, why the hell would I not end him now? And it weighed heavy on me until I heard twigs snapping in the darkness to my right—a bush line with several tall trees. I glanced across, hoping it was nothing more than a rabbit or monk jack roaming free; a heartbeat echoed to my ears, slow and steady. When out slithers Ruth.

"How long have you been watching?" I said, with a ferocious snap to my tone, fuelled by anger.

"A short while, you're not hard to find,"

"Well, here is your murderer. This is proof, now life the curse," I snatched the knife from Frederick's waistband, tossing it across the floor to Ruth's feet.

"It's been done already, was the moment you landed here. I told him and you that to keep you motivated. You seem to be the hot-shot detective your friend thinks you are. Especially in this fucked up world you find yourself balancing in. Juggling a werewolf's instincts and primal urges, the demon element and your humanity won't be easy," Ruth retrieved the knife before walking toward us slowly.

There was a look in her eyes I knew well, hatred. She had it fixed on Frederick. I wasn't sure if we could believe her, and there was no way of knowing. It's the best we could do—one thing I had to know for sure.

"Anna, you can drop the pretence now. How you managed it is crazy, the why is more important," I said, watching a cocky smile spread across her face.

"And my point is proven. You are quite clever. If only you hadn't been so rash earlier,"

"A lesson learnt,"

"For your sake, I hope so. When Frederick and Jean arrived, I fell for Jean rather quickly; we became inseparable. He taught me his world, and I got him accustomed to ours. Jean wrote everything down, a lifetime of instructions on how to harness the power of the earth and bend it to suit. Jean realised I had a natural affinity for the arts of druidism and witchcraft, separated by a fine line. He gave me the tools needed, and the village began to deteriorate. People started dying, Jean shared their fondness with me, and Frederick didn't like it. He thought I would ruin their chance of historical fame. Little did we know that Frederick was being used by something extremely evil to do his bidding.-

-Frederick eventually set the monster free. Jean thought he could take it on and imprison him once more. But feared for my safety and that of our unborn child, who was due any week now. He sent me away to my relatives in Denmark, saying he'd follow once it was over. Two months passed, and I'd heard nothing. The baby arrived healthy, but I couldn't settle. So, I instructed my relatives to look after my child. I went to fetch her father.-

-By the time I arrived, the village was almost dead. Frederick had become a vampire, along with many many others. Jean had formed a small army to take down the evil and all but succeeded. The 'evil' was entombed once more, costing Jean his life. I found him dead on those steps with his throat cut. Frederick had disappeared, leaving behind broken hearts and lives in ruins.-

-So much needed to happen; the village needed to be guarded. Soon, I realised just how powerful the earth could make someone, especially if they're sitting on telluric currents and a nemeton. Jean had discovered a natural source of power and ways to use it. I made it my mission to right wrongs and one day bring Jean back. Little did I know, an upside was an extended life, one I used to search for Frederick, hoping some good may still exist and he could help. Unfortunately, nothing," Ruth slowly dropped her pretence, changing to a version of 'Anna' I'd seen: tall, pale skin and long dark hair.

"So you used the pretence of solving a murder to get Jean back,"

"Sadly, yes. It's rare to find blood like yours tainted by demons. Mixed with an elder vampire's relentless thirst to live, the elements were there. But it had to be that particular lunar phase."

"Was it worth it? Was all this bloodshed worth it? That bastard has your ancestor, but as long as you get Jean back, you don't care," I fired back as the details sunk in.

"Did you think I wouldn't prepare for that? Who do you think synthesised those vials? It's a fail-safe for what happened last night and is about to," Ruth had me confused, and then a series of screeches filled the air.

"What do you mean?"

"I injected Ellena with a hybrid vervain concoction that may finally wake the supernatural in her. Once I knew her blood was viable. It also made her temporarily sick and weak. I know you saw the puncture; I relied on your attention to detail. But Ellena needed to be caught, and so did you. What the count thought would be the key to freedom is being rejected from his body, no doubt, from all of them."

"If she dies, it's on you. How fucking selfish could you be? Risk all this death for one person,"

"Love. A soulmate. A little like how you feel for Ellena, it's driven you to cut down anything in your path to find her. Trust me, she should be fine, in fact, better than fine. Unless she loses her head or anything farfetched like that," "But we're no nearer to finding her,"

"Oh, I wouldn't say that now; in fact, if my calculations are correct, you're about to be confronted by a very angry, very sick elder vampire wanting you to fix him. And he will bring the masses, Ellena included, to make you do it," At first, I was stunned to silence; Ruth or Anna had thought and planned for everything. All those years were used to get every detail. Two things, though: why six vials and what is to become of Jean?

"Why that number of vials? What's going to happen to him?" Anna…Christ, that's taking some to get used to after watching her morph. Anna smiled; with a flick of her wrist, the knife flew through the air, impaling Frederick in the heart. It took another flick to rip free from his chest, with Frederick's heart slicing down the blade.

"You can let go of him now. As for the vials, if one doesn't do, use two," I was in awe and disgusted in equal measure, longing for the nightmare to be over.

"The numbers don't add up,"

"Because you're immune. Why do you think you keep bouncing back? What because of a howl? The closest to death you came was the gunshots. Anything from a vampire will only slow you down, not kill you, never kill. The demon element sees to that. Which you need to embrace to realise how powerful you can be in this godforsaken crusade you have going against the bad people,"

"What will you do now? Did you bring Jean back?" I said, whizzing through the questions popping off in my brain while paranoid over an impending angry vampire. At least, according to Anna. However, most of what she says could be taken with a pinch of salt. She seemed too happy with herself, holding Frederick's heart on the knife.

My hackles rumbled with static that suddenly filled the air; an eerie rush of wind whipped into a frenzy around us. Anna's face changed; she dropped the knife before treating us to another Houdini escape. Anna melted before our eyes into a pool of bubbling clay, leaving a 'good luck' whisper trailing in the air. I felt sick and again impressed at how she pulled so many strings to get what she wanted before leaving us hanging on those questions.

'Did Anna manage to bring Jean back?'

'What will you do now? Well, she vanished after sacrificing what I could only assume to be her second golem.' Now, the winds of change are ushering in our final moments.

Skip and I stood, surrounded by Frederick Lasille, his shredded heart and the remains of a golem used by Anna, her last act before vanishing. Whether she'd be seen again was another story; Anna could be over-reliant on being close to the currents and nemeton. She answered my 'dots' like the injection point I noticed on Ellena and why she seemed so sick.

Anna used her cunning and intelligence to get what she wanted, and it has decimated a small village; at least the elder may be sick, too. I didn't understand how the other vampires could get sick, though, unless my blood had been tainted, too. Why wasn't I sick like Ellena? Unless, as Anna alluded to, my demon side keeps me resistant to many things. Anna loaded Ellena with that fancy vervain mix, hoping she'd get bitten. We could only hope, like Michael, to get the vials into her system. Michael may need another, a detail I wish had been in some kind of instructions. You know, 'take two and call me in the morning' that kind of thing.

The eerie kept whipping around; death was coming, hopefully not for us. Banshee whaling from vampires wreaked havoc through the air. Followed by frenzied, blood-curdling screams; if they were sick, they didn't sound it. Another Ruth-Anna misdirection, perhaps? Then I heard the familiar thunder-like cracking cradled by booming, swooping wings beating a path in our direction. I may not read much from them, but this time, I sensed anger, and it was getting closer.

The vampires were pissed about something, maybe Anna was right. Surely it wasn't because we had Michael back? He wasn't heavily guarded and was already on the turn. Details that had me thinking a sting in the tail could yet come. Dirt, blood and debris whipped into the air before being slapped in our direction. My heart sank after the first sign of a vampire army appeared on the main street.

There were hundreds of them. Far more than we could've imagined. Almost poignant that we were so close to a graveyard. We 'shifted'; I wasn't overthinking it anymore; there wasn't enough time to weigh up the should I, shouldn't I. The vampires were moving quickly; honestly, they could've whooshed here already, but something was off. Every gust carried the usual death stink, but now I was smelling something worse. Far more rotten, they were sick like Anna said.

"You ready for this?" I said, catching Skip daydreaming at the vamps.

"Not really, lad,"

"They're sick, just like Anna said,"

"So, the freaky bitch was telling the truth?"

"Well, it's more a law of averages. For every sentence that came out of her mouth, something had to be truthful at some point. I can't deny, I want to wring her neck thought,"

"Why's that lad?"

"She fucking engineered all of this. All for a bloody chance to get her 'loved one' back to life. Look how many people have died," I said, feeling my temper brewing as reality finally hit home.

"She didn't even have the nerve to be here in person. Instead, sends the walking, talking playdough think spoke of,"

"Exactly. The second one, too. If we survive this, I hope to god we run into her again,"

"You think that's wise. That bitch is dangerous; she fucking controlled a lump of lard to mimic her," He had a point; I daren't tell him what she did with the other golem and the police officers being controlled by the Count.

"Maybe not, but maybe we should try Logan and his pack; hopefully, they're not too far away," I said, preparing myself to roar. It felt bloody less natural being on the spot. The vampires were closing in; it was now or never. I dug deep, hoping it would be the last time.

'Three, Two, One,'

'Roooooaaaaaaaaaarrrrrrrrrrrrt,'

I surprised myself; it was loud, so goddam loud it shook the broken steps and the porch it led to. It echoed for miles, stopping the vampires' dead. After a minute or so of heart-pounding tension, they were on the move again. Until...

'Roooaaaarrrr,'

Logan hollered back, and a series of them followed, bouncing everywhere. They were close, hopefully, close enough to be in time. My arm hairs rumbled in anticipation; we moved further from the house in case any of the bloodsuckers decided on a sneak attack. Especially after what we'd already seen and taken on.

'Cuh...Cuh, help will be no use. Your time is up, and you don't even know it,' The elder pierced the tension as he's been in the habit of doing. This time, he coughed a little at the start; the vervain was getting to him.

"Is that right? Well, we have one of your little blood bitches down here missing a heart, that says otherwise. That's two of your key pieces off the board, not to mention the little pawns I've wiped out," I blasted back, feeling a surge of confidence after hearing him sound sick.

He didn't answer; the beating wings boomed to the ground. The elder's huge bat wings beat his wings a few more times, throwing gravel at our faces before phasing into his back. My stomach started to twist in knots; it was really happening. To make matters he had Ellna by the throat. I went to charge at him, but Skip flung an arm across my chest.

"Don't take the bait lad,"

"Can you not see? He has her by the fucking throat,"

"He wants you to try, look at all them fuckers coming. We need Logan and his pack here now,"

"Are you sure you want this back? She seems defective. Ever since I tasted her blood, I've been spewing up this black shit," I hadn't noticed at first, but black streaks were trickling from his eyes. It made me smile to see him suffering; I needed to get Ellena safe and a vial into her quickly.

'You need to shift George, fully shift now,'

I heard Logan in my head. They were near; I heard several heartbeats from the beach, with more by the barns. The Count had his vampires behind him now. This was going to get messy.

"If anyone here is defective, by the looks of it, it is you," The Count threw Ellena across the ground like trash. She wasn't moving.

"I'll get her lad, you worry about him,"

'Now, George,'

My head was in turmoil. I wanted to grab Ellena, but I had to trust Skip. The way the Count spoke about tasting her blood really pissed me off.

Every goddam thing that's happened this week has built toward this. Michael was being turned, and we didn't know if he would make it. Skip was used as a vampire pin cushion, and I barely got to him in time. Now Ellena looks all but dead. That's all I kept thinking as I headed for the Count, little by little, phasing, clinging to an image of Ellena before all this. Logan and his pack came steaming through just in time, pouncing through the middle of the vampire wall.

I dodged and weaved with one target on my mind. The Count crept behind the chaos as a vampire flew at my face; I caught his skinny head between my jaws. I tore through him like paper, sending his head spinning blood in the air and the bead across the floor. One by one, I ripped into any that got in my way, pouncing down on one, my claws scrunched through their chest, tearing out the heart. Up close, that black ooze stunk so bad. I finally had a clear path to the Count. Phasing back to normal. The Count was struggling badly, that ooze leaking from every orifice humanly or inhumanly imaginable.

"Georgie heads up," I turned to see Skip launch a stake. I caught the potent ash mix with a jump above an onrushing vamp, using the momentum to launch into the elder. I saw red like no other moment. Seeing Ellena the way she was, not knowing if she would live, not knowing if Michael would live, was killing me. That red had me tearing the stake into his bony chest, through his heart.

His smug, cocky demeanour was gone, all the horror could be over. Logan and his pack were ripping the vamps to shreds. In truth, we owed Anna more than I liked to admit. She caused all this, and we didn't know if she got what she wanted yet. At least she did one good deed. I guess love conquers all. I should know. If this nightmare has taught me anything, I was unequivocally and irrefutably in love with Ellena Walker, and the bastard I just staked may have ruined everything.

"Cuh...cuh... You think you've won. You don't even know who is who anymore,"

My jaw dropped; the world slowed down. An almost parting 'fuck you' or I really had no idea who was who. And that had my stomach falling out. The elder morphed into Michael.

"Georgie, it's me; what have you done? Help me, Georgie," Michael turned grey, blistering into the wind, slowly crumbling away. The body disappeared in the wind just as I wanted, leaving me sick at the thought that he told the truth. I stood holding the stake, stunned, watching one after the other, the remaining vampires crumbling to ash, swirling in the breeze.

Logan and his pack phased to humans, letting the vampire ash rain down on them as they whooped and cheered. I should've been happy, but I was too shockingly sick on so many levels. Was the nightmare over?

"Quick Georgie,"

I flipped the lid; Ellena was burning up, turning clammily pale. She already had fangs; I tipped one, and not taking chances, I tipped another. We may have already been too late, and we needed to get to the B & B, praying to god it was all for show to ruin the moment.

"Skip, the fucking elder became Michael; we need to get back quickly,"

While I was panicking, the ash aside, everything seemed almost normal. It would take a while for the village to recover, and there were too many unknowns, but it seemed we'd won this time.

"Go, run. We'll carry her," I nodded, sprinting, phasing to full wolf on the fly. The run became a glide until I reached the B & B. The front door was open, and nobody was guarding it like we thought.

I phased back, stepping through quietly. It's quite dark, I flashed my eyes. Someone stood by the unlit fireplace. My hackles didn't stir, but I didn't feel right in my stomach.

"Michael?" no one answered.

"Michael, that you?"

"Georgie?"

"Yeah, you okay, buddy?"

"I don't know, Georgie, some weird shit happened. I'm having all sorts of weird flashbacks. I was bitten, Georgie,"

"I know, buddy, but we saved you," He didn't answer, slowly turning to face me. I stepped back. The floor creaked, making goosebumps pop across my arms. No sooner had he turned than Michael steamed toward and grabbed me.

"Jesus, thank fuck you did. The vampires are some sick bastards," Michael's head popped up; he was normal, with a beating heart and everything. We breathed a sigh of relief. This could actually be over. The elder played me...I think.

"Georgie?" I knew that voice anywhere; it came from outside the doorway. Ellena was still cradled in Skip's arms.

"Are you okay?"

"I feel like shit, but I think so,"

Skip slid her to the floor; I rushed over, scooping her in my arms, her chest thumping loudly and fast. She looked a little pale still but alive, at least. I couldn't hold back any longer. I pulled her close, and we kissed like there was no tomorrow; for some of us, there very nearly wasn't. I had my friends back and safe. It felt over. The village felt safe for the most part, but I had an awful, niggling feeling Anna could come back to haunt us. Until then, we survived vampires and will survive anything else that comes our way. After all, we did solve a very old murder as requested. It was time to get out of this godforsaken place.

Synopsis

In Cruden Bay's enchanting yet eerie village, secrets as ancient as time lie beneath the tranquil facade. 'The Cursed Tides' beckons you to plunge into a supernatural realm where darkness and mystery reign supreme.

Having previously unravelled the enigma of the Black Widow, Detective George Reynolds and the brilliant forensic pathologist Ellena Walker embark on what they believe will be a romantic escapade to Cruden Bay, Scotland. Little do they know that their idyllic getaway will quickly transform into a dangerous mission to rescue the village from an age-old and malevolent adversary. They are compelled to investigate a series of inexplicable events and uncover a truth steeped in the supernatural, thrusting George into a dilemma that challenges his every conviction.

With Ellena Walker by his side, George must decipher the intricate links between the ancient village, Ellena's lineage, and the ominous intentions of ADI Locke. As they grapple with thwarting centuries-old vampires lurking in the shadows, George's immersion in the world of darkness intensifies, igniting a tormenting conflict within his soul.

While George and Ellena unearth more hidden truths, they must confront the perils of a concealed past, all while their blossoming relationship teeters on the precipice of malevolence. The sinister, heart-pounding forces they face threaten to unravel the very fabric of their love. But George refuses to surrender, fighting with an unwavering determination, even when confronted with the horrors of a world he once thought impossible.

As 'The Cursed Tides' wash over them, George and Ellena navigate treacherous waters, entangled in a web of darkness and deceit. If you delighted in the spine-tingling mystery of "Black Widow" and relish the notion of vampires engaged in a relentless battle amid a backdrop of corruption and organized crime, this emotionally charged rollercoaster ride with bared fangs and dripping blood awaits. Continue your journey into the heart of darkness in the realm of detectives and vampires.

Epilogue

Next in the Collection - The Devils Pages

"Demons are real, and it's time to sell your soul".

Are you ready to journey into the darkness and explore the terrifying power of 'The Devil's Pages'? In this thrilling horror novel, Gerald Ackerman is a good man from Newport Pagnell, England, struggling to cope after a tragic car crash took the life of his beloved wife.

When he stumbles upon a mysterious leather book at a seedy flea market in Northampton, England, he finds himself able to exact revenge - but at what cost? Read on to find out if Gerald will be brave enough to pay the price for justice or if someone can stop him and the mysterious book. If you enjoyed "The Detective Reynold's Series" by Ryan Holden or Stephen King's "The Stand", you'll love "The Devil's Pages"! Buy now if you have what it takes to beat the devil.

Chapter One Sample

Over the years, holy or unholy texts have been adaptations. Maybe as many talk of evil and the devil. What if there was a book waiting to be found? Old as time, it's full of blank pages ready to spill blood. A book capable of fulfilling your innermost evil desires.

All you have to do is let your imagination weave the chaos, doing the devil's work. Sit back and draw the savagery to appease your lust for revenge. It's passed through many hands and taken many a soul. More recently, it was discovered by Gerald Ackerman in 1990 near the town of Northampton on the outskirts of Towcester. Sat amongst a table of average, unwanted household goods at a seedy flea market. It appeared inconspicuous, yet the book was anything but normal within its grotesque leather.

This was just one of the many places it's appeared. Each time attracted someone in desperate need as they teetered on the edge of losing everything. Often, they're defined by tragedy or have been wronged in some way. The book consumes them until each holder is ripe to become the next horrifying chapter reaping for hell. On this occasion, Gerald Ackerman hadn't known what he wanted, scouring stall after stall, meandering his way around under the constant cover of another gloomy grey cloud day, much like the last six years.

Nothing caught Gerald's attention or was seen as adequate to inspire his resurgence in life. Advice was desperately given by Dr Nicholas Howsen, Gerald's psychiatrist, in a last-ditch roll of the dice to help Gerald find alternative ways to cope other than at the bottom of a Bourbon bottle and hopefully stop the spiral. Until Gerald came across a dirty, old, leather book, brown enthused with spooky red undertones that could easily pass for blood. Its spine appeared lined with bony fragments.

Blessed with horror-like hypnosis that held Gerald's attention with neither rhyme nor reason. A carbon black pencil that acted as evil's wand was tucked within a slim and almost fragile leather pouch. It's been said the seller could've passed for an undertaker or just an incarnation of the living dead. With a gaunt and pale complexion, the seller's protruding bony features looked ready to pierce his taut flesh. His haunting presence appeared from nowhere to help the evil book on its way.

This time, to Gerald Ackerman, who needed to regain control. A way to create some semblance of a future out of a life that had burnt out and turned to ash in the blink of an eye.

The heart-wrenching rot began on the M1, April 26th, 1984. A tragic car crash robbed Getald of his wife and young twin girls of their mother. Hailing from Newport Pagnell, a quaint, small town of around 15,000, mostly friendly people and rich in history. Its wonderful architecture was equally matched by rolling green hills, filling the air with the scent of freshly cut grass. Yet, Its over-friendly surface was just a facade that hid the darkness behind closed doors.

Gerald had lived there all his life, or as far back as he could remember. He knew his neighbours on both sides of the white picket fence well enough to have over for dinner and drinks one Saturday a month.

Like his father before him, Gerald worked for the town's major car manufacturer, Aston Martin. Prestigious automobiles helped the small town thrive beyond expectations. Gerald had made it to four years of loyal, hardworking service by the time his world shattered in the spring of 1984.

Acknowledgements

A huge thank you to 'Allie' from across the pond, who has listened, read and talked me around when I thought I couldn't make this or any of the first three. I owe my drive to do better to her and everyone that's put up with my procrastinating and second-guessing while taking the time to endure my rambling. A massive thank you to you all.

Milton Keynes UK
Ingram Content Group UK Ltd.
UKHW040631091123
432260UK00002B/109